Balkis hurdled over the side of the saddlebag and into his hands, then cuddled against his chest, purring like a nutmeg grater.

Not only had this cat stowed away, which was rather uncatlike behavior, but she had also managed to lie still and stay quiet, which spoke of either absolute terror or a degree of self-control that was unbelievable in an animal—and Matt didn't think he was all that terrifying.

Matt met her eyes, staring straight into them. Balkis stiffened in irritation and glared back at him, as though affronted by the temerity of any mere human who might try to outstare a cat.

Then Balkis opened her mouth, beginning with a yawn that developed into a meowing tone that shaped itself into words:

> *"No female thoughtless should comply*
> *With strange male's wishes, lacking facts.*
> *Each thought she should with conscience scry,*
> *And debate each issue ere she acts."*

Then she sat in his arms, glaring defiantly, every muscle tensed to spring and run.

Matt just stared, mind racing—talking cats just didn't happen. This creature was more than she seemed . . .

THE CRUSADING WIZARD

Christopher Stasheff

A Del Rey® Book
THE BALLANTINE PUBLISHING GROUP • NEW YORK

With thanks to my writing companions:

Katie (brown tabby)
Roxanne (white longhair)
Bonnie (black-and-white bicolor)
Besty (calico)

A Del Rey® Book
Published by The Ballantine Publishing Group
Copyright © 2000 by Christopher Stasheff

All rights reserved under International and Pan-American Copyright Conventions. Published in the United States by The Ballantine Publishing Group, a division of Random House, Inc., New York, and simultaneously in Canada by Random House of Canada Limited, Toronto.

Del Rey is a registered trademark and the Del Rey colophon is a trademark of Random House, Inc.

www.randomhouse.com/delrey/

Library of Congress Catalog Card Number: 99-91523

ISBN 0-345-39246-4

Manufactured in the United States of America

First Edition: March 2000

10   9   8   7   6   5   4   3   2

CHAPTER 1

The royal family was enjoying one of the rare hours when they could feel like a family. They sat in the palace garden in a secluded and high-hedged corner of the courtyard, Queen Alisande and her husband the Lord Wizard watching their son and daughter at play in the golden light of late afternoon.

"It is so good for them to be out of doors," Alisande sighed, "and with us. I could wish I were not a queen, that I could spend hours and hours with my babes if I wished."

"If you weren't a queen, you wouldn't have any choice," Matt pointed out. "You'd have to spend hours and hours with them, whether you wanted to or not."

"Oh . . . not if I were a countess or some such . . ."

"Well, that's true," Matt mused. "On the other hand, this country would be in real trouble if you *weren't* its queen."

"Oh, I am sure some other could rule it as well." But Alisande glowed at the compliment, then frowned. "Still, the poor babes must be quite sad now and again, with no company but one another."

"A pet," Matt said positively. "They need a pet."

"A pet?" Alisande stared, astounded. "A prince and princess, with an animal?"

"A family dog, to teach them responsibility and consideration."

"How could a dog teach consideration?"

"Because you have to be careful about its feelings," Matt explained. "If you pull its tail too hard, it lets you know about it in no uncertain terms—and if you do it too often, it won't come back to play. It doesn't care whether the child is a prince or a beggar, you see."

"Might it not bite?" Alisande said in apprehension.

1

"It has to be very well-trained," Matt explained, "and training it helps the children train themselves."

"A *princess*?" Alisande shuddered, and turned back to watch the children. "Whoever heard of such a thing?"

"Oh, I've noticed you seem to have a certain fondness for horses," Matt pointed out, "and you get along quite well with hounds."

"Well . . . yes, but that is in the hunt!" Alisande explained. "Assuredly, every prince and princess must learn to ride—but the grooms care for the horses and the houndsmen for the dogs. We do not make pets of our packs, and would scarcely keep a horse within doors!"

"Well, no," Matt admitted. "I had in mind something smaller—a nice, friendly, clumsy dog, maybe—a poodle or a retriever or something like that."

Alisande still looked scandalized, but she tried to be reasonable. "How would such a beast teach the children to be responsible?"

"By caring for it," Matt said. "Make it clear to them that nobody else is going to feed it or take it for a walk, because it's theirs. Simply having an animal that belongs to them will do wonders for their sense of self-worth, too—and it's great company if a child feels lonely."

"Royal children do feel alone quite often." Alisande lifted her head, gazing into her own past. "They have no playmates but their kin, and those seldom come . . ." She shook herself. "But to feed and water an animal? That is scarcely becoming to their rank!"

"It is, if nobody else is allowed to touch the royal pup," Matt pointed out.

Alisande still looked thoughtful, but she said, "A dog is too dirty and awkward a beast to keep within doors. A cat, now, would be another matter."

"Cats are better than nothing," Matt allowed, "but they don't need to be walked, and you can't train them, so they won't make you any more responsible than you are already. They won't come keep you company whenever you want them, either—they have this nasty little habit of only stopping by when *they* want company."

"But they are smaller, and more graceful," Alisande pointed

out, "far less likely to break a vase or a pitcher, and far better suited to life within doors."

"I had in mind a *small* dog," Matt said, "maybe a spaniel or a Scots terrier, something that can sit in your lap and be petted."

"Like a cat?" Alisande smiled. "Then why not *have* a cat?"

"Well, the dog can jump out of your lap and run to fetch a ball," Matt said. "It can play games with you."

"And bring the ball back in its mouth, and slobber all over it as the child picks it up?" Alisande shuddered. "Cats play games, too, by chasing bits of string. They are far less disgusting."

"Well, I would prefer a dog," Matt said, "but I'll settle for a cat. When shall we go find one?"

"Now, hold!" Alisande cried. "I have not said we shall have a pet! Only that if we do, it should be a cat!"

"Okay, so think about it for a few days," Matt said. "It's really a good idea, though. Why, I've even heard of a king who kept a dog in his lap when he was on the throne!" He didn't mention that Louis XIV had reigned in a world three hundred years older than Alisande's.

"We might set a fashion," Alisande admitted, her gaze on the children. "I shall consider it."

Kaprin suddenly gave his little sister a shove. She rolled back, squalling, then bounced up with a block in her chubby hand. She threw it with all her three-year-old might and very precocious accuracy; it hit her brother on the nose. He recoiled, hand to the offended member, squalling protest, then started toward her with blood in his eye.

"Children!" Alisande started up.

The nursemaid was there before her, though, separating the two children and chiding them equally. "For shame, Alice! Scold sharply if you will, but do not throw things! And you, Kaprin—you know full well that no gentleman should ever strike a lady!"

"I'm not a gentleman yet," the six-year-old grumbled.

"That is no excuse."

"There might be some advantage to a pet, after all," Alisande allowed.

"Just don't think it over for too long," Matt said.

The question was about to be answered for them, but it was an answer that had been growing for sixteen years. It began far to the east, in a northern valley nestled among the hills on the edge of the Gobi Desert. It began in the midst of chaos, but the setting was quite peaceful—for a few minutes.

The Oriental garden seemed magical in the moonlight, air fragrant with the perfume of exotic blossoms and stirred by a breeze, which rustled the leaves of flowering trees grown into fanciful shapes by patient gardeners over dozens of years. Wind chimes filled the night with music. The turquoise lawn seemed deep green in the moonlight, bejeweled with dew. Topiary shrubs in sculpted forms framed an ivory gazebo of ornate screens.

So lovely a garden should have lain tranquil under the moon, its only sound the susurrus of leaves and the tinkling of the brook that ran through it, turning model mill wheels and tugging at miniature boats moored for the night at tiny, fanciful boathouses.

It would be tranquil and still for a few minutes more, granting an illusion of peace and safety. But then, behind the scented trees, flames would roar high into the sky from the burning barracks of the horse-soldiers, and the breeze would blow the screams of horses and people alike through the garden, together with the roar and clangor of battle.

A woman hurried across the lawn, the train of her silken robe trailing across the dew-laden grass, her long sleeves sweeping almost as low. She held a small chest in her arms, and when she reached the brook, knelt down and lowered it into the water.

Lifting the lid, she took one last look at the little face of a six-month-old baby wrapped in a cloth-of-gold blanket, asleep from the drop of opium mixed into her milk.

The woman's eyes filled with tears. "Lie there, my treasure," she whispered, "and do not wake until the waters have borne you to safety."

Steel clashed against steel, much closer than before. She looked up with a gasp, then closed the lid of the little chest and pushed it out into the stream. "O Spirits of Brook and River," she called, "I beg you, protect my child! Carry her to safety far from these monstrous barbarians! Grant her some guise that will shield her from the cruelty of men!"

The little chest went bobbing away on the current as the woman watched, tears spilling down her cheeks, to dampen her robe.

Then a burst of shouting made her turn, gasping in terror. Three of the barbarians came galloping toward her on their small, hardy ponies, shouting in their uncouth language, sabers flashing in the moonlight.

"No!" she cried, and ran toward the gazebo—but one of the horsemen veered away from the others to come between herself and the slight safety of the screens. She stopped, uncertain, then turned to run to her left, but a horseman galloped wide to catch her by the arm. She screamed, but another horseman caught her other arm. She turned to bite his fingers, but the first struck the back of her head with his sword hilt, and she went limp.

Hauling her over the pommel of his saddle, he grinned at his fellow warriors. "One more for the sacrifice," he said. "Angra Mainyu will be pleased!"

"I know not why that foreign sorcerer must give such an outlandish name to the Lord of Demons," his companion replied, returning the grin, "but no matter what we call him, he will drink deeply this night."

Beneath the waters of the river, though, two spirits answered the mother's call, swimming up through the river weeds more from curiosity than from kindness. They seemed to be made of seaweed and water lilies themselves, but their upper bodies had arms with hands, and their faces were very much like those of young women.

"I thought these mortal mothers never parted with their children," said one as she caught the floating trunk with green, chilly fingers.

"There must be terror abroad to make her do so, Sister Shannai," the second said. She looked back toward shore, saw the barbarians riding away with the mother, saw the graceful form of the palace silhouetted against a sky filled with fire, and wrinkled her nose. "Those barbarians who daily pollute our streams! Well might she go in terror!"

"Then let us deprive the horsemen of this pleasure, at

least." Shannai opened the chest to look in at the baby, and smiled fondly, resting her pale green hand on the child's head. "Look, Arlassair! How sweetly she sleeps!"

"Sweet indeed." Arlassair laid her own hand over the child's heart. "Ah! How brave she will be! I feel it in her! Still, let us see that she does not waken till we have guided her to shore in some place so distant from these barbarians as to be safe."

"Indeed, let us be sure," Shannai agreed, and chanted a spell that would ensure the baby sweet dreams until the water spirits wished otherwise. Then she joined her sister in pushing the little chest along the stream.

Laughing like the brook itself, they batted the vessel back and forth between them until they came to a river. Then, still playing, they guided the chest a mile down, inviting a family of otters to join them in their game. Finally, tiring of the sport, they diverted the little trunk into a stream that branched off from the river to feed a still forest pool. There they left it, but as Shannai turned to follow her sister back underwater she called out, "Women of the trees, aid now a sprout! Within this trunk is a seed of a human newly sprung! Its mother has sent it to us to keep it safe from the horsemen who plague the plains! Aid this little fugitive, I pray you, for she is not of our element, and must live upon land!"

Her whim completed, she dove deep, following her sister, and forgetting about the baby on the instant.

All about the little chest, tree trunks bulged. The bulges moved, separated from their trees, and human, feminine forms stepped forth, skins brown and rough as bark, green leaves mantling their heads and shoulders in place of hair, more leaves covering them from breast to thigh—not clothing, but growth.

"What marvel is this?" one asked, stretching out a hand to the little trunk. "It is not made of wood, that's sure!"

"It is bound together in slabs made from the huge long teeth of elephants," another told her, "and its bindings are gold! Does not the moonlight show it prettily, my sisters?"

"It does indeed," said one adorned with oak leaves. She knelt to pry the lid open. "How pretty is the gem within?"

She folded the lid back to reveal the sleeping baby. The dryads gathered around with cries of delight.

"How lovely!"

"How sweetly she sleeps!"

"How darling a babe!"

"Rarely have I seen a mortal of pleasing shape," said Oak, "but this one is a treasure."

"How shall we keep her safe from the barbarians?" asked an elm-spirit.

"Hide her," suggested Maple.

"All well and good," Birch answered, "but who shall feed her and tend her?"

"Well asked." Oak frowned. "And where would we hide her?"

"Among the peasant folk?" Elm suggested.

"No, for the barbarians are likely to plunder them also," said Birch.

"With a caravan trader?" offered Thorn.

"Will they travel at all, with the barbarians abroad?" asked Oak.

"If they do," said Thorn, "it will be because they have made some arrangement to guarantee their safety, and that of their goods."

"Well thought," said Oak, "for even barbarians want the tea and silk of China. But no caravan will take a baby."

"Then let her not be a baby," Elm declared.

The others looked up at her in astonishment.

"You cannot make her grown in an instant," Birch said, "for her mind will still be an infant's, no matter her body!"

"Not if she is an animal," said Elm, "say an otter—or a cat!"

The others stared at her in amazement, then began to smile.

"A cat!" Thorn said. "What caravan would take an otter?"

"But any merchant would wish to protect his goods from mice and crickets," Oak agreed.

"Is it decided, then?" Elm lifted the baby and cradled her in the crook of an elbow.

"Yes!" "Yes!" "Yes!" "Yes!"

"But let us give her the power to change herself back into a human, when she is old enough to wish it," Thorn demurred.

"Aye, and to change back to a cat, if humans are once again in danger," Birch added.

"How clever we are!" Elm exulted. "Together, then, sisters! Lay your hands upon her and recite the spell with me!"

Woody hands covered the little bundle of flesh; voices like the rustling of leaves intoned a spell like the wind in the trees. As they chanted, the baby shrank, its form flowing here, bulging there, until a half-grown cat lay in the crook of Elm's arm, its fur the color of the cloth-of-gold that had swaddled the baby. The wind-rush of voices died away, then began again in separate words.

"Will she be strong and agile?"

"Yes, for a six-month kitten is quick and sure."

"Will she have sense enough to live?"

"Yes, for at six months a cat's mind is far more grown than a woman's."

"Will she know how to walk, how to hunt, how to hide?"

"No, and that we must teach her ere we let her go."

"Well, we cannot teach her sleeping," Thorn said, and touched the kitten's forehead. "Small one, awake!"

The kitten yawned hugely, then opened its eyes and looked about in curiosity.

"Do not be afraid, little one," Elm said, "for we are spirits who have already given you our love."

"We will guard you as long as you have need," Birch told the kitten, "and lay a spell upon you that will make all other spirits of grove and hill come to your aid."

The little cat sat up on Elm's palm and looked about her with bright-eyed interest, switching her tail. Then she stilled, eyes widening with surprise before she darted a quick glance at the twitching tip.

Smiling, Elm set her down on the ground. The tail twitched again; the kitten dove for it, and was instantly lost in the game of chasing her own tail-tip.

"She must have a name," Birch said. "Was there nothing writ on the little chest that held her?"

"No" said Thorn, "but I remember a word embroidered on her coverlet, in the strange letters that the Greek priests brought."

"I saw that, too," Elm said. " 'Balkis,' was it not?"

"Then let Balkis be her name," Birch said, and so they called her from that day forth.

"We must teach her," Oak reminded.

They taught. They scratched her paws in the dirt, and instinct took over; with no more teaching than that, she learned to cover her litter with earth. They showed her a mouse and taught her its scent, then forgot their own dignity long enough to stalk like a cat and pounce. She imitated them and caught a mouse of her own soon after, and they showed her crickets, locusts, june bugs, and all manner of kitten delicacies—but they did not teach her how to fish, indeed taught her not to, for the water-spirits had been her first friends.

When Balkis was nine months old, they cast a spell to keep her from going into heat until her human form was fourteen years of age. When she was ten months, a dryad at the fringe of the grove saw a caravan approaching. She told the others, and the word ran to Oak, who told the kitten, "We would dearly love to keep you by us always, but cruel men are riding through this land every day, and if they should see you in girl-form, they might kill you."

The kitten had learned their language, and within the cat-sized head the human brain understood the gist of the words. Her eyes widened and she trembled.

"Better far for you to ride with the caravan." Oak took her to the edge of the grove and pointed. "They will be glad to have a cat if they have none already. But you must make friends with them if you wish them to take you far to the west, where these horrible horsemen ride not."

Balkis-kitten nodded, but a tear formed at the corner of her eye.

"I know. We will miss you, too, little one," Oak said, "but your welfare is more important to us than your company. See, the merchants have stopped and are pitching their tents, for they wish the water in our grove for themselves and their horses! Go catch a mouse who seeks to nibble at their goods, and you will endear yourself to them forever! Or at least until they come to the lands of the Rus. Go now, make your way in the world!" She set the kitten down and gave it a push.

Hesitantly, and with many a backward glance, the kitten went to prowl around the caravan. Bravely, Oak and her fellow dryads gave her smiles of encouragement, for after all, she would still be near them for the evening.

* * *

The caravan drivers looked up at the sound of a sudden yowl. "What is that, so near our packs?" the master asked, frowning.

"A cat, by the sound of it," one of the drivers answered.

"Let us be sure," said the caravan-master. "Omar, go see!"

But Omar had scarcely come to his feet when a small golden cat came trotting from the huge panniers full of goods with a mouse in her mouth. She pranced straight up to Omar and dropped the little body at his feet, then looked up at him expectantly.

Omar stared down. "A mouse! By the stars, she has saved a bolt of cloth at least!"

"Perhaps even a pound of spices," the master agreed.

"But why does she stare at me so, Master Ivan?" Omar asked, completely at a loss, for he was very young.

"Raised with dogs, were you?" Master Ivan grinned. "Why, she seeks her pay, lad! Do you think one small mouse is enough dinner for her?"

"Oh, is that all!" Omar grinned, sitting down, and broke a piece of meat from his roast fowl to hold out to the kitten. She nipped it from his fingers and swallowed it in two bites, then ran back to the panniers.

"Well!" said Omar. "Not a thank you, not a backward glance—only gets what she came for and runs!"

"I've done that myself, on occasion," one of the other drivers said.

"Yes, we've all spoken with your wife, Sandar," a third driver said, and his fellows burst into ribald laughter, the more so because they knew Sandar had no wife. As the laughter was dying, the little yellow cat came trotting back to the campfire and dropped another mouse, this time at Sandar's feet. She stood looking up expectantly.

"Well caught!" he cried, and tossed her a scrap of meat. She pounced on it, gulped it down, and trotted back to the panniers.

"Why doesn't she just eat the mice?" the third driver asked.

"Would you, Menchin?" Master Ivan asked. "Especially if there is fowl to be nibbled?"

Another laugh answered him. As it lapsed, the cat came trotting back with a third mouse.

The drivers applauded, and Omar said, "She works as hard as any of us."

"We should take her along," Sandar said.

"We should indeed," Master Ivan agreed, and so it was decided.

As the sun rose the next morning, the drivers finished their breakfasts, drowned their fires, loaded their mules, and drove them onto the road. The little yellow cat clung to the harness-pad on the last mule's back. As they ambled away, she turned for a last look toward the grove, and the dryads. She gave a plaintive mew of farewell. Only her eyes could pick out the waving forms that were her friends and protectors.

Unseen by the men, the dryads raised hands in blessing as they chanted protective spells, tears trickling from their eyes—and that is why, if you look closely at the trees that grow in a grove about a pond, you will now and then see drops of water clinging to their trunks as dawn draws nigh.

Months later the caravan swayed into Novgorod, a city of timber surrounded by a sharpened-log palisade, the facades of its houses ornamented with fanciful carving, all wrought with no tool but an axe. The kitten looked about her wide-eyed, drinking in the wealth of strange sights and sounds and smells—then recoiled as a pack of dogs charged barking at the caravan. Balkis crouched hissing among the rolls of cloth in the pannier, ears laid flat and heart thumping wildly. What were these strange huge beasts with such loud voices and such huge teeth? She decided to stay with the caravan as long as she could.

As the drivers went to dine in a tavern, Omar held out his hands, clucking softly. Balkis jumped into them, and he tucked her away inside his tunic as he followed his companions into the inn. They called for ale and meat, and Balkis sniffed the air for the rank smell of those huge thunder-voiced beasts. Finding no trace of them, she dared to hop down from Omar's tunic to scout for fallen morsels under the table.

As she worried a sliver of tough meat, she heard the merchant and his drivers talking with others of their kind, and her wakening human mind in a maturing kitten's brain understood at least the gist of their words.

"Did you have trouble with Tartars, Ivan?" asked a strange voice.

"They gave us safe-conduct, Michael—for a tax," Ivan answered, "one bolt of cloth out of every ten, and one pound of each spice out of each twenty."

Dark mutterings greeted the news.

"Do you trust them?" another voice asked.

"Only so long as they do not ride to conquer Novgorod, Ilya, or any other of our Russian cities," Ivan answered. "While we were on this journey, their warriors were besieging Tashkent. Their chieftain boasted that their khan has even sent a horde against China, riding into Sinkiang. He assured us that Novgorod's hour has not come yet."

"Yet?" a new voice asked darkly.

"Yet," Ivan confirmed.

The atmosphere was suddenly tense, and Balkis looked up, uneasy and forgetting to swallow.

"When?" Michael asked.

"They gave no hint," Ivan answered, "but for myself, I will lead no more caravans to the east this year."

"What profits will you find, then?" Ilya argued.

"I will sell half my silks and spices here in Novgorod, of course," Ivan said, "then buy beads of amber and furs of sable. With those, and the rest of my silks and spices, I shall lead a caravan south and west, to Warszawa and Krakow in Poland, then farther west to Praha in Bohemia or north to Sachsburg in Bavaria."

Balkis had no idea where those strange-sounding places were, but she grasped the idea that they were farther from the horsemen of the steppes, and resolved that when Master Ivan's mules plodded west, she would be riding them.

It was a long journey through birch forests, and at night she stayed close by the campfire, for the darkness teemed with smells very much like those of the horrid beasts of Novgorod, whom she had learned were called "dogs." But the woods also teemed with mice and other small rodents, and she was able to lay quite a collection of gifts out for her merchant and drivers every morning. They rewarded her with scraps of many different meats, for they trapped and hunted for their dinners as often as they could; fresh meat was far better than the salt pork they carried with them. Balkis became quite a connoisseur of wildlife. Now and again, though, the traders would camp by a river and sieve the water with nets to catch their dinners. They would lay slivers of fish by Balkis, but at one sniff, something within her revolted against it, and she contented herself with mice, which were, after all, quite tasty, if one happened to be a cat at the moment. There were certainly enough of them.

There were bandits in those woods, and twice the drivers had to fight them off with staff and steel. Balkis burrowed in between bolts of silk when that happened, but stuck her head out and watched with wide eyes as axes swung against swords and men fell with arrows sticking in them. One of the drivers was killed and several others wounded, but the bandits fled as soon as they realized the merchant and his men were no easy targets. After all, what were cloth, spices, and furs against one's own life?

All in all, Balkis was quite relieved when they came out of the forest into broad plains, which were far nicer, for there were fewer of the doglike smells, but a host of mice coming to gnaw their way through the panniers to the spices within. There were also fewer streams. Somehow Balkis knew that it was wrong for a cat to dislike fish, but there it was, she couldn't stand the thought of eating one of the scaly aliens, and that was that. She did enjoy watching them, though, as they flashed golden and silver beneath the surface of the water. Now and again she dangled her paw in to play, but they never seemed gamesome when she was about.

At last they came to Warszawa, a city like Novgorod in many ways but unlike it in many others. A good number of the buildings were fashioned of brick or stone, for example, and fewer people wore fur or heavy woolen cloth. There were many who spoke a strange guttural language, moreover. Listening under the tables, Balkis learned that those people were called "Allustrians."

Master Ivan sold half of his remaining silks and spices, and with the gold he gained, bought so much more of Polish goods that he had to add three more mules to his string. In the taverns the talk was again of buying and selling, and there were a great number of worried questions about the barbarians. Master Ivan was in great demand, and so were his drivers. The other merchants did not seem happy to hear that the barbarians intended to ride west eventually, and there was much speculation as to how close they would venture. Would they come to Warszawa, or even to Sachsburg? No one knew, of course, but everyone guessed the worst, and a sense of doom thickened the atmosphere. All in all, Balkis was relieved when the mules ambled out of the city, and quite happy to be back on the plains again.

The land sloped upward gradually, until Balkis found herself looking at huge wooded hills ahead of her. They climbed into those hills, and she was greatly surprised to see the hillside shorn away into slabs of rock, cliffs adorned with ivy and creepers, slanting down to a broad river below. They were into wooded country again, and the rank smells of dogs-but-worse filled the night once more—but so did the calming calls of tree-spirits, whom the foolish men seemed unable to hear.

"What creature is that, who fairly glows with the traces of fairy magic?"

"It is only a cat, sister. Go back to sleep."

"Sleep! When her every breath bears the perfume of distant dryads?"

"It does indeed. Fear not, little one. No wolf shall come near you. We shall protect you."

And Balkis dozed through the nights, secure in the love and protection of the magical spirits.

Only dozed—she was quick to waken at the slightest sound of gnawing, and quicker to pounce. The forest spirits certainly felt no need to protect the mice who gnawed out dens beneath their own roots.

At last the forest gave way to river-meadow, and there, with steeple and tower gleaming above the waters in the morning sunshine, stood the city of Sachsburg.

Balkis looked about her with great interest as the caravan trailed through the gate and into the town. There was as much building with stone and brick as in Warszawa, but houses and inns were faced with stucco between the beams that held them up. The streets were cobbled, and though dogs ran barking after the mules as before, there was also the scent of many, many cats, some with a musky overtone that Balkis found exciting, though she could not say why. Still, some wariness within her held her aloof; she did not go out at night to find other felines. Somehow she knew they were not really her own kind. She stayed instead with her drivers and her merchant, and listened under the table.

"A toast to journey's end!" cried Master Ivan.

"Journey's end!" cried the drivers. Wooden tankards clacked against one another, and men drank deeply.

"How long shall we stay in Sachsburg?" Omar asked.

"A month, I think," Master Ivan said. "It shall take me some time to discover what Allustrian goods to buy, after all, and we can use the rest."

"With our wages in our pockets? Be sure we can!" Sandar said, grinning.

The other men all roared approval, and Master Ivan grinned through his beard—but when they had quieted a bit, he said, "Remember your wives, my lads."

"I shall buy mine a necklace and needles," Omar avowed, "and some skeins of Flemish wool."

"Then home to Novgorod?" asked Menchin.

Master Ivan nodded. "First to Krakow, I think—but then home, yes."

Amidst their feet, Balkis thought of the horse-riding barbarians, and decided that when they left for home, they would leave without her.

Accordingly, a month later, she perched atop a pannier as the caravan left the city, but as it plunged into the forest again, she hopped down and dashed away among the trees. She watched the last mule sway away down the track with Omar beside it on horseback, and felt a pang of longing, a sudden surge of loneliness.

Then a barky hand touched her with a feather-light caress.

CHAPTER 2

Balkis tensed beneath that touch, but a melodious voice said, "Fear not, little one. You have the aura of dryad-magic all about you, and that is reason enough to take you to our hearts."

Balkis mewed her thanks as she looked up into a brown and resin-painted face beneath a crown of green needles, and knew that wherever she roamed, she would always be home.

The Allustrian tree-spirits made much of her, petting her and crooning to her and watching her play as they trailed their branches temptingly for her to pounce at and miss, and sometimes catch. When she grew hungry, they showed her where small creatures burrowed, termites that might eat of their wood. At night, by herself, she found the mice. The forest was also filled with scents that frightened her, but she stayed near the trees and knew they would protect her. In fact, the tree-spirits taught her to climb up to their limbs for safety—then gently and with much reassurance and coaxing, taught her to climb down again.

At last, though, one dryad sighed and told her sisters, "She is not meant to be our pet, no matter how much we enjoy it."

"True, Sister Pine," another said. "She is more than she seems."

They all knew what.

"Come, then, little one," said Fir, "follow my needles." She trailed a branch along the ground, and pounce by pounce Balkis followed.

"Here, little one, come here," Cedar called, and her needles took up at the limit of Fir's reach.

Thus they led her, tree by tree, deeper and deeper into the wood, until the boughs opened out into a broad clearing. In its center stood a cottage with a thatched roof. Half the clearing was a vegetable garden, and a gray-haired woman plied her hoe there, in wooden shoes and long woolen skirts with a blouse of homespun.

"There is only one human word you need know," the last dryad told Balkis, "and that is 'Mama.' " Then she touched the little cat on her forehead and intoned,

> "You must be as you were born.
> Blood will tell, and Nature show.
> Kith and kind have made your form.
> As human henceforth you will go."

A wave of dizziness passed through Balkis. She shook it off and moved forward tentatively—but how clumsy she suddenly seemed! Looking down, she was appalled to see fat little arms where her legs should have been, and chubby hands instead of paws!

"Do not let it fret you, little sister," the dryad said, voice tender with sympathy. "You shall become used to it quickly, and be as deft and agile as ever you were."

Balkis mewed protest—but it came out as a wail.

In the garden, the old woman looked up in surprise and concern.

"Go now to that woman," the dryad said. "She will surely give you comfort and nurturing, for never has she had a child of her own, though dearly she has wished for one." She gave the baby a pat on the rump.

Confused and awkward, Balkis crawled from the underbrush toward the garden, crying.

The old woman dropped her hoe and came running. She found an eighteen-month-old baby with a golden blanket wrapped about her hips and torso, crawling toward her—for of course, at a year and a half a cat is fairly grown, but a human is still a baby.

"Oh, you poor little thing!" the old woman cried, and knelt down, holding out her arms.

Balkis looked up, blinking, and if the tilt of the eyes in that pale little face seemed odd to the old woman, she certainly did not say so. The rosebud mouth opened and spoke a single word: "Mama?"

The old woman's heart turned within her, making her all the more greedy to pick up the child and cradle it in her arms. "No, alas, I'm not your mother, pretty babe, but I shall find out who is. Come, come back to my cottage now, and I shall feed you warm milk and soft bread until my husband comes home. He shall spread the word throughout the wood and find your mother for you."

Old Ludwig was as delighted as his Greta to see the baby. Still, he dutifully went from cottage to cottage among the widespread, loose-knit community of forest dwellers, asking who had lost a girl-child. None had, and he and his wife exulted. Sooner or later, they knew, her parents would come looking for her, though they had heard of children being taken to the forest and abandoned. They kept her and hoped, and Greta held her to her heart. "I shall call you Leisel," she told the child.

But the little girl shook her head, her mouth firming with stubbornness, and spoke her second word: "Balkis."

Greta stared in surprise, then gave a laugh of pure delight. "Even so, if that is your true name. Balkis you shall always be."

The true parents never came, of course, and as she grew older, Greta and Ludwig ceased to think of her as a foundling and thought of her only as their daughter. At first she only mewed in answer to their fond chatter, and they found it endearing. When she could walk, though, she sometimes strolled into the forest in the early morning or evening to talk with the trees, and old Greta, watching her face, could have sworn she heard the firs and pines reply.

It was a year before Balkis happened to look out the doorway and see some kittens tumbling at play in the yard. She yearned to be with them, to be mock-fighting, though she knew she was too old for such things, a grown cat fit to have kittens of her own—but hard on the heels of the thought came an immense desire to snuggle a little body against her own, to feel its little nose nuzzling . . .

"Balkis?"

She looked up and saw Greta looking about, concerned. "Balkis, where are you?" she called.

"Here, Mama," Balkis answered, but heard only mewing from her own throat. Startled, she looked down at her feet, and saw hind legs and paws. The fur was tan, the color of the homespun gown Greta had made for her.

"Balkis!" Greta called, worried. "Come out of hiding, child! Don't make me fret!"

"But I'm right here, Mama," Balkis protested. She heard only mewing again, and dropped down to all four feet, heart thudding in fright. "Mama, help me!"

"Oh, out of the way, silly cat!" Greta flapped her apron. "Shoo! I must find my child!" She ran out into the yard, calling, "Balkis! Where are you, dear?"

Finally Balkis realized that the old woman saw only a cat, that she had indeed changed back into the shape she had worn for so long. She sprang to the side and, in the shadows, thought fiercely of her human shape, of chubby legs and small bare feet . . .

She looked down at her forepaws and saw hands.

With a sigh of relief, she ran toddling out the back door and around the cottage, calling, "Mamamamamamamama!"

"Balkis! There you are!" Greta came running and swept her up into an embrace. "Oh, you had me so worried, child! Never go outdoors without me! Never do that again!"

Balkis clung, trembling, and resolved that she never would "do that again"—at least, not where Greta might see her, or when she might worry.

Now that she had discovered she could change into a cat at will, though, she did, now and then—but only alone in her room at night, or when Greta allowed her to go into the underbrush to search for berries. Balkis found that a cat could go under the bushes and find the fruits that others never saw.

As she grew past five she began to think about the stories the old woman told her at bedtime—not only about the tales themselves, but what they showed as evil or frightening. Some of the stories were meant to scare, she realized—to make silly little children learn to be wary of dangerous things. The brother and sister who were abandoned in the forest and found a house of gingerbread where a witch lived, demonstrated what happened to children who wandered away into the trees—and the wolf who gobbled up the grandmother then donned her nightgown and bonnet to decoy the little girl in the red hood into coming close enough to catch, showed Balkis not to talk to strangers. But who were the wicked ones? Witches and wolves, night-walking spirits and fairy horses that could change themselves into men! Things of magic were evil and dangerous, wild animals were unpredictable and frightening.

What, then, would be a magical child who could change herself into a cat?

The mere thought of frightening Greta threw Balkis into a panic; she threw herself on her foster mother and wept bitterly, and when Greta stroked her hair and asked what had upset her so, Balkis only shook her head and wept harder. In the night, she dreamed of Greta and Ludwig staring at her in shock, then backing away, making signs to ward off evil and fleeing from the cottage. Balkis woke screaming, and it took Greta half an hour of rocking and murmuring before the child could sleep again.

So, though Balkis could not resist the temptation to go for a night's prowl now and then, she was very careful never to change where anyone could see her.

Now and again one of the monks from the monastery came by—the abbot thought of the forest-dwellers as part of his flock, and wished to be sure their souls were healthy. Greta and Ludwig walked long miles to hear Mass every Sunday, so they thought it only fitting that one of the monks should walk long miles to visit them now and then. He would talk with them and tell them the news of the world, then read from the Bible—the Old Testament, which they rarely heard in church. When first he did, Balkis was curious, so he taught her how to make the sounds the letters showed. Instantly, she felt consumed by a veritable hunger for the Book herself, and the stories the monk never had time to read. Ludwig and Greta had an old family Bible, an heirloom they kept more as a charm than as a source of knowledge, since, being peasants, they had never learned to read. Balkis, though, pored over the pages in the evenings, sounding out the letters until the words began to make sense, and thus learned another sort of magic.

When she was fourteen, her body began to change in a different way, and Greta had to teach her how women cope with their monthly difficulties. Soon after, the full moon summoned Balkis to change into a cat and go for a night's prowl—but she had no sooner leapt from the window when an unfamiliar sensation swept over her body, a prickling and tickling that nearly drove her crazy. She opened her mouth to mew in distress, but the sound that came out was loud and raucous, a yowling that she knew well from the cats in the barnyard. She sprang back through the window and changed to her human form, then sat on her bed, shaken and wary.

She had seen cats go into heat, of course, had heard them yowling for a tom to come and assuage their distress. She had watched them couple, but hadn't thought much of it. The next time it happened, though, she watched quite closely, and came away shaken, bound and determined that no such thing would ever happen to her. She was very careful about her timing after that, and if by chance she mistook and felt the craving in her cat-body, she transformed herself back into a girl on the instant. The craving was still there, of course, but was only a shadow of a cat's compulsion.

She kept studying the nearby cats though, and saw how having a litter too early stunted a cat's growth, saw how too many litters too close together wore them out. In fact, Balkis saw one mother cat die when her kittens were only a few weeks old, and afterward she adopted them and cared for them with a fierce devotion. She knew what it was to be an orphan kitten herself, and dependent on the whims of strangers.

Greta and Ludwig were pleased to see her compassion, but Ludwig told her sadly, "We can't afford to care for all the kittens in every litter every cat has, child. I can't chop and sell enough wood, and your mother can't raise enough vegetables in her little garden, even with all the help you give her."

"Don't worry, Papa. I shall tell the cats how to find their own homes and fend for themselves," Balkis said.

Ludwig smiled indulgently, not to say adoringly, and left her to her kittens. He was quite surprised when the cats really did wander away as soon as they were grown, not to come back. He couldn't know that a cat he had only rarely seen—and never the same color twice—had taught them at night how to hunt in the forest, then with more-than-feline intelligence had led them away to rich hunting grounds when they were grown. He would have been delighted, though, if he had known.

So Ludwig and Greta tolerated Balkis' hobby of raising orphaned kittens, and their house was seldom without a litter somewhere about the yard, or even indoors in the cellar in winter. They took it as a sign of Balkis' good heart—her positive passion for lost kittens, her untiring efforts to help the old couple in their chores, even chopping wood to lighten Ludwig's labors. They only thanked Heaven for such a willing and devoted daughter to brighten their latter years—and never noticed that she was truly, genuinely beautiful, for she had always been beautiful to them.

For her part, Balkis too thanked Heaven every night for such loving and gentle foster parents, and whenever she went into the woods, she thanked the dryads for having led her to them.

The town of Qushan in northwestern Persia lay white in the simmering heat of early afternoon. All was quiet, for most of the people were indoors, dozing away the heat of the day. A few men sat in the shade by the pool in the garden by the mosque, discussing the Koran. All else lay quiet. The people would rise when the worst of the heat was over and work till the sun sank.

On this particular day, though, they would not have the chance.

There was no warning but the rumble of hooves, a rumble that grew into thunder. The men in the garden ran to the western edge of the town to see what was making the noise. They saw a long dark line of horsemen racing toward them.

They ran, shouting, to waken their fellow citizens and bid them hide or take up arms. Sleepy men came stumbling from their houses carrying scythes, flails, here and there a sword.

Then the horsemen fell upon them.

They galloped down every street of the town, screaming with blood lust and loosing a volley of arrows from their short recurved bows.

Half the townsmen fell, transfixed by arrows. The lucky

ones died. The rest screamed as spears pierced their chests or bellies, or howled with rage as they swung their own weapons at the invaders—but the horsemen dropped their bows and drew broad-bladed, curved scimitars. They struck and struck again. The streets ran with blood.

When all the men had fallen, the invaders rode among them, seeking the wounded among the dead bodies. When they found one that still moved, they struck with lance or sword. Finally, sure that they had left none of the men of the town alive, they burst into the houses and dragged out the women and children. The barbarians set the townsfolk to digging graves as a way of learning what happened to those who dared defy them.

They didn't notice the one body that wormed its way, little by little, back into a house. There the young man found cloth to bandage his shoulder, then stole out the back door and into the granary, where he lay buried in grain until nightfall. When all was dark, he crept out, steeled himself against the wails of mourning, tried to ignore the wreckage and the sounds of pillaging and revelry inside the mosque, and ran off into the night to bear warning to the next village, that they might warn all others, perhaps even send word to the Caliph in Baghdad.

The Caliph's audience chamber was spacious, airy, and cool, while the land baked outside under the afternoon sun— but a fair quantity of its dust had come in with the messenger, who knelt at the foot of the Peacock Throne.

"Your pardon, O Shining One," he said. "Your forgiveness for the vile news this lowly one—"

"Be done with your apologies!" the Caliph snapped. "It is not my custom to punish the messenger for the news he brings—but I will punish you sorely if you do not tell it forthwith!"

The messenger raised his head to speak. "O Sun of Wisdom, barbarians have ridden through the passes in the western mountains and fallen upon your village of Qushan, in the shadow of the foothills! They have slain all the men and enslaved the women and children, they have looted and defiled the mosque and set up an altar with two heathen idols that guard a pile of cinders! There they rest, turning their horses out to graze the crops that were ripening in the fields, while more and more of their kind come pouring through the passes! Those who have seen them fear that they will march against your cities, that they may even threaten Baghdad!"

The Caliph sat glowering at the man, who shrank back, bowing his head, heart beating wildly until at last the ruler nodded brusquely and said, "I thank you for bringing this news so faithfully. Go now." He turned his eyes to the captain of the guard. "See that he is given rest and refreshment."

The messenger stammered. "I—I thank Your—"

"Praise Allah, not me. Go."

The messenger went.

The Caliph sat with head bowed, face thunderous. His vizier, Ali ben Oran, approached him warily. "O Light of Wisdom, we must shield your people from these monstrous horsemen!"

At last Caliph Suleiman raised his head. "We must indeed. More, we must beat them back from the lands they have already taken. Call up my generals and all of their armies."

The vizier gestured to an attendant, who turned, bowed, and ran.

"Send out agents," Suleiman told the vizier, "and summon my wizards. Tell the one to spy and the other to scry, that we may learn who these invaders are, whence they come, and why."

Ali bowed. "O Lord, it shall be done."

When Balkis was fifteen in human terms, Ludwig died, and Greta seemed to fade even as she followed his coffin to the churchyard. Balkis walked beside her, grieving herself, but even more concerned about her foster mother. When they came back to the cottage, Greta gave a sigh that seemed to send her soul with it after Ludwig's and sat down in a way that plainly said there was no point in ever getting up again.

Balkis was past concern now, and well into fear. She had been orphaned once, and had no wish to suffer it again. She bustled about the cottage, lighting the fire and swinging the kettle over it to heat, fetching a lap robe and tucking it about

Greta's knees. The old woman looked up at her with a smile in which some trace of life revived and said, "Bless you, child."

That was the way of it for the next half year—Balkis doing the housework and gardening, while Greta sat and prayed and told herself over and over again the stories she knew from the Bible—the ones she had learned by heart, from so many years of Sunday church—and gained comfort from them, comfort and reassurance that she would be with Ludwig again in Heaven. She yearned to be with him so ardently that she faded day by day, and would have gone much sooner to the Heaven for which she ardently longed had it not been for Balkis' love calling her back every evening. Together they would sit by the fire, Balkis reading the parts of the Bible that Greta had never heard, and the old woman would smile and bask in the care of the child she had reared.

But even Balkis' love could not hold her for long in the world of the living, and when the snow was melting and the first greening showed in twigs returning to life, Greta parted from it, and died in her chair by the fire with her hands on her Bible and a smile of utter peace on her lips. Balkis followed her coffin to the churchyard with only friends to support her now.

At the funeral, she noticed the speculative glances of the young men, and shuddered. Afterward, they called frequently, properly accompanied by mothers or sisters, to chat with Balkis and relieve her grief—but she noticed their gazes roaming the cottage, calculating its worth and the price of its furnishings, and she knew that their interest was not solely in the beauty of her face or the sweetness of her form. Nonetheless, she was glad of their company, for the little cottage was lonely indeed with neither Ludwig nor Greta there to embrace or to fuss over.

Accordingly, when April had taken the chill of winter from the land, and May sent flowers and warmth, she buried her most treasured mementoes of her foster parents in a wooden box beneath the roots of an oak, asked the tree to guard it for her, dressed in a brown traveling dress, walked into the forest, and changed into a cat.

She stood a moment, rigid with foreboding, but the aching, craving, and tickling did not come. Relieved, she set off deep and deeper into the wood, hurrying, but wary of wolves, wild-cats, and bears, hoping she could find the wise woman of whom everyone whispered before her cat-body might go into heat.

She found the cottage after four days, far deeper in the woods than she, or most folks, ever went. The little house stood in a small clearing, grass kept short by half a dozen grazing sheep. It was decorated with carvings that tugged faintly at a memory she hadn't known she'd had, and painted the green of new growth, with the decorations in pastels and the door and shutters sun-bright yellow.

Balkis watched from the shadows for several hours, until a woman came out to tend an herb garden. There were only a few streaks of gray in her black hair; she was still buxom and handsome, not at all the witch Balkis had pictured, clad not in black embroidered with arcane symbols, but in ordinary, everyday blouse and skirt of homespun cloth, with the wooden shoes of a peasant on her feet. The only thing special about her attire was a pendant of glittering crystal, worn about her neck on a silver chain. She hummed as she worked, and Balkis recognized the tune with a shock—it was a hymn!

The wise woman took a few herbs back into the hut with her and shut the door. Reassured by her appearance, Balkis changed back into human form, but still stood among the trees, trying to pluck up her courage to go knock on the door. Just as she was feeling that she would be horribly rude and in-trusive to do so, the door opened and the woman stepped forth again, this time with a black shawl over her white blouse and gray skirt. "Whoever you are, you might as well come out and stop bothering me with your lurking!"

Balkis stared in amazement, then took a faltering step.

Instantly the woman's eyes focused on that slight move-ment. "That's right, come forward, now. No need to hang back. You've nothing to fear, no matter what you've heard about me—if you mean no harm, that is."

"I mean none." Balkis stepped forth into the sunlight. "In fact, I seek protection from harm."

"Don't they all!" the woman said, with a sardonic smile. "Well then, come in, lass, and tell me your troubles." She turned on her heel and went back inside, leaving the door wide.

Balkis took a deep breath, plucked up her nerve, and followed.

Inside, the cottage was every bit as attractive as outside. It was all one room, perhaps thirty feet by twenty, with a fire-place against one wall and a bed across from it, a square table and two chairs between. A padded chair stood by the hearth in one inglenook, a low table beside it with a candlestick. There were windows in each inglenook, too, and to either side of the doorway and in the wall by the bed, with horn instead of glass—all a lonely woman could afford, surely, and even that was luxury. Each window wore damask curtains with a bright floral pattern, and the floor boasted an actual carpet with a similar motif. The walls were plastered and whitewashed. Against the far wall, across from the door, stood a long table with ceiling-high shelves, filled with jars with strange names painted on them, such as Wortroot, Umber, and Nightshade. From the rafters over the table hung bunches of dried herbs, lavender and thyme and savory among them.

Balkis stared. Could these be the stuff of witchcraft? Surely not! Some were as likely to be spices for cooking as others were poisonous—but none were strange or arcane.

"I am Idris." The wise woman seemed severe, but her eye glinted with pleasure at having company. "Who are you, lass?"

"I—I am Balkis, ma'am."

"An odd name." Idris frowned. "Come from a foreign land, have you?"

Balkis stared. That, just from a name? "I . . . I have a memory of such a journey, when I was very young—but I've been raised in Allustria since before I could walk."

"Allustrian enough, I warrant." Idris frowned and came closer, reaching out to touch Balkis' hair. Balkis steeled herself against the stranger's nearness.

"Don't be silly, I won't hurt you," Idris said impatiently. "You've the aura of magic about you, child. How did you come by it?"

Balkis stared. "I didn't know . . ."

"Did you not?" Idris frowned at the puzzle, then shrugged it off. "Enough. You haven't walked deep into the woods and braved the dangers of wolf and bear for idle chat. What is your errand?"

"I . . . I seek a potion to keep me from going into heat."

"Into heat?" Idris stared. "Odd choice of words for it. Well, there's nothing we can do about that, child—we feel the warmth and the tickling every month whether we will or no. The only cure for it would play havoc with your innards, and might keep you from ever having a baby. You wouldn't want that, now, would you?"

"Oh, no! And that kind of heat I can withstand easily enough . . ."

"That kind?" Idris frowned. "What other kind is there?"

"The . . . the kind a cat feels," Balkis stammered.

Idris' gaze sharpened. "How would you know what a cat feels?" When she saw Balkis hesitate, she cajoled, "Come now, child, I can't help you if I don't know what troubles you. If you feel you can't trust me, why, begone with you! But if you truly want my help, then truth you must tell, and all of it!"

"You'll think me mad," Balkis warned. "I'll have to show you."

"Show, then." Idris seemed mightily puzzled.

Balkis took a deep breath, hoped Idris could take it in stride, and changed into a cat.

CHAPTER 3

Idris stared, then took a deep breath and said, "Yes. No wonder there was an aura of magic about you. I can see why you'd want a potion to keep you from going into heat."

"Can you help me?" Balkis asked, forgetting her cat-shape for the moment.

Idris frowned. "What was that? I almost understood it."

Balkis stared up at her, amazed. It had never occurred to her to try to speak as a cat—she'd never been near anyone who wouldn't have called her a monster. She tried again, slowly and carefully, to shape her mewing into words. "Xhan ... eeeeyooo ... help ... mew?"

Idris nodded. "Yes, you can talk even in that form. Your 'kuh' and 'hih' sounds come out more like coughs than anything else, but if I strain, I can understand you. You'll have to practice that, my lass."

Balkis felt a thrill of accomplishment and pranced with delight.

"And as to my helping you," Idris said, "there's still no potion—but for a cat's heat, there is a spell. Hold still, now, and let me sing." She knelt by the little cat, hands almost touching, and began a tune in a language Balkis had never heard. Somehow she understood it, though, and wondered if it were akin to the songs of the wind in the leaves. Idris was calling upon the spirits of wood, water, wind, and earth to shelter Balkis and keep her body from its sexual urges for all but one week out of the year. Perspiration sprang out on her brow as she chanted, but at last she sat back on her heels, done. "There, now. You'll have to keep from changing into a cat during the week before and after the shortest day of the year, but even if you should forget and do so, there aren't all

29

that many male cats about then. Just pick yourself a house where you're the only one."

"I shall," Balkis mewed. "Oh, thankyouthankyouthankyou!"

Idris nodded. "It is my pleasure. But you can return the favor by telling me how you came to be able to change forms. Somehow I doubt you were born a shape-shifter. Come, change back to a lass and tell me."

Balkis willed it, and felt her body grow and swell until she stood before Idris again as a girl. "Thank you, good woman!"

"Show your thanks," Idris suggested. "Tell me how you learned this trick."

Balkis turned regretful. "I can't say—I don't remember. I've always been able to, that's all I know."

"But you say you have a dim memory of coming from a far place?"

"Yes, before I found Greta and Ludwig." Tears filled Balkis' eyes. "God rest their souls."

"Lost them this last year, did you?" Idris gave her a smile of sympathy. "A difficult time, I know. Tell me what you can remember, then—all that you can."

Balkis started to speak, but Idris turned away. "No, not standing here! For myself, I'm rather weary. Let's sit, and sip some brew."

The "brew" was powdered herbs in hot water. As they sat and sipped, Balkis told Idris the tale of her life. The older woman touched her hand with gentle sympathy when she spoke of losing her foster parents, then again when she explained why she had left her home.

"It comes to all of us sooner or later," Idris told her, "unless we're lucky enough to fall in love with a man who truly falls in love with us—but I've seen many a woman waste her life because she settled for a man she didn't truly love, in order to have a house and home and children." She shook her head sadly. "I don't know who to pity more, her or her brood."

"I've seen some, as you say." Balkis' tears dried in the contemplation of those less fortunate than herself. "Most of them seem able to convince themselves they're happy enough."

"And so do their men," Idris said grimly, "which only proves how well people can lie to themselves. No, you've made the right choice, lass, hard though it may be. Now see if you can remember in the other direction."

"Other direction?" Balkis frowned. "You mean back into infancy?"

"I mean that indeed." Idris took the chain from about her neck and held up the pendant—a polished crystal almost an inch across. She held it by the chain and let it swing, watching it thoughtfully, and Balkis followed her gaze, staring at the bauble. It glittered in the sunlight that came through the window, flashing reflections here and there. She felt the urge to bat at it with her paw, then remembered with a shock that she was in human form and told herself sternly to behave.

"Let your mind rest," Idris intoned. "Sit at your ease, let your limbs go loose. Let your thoughts roam, let them go back and back. Remember, but do not let the memories disturb your tranquility. Be at peace, but bring to mind the time that you first slipped your shape into that of a cat."

Perhaps it was the brew, or perhaps the slow, soft sound of Idris' voice, perhaps even the feeling of being safe and secure again—but no matter what it was, a delicious languor spread over Balkis' limbs and penetrated her whole body. Her eyelids grew heavy, but she couldn't bear to let them close and lose sight of that lovely whirling crystal and the flashes of light that coruscated off its surface. It seemed to swell, the room darkening about it, until it filled her sight completely. Then, in the maze of its flashing, she saw a face, a green face with hair like river weeds, and a green hand reaching down to touch her.

She stiffened. "I remember!"

But the face was gone, and the glittering crystal was only a bauble, tiny in a shadowed room suddenly huge.

Idris' voice stayed slow and calm. "What do you remember?"

"A—A green face, and a green hand." Balkis sank back in the chair again. "Huge, they were, filling the whole world."

"River spirits," Idris said thoughtfully, "and yourself a baby. Come, let yourself slip back into languor, let your thoughts roam free again, and drift back . . . drifting free . . . drifting back . . . drifting . . . drifting . . ."

The room darkened, the bauble shone, and heaviness stole over her limbs again. This time, though, Balkis couldn't keep her eyes open; they drooped shut, darkness came, the chair seemed to rise and fall beneath her, rise and fall with the flow of a current, and there were stars in the darkness, stars behind the green head and the green hand, a wooden rectangle about them, and she began to tell Idris what she saw, but somewhere in the telling, she fell asleep.

She woke to see the room quite dark, lit only by two tallow candles and the fire on the hearth. She blinked, looking up, and saw Idris busy with a wooden spoon, stirring a pot that hung over the fire. A delicious aroma came from it, a stew of some sort. Balkis stirred in her chair, and Idris looked up. "Awake, are you?"

"You used magic on me," Balkis accused.

"Call it that if you will," Idris told her. "I won't. What do you remember?"

The question caught her by surprise, but the host of images it evoked brought her to sit bolt-upright, staring into the flames. "I . . . I remember . . . I remember it all!"

"Very good, for so small a baby." Idris nodded. "I was quite impressed."

"But . . . but what were they?" Balkis pleaded. "The wood around me—I suppose that was a box of some sort, and I was in it, and I must have been floating in water, for I felt the rise and fall beneath me—but why would my mother have set me adrift?"

"You remembered voices shouting and screaming in the distance," Idris told her. "I would guess it was war, and your mother trying to save you. Amazing you heard, considering she had drugged you into sleep—but the sounds made you dream, and the drug made those dreams vivid."

"You mean the green faces were part of the dream?"

"They might have been, but they looked like the water-spirits we call 'nixies' here. I don't think an infant would have dreamt of such by herself. No, I think the drug had worn off by the time you saw them, and they were real enough—sprites who were struck by the novelty of a baby in a box, and took it into their heads to save you."

"You make it sound like a moment's whim!"

"It would have been," Idris said, musing. "They are flighty

things, nixies are, without the slightest notion of responsibility, and scarcely a germ of compassion. Life is only pleasure and gaming to them, and they've no patience with anything that does not please them. Indeed, I am surprised they paid attention long enough to take you to shore and call the dryads to help you."

"The women who came out of the trees! They were dryads?"

"They were indeed," Idris said. "Most trees have them, and the forest abounds with them—for those who can see. They are gentle, compassionate creatures, with a motherly instinct to them—as they'd have to be, to see their acorns grown to saplings."

"So they took pity on an orphan, even if she were not of their own kind?"

"They did indeed. There are children abandoned in the wood every year because their parents can no longer feed them, and those who survive do so because they let the dryads care for them. In your own case, though, what matters most is that they changed you into a cat, which saved your life, then touched you, as the nixies had—indeed, they petted you quite a bit, and each stroke left a trace of magical power in its wake. The dryads here in Allustria did the same, so it's no wonder you've such an aura of magic about you—they filled you with enough as to last your whole life, and then some!"

"But I don't know any magic," Balkis objected, then thought better. "At least, none but changing my form."

"Then you'll have to learn, won't you?" Idris said. "And I'll have to teach you."

Balkis' heart leaped with delight at the woman's kindness, but she protested, "I only came for a potion to keep me from going into heat!"

"And found it, so you'll be free to change shape whenever you wish," Idris said, "and I always did like having a cat about. No, my lass, you had better stay and learn, for you've a destiny upon you, and you'll need all the magic you can master to fulfill it."

"A destiny?" Balkis stared. "How can you tell that?"

"I have the Second Sight."

Balkis' heart leaped with hope. "Have I?"

"Too early to say," Idris replied, then with some asperity, "You might say thank you, you know."

"Thank you indeed," Balkis answered. "Thank you very much, and from the bottom of my heart."

Learning magic came easily, and Balkis couldn't understand why Idris kept warning her that it would take a great deal of hard work, that she must not let herself be downhearted if she didn't succeed at first, but must persevere in order to learn it. Balkis proved her wrong—she learned every spell by heart at one repetition, memorized every gesture at first sight, and somehow was able to turn her emotions and her will to the spell as easily as breathing.

"It's all that magic you were steeped in," Idris said, exasperated, "and the instinct for its use you've developed, changing your form all these years. You learn magic as easily as stalking a mouse! It's not fair, it's just not fair, when I had to work so long and hard to learn it!"

"But I've nowhere nearly so sharp a mind as you," Balkis protested.

"Nowhere? Everywhere, say rather! You've at least as much intelligence as I, and you put a project into motion as soon as you think of it!"

"Well, of course," Balkis said, surprised. "Why wait?"

"Why? Because you might not succeed, and there might be a deal of trouble if you don't!"

"Oh, I couldn't let that stop me," Balkis explained. "I mean, I had to discover why Mama couldn't see me, even though I was calling to her, didn't I? And when I realized I'd slipped into kitten form, of course I had to change myself back to a baby."

"Did you indeed!" Idris stared at her, arms akimbo. "Well, of course you had to, didn't you? How young were you then?"

"Oh . . ." Balkis gazed off into space. "A year, perhaps two."

"Few folk can remember so far."

"Well, yes, but a two-year-old cat can." Balkis flashed her a smile. "I remembered it as a cat when I was ten, so of course I remember it now as a human."

"Yes, of course again," Idris echoed, wondering. "But you

had to learn not to change into a cat where people could see, didn't you?"

"I did realize that, yes," Balkis admitted, "especially when Mama used to tell me tales of witches in the wood, and the frightful monsters who dwelt there, too."

"And after they died?" Idris asked, narrow-eyed. "How long did it take you to decide how to proceed with no guardians?"

Balkis' smile turned cynical. "As soon as I realized the neighbor boys and, aye, even old men, were eyeing my parents' cottage with as much greed as they were eyeing me. The answer was easy—turn to a cat, and go."

"Yes, easy," Idris said, looking rather numb. "Leave your possessions and your legacy, yes, nothing to it. But you might have changed into a cat in heat."

"I had to wait until I was sure the season had passed, then hope I could reach you before it started again," Balkis explained. "I'd heard tales of a witch who lived in the depths of the forest, and hoped you could help me—and would." Her smile turned dazzling. "And bless you, my friend and teacher, you did!"

"And right glad I am to have done so." But Idris frowned, considering. "So all your life you've had to solve problems and put the solutions into practice right away. No wonder you're so quick to solve the magical puzzles I give you, and quicker to put them into practice."

"I'd never thought of that," Balkis said slowly. "I suppose it is a gift."

"One well earned, if it is," Idris said. "Here's a new puzzle for you, then, child—in only six months you've learned all I can teach, but you clearly could learn a great deal more."

"I don't have to, though, do I?" Balkis cried. "Can't I stay here with you?"

Idris' manner softened, and she reached out to caress her pupil's hair. "As long as you like, child, and glad I am of your company—but you would do yourself an injustice if you do not become all that you can be. How, then, shall you learn more?"

Balkis balked, knowing the answer but trying to turn away from it. "By attempting new spells that I make up myself?"

"Possible, but dangerous," Idris said, "and a very long way of learning."

Balkis' heart sank. "You're telling me I must go find another teacher."

Idris nodded heavily. "I am. To do less would deny that destiny that I can see hovering about you, lass. Mind you, I'll not make you go, and when you do, I'll long for your visits—but go you must, or regret it all your days."

"Where could I go, then?" Balkis cried. "Where could I be safe?"

"For you, now?" Idris smiled without mirth. "Anyplace you like—you know enough magic to guard yourself well, and cope with anything but a magician who's even stronger than yourself. You can be sure you'll meet one sooner or later, lass, even if you stay here—and you would be better off by far to seek out a kindly one who draws his power from goodness, than to wait till an evil sorcerer finds you."

Balkis shuddered at the thought. "Where shall I find a good wizard, then?"

"In Merovence," Idris said, with decision, "for women are treated better there than anywhere else."

Balkis frowned. "Why in Merovence?"

Idris shrugged. "Belike because a woman rules there—Queen Alisande. Perhaps it is also because of her that the minstrels there have begun to sing of the glories of courtly love, of admiration so strong that it can kindle desire for a woman all by itself, a desire that need not be consummated but is ecstasy when it is. Such a notion exalts women far beyond the rest of the world, which regards us as little more than beasts of burden, and chattels that men trade like coins."

Balkis shuddered. "Merovence let it be, then! But to which wizard shall I go?"

"Why not begin with the best?" Idris gave her a sunny smile. "Ask the Lord Wizard himself—the queen's husband and consort, and by all tellings, the mightiest in the realm! If he turns you down, go to a lesser—but I've a notion that he'll take you as a pupil for his wife's sake, if not for his own."

Balkis turned thoughtful, and voiced what Idris hadn't.

"And because his wife is the queen, he would be unlikely to importune me for sexual favors?"

"For his wife," Idris agreed, "but more because, if he draws his power from Goodness, adultery would weaken him tremendously. No, child, seek you the Lord Wizard of Merovence and you'll be as safe as you may, and become tremendously learned in the bargain!"

"Let us hope I can bargain well indeed," Balkis said darkly.

Cat-memory served Balkis well, and she had no trouble joining a mule train bound for Merovence—as a mouser, of course. The merchants hired a full company of armed guards, ones who specialized in protecting commerce, for they had to pass through deep forests and cross broad rivers. Twice the soldiers had to beat back forest bandits, once they had to fight off river pirates, and they reached Merovence with only a dozen wounded. Some of those wounds would have killed the soldiers, though, had not Balkis crept among the groaning and fevered in the makeshift hospital wagon, and recited healing charms in her meowing voice. One or two soldiers later told of bizarre dreams in which the caravan's cat spoke to them, and all their mates enjoyed a good laugh over such an outlandish tale.

At last the morning sun burned away the mist, to show a small city lapping up the slopes of a long hill, on top of which stood a castle with high walls and graceful towers.

"Bordestang!" the merchants cried, and their eyes glinted in anticipation of sharp trading and good profits. "The Queen's Town!"

Balkis' pulse quickened, too, but whether it was in anticipation or dread she did not know. She had some hard dealing of her own to do.

Far to the east, Suleiman the Caliph had some hard decisions to make—in the thick of battle. But his wits worked at their quickest and most certain when they were encased by a steel helmet that rang with the echoes of battle-cries, screams of pain and rage, and the clash of steel, of sword against sword and lance against shield.

"Back!" he commanded his adjutant. "Our soldiers are

more skilled, but for every barbarian they slay, five more gallop in—and every single one of them is mounted!"

Cavalry was only half of his army. The adjutant nodded, grim-faced, never doubting his sovereign for a moment, and turned to signal to the trumpeter. The man set his instrument to his lips, and the signal for retreat blared out over the army. Other horns took it up, momentarily drowning the sounds of steel. The Arabic army pulled together and began their retreat, foot by foot, defending against overeager barbarians every inch of the way. Fired with triumph, many of the horde rode to the flanks to slay as many of the Muslims as possible, some even attempting to ride behind the army—but its back was to a river, and the rearguard defended the bridgehead well. Nomad after nomad rode against their grounded spears, and died.

On their own flanks, their comrades met similar fates, for the Arab crossbows thrummed and sent a message of death that the barbarians received before they could come near the army—received in their chests, fell from their horses, and died. Their companions turned, but loosed arrows from tough, short, compound bows before they fled. Many of their arrows fell short; those that did reach the Arabs clattered against light armor or shields and fell, to be trodden underfoot. Only a few found flesh; only a few of the retreating army fell on the flanks.

Their comrades in the van, though, fared far worse, for they were indeed outnumbered five to one. They had become the rearguard as the army retreated. They fought furiously. Crossbows and archers could do nothing, for the enemy followed within yards of them, charging again and again against their own blooded mares. Horses screamed and reared, lashing out at one another with sharpened hooves, and the barbarian horsemen rode against trained and disciplined Arab cavalry. Behind them waited infantrymen, hungering for a few feet of space to rush in, stab upward with their spears, and retreat. Those strokes were short, for the barbarians rode ponies, and if the Arab lances did not transfix the riders, they brought low the horses. The Caliph's cavalry struck downward at their opponents, and though it seemed to take ten strokes to slay even one of the tough little men, die they did.

Then hooves rang hollow on the pontoon bridge, and the army yielded their platform board by board. But as the rearguard passed the first of the boats that supported the bridge, they slashed the ropes that held them in place, then struck as deeply as they could with lances. The barbarians followed them onto the bridge—and sank, their horses screaming. They could not stop quickly, for hundreds of their fellows pressed them from behind, and a thousand barbarians plunged into the river as boat after boat drifted from the bridge, then sank.

A few barbarians had managed to thrust themselves so deeply into the Arabic army that they were carried away with the retreat, calling out in despair in a dozen different barbarous tongues—but as the soldiers swung scimitars high to slay, those same "barbarians" called out in good Arabic, "Not me, you fool! I'm a spy for the Caliph!"

The soldiers didn't believe them, of course, but they couldn't take the chance. They bound the barbarians and took them along.

When the army had finished the crossing and the remnants of the pontoon bridge were drifting away, the trumpets blew the halt, and the Arabs turned to digging a ditch to guard their perimeter, and to pitching their tents. As dusk closed in, campfires flared, cooking pots steamed, and the army paused to lick its wounds, sentries vigilant for the slightest sign of barbarians moving in the night—there was always the chance that they might find a way to cross in the darkness. It seemed unlikely, though, for they rode their horses like men who came from plains that stretched so wide they scarcely knew what a true river was.

By the Caliph's tent, braziers flared high as the captives were brought before him to be greeted by a coded question, to which they answered the password-answer—if they knew it.

"Who brought the Qaa'ba?"

"Ibrahim and Ishmael."

"What would you have of Toledo?"

"Steel."

"What is damascened?"

"Swords."

The Caliph's own wizards listened to the exchanges, and told those who truly knew from those who merely guessed—for there were a few barbarians who spoke Arabic with accents so thick it was clear they had learned it as a foreign tongue, and poorly at that. Some were indeed the Caliph's spies, though, recruited by other spies. Each, for his own reason, had come to hate the cause he served.

Those who did not answer the questions, or who tried and failed, were sent to a squadron of men who had lost brothers or fathers in that day's battle. When the true spies had been winnowed from the accidental captives, the Caliph asked them, grim-faced, "Whom do we fight?"

Now one or two spies interpreted for the barbarians who had taken the Caliph's coin, and who told more than the disguised Arabs, for they had known the answers for years.

"We all are members of hordes," one barbarian explained, "what you would call tribes. But we are of many nations—Turks, Pechenegs, Mongols, Kirkhiz, Kazakhs, Polovtsi, Manchus, and more—any whom Olgor Khan can sway to his service."

"Who is Olgor Khan?" Caliph Suleiman asked, his brow dark.

"You would call him a king," another barbarian answered. "He was born the son of the Khan of the Azov Horde, but when he came to power, a priest with burning eyes journeyed to him from the distant South, one who called himself Arjasp, and told him that if he worshiped the god of darkness and strove to bring all people into the god's power, that god would exalt him and make him emperor of the world."

"And he let himself be seduced by the lure of power?" Suleiman asked.

"Of power and riches," a third barbarian said, "for the priest promised him the wealth of all the world, masses of gold and gems by the bushel, if he would bow down and worship Arjasp's god."

"What name has this god?" Suleiman demanded.

The barbarians answered, "Angra Mainyu, or Ahriman."

The Caliph stiffened, staring at them in horror.

CHAPTER 4

"I know that name," said the general who stood nearby.

"Yes, I know it well," the Caliph said through stiffened lips. "There is a small district within my empire whose people still speak of Ahriman—but he is not the god they worship, he is the demon they abhor."

The barbarians stared. "It is no mere invention of this high priest, then?"

"Ahriman is the name they have given him of late," Suleiman replied. "The old name of this king of demons was Angra Mainyu, and he is the enemy of their true god, Ahura Mazda, the god of light. In times long past, his priests were called 'magi.' "

"Why, even so," said one barbarian, with a shudder. "Arjasp calls himself a 'magus.' "

"They are the oldest of the wizards," said the general, "and claim that all magic comes from them, for they have given their name to it."

" 'Magic' comes from 'magi'?" asked one barbarian, wide-eyed. "Then may the heavens defend us, for we are lost!"

"Not so," snapped an Arab wizard, "for we have learned a great deal since these magi invented their form of magic—and believe me, theirs is only one of many! We know something of theirs, and of others far older!"

The barbarians seemed to be a little reassured by the claim.

"What does this Khan Olgor with those he conquers?" the Caliph asked.

"Say 'emperor,' rather," said one of the Arab spies, "for he styles himself 'gur-khan,' which means Great Khan, or Khan of Khans."

"The audacity of him!" Suleiman fumed, but he could not

deny the validity of the claim, for a man who had brought many nations and their kings beneath his sway was indeed an emperor.

But not the only emperor—nor would he ever be, Suleiman swore to himself. "What happens to the peoples of the nations he conquers?"

"Those who join him of their own free will and seek places in his army are honored," said one barbarian, "and their wives and children dress in brocades, live in tents of silk, and eat meat every night. Those whom he commands to surrender, and who do so without battle, are left to live much as they did before, governing themselves, though their kings must obey the commands of the Great Khan. Their merchants, however, grow rich from trade with all other tribes and nations who have joined the empire."

"How long has it been growing?" the Caliph demanded.

"Nearly twenty years," a barbarian answered.

"What of the tribes who fight against the Great Khan's conquest?" the Caliph asked.

"He butchers all their men," a barbarian answered, grim-faced, "and builds a pyramid of their skulls to mark where a town was so foolish as to resist him. He makes eunuchs of those males who are still boys, then sells women and children all into slavery. Where there was a city before, there remains only a deserted ruin—deserted until he gives it to one of his wild tribes for their dwelling."

Even Suleiman had to suppress a shudder. "How much territory has he taken, this Great Khan?"

"His hordes have swept all through the center of the world, O Caliph," a barbarian said.

Suleiman turned to his Arab agents, frowning. "What does he mean?"

"It is their term for Central Asia, O Caliph," answered one. "Your empire and Europe sit on the western edge of the world and China on the eastern, with the land of the Hindus on the southern."

"What lies on the northern?"

"Ice, and people whose hides grow thick fur over everything except their faces."

In the heat of Persia, that almost sounded attractive. The

Caliph nodded and turned back to the barbarian. "How many nations has Olgor taken?"

"We Polovtsi, the Kirghiz, the Kazakhs, the Tartars . . ."

"The Afghans, the Pathans, the Mongols . . ." said another.

"The Uzbeks, the Huns, the Turks . . ."

Suleiman listened, dazed, as the names of Central Asian nations rolled before him.

"He has even conquered Fu-shien, a Chinese province that spreads beyond the Tien Shan Mountains," a last barbarian added. "All have fallen before him or joined him with eagerness, beguiled by the promise of loot and empire."

The Caliph drew breath. "Is there any part of Central Asia he has not conquered?"

One by one the spies shook their heads. Suleiman turned to his wizard, anger gathering. "Have you learned nothing with all your scrying that these men have not told me?"

"All is as they say." The oldest and most powerful of his wizards stepped forward. "We can only add that there are pockets of people here and there who have fled the cities that fell to Olgor and taken refuge in mountains, desert oases, and islands in the middle of vast lakes, who hold out against the Great Khan and stay free—but it seems they survive only because he does not think them worth his time when he has a world to conquer."

"We can say a bit more about the arguments with which Arjasp cozened Olgor," a middle-aged wizard added. "He told him tales of Iskander's empire, how that ancient Macedonian brought all the world under his sway, from Greece to the Indus River, in one short lifetime, not even a score of years. But he does not inspire his troops with Greek art and reason—he fires them with orgies and demon-worship."

The barbarians shuddered, and one pleaded, "Speak not against Angra Mainyu, or he will cast us into eternal night!"

"I shall speak against the demon king and condemn him indeed," the wizard told them, his face dark with anger, "for he cannot stand against the power of Allah, the One and Only God!"

The barbarians shrank from his words, moaning and making signs against evil.

"So Olgor's goal is nothing less than the conquest of the

whole world," Suleiman said, brooding, "though how a priest of the magi can preach the worship of Ahriman, I cannot understand. Still, it is not his ultimate purpose that must concern us here—it is his immediate target." He turned to a messenger. "Send word to Baghdad for all to leave the city and hide in the hills. We shall fall back and make a stand there; it may be that the city's walls will give us victory over these masses of uncouth horsemen."

The messenger bowed and turned away.

Suleiman turned back to the spies. "Will he be content with Baghdad, or must he come farther?"

"He will go to the edge of the world," said one.

Another said, "He means to conquer yourself and all your empire, of course, O Caliph—but he wishes most earnestly to conquer all of the Holy Lands, especially Jerusalem and Mecca, to desecrate them in order to gain power for his demonic lord. He thinks that with the holy places, he will take also the wills to resist of both Muslims and Christians."

A gasp of alarm echoed from every Arab, shocked at the audacity and impiety of such a thought.

"He may be right," said the oldest wizard grimly. "The common folk might well think that if God could not save the cities consecrated to Him, He could not also save His people."

"Such blasphemy," Suleiman said angrily, "and such falsehood! Allah is the only true God, though I will concede other nations may have other names for Him! None can triumph over Him, and we shall prove that upon Olgor's body!"

The barbarians trembled, and one screwed up his courage to say, "Know, O Sun of Wisdom, that these are not anti-Christian devil-worshipers, but anti-Muslim demonists. It is not the Christ whom they profane, but Allah."

"They will blaspheme the Christ soon enough," a wizard said darkly.

"I do not doubt it," Suleiman agreed. "Therefore must we make common cause with the Christians to stand against this corrupted khan."

The Arabs stared at him, shocked by the notion of such an alliance.

"How many of them are there?" Suleiman demanded of the spies.

The barbarians spread their hands, lost for words, and an Arab spy asked, "How many stalks of grass stand upon the steppes of Central Asia, my lord? His hordes are numbered by thousands, his subjects by hundreds of thousands. His warriors darken the plain to the horizon and beyond, and there are at least two camp-followers for each warrior, often more. They devastate the land like a plague of locusts."

Suleiman's face turned thunderous, but he only said, "Send word to King Richard in Bretanglia, to King Rinaldo in Ibile, to Queen Alisande in Merovence, to King Boncorro in Latruria, and to all the lesser monarchs of Europe. Send likewise to Tafas bin Daoud in Granada and all others of the governors of my empire, that they may know of this impious invader and send armies to crush him!"

"My lord," said his chief wizard, "it shall be done."

"Spoils 'em, I tell you!" one mule-driver claimed. "Spoils 'em rotten, both his wife and his children! Why, I hear tell he never even beats her!"

Balkis pricked up her cat-ears, very interested.

"Be sure he doesn't, Johann," another driver answered with a grin. "Would *you* beat your queen and sovereign?"

"Not if he wanted to keep living," a third said.

Johann frowned and avoided the question. "A man's *supposed* to beat his wife a little, Fritz! What kind of life can it be for a man, having his woman boss him around?"

"Come to think of it," Fritz said thoughtfully, "I've never heard of her bossing him around, either. He is a wizard, after all."

"There was that one time before they were married," the third driver offered. "The way I heard it, he swore some sort of foolish oath about taking the throne of Ibile from its sorcerer-ruler so's he'd be worthy to marry her, and the queen locked him up to keep him from going."

Balkis felt a tremor pass through her deep inside. This Lord Wizard sounded a most romantic fellow!

"Didn't work, Heinrich," Johann reminded him. "He magicked his way out and went questing anyway."

"Yah, but he didn't take the throne," Heinrich pointed out.

"No, he gave it back to King Rinaldo. *Then* he married Queen Alisande."

"Guess he'd proved her kingdom needed him," Heinrich said with a grin.

Balkis melted inside.

"But how about his little ones?" Johann demanded. "Kids're supposed to be spanked!"

"Not royal ones," Heinrich countered. "Why, I even hear some of 'em has servants to take their beatings for 'em!"

"Not Queen Alisande's," Johann said with disgust. "I hear that if Prince Kaprin is naughty, she doesn't let him practice sword drill that day—and if he's *really* bad, she won't let him go riding, either!"

"That's a punishment?" Fritz snorted.

"It is for a prince," Heinrich opined. "The royal ones take to swords and horses like most kids take to sweetmeats."

Johann sighed. "Well, I guess the Lord Wizard can always find a quick fumble with a serving maid. Who'd tell him no?"

"He would, from what I hear," Fritz said with disgust. "Matter of fact, he laid down the law with all the manservants and the soldiers even before his wife did!"

Heinrich stared. "You mean he won't even let the men sweet-talk the women into the hayloft?"

"He's put men out of jobs when he found out they wouldn't let the maids alone," Fritz averred.

"Now, that's going too far," Johann said with disgust. "Morals be all well and good, but not so many of 'em! A man's got a right to try, don't he?"

"Not if the woman don't want it," Heinrich told him, " 'leastways, according to the Lord Wizard."

Balkis decided that Idris had been right—the royal family was the one for her. It sounded as though the Lord Wizard might even be himself that ultimate rarity, a man whom a woman could trust—like her foster father. Besides, as her teacher had said, why not learn magic from the best?

The caravan swayed through the gates into Bordestang, and Balkis had no trouble deserting—the drivers went into

the first inn, leaving only one to watch the mule-train. She
slipped away, dodging between hooves, and set her course for
the castle, high above the town on its hill. She took a few false
twists and turns, and had a few bad moments when one of the
town mongrels decided she would make a good lunch—but
she was able to go straight up the corner of a half-timbered
building, leaving the nasty beast barking below in frustration.
She had no trouble leaping from roof to roof—they leaned so
closely together, scarcely a yard between—but as she went
uphill into the richer part of town, the houses grew larger and
drew apart. Finally she had to descend to the streets again,
and had a difficult time in an alley where a large tom refused
to believe she wasn't in heat. She glanced around, made sure
no one was watching, and changed back into a woman. The
tom yowled in fright and scurried over the nearest fence
without touching the wood.

Balkis turned back into a cat and stayed on the main road.
There were no more dogs in the streets—they all seemed to
be chained inside the yards of the great houses—so as dusk
turned into night, she came unscathed to the broad park that
fronted the castle's lower wall. She felt terribly exposed
crossing it, even in darkness, but she came to the wall without
incident. She followed it until she came to a wooden gate,
climbed it when the sentry was looking the other way, and
cat-footed her way along the top of the wall until she came to
a cherry tree espaliered against the stones. She climbed down
it and sprinted across the garden it contained—and nearly fell
into the moat.

She managed to claw her way to a stop, heart thudding, and
looked about her in the moonlight, wondering if she might
fare better as a girl now. But no one seemed to be about, except for the occasional sentry strolling his rounds, so she followed the moat, reasoning that there had to be a bridge
somewhere.

There was, and it was down. All she had to do was wait
until the sentries were looking the other way again, then
sprint across the wood and into the shadows of the gatehouse.
As she was catching her breath, she saw a small portal at
the end of the passage open. Half a dozen guards came out to

relieve the sentries. Quick as thought, she darted through the portal; it closed half an inch behind the tip of her tail.

She crouched in the shadows by the wall. The light of a torch high above showed her a spiral staircase. She sniffed, drinking in the smells of people washed too seldom, and of rats and mice sneaking about their nighttime business. She resisted the urge to go hunting and fairly flowed up the stone steps.

On the second floor she caught a whiff of a distant but familiar aroma, or a mixture of them, more accurately—cow's milk, soiled diapers, and sweet soap: the scent of a human baby. Nose twitching, she followed the aroma down halls and around corners until she came to a closed door. The baby-smell coming between the wood and the stone was quite strong, but there was also the scent of a grown woman—a nurse, no doubt. She padded along, identifying the aromas that went with a little boy—twigs and string, and the definite scent of a frog hidden somewhere—then past to a door that smelled of perfume. The one beyond reeked of leather and some sort of herb that evoked a memory from infancy, too evanescent to pin down, and Balkis knew better than to waste time trying, the more so because she saw an open door ahead of her at the end of the hallway.

She darted through it and found it a glare of moonlight. Instantly, her cat-eyes contracted until the light was comfortable, and she looked about her with interest, at a Persian carpet on the floor, oaken table and chairs, and clerestory windows filling a whole wall. She had never seen such a chamber, but had heard of them—it was a solar, a room that would be filled with the morning sun in a few hours, a place where people of the nobility passed their time when they were neither abed nor at work out of doors. The traces of perfume, baby-smell, boy-smell, leather, and that strange herb, told her, as clearly as though she could see them before her, that this was where the queen, the prince and princess, and the Lord Wizard gathered away from the public eye, to relax and be a family for a few hours each day.

What better place for a feline ambush? Balkis looked about her—and froze, astonished at the sight of a set of shelves eight feet wide that stretched to the ceiling, filled with books, real books! She had never seen so many in a single place, never more than a few together, and that only in the parsonage of the forest chapel. Whether they were about magic or not, she felt a sharp desire to read every one.

She would find a way to stay with this family, one way or another.

There were also tapestries hung as high as the bookcase, lower fringes brushing the floor. Balkis crept behind one to hide—and suddenly realized how tired she was. She kneaded the stone floor with her claws as she turned about and about, despaired of the flags growing any softer, and curled up in a ball to wait until daylight, and her chance to enchant the enchanter—or, at least, his wife and children.

Ramon Mantrell gazed fondly at his wife—fondly, and with something more than admiration, enough to make her lower her eyes demurely. "Ramon! Thirty years married, and still you stare?"

"I was only thinking how splendidly Renaissance gowns become you, my dear."

"And show a bit more bosom than is decent?" Jimena challenged him.

"Never too much," her husband assured her, "and our daughter-in-law's solar sets off your brocade perfectly. How many confirmed wives still glow in sunlight?"

Flooded by the sun, the whole room seemed vibrant and alive, as though it resonated with the vitality of the family that passed most of its free hours within it. The books seemed to radiate the spell of great stories, the tapestries almost to come to life, and even the granite blocks to warm with the morning's light. The wood of the table, chairs, and chest seemed to live in some fashion, and to delight in their part in the living gestalt that was the family.

"And I must say that doublet and hose become *you*." Jimena reached out a hand to caress his. "Enough to make me think most ungrandmotherly thoughts. Have you not heard of a grandfather's only regret?"

"What, that he is married to a grandmother?" Ramon's

grin widened. "There can never be regret, if the grandmother is you."

Footsteps sounded in the hall, and voices in earnest discussion, with smaller voices raised in salute to the dawn behind them.

"Hush, now." Jimena patted his hand. "Here come the children. Behave."

Their son Matthew and his wife, Queen Alisande, swept into the solar, followed by two nursemaids, a small boy and smaller girl, and a butler and two footmen. The queen was saying, "Yes, it is far away, but the presence of so many barbarians coming closer and closer to Europe concerns me."

"And if it concerns you, it concerns Merovence." Matt nodded. "But they're still far away, dear, and we can take half an hour away from them to enjoy breakfast with our family."

"Oh, of course!" Alisande said with chagrin, and turned to her parents-in-law contritely. "Good morning, lord and lady."

"Good morning, Your Majesty." Ramon gave a little bow, sure that she would be calling him "Father" in a few minutes.

Jimena didn't seem disturbed by Alisande's early morning formalities, either. She clasped her daughter-in-law's hand and said, "I am so glad you have accepted our custom of the family's dining together, my dear."

"It is wise council, my lady mother," Alisande said, "and I thank you for it."

They took their seats in hourglass chairs, and two small ones with very long legs, around an octagonal table set for breakfast. Sunlight filled them all with the morning's glow.

"Some of your fellow monarchs may sneer at our living like peasants in such a manner," Ramon cautioned her.

"True," Alisande agreed, "but it will endear us to the common folk, and what are we without their support?"

"A good point," said Papa, thinking of the last czar.

"Besides," Alisande said, "when we have so little time to be a family, we must make the most of each minute . . . Kaprin, your spoon!"

"Yes, Mama," the little boy grumbled, picking up his spoon and abandoning his dream of fistfuls of porridge. He dug the spoon in and eyed his sister as though estimating the range.

"It's for putting the food in your mouth," Matt said quickly, and Kaprin cast his father a guilty look, then brought the spoon to his lips, all injured innocence.

A nurse guided Princess Alice's hand as she plied her own spoon. The child swallowed, dropped the implement, and picked up her two-handed mug for a swallow of milk.

"She develops well," Grandma said with pride.

"Yes, and I see that it is good for her," Alisande said. "She manages well enough with her toy sword, but you were right, Lady Mother—this does require more control."

"Call me 'Grandmother,' dear," Jimena reproved gently.

"But the children will think that is your name!"

"They will learn to say 'Jimena' soon enough, and 'Grandmother' is a title of which I am far more proud than the peerage you have granted me."

"Very well—" Alisande relaxed enough to beam fondly at her mother-in-law. "—Grandmother."

They finished breakfast, and the butler poured tea, his face screwed into lines of disapproval at the foreign beverage. He couldn't deny, however, that it cost so much as to be worthy of a queen. The nursemaids released Kaprin and Alice from the bondage of their feeding chairs, and the prince ran to the blocks set aside for him under a side table to begin building his first castle of the day. Alice toddled over to join him, but Grandma, sensing an imminent territorial dispute, side-tracked her by picking up a doll and making it dance on her lap. In a squeaky voice, she called out, "A-A-A-A-lice!"

The little girl stopped, turned, looked, and padded over toward her grandmother with a laugh of delight. Unfortunately, her fat little legs became tangled and she sat down rather abruptly. Her face twisted, mouth opening in a wail.

"Oh, dear!" Jimena laid aside the doll and reached down.

Before she could touch the child, though, a tapestry moved and bulged near the floor.

Alisande instantly tensed, hand going to the dagger at her side. "Husband!"

But Jimena beat her son to the song.

> "No assassin harm us!
> Nor no witchcraft charm us!
> Ghost unlaid forbear us!

Nothing ill come near us!
Naught that's foul at us shall rave!
Peace and quiet we shall have!"

But the tapestry lifted, and a small calico cat with outsized ears crept out.

Matt stared. "Where did *that* come from?"

The baby took one look at the furry stranger and broke off crying, staring in wonder.

The nursemaids gasped and started for the intruder.

Jimena waved them back. "Well, we can be sure it intends no ill, at least. In fact, its entrance is quite welcome."

"But how *did* it get here?"

"With a kitchen maid, like as not," Alisande said, "and crept out of the scullery looking for mice in the night." She shrugged. "My castle is proof against wolf and lion, army and knight, husband—but not against so small a thing as a mouse, nor she who hunts it."

The cat stepped toward little Alice, ears forward and alert. The baby gurgled and reached with a hand that hadn't yet learned to control its strength. The cat shied away, then batted at the little fist with a paw. Alice laughed and pushed up to hands and knees to pursue.

Across the room Kaprin looked up, then came toward the cat, eyes kindling with interest.

"She is only a kitten!" Grandpa cried.

"No, I think full grown," Jimena said. "I have seen a cat like that before—an Abyssinian, it was, small and with large ears. This one looks somewhat different, not quite of so southern a breed, but has that same air of maturity. She is young, yes, but I am sure the toms think she is full grown."

The cat neatly evaded a clutch by Kaprin and scooted underneath Alice. The little girl cooed with delight and sat back on her heels, exposing the cat. Kaprin reached down . . .

Grandma's hand arrested him. "Gently, Kaprin, gently! They are delicate, you know, and wary. You must earn her trust."

"Yeah, you have to make friends with them," Matt seconded. "Cats choose you, not the other way around. Hold out your hand and let her sniff it. Then if she decides to take a chance on you, pet her very, very gently."

Kaprin reached out a hand. Alice squalled objection—it was her cat, after all—and reached for a tail. But the cat turned back in one lithe movement, tail slipping from between fat little fingers even as they closed, and sniffed at the little hand, then touched it with a cold nose. The baby cooed with delight.

"Sniff *me*!" Kaprin demanded.

Nothing loath, the cat turned and sniffed at his palm, then gave it a lick. Kaprin chortled with joy, and the little beast turned back to flow under Alice's reaching hand, forcing an involuntary petting. Alice gurgled with pleasure.

"That," Matt said, "is one smart cat."

"She does seem experienced with babes," Alisande agreed.

Matt grinned at her. "Well, the decision about what kind of pet the family needs seems to have been made for us, dear. Now all you have to do is decide whether you want one or not."

The cat arched its back as it stepped past Alice, brushing its fur under her chin. Alice crowed and Kaprin turned thunderous with jealousy.

"A bit of string," Jimena said to a nursemaid.

The woman looked startled, then pulled some yarn from a capacious pocket and broke off a length.

Jimena handed it to Kaprin and said, "Let its end touch the floor and shake it."

With total faith in Grandma, the little boy did just that. The cat went stiff as a pointer, staring, then crouched down, tail-tip twitching.

"Try to keep it from her," Grandma told him.

The cat pounced, but Kaprin managed to twist the bit of string out of the way at the last second. The cat followed, batting at the yarn, and both children cried out with excitement.

"Is there a decision to be made?" Grandma asked.

"Yes, and the children have made it," Alisande said with a sigh. "They would be devastated if we took the beast from them now. Only make sure it comes from no evil sorcerer, husband, and carries no pestilence."

"Just a few spells," Matt acknowledged. "No problem. We

can't just call it 'cat,' though—at least, not if it's going to be a member of the family."

"If it is Abyssinian," said Grandpa, "we should call it Sheba, the biblical name for that land. After all, should not the royal cat be royal herself?"

"Call her after Sheba's queen, you mean?" Grandma nodded. "A good thought—but let us use her name, not her land."

"I didn't know it was ever recorded," Matt said, frowning.

"Do you not remember your Kipling?" Grandma chided. " 'The Butterfly Who Stamped'?"

"Of course!" Grandpa cried, with a smile of delight. "Balkis, the Best Beloved!"

The cat's head snapped around, staring at them in amazement.

CHAPTER 5

"See how she stares!" Mama cried. "Perhaps we have guessed better than we knew."

"You do not mean I have struck upon the name someone else has already given her!" Ramon protested.

"Let us see." Mama patted her lap. "Come talk with me, Balkis."

The little cat padded over to her, jumped up into her lap, reared up to set her feet on Jimena's chest, and stared into her eyes.

"Never try to outstare a cat," Ramon cautioned.

"I would not be so foolish," Jimena assured him, but she looked directly into the cat's eyes anyway and recited,

> "What you are stands over you,
> Glaring so I cannot see
> What you show as mask untrue.
> If you mean ill to any here,
> Let it flare in nimbus 'round you,
> Good intentions showing blue,
> Selfishness as yellow sere,
> Red for meanings we should fear!"

A green aura sprang up about the cat. She blinked in surprise, then cowered, gathering herself to spring.

"Green?" Matt said. "She means us well, but is selfish about it?"

"Isn't every cat?" Jimena returned, and stroked gently to reassure Balkis. "But her interests must coincide with our own, and therefore she means us no ill, at least, and perhaps well."

"Because if she makes the children happy, we'll make her happy?" Matt nodded. "Enlightened self-interest—very dependable. Okay, Balkis, we offer steady food, petting when you want it, and a garden for bird-chasing and natural functions. How's that for a good deal?"

The little cat turned to stare at him.

"She certainly recognizes her name," Ramon said. "She could not have understood anything else you said."

"Well, maybe the word 'food,' " Matt demurred.

"Be assured that you are welcome, Balkis," Alisande said with a smile.

"There!" Matt said. "If the queen herself says it, you know you can trust it!"

The cat mewed plaintively.

"I think she wishes to test your promise of food." Jimena took a scrap of meat from her plate, offering it to the cat. Balkis nibbled daintily. "You shall have as much nourishment as you wish."

Balkis stopped nibbling and looked up at the shelves of books.

The adults laughed, and Jimena said gently, "You would not find parchment and ink to your liking, little one."

Balkis gave a mew of disappointment and went back to the meat. The others gave another gentle laugh, but Matt took on a thoughtful expression.

Little Kaprin came up and reached out to touch the cat's head.

"Gently," Grandma reminded, and the touch became feather-light as Kaprin said, "Good boy!"

"No, Kaprin," Grandma said, "this is a girl cat."

Kaprin looked disappointed. "How do you know, Grandma?"

"Because if it had been a boy cat, it would be obvious," she said. "Your father will explain it to you when you are older."

"Yeah, by about two hours," Matt warned her. "I will admit that it should be a private discussion, though."

Balkis looked up from her food to glare at Grandma, switching her tail.

"Yes, I know it is a rather intimate detail to discuss in

public," Grandma said apologetically, "but Kaprin is old enough to need to know."

Balkis gave an indignant sniff, then thawed enough to rub her head against Grandma's hand.

Jimena relaxed. "I have been accepted."

Balkis pivoted and sprang to Alisande's lap.

"Oh!" the queen cried in delight. "I too pass inspection?"

Balkis reared back, feet on Alisande's neckline, and stared into her eyes.

"Inspection, yes," Matt said. "Passing remains to be seen."

Balkis rubbed her head against Alisande's hand.

Alisande laughed. "Why, how is this, husband? Am I to be judged, and chosen or cast out, here in my own castle?"

"You bet," Matt said. "Cats know they're the real owners."

"And no matter where they are, they can send you to Coventry in an instant," Ramon assured her.

"Send me to Coventry?" Alisande asked, puzzled.

"Forget that you exist," Matt explained, "and make you wonder about it, too."

"Be glad she has accepted you, dear," Jimena said, "or you might have had to move out."

Balkis jumped into Matt's lap.

"Who shall have to move out now, husband?" Alisande challenged.

Balkis gave Matt a good sniffing and looked doubtful.

Suleiman sat his horse on the plain around the city of Baghdad, watching his army file through the gate into the nearly empty town. Now and again he glanced apprehensively at the pillar of dust to the east which marked the barbarians' progress.

"Be easy, my lord," said the battle-worn general beside him. "They will all be inside and the gates closed and barred before the wild men come in view."

"In, yes," Suleiman replied, "but how shall we come out again?"

A much smaller plume of dust rose from the west. The general braced himself. Two cavalrymen broke off from the inbound column and rode up beside the plume, matching speed with it.

"Your soldiers must have approved of whoever rides," the Caliph said, "for he still approaches, and they with him."

"A courier?" the general guessed.

It was a courier indeed, his skin a bit darker than theirs, his robes bright with the patterns of the Berbers. He reined in his lathered horse and fell more than dismounted, then dropped to his knees, haggard with weariness. "Hail, O Father of All the Faithful!"

"Hail, steadfast soldier," the Caliph returned. "What word do you bring?"

"Salutations from Tafas bin Daoud!" The messenger fumbled a scroll from his belt and offered it. One of the soldiers reached down, took it, and passed it to the general as the courier explained, "He greets you with love and reverence, and tells you that he has gathered a host of Moors and rides at their head to defend the holy places."

"He is a devout son of Islam," Suleiman said with ill-disguised relief, "and praised be Allah that he marches!"

"He will be a month and more, riding across North Africa and Arabia to join us," the general warned. "Can we hold the city till he comes?"

"We shall have to," the Caliph said simply. Then he smiled with a touch of his old bravado; his teeth flashed as he said, "With Allah to strengthen us, how can we fail?"

"Let it be as He wills," the general said somberly, "but I would be more reassured if some of the Christian monarchs had answered, too."

"Peace be within your breast," Suleiman told him. "They are farther distant than Tafas, and belike only now receive our summons."

" 'Therefore do we ask that you join us without delay in defending the city of Jerusalem, and the sites that are holy to Muslim, Jew, and Christian alike,' " Jimena read, and rolled up the scroll. "He ends with the usual compliments and titles, and assurances of brotherhood."

"I thank you." Alisande gazed down from her throne at the

dusty Arabian messenger, who had been hauled up off his knees by two stout Merovencian guardsmen. They still held his arms, because his legs were likely to collapse again with sheer fatigue. The queen said to one, "Take him to a bed, and bring him food and drink—if he can stay awake long enough to take them."

"As Your Majesty wishes." The guardsman looked strongly disapproving of hospitality to a pagan.

"I thank you, stalwart soldier," Alisande said to the courier. "You have ridden long and hard, and have shown great devotion to your caliph and your cause. Go now and rest, for you have earned it well."

The man blinked in surprise at being thanked so directly by a sovereign, then detached an arm from one of the guardsmen and touched fingers to brow, lips, and breast as he bowed to the queen. He started to back away, but the guardsmen turned him around and half escorted, half carried him from the throne room.

"You are a marvel, Mother Mantrell, and a godsend," Alisande said. "How is it you can read the Arabian script?"

"It is useful, if you wish to study the history of the Spain of our world," Jimena told her. "Still, if they had not written in the language of Merovence, my knowledge of their script would have done little good."

Alisande turned to Matt and asked, "What do you think of this news, my husband?"

"It has the ring of truth," Matt told her. "The Caliph would scarcely admit weakness to a Frankish monarch otherwise."

"That is true," Alisande said, "and confirms the verity that I feel within me. But how can an army so distant be a threat to my Merovence?"

"Because it contains so many soldiers," Matt said grimly, "and all of them are horsemen. Worse, they're fanatics. They seek loot and plunder, but they think they ride in a god's cause, and that they'll go directly to a reward of extravagant pleasure if they die in his service." Thinking of the Huns, Turks, and Mongols of his own universe, he assured her, "No, my dear, there's no doubt—anything riding in off the plains of Central Asia is a very real threat, not only to the Arabian empire, but also to Europe."

"In fact, one could find room to wonder why the Arabian empire still holds," Ramon mused, "and has not yet fallen to the Turks."

"I can only think that the Turks have not ridden west—till now," Jimena said, "though it seems they are subservient to the Mongol barbarians."

"You must tell me of these barbarians another time," Alisande said, frowning. "For the moment, we must decide whether to march, and with how large a force."

"Doesn't the size of the army depend on how many Allustria, Ibile, and Latruria will send?" Matt asked.

"Even so," Alisande confirmed. "I cannot leave my country defenseless if my neighbors keep all their armies home. Well then, we must send to King Richard in Bretanglia, Frisson the Regent in Allustria, King Rinaldo in Ibile, and King Boncorro in Latruria. But we must send *some* force to the Holy Land, I can feel the necessity in my bones."

In a universe in which, when the country was in danger, the monarch's bones ached, that was no small evidence. Alisande was queen by Divine Right, which created a bond of enchantment between herself, her people, and her land. She instinctively knew what was right or wrong for Merovence, and ignored her intuition at all their peril.

"I shall ask you to be castellans and regents again, lord and lady," Alisande said formally to her in-laws.

"Must you lead the army yourself, my dear?" Jimena asked anxiously.

Alisande hesitated.

Matt read her expression of doubt correctly. "Not until you're sure your sibling monarchs won't try to invade, is that it?"

"It is." Alisande flashed him a quick look of gratitude. "I shall send my expedition under Lord Sauvignon's command, then ride posthaste to join them if I am certain I am not needed here."

"Should you invite the Witch Doctor to ride with them?" Ramon asked.

"Saul was never too enthusiastic about the Muslims," Matt said. "His fascinations lay farther east."

"India and China, you mean?" Ramon nodded. "Still, we speak of him as a wizard, not a scholar."

"I am loath to tear him again from his wife and babes," Alisande said.

"Why not make use of Saul here, then," Matt said, "after you are gone and I've ridden ahead?"

The throne room was very quiet.

Then Alisande exploded. "I knew this would come! Am I so boring, husband, that you must take to the high road at every chance of adventure?"

"Never," Matt said, looking directly into her eyes, "but you are so precious to me that if I can stop a threat before it reaches you, I will."

Alisande met his gaze, but only held it about ten seconds before she melted and reached out to grasp his hand. "It seems, though, that you are forever leaving me!"

"Never willingly." Matt returned the pressure. "And never for more than a few months every year or three. It's just bad luck, darling, that you were born to be queen at a time when the powers of Hell are making a very good try at dragging down all the nations of Europe. Sure, we've managed to win the lands back so far, but they're still trying to set us against one another."

Alisande looked deeply into his eyes, searching for reassurance, and when she found it, closed her eyes and lowered her chin in assent. "You speak truly, husband. Nay, I must let you go forth again." Her eyes flew open and she glared at him in command. "But only to gather information, mind you! You must not risk yourself unless it is absolutely necessary!"

"Only to protect the weak," Matt assured her. "I may have to travel a long way to find out what lies behind this invasion, though."

"Be of good heart, my dear," Jimena consoled. "Lord Sauvignon and your army shall be following, if there is any real threat."

"Even a week can be far too long a time," Alisande countered, "when my love is in peril."

"Hey, I'll be safe as long as I'm behind the Caliph's lines," Matt cajoled. "I've always wanted to see Jerusalem, anyway."

The question, though, was whether the Caliph's lines would hold.

Holes suddenly caved in all along the eastern wall of Baghdad, and barbarians boiled out of them, small hard-muscled men with flowing moustaches and ugly hairless heads ridged with scar tissue. They shouted war-cries as they charged the inside of the gate, slashing with short heavy sabers—but they ran with a bow-legged, ungainly gait.

Archers on the wall spun about and sent flights of arrows into the attackers. Dozens of barbarians fell, but dozens more jumped clumsily over their bodies and flailed at the gate guards. The porters swung their pole-arms to block, then to counter. Two of the four fell, but a score of Arabs came pounding up to aid them, small round shields up to block the Mongols' blows, scimitars flashing. Unlike the attackers, they hadn't lived all their lives on horseback, and were far quicker runners.

But fifty more Mongols clambered out of the tunnels and ran toward a corral of Arabian mares. It wasn't guarded— who would need to ward horses within a city? Too late, Arabian soldiers saw them coming and shouted in anger, running to cut them off—but the Mongols caught the horses' manes and sprang high, landing on their backs as though they had been there since birth, then leaned down to cut the horses' tethers with single strokes of their curved swords. They whirled their mounts and rode down the Arabs, screaming their war-cry.

The Arabs sprang aside, though, and hurled swords, shields, anything they had, at the invaders. A dozen hit their marks, a dozen Mongols fell, but the rest charged into the fray around the gates, screaming like demons and laying about them with their swords. Their own men parted to let them through.

With cries of anger and despair, the guards set their pole-arms so that the Mongols' prized horses ran upon the points.

The horses screamed and reared, then fell. The Mongols sprang from their backs in the nick of time and turned to face the scimitars of the Arabs with their own yataghans—to little effect; Damascus steel cut through their untempered blades. One or two Arabs fell, but more of the Mongols.

Their companions, screaming in frustration, tried to force their mounts through to the gate, but couldn't get them over the fallen horses. They wheeled to ride away so they could turn and gallop back with enough momentum to hurdle the dead, but a squad of Arab cavalry rode down on them with howls of rage. Mongol met Arab in their natural element, the backs of horses, and proved very quickly that they were evenly matched when mounted.

"The slope!" cried the captain of the guard. "Ward the slope!"

Half the archers on the wall turned to see a thousand barbarians gallop up the scree toward the gate. Bows thrummed on both sides, but the horsemen were too far away, and their arrows fell short. The Arabs, though, with longer bows, had longer range, and the front rank of barbarians fell. The second rank hurdled them as though they weren't there and charged on toward the gate, only six abreast, but with thousands of reinforcements behind them.

More archers came running; more bowstrings sang of death and blood. The barbarians fell in windrows, and at last their captain, convinced of the futility, turned his men and rode away.

At the gate, superior numbers won the day, and the Mongols died to a man, each still screaming his war-cry. When all lay still, the Arabs stood glaring down at them, chests heaving. As the heat of battle cooled, first one, then many, lifted their swords in grudging salute.

"They are fearless," said one soldier, "and mighty fighters, when they are horsed."

Even the Caliph came down to pay homage to worthy enemies. "Lay their bodies upon the slope outside the gate," he commanded, "so that their fellows may bear them away during the night. When all are laid out as befits warriors, play a dirge from the wall to do them honor."

He turned away, but his chief wizard fell into step beside him and said, "They are mighty warriors, as you say, lord. How shall we hold the city against so many of them?"

"With faith in Allah," the Caliph answered, "and hope that my governors can bring their armies while we can still hold off these barbarians."

Matt always tried to go spying without his friend Stegoman the Dragon. True, the mighty beast was worth an army of bodyguards, and was excellent transportation as well as very good company—but he did tend to make a man somewhat conspicuous, and when you were trying to pick up gossip from roadside inns, that could be a noticeable handicap. Stegoman could definitely be classed as a conversation stopper.

Matt did, however, ride a horse, which automatically boosted him a social class or two higher than the average citizens he usually wanted to listen to—but he needed speed first, and didn't really need to eavesdrop until he reached the Holy Land. There, he could sell the horse if he had to, but he couldn't sell a dragon, and Stegoman was very hard to send away for more than a night or two.

In spite of his reassurances to Alisande, Matt did feel a lifting of the soul as the skyline of the capital city fell below the horizon. For a few months now he would be free of his daily responsibilities and liberated from the intrigues and social infighting of the court, which sometimes made him so heartsick he was tempted to give everybody a magical brainwashing. So far he had always resisted, out of respect for free will if nothing else. Out here on the open road, though, it was emotionally clean if physically dusty, and the sweep of the countryside made the air seem fresher.

Unfortunately, the countryside was still sweeping when the sun set. Matt resigned himself to a night in the open. He chose a campsite just off the road, under some pine trees near a brook. Tethering his horse in the middle of plenty of rich green grass, he unsaddled and combed the beast, then decided to cut some boughs for a mattress while there was still twilight. He reached into his saddlebag for his camp hatchet.

Warm fur moved against his fingers.

Matt snatched his hand out, stifling a curse, then opened the saddlebag wide and turned it so he could see in.

Two large pointed ears pushed up over the rim, then two

large slit-pupiled eyes in a round brindle head. Balkis opened her mouth and meowed reproach at him.

Matt stared.

Then he laughed and held out cupped hands. "Wanted to go adventuring, huh? Well, hop out and help pitch camp!"

Balkis hurdled over the side of the saddlebag and into his hands, then cuddled against his chest, purring like a nutmeg grater.

Matt fondled her head. "Now, why would you want to go to the discomfort of being crammed into that saddlebag all day?" He asked the question with a lighthearted note, but his nasty suspicious nature was working overtime. Not only had this cat stowed away, which was rather uncatlike behavior, but she had also managed to lie still and stay quiet, which spoke of either absolute terror or a degree of self-control that was unbelievable in an animal—and Matt didn't think he was all that terrifying. "This isn't the job you signed up for, you know. You were supposed to be a babysitter."

Balkis looked up indignantly, as though to say any actual job would be beneath her dignity.

Matt met her eyes, staring straight into them. Balkis stiffened in irritation and glared back at him, as though affronted by the temerity of any mere human who might try to outstare a cat.

Sure that she wouldn't look away, Matt crooned,

"To your wizard pay some heed,
Follow you his every lead.
Him in all respects obey,
His bidding do in every way."

The cat's stare glazed; he could see her natural independence struggling against his spell, and wondered which would win.

Then Balkis opened her mouth, beginning with a yawn that developed into a meowing tone that shaped itself into words:

"No female thoughtless should comply
With strange male's wishes, lacking facts.

Each thought she should with conscience scry,
And debate each issue ere she acts."

Then she sat in his arms, glaring defiantly, every muscle tensed to spring and run.

Matt just stared, mind racing—talking cats just didn't happen. This creature was more than she seemed.

He took a deep breath. "So. You won't be taking my orders to explain why you came along."

"A spell to counter a spell," Balkis mewed. "How could I have told without words?"

"Cats have always found ways to make their wishes known." Matt didn't bother mentioning that the next spell would have given her the power of speech she already had.

Balkis turned her head, eyeing him sideways. "You seem to know a great deal about our breed."

"My mother had a knack of taking care of strays," Matt explained. "She wouldn't let them into the house, but she had a very lively backyard." He didn't mention that she had also been very careful about letting the family cocker spaniel out.

"I knew there was reason for liking her," Balkis purred.

"There surely is," Matt agreed. "So who taught you how to talk?"

"My sire and dam," Balkis replied flippantly.

"Very unusual cats," Matt said. "Whoever taught them must have taught you a bit of magic."

"I can cast simple spells," Balkis said, her eyes wary.

"Look, you had a really soft berth set up in the castle," Matt pointed out. "Why come along to share the discomforts and dangers of the road with me?"

"I am no stranger to the road," Balkis told him, "and I doubt there will truly be much danger."

"Then you should pay a bit more attention to the reports of the barbarians who're invading the Arabian empire. That still doesn't explain why you would leave a full food bowl and a soft cushion to come camping."

"Do you dislike my company?" Balkis challenged.

"I've learned to value solitude," Matt said, then tried a different tack. "Why did you come to Merovence?"

"Because I learned that you have a much more favorable

attitude toward females than I would find in my homeland," Balkis replied.

So she wasn't a native. That explained the exotic look. "What homeland was that?"

"Allustria."

Matt frowned; Allustria favored the alley variety of feline, not rare breeds. "*You* were born in Allustria?"

"I grew up there," Balkis prevaricated.

Matt decided to let the question of origins alone for the moment. "Why did you come to the castle?"

Balkis turned shifty-eyed. "I heard the queen had children, and where there are little ones, a cat will be welcome."

"Seems you know a lot about people," Matt said. "Okay, so you played patty-paw and got yourself a soft berth with my very understanding mother and my overworked wife. Why leave it all to come along with me?"

Balkis was caught; she knew it, and didn't like it. Glaring at Matt, she admitted, "I wish to learn more about magic than I know, and I shall not learn it playing with your babes in your absence."

Matt frowned down at her, considering. He was beginning to develop doubts about her species, and he ordinarily screened his helpers very thoroughly. "There are many wise women and village wizards who could teach you."

"I've learned all the best of them can teach," Balkis snapped. "She bade me seek out you."

"Oh, she did?" Matt felt unreasonably flattered. "Who was this woman?"

"Idris."

"Don't know her." Matt frowned. "Where does she dwell?"

"In the Black Forest."

"I'll have to look her up the next time I'm out that way." Matt saw Balkis' look of alarm and hastened to reassure her. "Don't worry, I don't pick quarrels with good magicians—I have too much need of every one I can find."

Again the guarded look. "Need for what?"

"To combat evil, and most especially evil magic," Matt explained. "It helps to know who I can call on in every place I may find myself. You don't really think you're going to learn magic just from watching me, do you?" He had a notion she had intended just that, and realized with a start why she'd been so interested in the bookshelves.

Balkis watched him with a cat-steady stare, then said, "I had hopes you might teach me."

"But just in case I wouldn't, you planned to spy on me as much as possible?"

"Cats have the right to observe everything everywhere," Balkis told him loftily.

Matt stared deeply into her eyes, frowning. "There's something more you're not telling me."

Balkis' gaze shifted, then came back to him. "How did you know?"

Matt shrugged. "Call it a wizard's hunch. What is it?"

"Nothing for which I can find words," Balkis said slowly, "only that, when I heard you were going to the Orient, something within me compelled me to go along, much though I mislike the discomforts."

"I never argue with a geas." Matt had labored under just such a compulsion himself once. "But you could have gone with Lord Sauvignon and the army, with a good deal more safety—at least until they reached the Holy Land. Why didn't you simply wait for them to march?"

"I might have been left behind, deemed unfit to accompany an army," Balkis said.

Matt shook his head. "You're fishing for excuses."

The cat looked angry, but admitted, "My compulsion is too strong to let me wait."

Matt stared into her eyes again, weighing her words and judging that they smacked of truth. He decided to let her off the hook. "You sure this doesn't have anything to do with wanting to get away from a couple of kids?"

Balkis looked surprised, then sheepish, if you can describe a cat that way. "They are too small to know how to treat a cat properly," she admitted.

"Wolves and bears might be less of a danger," Matt agreed, then let a little admiration show. "Definitely smarter than the average cat."

Balkis fluffed herself up in indignation. "There is no such

thing as an average cat! We are all superior to every other species of creature, and *I* am superior to all other cats."

Said with all feline modesty, Matt reflected—every cat seemed to feel that way. "I suppose 'every other species' includes humans?"

"Of course," said Balkis in surprise. "Why else would you be willing to serve our food and open and close your doors to let us in and out?"

CHAPTER 6

From the ramparts, Caliph Suleiman could see nothing but tents stretching away from northeast to southeast, all the way to the horizon and, said his spies, well beyond it. The clangor of smiths at work rang over the plain, echoed by the banging of carpenters' hammers.

"I can see a catapult taking shape," reported a sharp-eyed sentry.

"Yonder is a rude wheeled tower." Another sentry pointed toward the east, where a rectangular shape was rising.

"Rude, but effective," Suleiman said grimly. "In a day, perhaps two, they will strike."

"We cannot hold against them," his general said, watching him with dread. He feared to say unwelcome words, but pressed on from the need to have them said. "Their catapults will break our gates, they will pour over our walls from their siege towers. Our soldiers will slay them by the dozens, but will themselves be slain, and in the end there will be none to hinder these barbarians from running loose in the city."

"There is no help for it," the Caliph said darkly. "We cannot wait, for the armies from North Africa and Ibile may come too late. We must retreat."

A barely heard sigh of relief breathed all about him.

"They will slay us all if they see us sally forth," the general pointed out.

The Caliph nodded. "But they have only a few scouts watching the western walls. Let our footmen and archers build ladders and go pouring down from the ramparts even as our cavalry goes charging out the western gate."

"Well thought, my lord." The general nodded slowly. "By

70

the time their scouts can bring their main army, perhaps we will have found a proper ground for a battle."

"High ground, where our archers can slay them by the hundred," Suleiman agreed, "and in their eagerness to catch us, perhaps they will neglect the city."

"When they have finished with us?" the general asked dubiously.

Suleiman's grin flashed in the sunlight. "Then we must make sure they do *not* finish with us. Give the orders for the retreat. We shall quit this city when the left hand of dawn is in the sky."

As the sun rose, Matt drowned his campfire, shouldered his pack, mounted his horse, and set off down the southern road.

Balkis poked her head out of the saddlebag and complained, "You choose a horribly early hour to be on your way!"

"Serves you right for staying out all night," Matt retorted. "How was the hunting?"

"Very poor," the cat said, disgusted. "There are many owls by this stream, and they took all the mice. I caught only three voles."

"How were they?"

"Not as good as those of Allustria."

"Must be the soil," Matt said judiciously. "Merovence grows great grapes, but that doesn't say it'll do as well for minor mammals."

"They were tough and stringy."

Matt nodded. "Had to burrow through. Too much clay, no doubt. Made 'em muscular."

"Scarcely worth the effort," Balkis agreed. "You could at least let me sleep."

"Hey, what're you griping about?" Matt countered. "You've got a nice comfortable saddlebag all to yourself—I moved the rest of the cargo into the other one. Just settle down and nap."

"If I can, on a swaying beast," Balkis griped, but the small head disappeared. The saddlebag rippled for a bit, then stilled.

Matt shook his head. "Just had to have the last word."

"I did not," snapped a meowly voice.

Matt grinned and had sense enough not to answer.

It was a pleasant ride, in the early morning—down a winding road by a stream, leaves stirring in the dawn breeze. Even as the day grew hotter and the road swung away from the water, the landscape was pleasant to watch—hedges dividing fields into a patchwork of different shades of green, lavender, or rose where a fallow field had sprouted flowers. Yes, it was a very pleasant ride until the blunt object struck the back of Matt's head. He had only time for a feeling of outrage before the darkness closed in.

The eastern sky washed pale with the predawn twilight, and in its silence hundreds of scaling ladders thrust over the western walls of Baghdad, lowered to the ground, and filled with a steady stream of soldiers. They climbed down as quickly as they could, none speaking, all moving as quietly as possible. In similar noiselessness, the doors of the great western gate swung open, and the cavalry rode out at a trot that turned quickly to a canter.

Their silence was laudable, but useless—Turkish sentries in the hills saw, stared in disbelief, then sent horsemen galloping to the khan with the news. Still, it took time for the couriers to arrive and longer for the warriors to leave their tents, strap on swords, sling their bows, and mount their horses. By the time they came shrilling and galloping over the plain, the last of the Arabs had cleared the wall.

The barbarians rode all out, trying to catch up—but the khan, with a cooler head than Suleiman had hoped, held back half his force. A hundred riders charged through the open western gate into the empty city. Not long after, the eastern gate swung open and barbarians poured into Baghdad.

"There!" The Caliph pointed to rising ground between two rivers. "Give the command for all to ride to that plateau!"

"So slight as that?" the general cried, aghast. "They shall thunder upon us without the slightest slackening of speed, lord! There shall be no chance for our archers to bring them down!"

"There shall, for between us and that table land lie the marshes! Around and up, Emir, quickly!"

The general gave the order, and trumpets blared. The vanguard turned, fording the rivers on each side and turning again to ride up onto the high ground.

As the rear guard rode up, the general looked about him with pleased surprise. "That neck of land is so narrow, only half a dozen barbarians can ride up abreast! How did you know of this, lord?"

"I have heard of this confluence often," the Caliph replied. "One of my ancestors was balked by a small army here; they held off his horsemen for days, until he tired of assaulting them and rode past to capture Damascus." He turned to look eastward toward the advancing horde, hooves beginning to be heard as thunder. "We have a river to each side of us and marshland before—but since the ground slopes down gently to those marshes, the barbarians may try to ride directly toward us."

"They shall succeed!"

"I think not," the Caliph said, and waited.

The thunder grew louder; it filled the world, and the ground began to tremble under their feet. The Arabs' horses began to grow restive, tossing their heads and fighting the bridles, but their riders held them steady. Then the horde burst into the marshes, waving their swords and shrilling their war-cries.

Their ponies stumbled in the mud, fell to their knees, and could not rise again.

Riders leaped off, cursing, and tried to help their mounts up. Many struggled back to their feet, but some had ridden into quagmires and, thrash though they might, only sank deeper. Other barbarians threw ropes to the riders and pulled them free. Here and there they even saved a horse or two— but more barbarians, not seeing the fate of the first, galloped into the marshes and bogged down. In minutes the whole breadth of the wetland was filled with barbarians struggling to free their horses from the agglutinative mud.

"Bid the archers loose," the Caliph said.

The general signaled and the trumpets sang. Archers lifted bows, strings thrummed, and hundreds of barbarians fell with arrows in thigh or chest. Horses, too, died with barbs in them, which was a quicker death than the mud gave.

"Loose again!" the general cried. "Again, and again!"

The air filled with arrows. The barbarians returned the fire, but their bows were made for power, not range, and their arrows fell far short. Immune, the Arabs stood high above and rained arrows upon them. At last the barbarians turned and scrambled for the odd bits of dry land, trying to make their way out of the marshes.

Their khan must have seen their plight, for he sent a diversion to draw the Arabs' arrows—thousands of horsemen scouting the rivers to find fords, then splashing across to charge the rising ground. Their horses were smaller, though, and had a more difficult time wading, so the rout was well under way before the first horsemen came charging up the slope.

The general bawled orders. Half the archers turned, ran to the rear, and loosed their shafts at the galloping ponies. The front rank went down. The second hurdled them and fell upon the Arab infantrymen with screams of rage—but they could only ride six abreast, and the footmen set their spears for horses to run upon, then struck down the riders with their swords. Here and there a barbarian proved skilled enough to exchange three or four strokes with an Arab, but Damascus steel bit through the softer blades of the barbarians, and they died by scores. Arabs fell, too, but only one for every fifty barbarians. Fearless, the barbarians rode and kept riding, trying to drown the Arabs under sheer weight of bodies, but they succeeded only in building a wall of their dead that quickly rose high enough that even with their skill, they could not hurdle it. The Arabs drew back, wary and watchful, but the wall of flesh held. As the sun reached noon, the barbarians retreated.

They pitched camp, though, round about the low plateau, and settled down with an air that said they meant to stay.

"We are besieged, my lord," the general said, "and the dead will quickly bring a pestilence."

"Not to us, though," the Caliph said. "Bid our men roll their dead back down to them. As to the fallen horses, butcher them for stew and boil their bones for soup."

The general nodded slowly. "If we keep the stewpots boiling, we can last for weeks—and one of the men has found a spring at the top of this rising land."

"I had hoped for that, with so much water about it." The Caliph tried not to show the relief he felt. "We can wait, then, for armies to relieve us."

There was a shout of delight, and Arabs began to sing a victory song.

"They celebrate too quickly," the general said, frowning. "Wars are not won by retreats."

"This one may be," Suleiman said. "They have proved for themselves that the barbarians can be beaten, for all their numbers. More importantly, the barbarians have learned that they can lose, that their ancient god cannot always give them victory. They will charge with less assurance now."

The general lifted his head in understanding. "You do not think their khan will wait for Tafas bin Daoud and the other emirs."

"I think that, as soon as his spies tell him of an army advancing, he will raise the siege and ride for Jerusalem," the Caliph said, "but Tafas has his own spies, and will invest the Holy City before the khan comes."

"Then we shall attack from the rear, and catch him between two forces!" The general grinned. "Well planned, my lord! We may yet win this war!"

"We may," the Caliph said, frowning, "but we will need many more stratagems than these to counter so many men. Bid my wizards come to me, Emir—and bid the muezzin call the faithful to prayer. We have much for which to thank Allah."

"Do not let him talk," cautioned a voice with an accent that sounded vaguely Pakistani. "He is a wizard, after all."

"Doesn't look like one," grunted another in common old Merovencian—very common indeed. "More like a mercenary soldier looking for a job."

"He is not what he seems!"

"How would a wizard not see us jumping out of that hedgerow nor hear us running toward him?"

"Because I know a little magic myself, and used a spell to hide our approach!" said the Asian voice. "Bind that gag tightly, or I shall try another verse I know and see if it really will turn a man to a toad!"

Quickly then, a smelly rag tightened around Matt's mouth, so smelly that it brought him out of grogginess into full consciousness—and made him aware of the worst headache he'd had since the last time someone had sneaked up behind him and sapped him on the head.

"Sap" was right . . .

Matt scolded himself for not paying more attention to his surroundings. The fact that his assailant had silenced his approach with magic didn't help much. Made it worse, really—he should have been aware of hostile magic swirling around. The need for vigilance had never occurred to him, though, in the middle of a peaceful countryside in his own land. In the woods, you expected bandits, but not in open fields.

Which meant this duo had been sent after him in particular. Matt took a closer look at the foreigner, but he didn't look all that Asian—black haired and olive skinned, maybe, but so were a third of the men in Merovence, especially in the south, near the Middle Sea. Still, by his accent, he was an outlander, and that raised the little question of how the two had known where to find him. But headache stabbed again, and Matt had to shelve the item for future consideration. To make it worse, whatever kind of surface he was on seemed to lift up, then sink down, and his stomach rebelled. Frantically, he tried to stifle the nausea—with a gag on, the law of reverse gravity had even less to recommend it than usual: "What goes down, must come up." Matt had no wish to choke on his own vomit.

He cracked an eye, peering through his lashes, and was amazed to see planking in front of his face. The surface tilted under him, rolling him onto his back; looking up, he saw a low rail and a single mast. Then the surface tilted back, he rolled onto his side again, but that had been enough—he was on a boat, and the rocking and rolling was due to waves.

He wondered where he was going. One way or another he was certainly going to find out—his verse-chanting wizardry doubly disabled by headache and gag, there wasn't much he could do to change things. When the pain stopped, it might be another matter—he had found out by experience that he could work a few spells without speech, if he concentrated hard enough. But even in misery, curiosity poked through—he had been most definitely kidnapped, and began to wonder why.

"You have slept long enough," a meowing voice said sarcastically.

Matt tilted his head enough to see Balkis, brown fur shading into the shadow behind an upright, lying with paws tucked under and eyeing him with disgust. Matt shrugged apologetically.

"If you are so mighty a wizard," the little cat said, "free yourself from your bonds! Whisk us out of here!"

Matt considered for a moment, then shook his head.

"No?" Balkis demanded, scandalized, "For Heaven's sake, why not?"

Matt raised his right hand, found the left came with it, bound, and pointed with both toward the sun.

Balkis followed his gaze, frowning—as much as a cat can. "The sun? What of it? . . . Oh!"

Matt nodded.

"You mean that they take us where we wish to go!"

Matt nodded.

"How if they try to slay you?" Balkis demanded. "What then?"

Matt grinned behind his gag. Balkis read the wrinkles at the corners of his eyes correctly and shuddered. "You are quite sure of yourself."

Matt wasn't, but he nodded anyway.

"Would it not be safer to go on our own?"

Matt raised his bound hands and pointed to his ear.

The cat stared, puzzling out his pantomime, then said, "You believe you can learn of our enemy from what they say?"

Matt nodded again.

"It is most horribly dangerous," Balkis said, coming to her feet, "and I'll have nothing to do with it!" She stalked away, her tail straight as an exclamation point.

She'd stay, though, Matt knew. After all, if she didn't, how would she learn his magic? Besides, they were in a boat, and he knew how cats felt about water.

In the middle of the day they fed him and gave him a drink—but the hulking Merovencian stood over him with a raised club as the foreigner took his gag off, promising, "Say one word and my companion will knock you senseless again."

Matt nodded to show he understood, then ate with bound hands. He gave a groan of pleasure at the first taste of food, then made noises of delight with each spoonful. Of course, those moans and burps had consonants in them, and when strung together they added up to:

> *"J'attends quelq'un qui parle,*
> *Et les comprends,*
> *Malgre la langue*
> *Dans ceux qu'ils réponds!"*

Which was French for:

> I listen to whoever speaks,
> And understand them,
> In spite of the language
> In which they respond!

"That had the sound of a word," the thug said suspiciously.

The foreigner frowned, listening for the next groan of delight, then shook his head. "Not in any language I ever heard."

That was nothing but plain truth, of course, for the French of Matt's home universe was quite different from the Merovencian of Alisande's. Nonetheless, the verse, rude though it was, worked quite well, as Matt discovered the next time the Asian muttered to himself under his breath. What he said was enough to make Matt sorry he'd understood, and to hope the cat didn't—though it took a lot to embarrass a cat.

They retied the gag and, before they again shortened the rope that held him to the mast, gave him a chance to take care of sanitary functions at the gunwale. This involved standing up, so Matt was able to see that they were sailing down a river. From what he knew of the geography, he guessed which one, and had it borne out several days later when they docked at Playamer, the greatest of Merovence's southern ports.

Matt's first hint was the increase in river traffic—small sailboats scudding past, or at least the tops of their sails, and shouts and curses to give way—Matt himself had introduced the tiller, but the sailors were slow taking to the newfangled invention, and couldn't see any sense in his triangular sails. As the number of masts increased, so did the noise, until, when they jarred against a dock, he was surrounded by a forest of bare poles and a cacophony of voices in a number of different languages, shouting, cursing, and calling their wares. Matt began to regret he'd laid the translation spell, once he understood what some of the voices were saying.

The Asian and the thug untied him from the mast and hoisted him onto his feet. Something sharp poked into his ribs and the Asian hissed, "Put one foot wrong and I'll skewer your spleen."

Matt took a step and stumbled, more or less deliberately.

"All right, all right, so it will take you a minute or so to regain your land legs," the foreigner snapped. "Even so, be wary how you walk."

Matt was very careful—in fact, as slow as he could be. He wanted to leave Balkis plenty of opportunity to follow. Obviously the little cat had decided to go along with his plan, or at the very least, she would have turned his bonds into mice and chased them away.

"I thought we were supposed to kill him," the thug grunted.

"We were," said the Asian, "but why not make a bit of a profit off him while we can? Levantine galleys will ply the Middle Sea until my masters conquer their caliph, and they always want more slaves for their oars. Why not make a bit of cash while we can? He will be dead soon enough aboard one of those ships."

Matt felt a cold chill down his back, but pretended not to have heard them.

The galley they chose was a merchantman; its master looked as though his home port was Tripoli and honest trading was a sideline. He wore a gold ring in his ear, a colorful scarf instead of a turban, a vest over a bare chest, and knee-length loose trousers. He grinned under a huge black moustache and said, "You would sell me a man with a gag? What is he, a Finn?"

"Finn?" the Asian asked, frowning, but the Merovencian said quickly, "Aye, a Finn he is, and a sorcerer, like all his race! Keep his mouth bound or he'll sing up a storm to sink you!"

"Why then should I buy him?" the captain challenged.

"Because he is strong—look at the broadness of his back, the thickness of his arms! Only see to it his mouth stays shut, and you will have much work from him!"

"Well, I've a wizard of my own on this ship: that should be protection enough," the captain allowed. "I will give you fifty doubloons for him."

Matt was surprised to hear the Spanish coin mentioned, then realized that it was probably a standard medium of exchange throughout the Eastern Mediterranean. They were still close to Ibile, after all.

"Fifty!" the Asian protested. "He is worth two hundred."

"Perhaps seventy-five . . ."

Matt listened to them bargaining over him, with the Asian pointing out his finer features to boost the price, and the captain pointing to old scars and new sunburn to beat the Asian down. In the end Matt went for ninety-four doubloons and a flask of brandy, and felt thoroughly mortified.

The Asian and the Merovencian went their way, but Matt noticed a small brown shape slipping between the legs of the crowd to follow them. He wondered if Balkis would come back, and if she did, what tales she would have to tell.

Then the captain kicked his legs out from under him and said, "Now, Rosandry! Bind his tongue so we may dispense with that gag!"

Matt looked up into a face of wrinkles that cleverly disguised a mouth and eyes. The blade of nose was easy to make out, and so were the lips, after they opened to reveal a grin featuring a few yellow teeth. Matt could have sworn the man had discovered tobacco.

"What have we here, then?" Rosandry leaned over to peer at Matt, who realized the Berber's magic didn't include a cure for nearsightedness. "This is one who has seen little work with his hands."

"He will learn it, never fear. Now lock his tongue!"

"Easily done," Rosandry sniffed, and tossed some powder into a brazier that sat in front of his crossed legs. He chanted in his own language, and thanks to his French translation spell, Matt caught the sense of it, if not the poetry. It came down to the fact that his lips would be able to open, but would be stiff and numb, as would his tongue—able to move enough to swallow, but not enough to form syllables. Even as he chanted, Matt felt the heaviness stealing over his mouth. It felt as though he'd had a complete treatment with novocaine.

Rosandry finished the verse with a triumphant flourish and said, "Remove his gag."

The captain summoned a sailor, who held his scimitar above Matt's head, then cut the strip of cloth with his dagger. Matt opened and closed his mouth, waggled his jaw, and decided that even filled with the stench of rotting fish, the waterfront air tasted marvelous.

"What is your name?" the captain demanded.

Matt turned wary and tried an alias—but somehow "William Shakespeare" didn't sound the same without consonants. Matt stared, thunderstruck—Rosandry's spell had worked, and all too well!

The sorcerer cackled with glee.

"He might be faking," the captain said, scowling, and stamped on Matt's foot.

Matt howled and turned on the man, swinging his bound hands up and shouting, "You blasted runt, get back to Tripoli or I'll send the Marines after you!"

Unfortunately, all that came out was a sort of modulated bellowing. Matt froze in shock.

The captain laughed. "Well done, Rosandry, well done! Take him below, Hakim, and chain him to his oar. Be quick about it—I wish to catch the evening tide for Said!"

All Matt could think, as the mate hustled him below, was that he was still going in the right direction, so he might as well play along. Hard work didn't bother him—he needed to get back into shape, anyway. He could always jump ship in Egypt.

The mate manacled him to five feet of oar and said, "Row as the others do and when they do, or the oar itself will break your neck!" With those words of tender consideration, he stamped away down the aisle between the benches, bending low because the whole space was only four feet high, and disappeared up through a hatch into the realm of sunlight and fresh air.

The boss could certainly learn a thing or two about ventilation, Matt decided, and wondered if he'd smell as badly as the others by the time they reached Port Said. He looked around, picking out human forms in the gloom, and wondered how men could be so muscular and still so emaciated.

Then his gaze took in the glowing yellow eyes and the furry brown body wedged into a cranny in the side of the ship.

"You certainly must be able to find a more comfortable way to travel to the east," Balkis said, and at his look of alarm to the slaves in front and in back of him, she said, "Be not anxious, I have cast a sleep over them, not that they needed much aid."

Matt decided his new apprentice had some ability after all.

"Can you not find a safer way to travel?" Balkis repeated.

Matt grinned, as much as he could with numb lips, and shook his head.

"Can you not talk?" the cat asked with anxiety.

Matt shook his head and made a cawing sound to prove it.

"That could be troublesome." The cat fluffed herself, unnerved. "Well, would it interest you to learn where your captors went?"

Matt nodded, and his eyes gleamed in the gloom as he fantasized revenge.

CHAPTER 7

"The two went their separate ways," Balkis reported. "When they came to a tavern, the foreigner gave the thug half the money they had from selling you, and that half has probably rolled down his throat in the form of ale already."

Matt nodded agreement; she knew the type. Just what kind of a past had this cat had, anyhow? He raised his eyebrows in question.

"The foreigner wound his way through the alleyways till he found a cellar where he knocked, spoke some words in his senseless tongue, and was admitted," Balkis said. "Before the door closed I heard men's voices chanting, and somber and off-key they seemed. I squeezed through where a piece of board was missing and descended some stairs to a pagan temple, ill-lit by rushlights. At least, I would have thought it a temple, but it had no idol—only a cavity in the back wall where no light fell, dark as the deepest night. Nonetheless, the men there seemed to be praying to it. An odd lot they were, three in dark blue robes, one with a hat and two with headbands. Behind them knelt a dozen or so men of every kind, fat and prosperous, skinny and poor, tough and mild, and soft-handed and work-hardened. Most, I think, were sailors, or had been. Almost all were like your captain and the foreigner who sold you."

Matt scowled. It sounded as though the high priest of the barbarians had managed to open a branch office in Merovence, and he didn't like the sound of that at all.

The boat lurched, the slaves came awake, and Balkis disappeared. A man came walking down the aisle lashing everyone on the back. The sting of the lash was enough to shock, not to injure, but its pain still caught Matt by surprise.

Matt grasped his oar and sat up straight, smarting from the lash, trying to channel his anger into rowing, and privately swearing that he would one day decorate the back of the slavemaster with his own whip.

A drum began to beat and the slaves began to shout, counting as they swung their oars. Matt imitated them as best he could, but he was out of sync at first, and his oar must have clashed against someone else's, for it jumped in his hands and rammed him in the stomach. Swearing without consonants, he took firmer hold and forced himself to bend forward, then lean back, in unison with the rest.

Slowly, the ship moved away from the dock. As it came into open water, the beat accelerated. Matt found himself gasping and decided he should have considered his entry into slavery a little more carefully.

Out the ship moved into the evening sea, heading southeast, and Matt consoled himself with the thought that he was, at least, safe from ambush and assassins, for nobody would have thought to look for him there.

Tafas bin Daoud rode at the head of an army that filled the plain. He eschewed the usual signs of rank—no canopy, only his battle-standard; no band of musicians capering before him with a droning of pipes and rippling of harps, only a marching drum slung between two horses and sounding the tempo of the procession—though a trumpeter rode nearby, ready to sound signals to all who could hear him. His raiment, although it was rich, was not of cloth-of-gold or any other sort of awe-inspiring luxury. No, his robes and turban were of the finest cotton, died the purple of murex, but were withal a soldier's clothes, and would both shield him from the sun and withstand the strain of battle. His one concession to rank was his snow-white mare, so that all might see at a glance where the emir rode.

This was especially important for his brother emirs, so they might know where to send their riders for battle-orders. They were distributed throughout the host, for they rode at the heads of their own armies. They had chosen Tafas their leader without demur, for his battle-genius was legendary already, though he was not yet thirty. If he thought to exploit that position after the war was won, well, they knew how to deal with an upstart quickly and thoroughly. Not a one of them doubted that the boy, though a mighty strategist, was still incredibly naive. After all, when he gave Allah the credit for winning his battles, he really meant it.

A plume of dust rose from the plain, growing taller as it came toward them. "Your pardon, Emir," Tafas said to the Emir of Algiers, with whom he had been discussing the barbarians' style of charge, and turned to one of the officers beside him. "Send a dozen riders to escort he who comes."

"My lord, I shall." The officer turned to snap commands to the men behind him. They galloped off. Their column of dust met and swallowed the plume, then swept back toward them.

Tafas held up his hand, and the advance stopped.

The scout drew rein and all but fell off his horse. "Hail, lord! I have seen the barbarian horde!"

"Tell me of them," Tafas said, his face bland.

"They are of many nations, lord, and they filled all the earth that I could see from my hilltop! They surrounded a plateau atop which camped the Caliph's army!"

Tafas saw the implications immediately. "If you bring me this news, one of the khan's scouts is even now telling him of our approach."

"They will be ready for battle when we come in sight," said his aide heavily.

"They will not wait," Tafas said with total conviction. "When he hears of our approach, the khan will leave a force large enough to hold the Caliph where he is, and will ride to conquer Damascus before we come."

A murmur of shock went through all the leaders who rode near him, but the scout said, "We are a day's ride from Damascus, and he is three days!"

"Be sure that his men will ride like the wind," Tafas said.

"Praise Allah that we are all mounted, even the spearmen and archers!" said his aide.

The Emir of Algiers nodded heavily. "You were wise to insist on that, Lord Tafas."

"I thank you, my lord," Tafas said, but he was clearly preoccupied with the problem at hand. "Bid all to canter half a mile, then trot half a mile, so that we may pace the horses but still ride as fast as the horde, or faster. We must be in Jerusalem by this time tomorrow!"

When the ship set its sea anchor for the night, the slaves were able to rest a little. Matt sagged on his oar, his body one huge ache, and was almost too weary to notice how well his translation spell was paying off. The rowers spoke a variety of different languages—Berber, Algerian, Arabic, and Farsi, the language of the Iranians. Matt could even hear a few men talking in the Latrurian dialect and the Ibilean, and several of the slaves were conversing in Hebrew. The pirates were very democratic—they didn't care who they captured or bought.

Any doubts Matt might have had about his captors' profession were settled the second day out, when there was a sudden flurry of activity overhead, feet running to and fro, then the drumbeat picking up until the slaves were rowing as hard as they could and he was so breathless he was seeing spots. Above, the captain was shouting, "To starboard, to starboard! Faster, faster! We almost have him!"

Suddenly, there was a jarring crash, and several of the oars on the starboard side shot back through their holes. Two caught their luckless rowers in the belly; one cracked under a slave's chin, breaking his neck. Matt barely managed to duck as his oar jolted out of his hands and slammed toward his head. He concentrated on staying out of its way and tried to keep its swings from hitting the men in front of him. Then the oar behind him cracked into his head, and he missed the rest of the battle.

The overseer's lash jolted him back to consciousness, howling, "Sit straight! Push the butt of your oar out!"

Matt did, fighting a headache as big as the sea. The broken oar disappeared; then a new one poked through. Matt stared.

"Seize it!" the overseer snapped.

Matt heard the thongs of his whip whistle up, and he grabbed the new oar before the man had a chance to bring them down. He realized other pirates must be outside in a rowboat, pushing replacement oars through.

A blacksmith stepped up and cut open the manacles that held the dead rowers.

"You new men!" the overseer snarled. "Haul those corpses out and throw them to the sharks! Then back you come, for these will be your places now."

The newcomers hesitated. With a shock, Matt recognized them as Latrurians, and one of them was middle-aged and dressed in expensive-looking red robes. The merchant must have been traveling with his cargo, and the pirates were no respecters of persons.

The blacksmith pounded new rivets through the manacles, shackling the sailors and their supercargo to their oars and benches. Matt sent up a quick prayer for the merchant—between the shock of capture and his being somewhat out of shape, he might not last long at the oar.

Above, he could hear the captain ordering half a dozen of his crew to take the captured ship to Tripoli. That was good news—if the ship were still whole, more of the crew might have survived. In fact, that would explain why the captain could send only half a dozen men—enough to browbeat the merchant's crew, who would no doubt be shackled to their stations, too.

His headache throbbed, and not until the lash streaked fire across his back did he realize it was the drum beating, not his pulse. He bent his back to the work and heartily wished he'd decided to fly. He wondered if it were too late to call Stegoman.

The people of Damascus ran up to the walls to cheer as the North African army rode up to the Holy City. The gates swung wide, and Tafas set the example by waving and smiling. The other emirs followed suit, and their men imitated them. Grinning and calling out greetings, the army rode in.

The cheering slackened as the people began to realize just how many soldiers there were. They seemed mightily relieved when most of the riders dismounted outside the walls and pitched camp.

Within the palace, Tafas was already in earnest conference with the governor of the town.

"The civilians may stay, of course," he agreed, "though I do not doubt we will press them into service on the walls."

The governor frowned. "It has been long since these tradesmen have served in an army."

"They will be of little use, I agree," Tafas said, "but better than nothing. They must begin training tomorrow morning, and the whole town must begin to eat and drink sparingly."

The governor nodded, face dark. "This will be hard on them—but we shall make it clear that the barbarians would be harder still."

"They would indeed. Any who wish to leave, my men shall guard for a day's ride away."

"Pray Allah that all shall wish it!"

They did. Criers went out into every street and alley, telling the whole populace what they could expect during the siege, and what their fates would be if the horde unthinkably won. By morning all the civilians had packed their valuables, loaded their carts, and lined up at the gate to wait for dawn. The sun rose, and the train of civilians rolled out. Soldiers fell in on each side of the caravan to guard them for the promised day's ride. Couriers had already gone ahead to plead for sanctuary from other cities. Only a thousand men remained within Jerusalem, and they marched on the palace in a body. Warned by a sentry, the governor came out to meet them. "What means this assembly?" he called.

All the men bowed, and the oldest, a stocky man with grizzled hair and beard, called out, "We wish to share our city's fate, my lord! All here have ridden as soldiers except the youngest, men in their late teens who wish to learn. We shall join your army, if you will have us!"

The governor grinned and said with pride, "Glad I am to have you. Now it can never be said that the men of Damascus all ran when the invader came. Sit down upon the ground and wait—my officers shall come to give you weapons and begin your drill."

The order went out for the soldiers to enter the town, to take whatever housing they could find, but not under any circumstances to steal or defile the residences in any way. Tafas also made it clear that when they had beaten the barbarians and ridden out of the city, every house should be as they had found it, only cleaner. Mindful of the punishments the

Koran imposed, the men took his orders seriously. Most of the soldiers found shelter. The few remaining set up tents in public squares that had formerly held bazaars. When the muezzin called the faithful to evening prayer, Damascus was once again full, and only the holes made by tent pegs showed where the army had camped outside the walls the night before.

But in the hills, a quarter of the army were camped unseen under the boughs of trees, small fires smokeless. The soldiers returning from escorting the civilian caravan rode in to join those camps. They spoke softly, laughed even more softly, and waited for the barbarians to surround the city.

When the prayers were done, Tafas bin Daoud stepped forth before his men on a balcony of the palace. "Here we are, and here we shall stay," he called out, "until the invader has been banished!"

The army roared approval.

Tafas raised his hand and looked up to heaven, his face solemn. "May Heaven be my witness! I swear that I shall stop these barbarians or die in the attempt!"

A buzz of awed conversation answered him as the men realized for the first time how close they were to death. Then, faces firmed, brows darkened, the soldiers raised their hands and looked up to heaven to bear witness as they shouted the same oath their leader had.

Tafas beamed down upon them and called out, "Many of us will die, but we shall stop the barbarian here, then chase him back whence he came! We who die will be the most blessed, for we will surely waken in Paradise!" His fist punched high into the air and he shouted, "Death to the invader, freedom for Islam, and Paradise for us!"

The men stared, spellbound, for he seemed to swell, to grow, to become something more than a mere man. Once again he was the Mahdi; once again, they realized, they had enlisted in a holy war.

Then all their fists punched high and they shouted, "Death to the invader, and Paradise for us!"

* * *

At last the drumbeat slowed and the overseer commanded, "Ship oars!"

With groans of relief the slaves heaved their oars out of the sea, pushed forward until the handle was near the side of the ship, and lowered them. Matt followed suit and could feel the huge blade jar into whatever device held it in place, out of the way of heavy water traffic. A few minutes later the whole ship slowed abruptly, pitching the slaves forward, but the old hands were ready for it and braced themselves on overhead beams. Matt, not being an old hand, slammed into the small of the back of the man in front of him.

"Watch out, you landlubber!" the man snarled in Hebrew.

"Sorry," Matt answered in Merovencian, but it came out as an apologetic mumble—he still couldn't move his lips and tongue enough to form words.

"Oh, mute, are you?" the Jew said, softening. "Well, you know what happens now, lad, after we ship oars. Brace yourself and hold your seat!"

"Mmm-*mmm*-mm!" Matt nodded and slid back onto his bench.

"You always so kind to dumbies, Jew?" sneered a neighboring oarsman in a pidgin dialect made up of all the oarsmen's languages.

"*Our* God teaches us to be merciful to the unfortunate, Moor," the kind one retorted. "I thought your Koran said something about alms-giving."

"Well, yes," the Moor conceded, "but that's money."

"Oh, you have money?" The Jew shrugged. "Myself, I have no coins—but I can at least give a little kindness."

Matt's heart warmed to the man. He hoped he'd be able to find him again, after he got out of this.

He did sooner than he thought. The ship docked with a jar that shook his molars—that was what the Jew had meant by saying "You know what comes now," and Matt hadn't. He'd braced himself, though, thanks to the man's advice, so he was sitting straight when the blacksmith came down the row, striking off the shackles of half a dozen slaves—those captured at sea, and one or two others besides.

"This one, too," the overseer said, pointing his whip at Matt.

"Why?" The blacksmith frowned. "He's just learning his trade."

"Captain says he can make a nice profit off him, and buy two for the price." The overseer shrugged. "Myself, I wouldn't think he's worth that much, but Captain says some people will pay through the nose for a mute."

Matt considered the implications and shuddered. He hoped his potential buyer only wanted a confidential servant.

The slave market was a new low in humiliation, with people yanking his mouth open to look at his teeth, poking him in the ribs, squeezing his shoulders, and punching his arms. He kept reminding himself that he could get out whenever he wanted, and felt a huge surge of sympathy for his fellow slaves, who couldn't. He wondered how successful he would be in mounting a worldwide antislavery campaign. His mind started considering possible ways and means, and he found himself including the little brown cat in them. Talk about the perfect spy . . .

Though maybe he would prefer one who couldn't be bribed with tuna.

He went for a decent price, but nothing earthshaking. His new owner led him away by the rope that tied his hands, and Matt reflected that the police must be very good in Egypt, because any determined slave could have knocked down such a buyer and escaped easily.

The buyer led him to a rowboat, said, "Get in and take the oars!" then knelt down to tie Matt's rope to a thwart, loosed one hand from it, then boarded behind him. He cast off the mooring line and said, "Row straight out to sea."

Matt turned and stared at the man as though he were crazy.

"Row!" The buyer produced a mean-looking little whip from inside his robe. "Straight out, as I tell you, or you'll be sorry for it!"

Matt revised his opinion of the police. This man, apparently, was sure of his ability to win if he tried to fight him. Well, he hadn't been planning a mutiny anyway—he was curious enough to want to see where the journey led.

He rowed, considering. The man was round-faced, his skin darker than the Berbers' and his hair and moustache jet-black. From the accent in which he spoke Arabic, Matt guessed he was from India. Too far south to put him in contact with the barbarians, really, but he'd picked up a lot of interesting rumors from his fellow galley slaves, and decided to play along for a while yet.

As he rowed he happened to notice a pair of yellow eyes watching him from the shadows at the stern. He tried to grin, and felt an illogical fondness for the little cat. She might have had her own purely selfish reasons for it, but she was loyal.

He rowed hour after hour, and realized that he was rowing east along the shoreline. When darkness fell, the man told him to beach the craft, then drove him ahead on a long, long walk through the darkness. His captor didn't enlighten him, but Matt glanced at the stars and guessed he was hiking south. He guessed that if they went far enough, they would come to the Red Sea. After a long while he smelled salt air again and knew they were approaching. His captor drove him down a rocky beach to another rowboat.

"Get in."

Matt did and, as he took up the oars, wondered how Balkis was ever going to find him—it had been an awfully long distance for a little cat. But as his captor pushed the bow free, Matt saw a shadow flow over the gunwale. His heart warmed.

The captor jumped in, and Matt started to row. He rowed for an hour and more. Then suddenly, black against black, a small galley loomed beside him.

"Stop."

Matt did, with massive relief. He reflected that he never could have rowed for so long only a few weeks ago, when he'd left home. He turned and looked over his shoulder to see a rope come flying down from the galley. His owner caught it, then untied his tether and gestured to the rope. "Climb."

Matt climbed. His owner climbed up right behind him. He wondered if they'd leave the rope down long enough for Balkis, then remembered that they would probably tie the rowboat to the galley.

His owner bowed to an older man resplendent in a brocade robe, even this late at night. "Your new slave, my captain."

The captain gave Matt an assessing glance. "Where is your home?"

Matt tried to say "Merovence," but only heard the familiar cawing.

The captain nodded, satisfied. "He will do for crew aboard a smuggler. Shackle him to his bench."

As the blacksmith hammered the rivets home, Matt reflected that the ship had to be a rather special smuggler. Of course, any illegal ship would be painted black and running only at night—but this one was long, low, and slender, built for speed rather than cargo capacity. Admittedly, smugglers needed to be able to outrun the tax police, but they usually tried to carry enough goods to make the journey worthwhile. Gold? Diamonds? Matt couldn't offhand think of anything of high enough value that would be cheaper smuggled than bought and sold openly.

Except, perhaps, information . . .

He felt a chill down his back, and wondered whose spy network he'd blundered into. It did make sense for even the oarsmen to be mute, though—not only could they not tell what they didn't know, they couldn't even tell what they *did* know. Apparently nobody had considered the possibility that he might be able to read and write—but how many slaves could?

"Out of the kettle and into the flames," hissed a barely heard voice overhead.

Matt looked up at the brindle bundle stuffed into a niche where the overhead deck met the side, and bared his teeth, hoping Balkis would understand it as a grin.

They rowed all night, but at the first hint of dawn the captain ordered them into hiding—a river-mouth with a sea-cave large enough to hold the little ship; he had obviously come this way before. In fact, Matt suspected it was his regular route, running information between India and the Arab world. There in the gloom, the slaves rested on their oars, pillowing their heads on their arms, to sleep as well as they could.

Matt, however, discovered one advantage to the smuggler-ship—it didn't have a resident wizard. With no need to worry about alerting a magical rival, Matt peered up through the gloom to discover the glowing yellow eyes still on him. He stared at Balkis, pantomimed unzipping his mouth, then wondered if the cat was really frowning. He tried again, opening his mouth, taking hold of his lips with both hands and wriggling them into letter shapes.

Balkis stared, frown disappearing.

Matt stuck out his tongue and twisted it up and down with his fingers.

"And the same to you," Balkis hissed. "Do you tell me that your tongue is still tied?"

Matt nodded.

"A fine master I have chosen!" the little cat huffed, but she went ahead and recited in a cat-whisper,

> "Unbind the tie that stiffens his lips,
> Untwist the knot that his tongue girds!
> Free his voice and mouth to speak . . ."

Balkis hesitated, looking uncertain, then concentrated so fiercely that her slit-eyes crossed.

Matt realized, with a sinking heart, that she was stuck for a rhyme. *Heard,* he thought, desperately hoping Balkis was a telepath, *Heard!*

The little cat might not have been a mind reader, but she came through for him anyway:

> "Loose the torrent of his words!"

Matt heaved a sigh of relief and whispered, "Thanks, Balkis." He had never liked the sound of his own voice as much.

"You are welcome," the cat hissed, then added almost apologetically, "I have difficulty with final lines, or last verses, if there are more than one."

A flag went up in the back of Matt's mind—cats didn't apologize. On the other hand, of course, cats didn't talk. He let surprise take over. "You mean you improvise all your spells—make them up on the spot?"

"When I have not learned a spell for the situation, yes," the cat sniffed. "Do not all wizards?"

Matt took a deep breath, then said, "Yes, but I'll obviously have to teach you a broader range of verses." His heart thrilled at the thought of actually teaching literature again. In fact, though, he wondered if one small feline head could hold any spells at all. Cats weren't reputed to have very long memories.

Of course, anybody who thought that hadn't tried to open a rustling bag of cat food when he thought he was alone.

Down the Red Sea they rowed, the slaves getting a break when the offshore breeze took them out into the midnight sea. They crossed the Persian Gulf, and the temperature grew hotter and hotter. Then Matt lost track of how many days they were at sea, or how many times the overseer came down the aisle with water, interrupting the slaves' sleep. They sweated the water right back out at night, bending to their oars in the tropical warmth.

Finally the order came to ship oars, and the smuggler slipped into its berth. Matt was amazed at how slight the jar of docking was, then remembered that these were men accustomed to secrecy and who practiced it by habit even in their home port.

If this was their home port. Balkis went out to scout.

But when the sun sent shafts of light through the oar-holes, Matt knew they weren't in a cave or forest. Not long after, Balkis came back to report.

"We have come to a great city that stretches as far as the eye can see! The houses are white, there are gilded temples, and the palace is trimmed with gold!"

"Sounds rich," Matt agreed. "How about green space?"

"There are trees everywhere, but some of them are only tall straight trunks with a bunch of slender leaves at the top."

"Palms," Matt said, frowning. "We're pretty far south, all right."

They had to delay further conversation because the overseer came through with dinner—wooden bowls of gruel, as usual.

There was another merchant among the crew—at least Matt guessed him to be a fellow pirate victim. Stripped to breechcloth and covered with sweat and dirt, he looked like any of the other middle-aged slaves, except his flesh was sagging where he had recently been fat, and his body wasn't as hard as the others' yet. The constant sorrow and resignation of all the others was absent from his face, as was all other emotion. Now, though, he came out of his daze, looking up from his oar, and his vacant expression livened with a trace of hope. "Where are we?"

"Bombay, they call it," a Moor hissed in answer, "this ship's home port. Be still, if you wish to keep your tongue! They think we're all mutes, and too stupid to learn to talk."

The merchant shuddered and let his eyes glaze again.

Bombay! Matt's blood thrilled at the exotic name. He'd never been to India, and he'd always wanted to, more than a dream, less than a plan. Admittedly, he hadn't intended to travel in quite this way, but it was Bombay nonetheless, and even better, untouched by the twentieth century! He could hardly wait to jump ship and start exploring.

He had sense enough, though, not to try it by day. They waited for night; then Matt asked Balkis, "Are there lots of people?"

"Everywhere," Balkis said with disgust. "It is packed and thronged with folk! I am amazed they can find houses for them all."

"They can't," Matt told her, "but the more of them there are, the easier it is for us to lose ourselves among them."

Balkis eyed him critically. "You will stand out like a jay among robins."

"Not for long," Matt assured her. "We've come as far east as this ship will take us. Time to find transport north."

"You seem to forget the small matter of escape from this vessel," Balkis said tartly.

"Yes, that is a small matter," Matt agreed, and recited softly,

"Rivets shall shatter and manacles spring wide!
Don John of Austria to freedom be our guide,
Hacking out a pathway for the captured and the sold,

Breaking of the hatches up and bursting of the holds,
Throning of the slave-men who all labor under sea,
White for bliss, blind for sun, stunned for liberty,
Don John of Austria will set his people free!"

The shackles cracked open. Matt ducked flying rivet-heads. When he looked up, he saw a huge man in conquistador armor standing in the middle of the galley slaves.

CHAPTER 8

The apparition seemed eight feet tall, but Matt told himself it couldn't be, the deck was scarcely more than six feet overhead. But for an apparition, the intruder was very solid, as he proved by whirling to fell the overseer with the flat of his blade and crying, "Up, all you who thirst for freedom! Up, slaves, and fight for your liberty!"

The rowers stared in shock. Then, with a shout, they surged up from their benches and followed the huge bearded figure.

Don John swung his broadsword two-handed and chopped through the hatchway. Three more strokes, and he kicked scrapwood out of his way to step onto the deck.

There the smugglers came running, or at least the half-dozen men left to guard the ship, howling in rage, scimitars swinging high.

Don John bellowed with the joy of battle and swung his broadsword. Most of the pirates had sense enough to leap back, but two were slow and fell bleeding. Matt leaped in to snatch up their swords, then stepped back to hand one to the healthiest-looking of the slaves.

The other four smugglers shouted in rage and charged back in as Don John was recovering his stroke, vulnerable for a few seconds. A scimitar clashed off his breastplate, another jabbed at his naked face, but Matt's sword rang against it, and the stroke glanced harmlessly off the hero's helmet. His fellow slave leaped at the other two smugglers, slashing and whirling like a dervish and howling like a maniac. The smugglers gave way, then gave again as the bearded armored man followed, demonic in the torchlight. The smugglers ran, calling for help.

Don John turned to the slaves. "Away with you now, and quickly! Find Christian ships and stow away! Find churches and cry sanctuary! Find native robes and disguise yourselves—but flee!"

Matt fled. He pounded across the paving-stones to an alleyway. There he paused to look back, and saw Don John in the light of the torches, both hands around his blade, holding the hilt up like a cross, his gaze on it in rapt devotion, crying, *"Vivat Hispania! Domino Gloria!"* And, praising God and country, he faded, became transparent, and disappeared.

"Surely such a man never came from this world!"

Matt looked up and saw Balkis crouched on top of a stack of baskets, staring at the now empty ship. "No, not from this world—not yet, anyway."

"Then from where?" His new apprentice turned searching eyes upon him.

"From G. K. Chesterton's pen," Matt told her. "Come on! Soldiers will be searching these docks any minute now! We've got to hide."

He turned away, but there was no answer, and he turned right back, frowning up at Balkis, who was staring at him wide-eyed. Matt repressed a smile and shrugged. "Hey, you knew what I was."

"Yes," the little cat hissed, "but I had not seen it."

"Better get used to it," Matt said. "Hop onto my shoulders."

"Very well." Balkis sprang onto his shoulder.

Matt gasped. "Velvet paws! I'm not made of oak, you know!"

"I thought your bark was worse than your bite," Balkis retorted.

"You haven't seen me bite yet." Matt started off down the dark alley. "Time to hide."

"Where?" Balkis looked blank. "I can dodge to any shadow, but you . . . ?"

"I think I'll take Don John's advice and go native," Matt said. "Let's see if we can find somebody's laundry line."

Murk moved out of murk, and a dagger-point pressed against Matt's throat. "Your purse, foreigner!"

"On the other hand," Matt told Balkis, "there might be a

closer source." Then, to the thief, "All I'm wearing is a loin-cloth. Where would I hide a purse?"

The knife pricked at his throat, and the voice said, "Your sword, then."

"Sure." Matt swung the tip up against the man's belly. "How deep do you want it?"

The thief froze in surprise, and Balkis sprang.

She hit the thief's face with all four sets of claws, yowling like a snow tiger. The thief recoiled, dropping his dagger in shock.

"That's enough," Matt said.

Balkis' weight landed on his shoulder again, and the thief stared in dread at the blade of the sword vanishing under his chin. He could feel the point against his throat.

"Not a good idea to attack armed men," Matt explained, "even if they are only lousy galley slaves. Off with the clothes, fella."

"*Me* give to a *victim*?" the thief squalled in protest.

"Almost enough to get you kicked out of the footpad's guild, isn't it?" Matt asked sympathetically. "Don't worry, you can tell your shop steward the slave you picked on turned out to be a wizard in disguise."

"Who would believe so foolish a tale?" the thief sneered.

"You would," Matt told him, and chanted in English,

> "He can fill you crowds of shrouds
> and horrify you vastly!
> He can rack your brains with chains
> and gibberings grim and ghastly!"

Since there weren't any shrouds to fill, all that happened was a sudden heavy jangling all around them, underlying gloating voices uttering jumbles of nonsense syllables and giggling in deep, liquid tones.

The thief cried out in horror and shrank back. Matt followed with the sword, chanting,

> "Silence is golden,
> And talk overrated.

Let all noise I've called up
Forthwith be abated!"

The darkness was silent again, or as much as night in a big
city can be. There were still voices calling out here and there
in the distance, the creaking of ships tied up at the wharf,
scurryings and chirpings of small life-forms that weren't
willing to admit the forest had been cut out from under them,
and over it all, the shouting of soldiers coming nearer.

"You won't be lying," Matt told the thief. "Out of the
clothes, now, before I make them jump off you!"

With alacrity, the thief pulled off his robes.

"Go on, now, get lost!" Matt snapped. "You can keep your
knife, if you promise not to use it unless you're attacked."

"I promise!" The thief dashed past him and out the alleyway. Angry voices shouted, and boots clattered on cobbles.

"The soldiers have seen him," Matt told Balkis. "We've
got to move fast." He pulled on the dark robe and tunic,
muttering,

"Classifications of pesties I do not distinguish!
Let all lice and germs from these clothes be extinguished!"

"You are indeed a wizard!" Balkis said in a shaky meow,
"and you cast your spells with such ease!"

"All it takes is a good memory and practice improvising."
Matt patted his shoulder. "Come on, let's get out of here!"

Balkis jumped onto his shoulder again, and Matt hurried
away down the alley. He heard the thief squalling excuses and
knew the soldiers had caught him. That meant they'd be running down the alley in minutes—as soon as they could calm
the footpad enough to get some intelligible sentences out of
him. As he hurried he explained, "I don't like to sling magic
around so lightly, but there wasn't time to reason with him."

"Why should you hesitate to work magic?" Balkis wondered.

Matt dodged around a series of close corners, explaining,
"Because you never know whose attention you might be
attracting."

Light exploded in front of him, then condensed into a roughly human form.

"Someone like that?" Balkis asked in a shaky voice.

"Yes." Matt swallowed. "What were you saying about the nearest shadow?"

The glowing humanoid shape shrank in on itself until it was only an ordinary human male, and a rather old one at that, dressed in a midnight-blue robe with a matching cylindrical hat with a curving taper, which contrasted nicely with the white moustache, snowy beard, and bushy white hair falling to his shoulders. He didn't look Hindu—his face too long, nose too prominent, eyes too light. Something about him reminded Matt of the Ayatollahs he had seen in the newspapers, maybe the eyes; they blazed with anger and fanatical purpose.

The apparition raised an arm slowly, forefinger pointing straight at Matt and trembling with rage. "Who are you who dares obstruct Angra Mainyu from his dominion? Pale, whey-blooded fool! Do you not know it is the Great Khan's destiny to sweep all before him? Do you not know he must yield all the earth to the reign of Ahriman, that the Lord of Darkness must rule this corrupted world for a time? For if he does not, Ahura Mazda cannot rise to overthrow him and triumph, to free all from the bondage of Evil and rule the world in peace and joy! Would you block all of mankind from this earthly paradise? Do you have the gall and effrontery to stand against the gods?"

"Yes, now that you mention it." The mad old man had gone on long enough so that Matt had recovered from his first shock. "I always thought that people were perfectly capable of ruling their world by themselves—with the support of God, of course, but everything needs that support, anyway. Nothing can exist without it."

"Heresy!" the madman fumed. "You have been corrupted by these lingam-worshiping Hindus! Do you not know that the world is balanced between a force of darkness and one of light, between evil and good, between Angra Mainyu and Ahura Mazda? Do you not know they are equally strong, each seeking to conquer the earth, and that man is the key to the struggle, that we must fight it out on earth, for whichever god's people win man's war, that god will also triumph over his enemy?"

"That delicate a balance, huh?" Matt shook his head regretfully. " 'Fraid I can't agree, old man."

"You shall speak with respect!" the old man thundered. "You shall call me Arjasp, you shall call me High Priest!"

"I'll call you mistaken," Matt said evenly, "for I believe that the God of Good is all-powerful, and the Evil One lives only by His sufferance."

Arjasp leveled an arm, pointing a trembling finger at Matt. "You are one of these Jewish heretics!"

"Well, I suppose so." Matt pursed his lips, considering. "I'm a Christian, and I'd say that is a heresy of Judaism, yes."

"You shall fail, you shall die!" Arjasp ranted. "I shall slay you with magicks, I shall send a sorcerous horde against you! None must stay the reign of Ahriman! No one may prevent the conquest of Angra Mainyu! The Lord of Night must triumph, so that the Wheel may turn to bring once again the dominion of Ahura Mazda!"

Matt frowned. "Where did you get hold of the idea of—"

"Behind you!" Balkis squalled as she jumped from his shoulder. Matt whirled, but too late. The club landed on the side of his head, not the back, and he slumped down into darkness.

The army waited in the outer bailey, knights by war-horses that curvetted and danced, waiting for their masters to mount. The infantry leaned on their spears, sipping at last mugs of mulled ale and gossiping about the shortcomings of their leaders, as soldiers have always done. They waited with growing impatience for their queen to lead them forth.

Alisande watched from the battlements of the keep, clad in light mail, helm, and gauntlets, having a few last words with her viceroy and castellan.

"There are only a thousand of them," Jimena said, her eyes shadowed with worry.

"They are only my personal guard, Mother Mantrell," Alisande assured her. "My barons shall bring their own men as they join my banner. Ere we come to Seilmar to take ship, we shall number them by the thousand."

"The herald told us a week ago that King Rinaldo's troops were sailing from Gibraltar," Ramon noted.

Alisande nodded. "We shall meet him at Knossos on the isle of Crete, and Frisson's troops also."

"But not himself?"

Alisande smiled. "He has proved skilled at governance, but not at war. His barons vied for command, and he dispatched them under the Graf von Wegensburg, with lesser noblemen in his train."

"And thereby rid himself of several of the worst thorns in his side," Mama said, smiling.

"Even so."

"So you will not take ship at Venoga?" Ramon asked.

Alisande smiled. "King Boncorro is a congenial neighbor when it suits him—but I am not about to test his friendship by marching an army of thousands through half his land."

"Wise," Ramon admitted. "Still, it seems the least he could do to help forestall the horde from attacking Europe, considering that he is not going himself, nor even sending anything but a token force."

"This, of course, leaves him well-equipped to attack Merovence while you are gone," Jimena pointed out.

"Yes, but I trust him not to—provided I leave a sufficient force of wizards and warriors to cost him dearly if he tries." Alisande turned to Ramon with a frown of anxiety. "You will not risk yourself in the land's defense?"

"Not foolishly, no."

"Not at all." Mama glared at him. "Leave the actual leading of the troops to young noblemen eager to prove themselves, and content yourself with planning the battles with me, while Saul plans the magical assault."

"I would never forgive myself if you were slain or maimed in my place," Alisande told him, huge-eyed.

Ramon sighed. "What can a gentleman do when the ladies league against him? As you will, my love and my daughter— I shall take all possible care. Let us hope, though, that the tournament we have planned at Avignon will give Boncorro pause enough so that he finds attack unnecessary."

"Let us hope so," Jimena agreed.

Ramon frowned, troubled. "We may wrong a good man."

"If so, he shall never know of it," Jimena pointed out.

"I shall be delighted to be proved wrong in having borrowed trouble," Alisande assured him, "the more so because I will not have to repay it."

Below, hooves thundered on the drawbridge, and the last knight came trotting in from his fief with six squires riding behind him, leading fifty archers.

"The time has come; I am gone." Alisande turned to embrace each of her parents-in-law, briefly but fiercely. "I left you Lady Eldori and three other nursemaids, but it is to you whom I entrust my children. Protect them for me, and care for them! I praise God that you are here, and pray Heaven to protect you!"

"May Mother Mary watch over us," Jimena returned, "and St. Michael protect you. Go, daughter, and have no fear for your kingdom or children."

A shining figure was shadow-boxing—or shadow-fencing, Matt realized, for both figure and umbra fought with sword and shield, the dark one slashing at the bright one's target. But how could its right hand be striking its opponent's right? This, Matt decided, was an awfully independent shadow.

Only it wasn't a mere shadow, not simply a darkening of the pale wall of mist behind it—rather, a total absence of light, an even deeper darkness than a moonless, starless night, even more profound than the lightlessness of a small shut-up room. The manlike figure seemed to drink light, to soak it up, to be a window into the primal Void beyond space and time, where all light streamed in but none came out. It was no mere absence of light, but a presence of darkness.

The Light-Drinker swung high, the bright figure raised its shield to ward off the blow—and Matt felt shock reverberate through him, for the shield was his own face. The bright figure smashed that shield into the dark one's head, and the Light-Drinker fell—fell and fell into his own darkness until it closed up behind him, and the shining one turned, came closer to Matt, his face filling the world, clean-featured and handsome, smile quirking with humor, hair so pale as to be almost white, and the face said, "Behold your destiny!"

Matt ran howling. He didn't want anything to do with either of the maniacs. The bright figure was gone, though, and he was fleeing through darkness now. He realized his wailing wasn't his own voice, it was a dozen, and it wasn't howling, it was droning.

A droning chant in his ears, Matt realized the only reason he fled through darkness was because his eyes were closed. Something seemed to swim up and press against his whole body from behind, and he was astounded to discover he was lying down, not running. Then came the thunderous realization that he was awake, that the hard surface beneath him and the droning around him were real, and the fencing figures had been a dream.

Or a vision?

He shoved the thought away and opened his eyes—a little.

He saw a figure that made him jump, or would have if he could have, but he couldn't, because he was bound hand and foot. The figure was female, but certainly not in the slightest bit voluptuous—at least, not unless you were aroused by necklaces of skulls. It was human, too—technically, and if you didn't count the extra arms. The face was contorted into a ferocious snarl, and Matt finally recognized her—Kali, the Hindu goddess of death.

He looked away, both out of a need to see where he was and a greater need not to look upon the image of doom. He saw a barrel-vaulted ceiling held up by stone columns and filled with muslin-clad worshipers, bowing to the statue and chanting. There were no windows; if the place wasn't underground, it might as well have been.

Matt turned his head a little farther and saw the girl.

She was only a teenager, and a very pretty one, though clearly no Hindu—her skin was too pale, and had a golden tinge; her eyes slanted slightly; her mahogany tresses were long and abundant, framing her head and shoulders. Seventeen, perhaps, but her simple white robe revealed adult contours, for she lay on a slab of rock, wrists bound before her, eyes wide open but glazed, her face peacefully entranced.

At least, Matt hoped it was a trance.

He realized that he was lying on just such a slab of rock, too. His stomach sank, for he knew what Kali's worshipers, the Thuggee, did with the people they kidnapped—strangled them, as sacrifices to their goddess.

He heard voices above his head and craned his neck enough to see two men robed as priests with scarlet silken cords in their hands. They didn't look ready for business, were only reviewing the facts. They were speaking Hindi, but his translation spell was still working.

"She fought so hard to save him that perhaps she is already consecrated to the goddess."

"No," the other priest replied, "for she did not slay."

"Not for lack of trying! Three of our staunchest men will bear the marks of her claws for a month or more."

"If she were of Kali," the older priest said dogmatically, "she would not have failed to kill."

That decided it, not that Matt had had any doubts—he had to save the girl. Of course, that involved saving himself, but he'd been planning on that anyway.

"There is no doubt we must sacrifice her," the older priest went on, "for she is of great importance to the enemies of the horde, and the horde brings destruction."

"Surely, then, the barbarians' enemies are ours," the younger agreed. "How, though, can she be of such importance? She is so young!"

"We cannot know," the older priest said heavily, "only be sure that sacrificing her to Kali will help to assure the horde's success."

Definitely, he had to save her, Matt thought. As softly as he could, he began to chant—but found that his lips and tongue scarcely moved, felt as though he were trying to talk through heavy syrup. Panic struck for a moment, and he thought he had fallen back into the tongue-tied spell again. He looked about frantically for Balkis but didn't see her.

But he did see the girl's glazed eyes again, and this time he recognized the look—drugged! Presumably the priests had given him the same dose—that was why his head wasn't hurting yet—but having more body mass, his had worn off faster.

It felt like trying to talk with a mouthful of cotton, but Matt forced his lips and tongue to move:

> "Juice of the poppy or leaves of sativa,
> Begone from my fluids, blood, tears, and saliva!
> Lethe or lotus, clear out of my brain!
> Narcotics all leave me! I'll welcome the pain!"

The headache hit like a jackhammer, and he instantly regretted making the spell so comprehensive. Still, what had to be, had to be, and the younger priest was stepping forward with his cord tight between his hands. The older priest was only a step behind him, cord swinging down toward the girl's neck. Matt talked faster than he ever had.

> "Take us somewhere blocks from Thuggee,
>   where the best is like the worst,
> And the streets are jammed with people,
>   with karma blessed and cursed,
> For the temple bells are callin',
>   and it's there that we would be,
> Free and standing on the pavement,
>   out of sight and sound of sea!"

Vertigo seized him, and it was the first time in his life he'd ever been glad of nausea. The spell whirled them clockwise around and away . . .

. . . then counterclockwise, and the slab of stone jarred up against his back. The room steadied, and he found himself looking up into the furious face of the older priest.

The man knew some magic of his own, Matt realized. In fact, he was droning in Sanskrit right now, looking smug because he was talking in the sacred language, the old language that only the priests understood anymore.

But Matt's translation spell was working overtime, and he could understand what the priest was saying—something about tying his tongue and sealing his lips. Couldn't let that happen! He chanted right back, in English.

> "Tongue and lips, stay loose, stay loose!
> Unlock the jaw he'd freeze!
> Tetanus be banned! I've had my shots!
> Let his own spell on him seize!"

The priest finished his chant, grinning, and Matt panicked as the pain of cramp bit his tongue and his lips went numb. A second later, though, the pain and numbness were gone, and the priest howled an inarticulate shout as he turned away, bent in agony as his own tongue cramped.

The younger priest stared in shock, then snapped out a verse in Sanskrit, an all-purpose counterspell. The old priest stopped shouting, but could only mumble his thanks as he straightened and turned back to his junior.

Generalities never really did work all that well, Matt decided, but figured he'd better get his licks in before the young priest managed to get specific and really free up his elder's vocal apparatus. Matt chanted,

> "As ever the golden bowl be broken,
> Or the leaden coin told by its hue,
> Or the pitcher be smashed at the cistern,
> Let the scarlet cord now break in two!"

The older priest apparently wasn't waiting to get his spell-checker back in action. With a snarl, he stretched his scarlet cord between his hands and advanced on the girl. Matt was sure the younger priest was doing the same to him, but he didn't worry about it, only recited,

> "Sleeping beauty, wake and rise!
> No prince here will ope your eyes,
> Only thugs who'd steal your breath.
> Lass, awake from certain death!"

The girl's eyes fluttered, opened—and saw the contorted face bending over her, the strong arms sweeping down to stretch the garrote across her neck. She screamed and sat up convulsively, but that only made it easier for the priest to wrap the cord around her neck and pull.

It snapped.

The priest stared down at the broken ends in his hand, dumb with shock, just as the younger priest jerked Matt up and wrapped his cord. There was a moment of pain, then a loud snap, and Matt spoke while he could, reciting the escape spell again. The older priest, hearing his voice, turned livid and yanked another strangling cord from someplace, but just as he was stretching it between his hands, Matt shouted,

". . . out of sight and sound of sea!"

and the vertigo seized him again.

This time, mist seemed to boil up, and he whirled away into it, hoping against hope that the girl was coming with him. Then a smooth, loose surface pressed up against his feet and the mist dissipated, showing him hovels all about him in the dark, and above them in the distance, a gorgeous palace.

His knees gave way, and he sank down in the dirt of the alleyway with a silent prayer of thanks, the more so because he saw the girl in the white robe kneeling a few feet away from him, head bowed, probably trying to choke down nausea.

The world steadied and Matt climbed to his feet, albeit shakily. He started to walk and fell heavily, managing to fall and land on his side. Of course—he'd transported them out of Kali's temple, but their feet and hands were still bound. He wished for Balkis and her sharp teeth, but since she wasn't there, he'd have to untie the girl's bonds himself, then ask her to do the same for him. He just hoped the translation spell would let him speak Hindi as well as understand it.

At least he'd fallen only a foot or so from her. He reached out his bound hands toward hers, but she yanked them back with a gasp, then saw his face and seemed to lose her fear.

"That's right," Matt told her, "I'm your fellow captive. Hold still, now, and I'll untie you. Then you can do the same for me."

Slowly, the girl lowered her hands and held them out. She had to be very brave or very naive, Matt decided, since she didn't seem to be wary of him at all. He'd have to warn her about strange men, especially since there were very many a lot stranger than himself.

He picked at the knot, pulled a rope-end loose, then untied the whole intricate mess in a minute. "The first one is always the hardest," he told the girl. "My turn, now."

He held up his hands, lying on his back. She picked at the knot with slender fingers that scarcely seemed up to the task but were apparently much stronger than they looked, for she slid the rope free more quickly than Matt had.

"Thanks," he said. "I think I can manage the feet myself." He sat up and started on the knot at his ankles. By the time he finished, he found her standing before him. "Quick work," he said approvingly, and climbed to his feet. "My name is Matthew Mantrell."

"I am . . . Helga," she said in amazingly good Merovencian.

Matt stared. Then he said, "Little far from home, aren't you?"

"I come from the north," she said noncommittally.

Matt frowned; she didn't look Allustrian—but that was her own affair. He shrugged. "Well, the first order of business is to get you home. Where do you live?"

"The north," Helga repeated, spreading her hands. "I cannot tell you more."

"Well, the road back to Allustria leads through lands I have to visit anyway," Matt mused. "I'm afraid it's going to be a long trip. How did you get here, young woman?"

"By sea," she said.

Not very helpful, was she? "Father a merchant?" Matt asked. "What happened to him?"

"Pirates," she answered.

Matt felt a stab of sympathy for the girl and wondered if she'd been part of the spoils his Mediterranean pirates had taken from the merchant who had become his fellow galley-slave. After all, if the smuggler had bought him from the slave market, why not her?

But he wasn't about to ask—he didn't want to arouse bad memories. "Well, let's find our way to one of the city gates," he said. "Maybe we can join a caravan going west."

Helga nodded without saying anything, and Matt turned away with a sigh. She wasn't going to be much company, was she? But that didn't lessen the responsibility he'd taken on, of returning her to her home. For a moment he had a vision of what his own little girl might look like at fifteen or sixteen—very much like Alisande, probably, but with Jimena's bone structure. If she were lost in a foreign land, wouldn't he want some other young father to take her home? Definitely he had to lead Helga home, even if her father didn't manage to escape.

He turned back to see if she was following—but she wasn't. The slovenly street was still and empty. The girl had vanished.

CHAPTER 9

Matt looked around frantically, but the narrow street was completely empty. Apparently Helga had been afraid of him after all. But she couldn't have gone far—he'd only turned his back for a few minutes. "Helga!" he called, then winced at the loudness of his own voice in the alleyway. He lowered his tone, hissing, "Helga! Where are you? I won't hurt you, but nightwalkers might!"

His answer was a plaintive mew from his feet.

Matt looked down and saw a small white cat looking up at him pathetically.

"Later, kitty," he said. "I have a girl to find." He set off toward the narrow space between two hovels, thinking he might find a hiding place behind. The cat followed him, mews changing from plaintive to demanding—and growing louder and louder. As they neared the hovel, Matt realized the windows were only square holes and the door nothing but a piece of rough cloth. At that pitch and volume, Small-and-Furry would wake the neighbors! He turned around to the cat and knelt, exasperated. "Look, I have to try to find someone, and you're not helping! You'll wake half the neighborhood, and they'll chase me away, and I'll never find her, and I have to keep her safe!"

The little cat sat down and gave a determined but softer meow.

Something about the tone seemed familiar. Matt looked more closely and recognized the outsized ears, the small and slender form. "Balkis!" he hissed.

The cat looked at him as though he were crazy.

"No, you can't be," Matt sighed. "Wrong color. Well, I'll tell you what—you go your way and I'll go mine, and if you find a young girl wearing a white robe, you meow loudly, okay?"

For answer, the cat leaped onto his thigh and scooted up to his shoulders.

"Ouch!" Matt said aloud, then cut back to an agonized whisper. "Velvet paws! Velvet paws!" He went still, remembering the last time he had said that—and reminded by his own words that Helga had been wearing a white robe.

Purring in his left ear. He turned his head and found he was looking directly into the cat's eyes. "You are Balkis, aren't you? But you're also Helga. How else did your coat change color?"

The cat gave an indignant meow.

"No use denying it," Matt told her. "I've found you out." Softly, he sang,

> "Sweet sixteen goes as a cat
> Just to spy on boys.
> She hisses and she purrs aloud
> At every little noise."

The cat meowed in outrage.

> "Let's see her in her true form
> For a very little while,
> For she can't hide that she's just
> Putting on the style!"

The cat leaped down from his shoulder, then squalled protest as her form fluxed, stretched, then steadied into Helga's. She spat a verse in Allustrian, though, and instantly flowed back into the form of a small white cat.

"Gotcha!" Matt whispered triumphantly. "So that's why you're white—you're wearing a white robe now! What were you wearing before, a brown dress?"

Balkis turned about and, with great aplomb, sat with her back to him.

"So now I'm being punished, am I? To think that all this time I've been traveling with a teenager! Wise of you to disguise yourself as a cat, though," Matt said thoughtfully, "especially on a ship full of pirates. You wouldn't want to have appeared as a pretty, voluptuous girl there."

The cat peered over her shoulder at him with a feline frown.

"Oh yes, I know you're pretty." Matt remembered that cats were very susceptible to flattery. "A uniquely attractive cat, in fact. The touch of the exotic is fascinating, and the huge eyes and shiny coat would make any mouser yowl with envy."

Languidly, Balkis stood up and stretched, arching her back, then sat down again, just happening to be in profile.

Matt saw he was making progress, but he wasn't getting her back into human form. Transformation spells wouldn't work—she'd proved that was one bit of magic she had down pat, probably didn't even need to think about.

He decided on shock tactics. "Is that why you stay in cat disguise? Because you don't think your human form is pretty?"

Balkis leaped up and glared at him.

"Probably right," Matt said judiciously. "After all, if you didn't have any boys buzzing around you, you'd prefer the toms."

Balkis arched her back, spitting, even as she seemed to flow and swell and writhe into an amorphous white-and-tan giant egg that pulled in on itself to take human form, Helga's form. "A lass might also seek refuge if she suspects the boys want only her pretty body, her father's fields, and her mother's house!"

Matt caught his breath; fired by anger, she was beautiful indeed. "Quite right, too," he said, "and I can see why they wouldn't let you alone. You really are a beauty."

Balkis stared, confused by his change in direction—and suddenly wary.

Time for a touch of fatherly reassurance, Matt decided. "I hope my little daughter will be as pretty as you when she grows up."

Balkis eyed him uncertainly. "You do not wish her to look like her mother?"

"Oh, definitely I do," Matt said. "After all, I married the most beautiful woman in the world."

Balkis' eyes sparked with jealousy—but also with reassurance. "How will you manage to return to her, then?"

"By finding out who's threatening her, along with the rest

of Europe," Matt said, "then taking passage on a ship. Of course, I might call up a friendly dragon and hitch a ride, or even see if my transportation spells will take me halfway around the world."

"You have not even thought of it, then."

"Not really," Matt admitted. "Not time to think of going home, you see—I haven't found out what Alisande needs to know."

Balkis stared at him in frank disbelief. "You have never doubted for a moment that you can return whenever you wish!"

Matt nodded. "I've had experience along those lines. How about you?"

"What of me?" Instantly, Balkis was on the defensive. "I have had very little experience of any kind, except in dealing with bumptious males!"

Matt took the warning even if it wasn't needed. "Did you really come to Merovence to learn magic from me?"

"Even as Idris advised, aye."

"Really must meet this Idris someday," Matt muttered, then aloud, "Where did you come from?"

"From Allustria, as I've told you."

Matt shook his head. "You're too exotic. They don't grow eyes like yours, or skin that tone, in southern Allustria. Where did you come from before that?"

"I—I do not know." Balkis' voice faltered. "Idris enchanted me and drew out memories of women with skin like bark and green hair who helped me—she called them dryads—and of others whose tresses were like seaweed and whose skin was greenly tinted. She called them nixies."

"Water-spirits." Matt nodded. "They have different names in different countries. They helped you?"

"Aye, nixies and dryads both. The nixies took me to the dryads, who cared for me, gave me the power to turn into a cat, and directed me to join a caravan that took me to a place called Novgorod."

"Novgorod?" Matt stared. "That's in Russia!"

"What is Russia?"

"A country far to the east of Merovence." Matt frowned. "How old were you when you made this journey?"

Balkis gazed off into space, remembering. "My mother said I was two when I came to them."

"Two years old?" Matt stared. "How did you survive?"

"As a cat," Balkis said with irritation. "With four legs, claws, and sharp teeth, I was well enough grown to make my own way when I was only a year old."

"Clever, clever," Matt said, marveling. "Your dryads may have had wooden heads, but they were filled with brains." Then another thought struck. "It was they who gave you your magical talent!"

"Aye—or so said Idris. She guessed that I had spent most of my first year in the forest, and that the dryads had stroked my fur many times . . ."

"And left a charge of static magic every time. Yes." Matt nodded. "No wonder you can learn wizardry."

"Idris said I was an apt pupil, that I learned all she knew in a year."

Matt shuddered. "Major talent indeed. I'll have to be careful what spells I work while you're around."

"Why?" Balkis' gaze sharpened. "Do you not want me to learn?"

"No, I do want you to learn." Matt sighed, remembering this same conversation with student after student when he'd been a teaching fellow. "But you have to learn to walk before you can learn to run."

"What does that mean?" Balkis challenged.

"That you have to understand the intermediate spells before you try the advanced ones, because if you try to use the tougher spells right away, you're liable to kill yourself and everyone near you."

Balkis shrank. "Is magic so dangerous as that?"

"Oh, yes," Matt said softly. "Very dangerous indeed." He remembered the ocean roaring in over the land bridge between Merovence and Bretanglia when he'd made it sink by a spell the druids had given him, and shuddered. "You bet it can be dangerous. Ask me before you try anything you've heard me chant, okay?"

"If you wish." Balkis' eyes were wide and frightened.

"Hey, don't be that put off!" Matt reached out a reassuring

hand, brushed her fingers. "You shouldn't be afraid of magic—just have a very healthy respect for it."

Balkis stared at him a moment longer, then relaxed enough to smile.

"See? Caution doesn't mean fear." Matt grinned, then turned serious again. "A caravan to Novgorod, you said? What kinds of animals?"

"Tall ones, each with two humps on its back."

"Bactrian camels." Matt pursed his lips. "Do you remember whether the sun was behind you when you started out in the mornings, or in front of you?"

Balkis' eyes lost focus as she gazed back into the very early pictures Idris had called up within her. "Behind."

"And the sunset was in front?"

Again the look back into memory, again the nod. "Aye."

"Then you were traveling from the east toward the west." Matt nodded. "That accounts for your skin tone and eyes—but how far east, I wonder?"

Balkis stared. "What could the east have to do with my appearance?"

"Because the people far to the east, in Mongolia, Manchuria, Korea, China, and Japan, have golden skin, and folds at the outer corners of their eyes that make them look slanted."

Balkis touched her eyes. "Like mine!"

"Yes, but your skin has only a touch of gold to it, your eyes only a hint of a tilt, and your hair is dark brown, not black like theirs," Matt pointed out. "At a guess, your people are hybrids between the European type of people, like me, and the Mongolian type farther east."

He could see the excitement in Balkis' eyes. "Can you say where I was born, then?"

Matt shook his head with a smile of regret. "Only that it was somewhere in Central Asia, I'm afraid, and that's a very big place."

"Oh." Balkis lowered her gaze, crestfallen for a moment, then looked up with a brave smile. "Still, you know that I am neither from Europe nor this China you spoke of. That is a great matter, is it not?"

"Definite progress, yes." Matt smiled, warmed by her

courage. He decided not to tell her that she'd been born where the horde came from—but that reminded him of the older priest's words. "Did you understand what they said, the priests who tried to strangle us?"

"Priests?" Balkis asked, wide-eyed. "What manner of priests seek to slay?"

"Ones who worship Kali, the destructive aspect of a great goddess," Matt explained. "Could you understand their words?"

"Not a one! Could you?"

Matt nodded. "Back there on the galley, I recited a spell that let me understand any language spoken near me. I'll give you the same treatment just in case we become separated."

But Balkis wasn't to be deterred from the point. "What did they say, these priests?"

Matt took a deep breath, then gave it to her straight. "That you're a threat to the horde's plans for world conquest."

"I?" Balkis stared at him, shocked and, finally, frightened.

She saw the implications quickly, Matt realized, and he was impressed by her intelligence. "Do you have any idea why you might be the key to stopping the horde?"

"None at all!" But cynicism rose behind the fright in her eyes. "If you can discover that, you will use me as a weapon, will you not?"

"Not a weapon, no," Matt said slowly, "but as an ally. Can you honestly say the Caliph is using Queen Alisande as a weapon?"

"There would be some truth to it," Balkis said slowly, "but you might as easily say she uses him. I take your point."

Amazingly quickly, Matt thought, and with no explanation. "What I had in mind goes beyond that, though. It's a matter of common interests. If stopping the horde helped you regain your homeland and your heritage, wouldn't you want to foil their plans?"

"Yes!" Balkis' eyes burned with sudden fervor.

Matt nodded. "Not a weapon, then, but someone who shares a common goal with me."

"I see why you seek to learn more about this enemy," Balkis said slowly, "but was that he, the man in midnight-blue robes who appeared in front of you?"

"And held my attention long enough for the Thuggee to

sneak up behind me and knock me out, yes," Matt said sardonically, looking away. "I really should have been more aware of my surroundings."

"With a surprise like his appearance, it would be a wonder if you had been," Balkis said dryly.

Matt looked back at her with surprised gratitude—but Balkis seemed unaware that she had made an excuse for him, only that she was dealing in facts. "Why did he not smite you with magic himself?"

"Good question," Matt said, "and the obvious answer is that he couldn't."

"He is no magician, then?"

"Oh, he definitely is, if he could appear out of nowhere that way," Matt said, "but I suspect he's cautious, too. He seems to have some idea who I am, so he would have been wary of my magic."

"That was why he bade the Thuggee strike you unconscious!"

"Good point," Matt said. "How did they catch you?"

"As one struck your head, another pounced on me where I lay behind a basket and held some foul-smelling rag over my nose."

"A drug," Matt frowned. "So Arjasp knows how to make ether or chloroform or some such, and knew where you were. Difficult to do, if he wasn't there."

"But he was!"

"No, his image was," Matt explained. "If he'd been there himself, he could have hit us with major magic, and would have. But if he were a thousand miles away, just projecting a sort of picture-in-the-round of himself, he couldn't do much here—not too many spells work over long distances, and the ones that do take a lot of energy and concentration. He was probably using up half his resources just sending his image."

"Why not come himself, if such a sending were so tiring?" Balkis asked, frowning.

"Because he would have arrived already tired, and being considerably older than me, he'd tire more easily," Matt explained, "whereas I would have been full of energy."

"And you might have struck him low with your magic!"

"Yes." Matt nodded. "Definitely safer to stay home and send instructions to the Thuggee. Of course, there's the little question of why they obeyed him, but what I said about common goals might have something to do with that."

"At the very least," Balkis said, "they would have had assistance in finding two victims for sacrifice."

"Good point." Matt wondered how long it would take her to learn everything *he* knew. "And it should have worked. I shouldn't have woken up quickly enough to get us out of that temple, and he probably didn't suspect that I knew who Kali was, or could understand Hindi and Sanskrit."

"How *did* you know that goddess?" Balkis eyed him askance.

"It's called a good liberal arts education," Matt told her. "That's also how I'd know Arjasp was a magician even if he hadn't appeared out of nowhere."

"By these 'liberal arts' of yours?" Balkis frowned.

"By history, anyway," Matt said. "He was talking about Ahura Mazda, the Zoroastrian god of light, and Angra Mainyu, the Zoroastrian god of darkness—from which I would guess he's a Zoroastrian."

"There is sense in that." Balkis nodded. "What is a Zoroastrian?"

"A person who believes the religion preached by a prophet named Zoroaster," Matt said, "though it had been around a long time before him; he just gave it its final form. The priests were called 'magi,' and they had so great a reputation for spells and supernatural power that people based the word 'magic' on them."

Balkis shivered. "Powerful wizards indeed! But who was this Ahriman that Arjasp spoke of ?"

"Just a more modern name for Angra Mainyu," Matt said, "just as the more recent name for Ahura Mazda is Ormuzd. Before Zoroaster, the Mazdaeans believed that the world is a battleground between Ahura Mazda, the god of goodness, and Ahriman, the god of evil. They were equal in power, so humanity had to decide the issue by rallying to support Ahura Mazda and giving him more power by living good lives and doing good to one another."

"Then Ahriman must tempt people to hurt one another and live evil lives," Balkis said slowly.

"You understand quickly," Matt told her.

"But if Arjasp is a . . . what is one of the magi?"

"A magus," Matt said, "at least, in Latin."

"What is Latin?"

"The language of an empire that has seen its day and fallen apart," Matt sighed. "But the magi in the pictures I've seen wore white robes and hats. I think Arjasp is a magus who has decided to turn his coat and become a priest of Ahriman."

"For heaven's sake, why?" Balkis cried.

"You heard him," Matt said. "He's dreamed up the idea that Ahriman has to win the fight and conquer the whole world before Ahura Mazda can begin to win it back. Then, presumably, the god of light will win more and more battles until he conquers the world and Right and Goodness prevail. Of course, the Zoroastrians never believed any such thing."

Balkis frowned, beginning to understand. "So if this Arjasp is devoted to Ahura Mazda, he must do all he can to see that Ahriman wins the whole world as quickly as possible?"

Matt nodded. "That's how I figure him."

"Then his mind is crazed!" Balkis cried. "It is split into fragments as surely as the glaze of a pot that has baked too long in the kiln!"

"Crazy he is," Matt confirmed.

"What could have thrown him so far from good sense?"

"Who knows?" Matt shrugged. "I'm not a psychiatrist— a doctor of the mind. Maybe he came into contact with a Chinese merchant and learned about the Taoists—they believe that the world goes through cycles from bad to better to good, then to worse and to bad again. Or he could have heard about it from the Germans, with their belief in an endless winter followed by a war of gods that engulfs the whole world and destroys it so that a whole new world can be born. Or maybe something just went wrong with his biochemistry or something broke inside his brain, and he brooded about his own sufferings and the unfairness of life, and decided the only way to cure it was to hurry up and get the battle between Angra Mainyu and Ahura Mazda over with, so that Ahura Mazda could start winning again and punish Angra Mainyu for him." He spread his hands, at a loss. "No way we can really know, Balkis. All we can be sure of is that he was one of the magi, but went wrong somehow and turned against his own kind and Ahura Mazda."

Balkis shuddered. "It is horrible to think that a man could be so twisted as that!"

"Yes, using the magic of goodness for evil purposes," Matt agreed. "One way or another, he certainly seems to have recruited a military genius and made a gur-khan of him."

"Yes, and convinced whole peoples of their right to conquer!"

"We'll have to set them straight about that, won't we?" Matt flashed her a grin.

Balkis stared, startled by his optimism. Then, slowly, she returned the smile.

"But before we can convince them, we have to find them." Matt turned toward the end of the street and offered her his arm.

Tentatively, she slipped her hand through the crook of his elbow, but her smile faded. "You do not truly mean to beard the horde by ourselves!"

"No, but the closer we get to them, the more we'll learn," Matt said. "When we know enough, we'll turn west and travel till we meet my wife's army. Then we'll tell her what we've learned and let her deal with the horde—her, her allies, and about fifty thousand soldiers."

Balkis' smile came back, and they walked together between the rows of hovels. "What lies north?"

"More of this land of Hind—India, some people call it—a lot more. Beyond that, though, there's a range of huge mountains, and on the far side of that range, Central Asia begins."

"Central Asia!" Balkis' eyes widened. "Is that not where you said I was born?"

"That's my guess, yes."

"Might we not also learn some more of my homeland?"

"That's possible," Matt conceded. He didn't tell her he'd been planning on it.

"Only possible." She seemed crestfallen.

Matt shrugged. "The horde is off in the west fighting the Arabs. We'll be going through conquered territory, so it should be peaceful, as long as we don't attract the attention of the garrisons the barbarians have left to oversee the local government. When we find a land where all the people look like you, we'll know."

Balkis walked silently beside him for a while, digesting the idea. When she spoke, it was about a much more immediate issue. "How shall we pass the gates? For surely so vast a city as this must be walled."

"I expect it is," Matt agreed, "but I didn't notice any walls along the waterfront. Of course, I couldn't see much, running away from my erstwhile owner. We'll just follow the water until we're out of town."

"Will the city's wall not come down to the shore?" Balkis asked doubtfully.

Matt nodded. "But you can change into a cat, and I'll boost you up to the top. Then I'll swim around and catch you as you jump."

"I trust you are skilled at such catching," Balkis said with asperity.

Matt dismissed the problem with an airy wave. "Just keep your claws in when you leap. Besides, don't cats have nine lives?"

"I am not eager to test the notion," Balkis said dryly.

Actually, Matt wouldn't have minded a few extra lives now and then; he'd heard about the crocodiles in Indian waters. He consoled himself with the idea that he wouldn't be in very long, but just in case, he started working up an anticroc verse.

Either the spell worked or the giant lizards were taking the night off. Luck or good planning, he collected Balkis from the wall, catching her as promised—though he suspected it was due more to her skill than his. Once in cat form, she decided to stay that way, riding his shoulders with indolent ease.

The heat rose with the sun, but it was bearable, and Matt was enchanted by the land itself. The air was fragrant with exotic blossoms, and the peasants at work in the fields seemed picturesque and happy. The soft air caressed him, the breeze in the tamarinds and deodars sang to him, and every Kipling story he'd ever read came alive again in his mind.

By mid-morning, though, the sun was beating down with a fiercer heat than he had ever known, and it was heavy going.

Matt found a stream and followed its banks, shielded by the low trees that grew there, and managed to keep on until noon with a sleeping cat on his shoulders. When the sun was directly overhead, though, even the leaves couldn't stop the heat, and Matt found a stand of underbrush to crawl into. Balkis woke as he sat, and he whinnied as her claws came out to hold on. "Velvet paws, velvet paws!" he pleaded, and she withdrew her miniature scimitars, meowing, "You might have warned me."

"Didn't want to wake you," Matt told her. "A nap is the best shield from this heat. Go back to sleep."

Balkis looked around her, then back at him. "You will sleep, too?"

"You bet," Matt said, and closed his eyes. He felt her curl up on his stomach, and did manage to recite a brief warding spell before he fell asleep.

He woke to find the sun much lower in the sky and an evening breeze already stirring the jacarandas. Groggily, he lifted his head—and saw Balkis lying on his stomach like a little sphinx, head up and eyes open. He stared. "Have you been awake this whole time?"

"Someone had to stand guard." Her mew sounded leaden.

"You poor thing!" Matt lifted her as he sat up, then set her on the ground. "You must have broiled!"

"There was shade," Balkis said. "Still, let us find somewhere cooler to sleep tomorrow, shall we?"

"Good idea." Matt shoved himself to his feet, then lifted her to his shoulders. "Your turn to sleep, then."

The cat hung herself around his neck and promptly dozed off.

Matt walked slowly, waiting for his body to work its metabolism up to cruising speed. All in all, he decided, it was definitely better for Balkis to travel as a cat—she might prove all too interesting to any passing nobleman, and they had no patron to protect them from being seized.

She also might prove all too interesting to himself, he had to admit. She was, after all, a very beautiful sample of teenage womanhood.

Oddly, though, he found that his appreciation of her good looks was entirely aesthetic. He wondered about that. Weren't men supposed to respond to feminine beauty, whether they

were married or not? Of course, he hadn't felt any great lust
for Lakshmi the djinn princess, except on the rare occasions
when she had assumed human size and deliberately tried to be
sultry—but it was hard to feel desire toward a woman as tall as
a house, no matter how voluptuous she was.

As tall as a house, or as small as a child?

Matt considered that possibility. Maybe there was something about being thirty-four and having been a teaching
fellow, plus being married to a very beautiful woman in her
thirties. He'd had a few students rather obviously fall in love
with him, but hadn't felt any answering surge of emotion,
though he knew some faculty members who had. He had put
it down to his hopelessly romantic nature, with his vision
of the ideal woman before him in his loneliest hours—
and, against all odds and the logic of his home universe, he
had found her. More amazingly yet, she had fallen in love
with him, and thanks to some spells cast on him in his first
few months in Merovence, he had even become handsome
enough and courageous enough to believe himself worthy of
her and to be able to love her. Sayeesa the lust-witch, and the
ceremony of knighting, conferred by a legendary emperor
and his descendant, had raised his self-esteem to the point at
which he could dare to love a queen, and a very beautiful one
at that.

Little Balkis couldn't hold a candle to Alisande, though of
course he didn't tell her that. But she was a pleasant child.

At sunset they came into a village. The smells of cardamom and curry made Matt's mouth water, and he knew he
would have to take a chance on conjuring up some money.
Accordingly, he went back to the edge of town, gathered a
few pebbles, then chanted,

> "Even pebbles share in beauty's bliss.
> Beauty is Nature's coin, must not be hoarded,
> But on the hungry stranger be awarded,
> Their virtue known by gold and silver's kiss."

Balkis watched every gesture, wide-eyed, soaking up the
words of the verse. When the pebbles flattened and grew

shiny, turning into coins, she sucked in her breath and asked, "Dare I work that spell?"

"You? Yeah, you know the basics, and it's pretty simple, no built-in booby traps." Matt gathered a few more pebbles. "Go ahead and try."

Balkis recited the verse word-perfect in her meowing voice. The pebbles glimmered and turned into coins.

Matt caught his breath. She had heard the words once, only once, and already knew them by heart. She might forget them as quickly as she'd learned them, but somehow he doubted that.

They went back into the village and bought some chap-patis and curry with a single coin. The couple who sold it gave them a look that said plainly they must be insane to pay so much for so little. Warmed by the thought that they might have made life a little easier for the baby in the woman's arms, Matt and Balkis ate their dinner in the village square.

"Shall we travel at night?" Balkis asked, dilating her slit pupils.

"Maybe early night," Matt said doubtfully, "but I'd rather not find out the hard way what kinds of supernatural long-legged beasties inhabit the Indian countryside."

"Do you fear them, then?" Balkis asked in surprise.

"Let's just say that I'm rather cautious," Matt told her. "After all, we've just worked some magic, no matter how minor, and if Arjasp is on the lookout for us, even that little bit could be enough to tell him where we are."

Balkis shivered, a ripple that began at her shoulders and went in a wave down to her tail-tip. "Would not the land be filled with such minor spells sung by village witches?"

"That's our only hope," Matt said, "and yes, I expect that's true, which is why I took the chance of making money."

Balkis cocked her head on one side, frowning at him. "You have not looked at me once while you have talked," she pointed out. "You have only gazed at that mud-brick building on the western side of the square."

"Yes," Matt said. "Odd, don't you think? So much bigger than the others, and with so many people coming in and going out."

Balkis shrugged—cat-style; a toss of the head. "A temple to their local god, like as not."

"Yes, but what god is that?" Matt asked, and stood up. "I see a few villagers going in. Let's join them."

"But we are not of their faith!" Balkis said, surprised.

"True," Matt agreed, "but some faiths welcome visitors. Let's see if this is one of those, shall we?"

"No matter how tolerant," Balkis told him, "I doubt they will admit a cat—and I have no wish to assume my human shape and be stretched upon an altar again."

"If they were Thuggee, we'd already be inside and tied up," Matt told her, "being strangers. Still, your caution is prudent. Think you can find a way to sneak in?"

Balkis sniffed with indignation and reminded him, "I am a cat!" She stalked away, tail high and waving.

Matt waited for her to step out of sight around the curve of the temple, then joined the stream of visitors filing in, chatting with one another. As they passed the portal, though, they fell silent, and moved away from one another, each standing apart in silence. Matt glanced at rapt, intent faces and assumed they were praying.

Matt blinked, startled. At the far side of the dome where he'd expected to see an idol, there stood no brazen-bellied Baal or multiarmed deity, but a fire, tended by two white-robed priests with small white cylindrical hats and white veils over their noses and mouths. One's beard and hair was white, the other's was black.

A man nearby was muttering softly, apparently not able to pray in complete silence like the others. Feeling ashamed of himself, Matt strained to hear, and with enough concentration the words became clear. What he had thought were untranslatable syllables resolved themselves into a name he knew well. The man was praying to Ormuzd—to Ahura Mazda.

That meant the priests were magi.

CHAPTER 10

There was no service as such, no liturgy, no singing, only individual people facing the fire and praying. It looked as though they were worshiping the flames, but Matt's Asian Literature courses had taught him that the flame, like the sun, was only a symbol to these people, a reminder of Ahura Mazda, and an aid to focusing their prayers. If he was up and about at dawn, he knew he'd find them out in the village common, gazing at the rising sun.

Seemed perfectly reasonable. As long as he was there, he decided to say a few prayers to his own god—or rather, his own conception of the One.

After half an hour people began to leave. In ten minutes or so the temple was almost empty, only half a dozen people still praying. Matt realized there was no set time for this worship—it was just that most of them wanted to pray when they came in from the fields. He had a notion he'd find many of them back, probably as families, after dinner.

He contrived to find a shadowed corner near the door, hoping the dark robe and tunic he'd taken from the thief would keep him from being noticed.

It almost worked.

The younger priest happened to turn his way and froze, staring at Matt, then turned back to the older priest. "The stranger is still here, Dastoor."

So much for passing as one of the natives, Matt thought. He should have known better, in a village in which everybody no doubt knew everybody else.

"Bid him come nigh," the older priest said. "He is the one who was foreseen."

Matt stood very still. Foreseen? How? By whom—and what magic?

Then he remembered—the magi were excellent astrologers.

The younger priest approached him. "Come to my master," he invited.

Matt gave him a little bow. "You are gracious."

The younger priest returned the bow, then went back to his elder. Matt followed.

"Why have you come, stranger?" the priest asked. "Are you a follower of the teachings of Zoroaster?"

"I'm afraid not." Matt tried another little bow. "I thank you for your hospitality in letting me pray in your temple."

"All are welcome," the old priest said with a smile, "but you have not answered my question."

"Noticed that, did you?" Matt forced a smile of his own. "Well, uh . . . I wanted to ask some questions, but I don't know if the temple is the right place."

"Do they concern the Lord of Light?"

"No. His . . . adversary."

Both priests stiffened, but the older one only nodded and said, "Come."

Matt followed him out the side door, noticing that the younger priest stayed to watch the fire. He wondered if one of them was always on duty, night and day. If they were, where did they ever find time to study the stars?

They passed out a small door at the back of the temple, where the old priest turned and said, "Ask now your questions."

"I have heard of the magi, the priests of Ahura Mazda," Matt said slowly.

The old priest waved his hand in negation, shaking his head. "No longer. Zoroaster freed us from the reign of the magicians. You may call me 'dastoor' if you wish—that is my title."

"Dastoor, then, for a priest of Ormuzd?"

"No, an ordinary priest like my young associate is a mobed. A dastoor is a high priest."

"A bishop, in our terms, I guess." Matt nodded slowly. "No offense, Dastoor, but I've never heard of a priest of Angra Mainyu."

The old priest nodded. "There are none."

"I met one," Matt said.

The old priest stiffened again, his eyes flashing. "If that is so, he would be a daivayasni—a demon-worshiper—for Ahriman is the greatest of demons. I earnestly hope there is no one who would be a sincere daivayasni. He must have been a rogue and impostor."

"I think he's more likely a madman," Matt said slowly. "He wore garments like yours, but of midnight-blue, and ranted at me that Angra Mainyu must triumph in the battle for control of the world so that Ahura Mazda can begin winning again."

"We have never taught such nonsense!"

"I thought not," Matt said. "What do you teach?"

The old priest shrugged and spread his hands. "That Ahura Mazda will win when the world ends. That is all."

"And Angra Mainyu will never win?"

"Never fully, or forever." The old priest smiled sadly. "Though when the Arabs conquered Persia and converted so many of the faithful, there were many who thought the Dark One had triumphed. Our ancestors, loyal to the Lord of Light, held fast. Some few were in small enclaves in the hills of Persia, and there are still some there. Most, though, took ship and sailed to the island of Hormuz. After some years, they had need to set sail again, and landed on the seacoast not far from here. We are seeds from which Ahura Mazda can begin once again to raise a forest of faith."

"Only of faith?" Matt asked. "You're not planning to start a holy war for him?"

The old priest shook his head, again with his sad smile. "The day of the Persian Empire is done, my friend. It is in the spirit, and in the hearts and minds of men, that Ahura Mazda will conquer."

"Reassuring," Matt said, "but Arjasp isn't willing to keep the fight on so noble a plane."

The old priest went rigid, eyes wide with anger. "Arjasp! Calls he himself that?"

"Yes, he does." Matt frowned. "What's wrong with the name?"

"Arjasp was the general who defeated the last emperor of old Persia," the old priest told him. "Taking that name is as good as a declaration that he intends to conquer all the world!

Even worse, it was one of his soldiers who slew the prophet Zoroaster himself. Only that soldier's name would have been more abhorrent to us than that of Arjasp!"

Matt stared. "You don't think it's the same person, do you?"

The old priest shook his head, still angry. "As a soldier, though the real Arjasp's actions against us were evil, I have always sought to remember that he quite likely believed himself right in what he did. To us that was evil, of course, and a stroke for Ahriman, but I doubt Arjasp intended it so. Moreover, he died two thousand years ago."

"So this renegade magus deliberately took a name that would be insulting to you?"

"Perhaps." The priest frowned, looking away, thinking. "It is my habit, though, to be slow in imputing evil to people's reasons—to their actions, yes, but not to their motives. He may believe the real Arjasp's deeds were, as I have said, blows for Angra Mainyu, and taken the name as a way of declaring whose work he seeks to do. Where is this man, my friend?"

"I don't know," Matt said slowly, "but he seems to be the one who convinced a barbarian chieftain he could conquer the world, and is using his magic to help the man do just that."

The old priest stared. "You do not mean it is this Arjasp who is the power behind the horde and its conquests!"

"I'm afraid it looks that way, yes."

The old man looked away in horror, grasping Matt's shoulder to support a suddenly trembling body. "Oh, my friend, then the world is in deep and deadly danger indeed, for if Arjasp's gur-khan conquers in the name of Ahriman, there is no end to the evil he may do!"

Matt stepped closer, putting an arm around the old man to hold him up. "I'm sorry—I didn't realize this news would affect you so deeply."

"How could it do aught else?" the old man asked. He lifted his eyes to Matt's again, deeply agitated. "Is there nothing we can do to stop this man?"

"Actually," Matt said, "I was going to ask you that."

With a cry of despair, the old priest looked away again. "I shall pray . . . I shall pray to Ahura Mazda to strike stronger blows against Angra Mainyu . . ."

"Yes, attack the source of the trouble." But Matt knew that if Ahura Mazda wasn't supposed to win until the world ended, it wasn't going to do him and his beloved much good right now. Only a bigger and stronger army would. An army, or . . .

The old priest lifted reddened, frightened eyes to Matt's. "What more can I do?"

"Actually," Matt said, "I was thinking you might teach me your magic—but if the magi are gone . . ."

"Gone, but we were careful to preserve knowledge of their ways, so they might never rise to their despotism again," the dastoor said darkly.

Matt lifted his head slowly. "Which is what Arjasp is trying to do!"

The dastoor nodded. "I shall teach you."

Matt stayed with the dastoor for two weeks, learning the essential spells and the basic approach to magic. It seemed to be based on astrology, on reading the future, and he was astounded at how accurate and detailed the priests were able to be. Of course, they reinforced the stargazing with some highly secret verses in an ancient and arcane language, but with his translation spell still going strong, Matt had no trouble learning them. Memorizing the sounds of the alien syllables took a bit more doing, but he managed it.

Somehow, he had a notion that the dastoors of his own universe didn't know a thing about magic, and probably avoided the idea like the plague—but they didn't live in a universe in which magic really worked.

He found that the priests didn't really see *the* future—they saw a whole range of futures, from the disastrous to the supremely fortunate, and the events that caused each to happen.

"Can you foresee that for a single individual's life?" Matt asked, awed by the panorama of the heavens as seen from the top of the hill near the town.

"Only the broad sweep of it," the old priest told him, "only the major events, such as births, marriages, and deaths. We can advise overall policies that will lead to prosperity, and warn against others that will lead to ruin."

Matt frowned. "But that's what you can foresee for your whole people, too, and even for the world."

"Even so," the old priest agreed. "For nations, though, details are the whole lives of individual people. We cannot see so finely for any one person."

"Because he or she *is* the detail." Matt nodded.

But once they knew the range of possible futures, the priests were able to see which events would lead to each, and were then able to compose verses that would strengthen Ahura Mazda's struggle to bring those events to pass.

"Then all the congregations of Parsis include those prayers in their daily worship," the old priest explained, "each yielding his own tiny bit of power to the Lord of Light."

Matt knew it wouldn't happen in his home world, of course. "But thousands of those bits of energy add up to a huge increase in strength," he said. "And since Angra Mainyu doesn't have such congregations giving him power, Ahura Mazda wins."

"Now, though," the old priest said, "Angra Mainyu has such worshipers."

"Yes," Matt said grimly, "thanks to Arjasp." Then a thought struck him. "If Angra Mainyu didn't have priests and congregations, though, where did he get the strength to fight Ahura Mazda in the first place?"

"Every evil thought, word, or action anyone commits strengthens Angra Mainyu," the old priest said.

"And every good thought, word, and deed strengthens Ahura Mazda?"

"Exactly." The old priest beamed. "You have understood the essence of our purpose on this earth."

Matt thought of the number of atrocities the horde was committing, and shuddered.

He learned the Parsi rules of versification, learned how to craft a poem that would strengthen Ahura Mazda for battle in a specific event. The old priest was delighted with his progress and amused by his extra student.

He chuckled. "Your cat seems as interested in our lore as you yourself."

"She's a very patient one," Matt said.

Finally the fortnight was over, and the old dastoor had taught him as much as he could in that time. The priest regretted that Matt couldn't stay to study longer, but understood that he had to forge ahead northward to discover the horde's Achilles' heel, if it had one. The villagers held a farewell banquet for him, then all turned out the next morning to see him off.

As the collection of cottages receded behind them, Balkis asked, from her seat on his shoulders, "Are they cheering us on, or glad to see us go?"

"Their hearts are with us," Matt answered, then changed the subject. "If you do try any of that Zoroastrian magic, remember to keep it simple! I don't want you getting blasted by an advanced spell you don't know how to control."

"You have scant faith in me," the cat sniffed. "Even I have seen that those spells will hasten a favorable event, no matter whether they are addressed to Ahura Mazda or to the Christian God."

"They'd better," Matt said, "or they won't be any use to us."

Privately, he was sure that the Supreme Being was the same everywhere, and would hear and understand the petitions of any people, no matter what language they spoke or in what name they prayed, or which limited image of the Limitless they envisioned. Even more, though, he was increasingly suspecting that even in this universe, magic worked by poetry itself more than by the Being to whom those spells were addressed—by symbolism and intent, not direct intervention. Good intentions resulted in good effects here, though they sometimes did not in his home universe. Surely the Source of Goodness could read what a human heart intended and respond to the symbols to which those intentions gave rise. But most of the minor spells, such as those for lighting a fire or removing a wart, seemed an imposition on such a Being, even though God must indeed have had an infinite capacity for attention to detail. Matt suspected that simple magic worked by manipulating the laws of nature, here as well as at home. But in this universe they were manipulated by poetry and song, not mathematics and exotic hardware. He had a notion that computers wouldn't work here, and wondered if that was a good thing.

* * *

As the sun neared the zenith, they found some shade under a deodar and broke out the leftovers the villagers had packed for journey rations.

"Another advantage to traveling as a cat," Matt noted. "You don't eat as much."

"Yes, but the tastes are as delicious and last as long as a larger meal would for my human body," Balkis answered, then took another bite of curry. She swallowed and said, "I quite approve of their cooking."

Matt agreed, though he did leave the really hot foods to her. He was amazed that a cat could purr while she ate.

After lunch he stretched out for a nap, and Balkis curled up on his stomach. He was just dozing off when the cat squalled and sprang away. "Oof!" Matt said, and sat bolt-upright just in time to see a turbaned maniac in loincloth and bushy beard swinging a club at his sinuses.

Matt rolled to the side at the last moment, and the club thudded into the earth. He lashed out with a kick and caught the attacker in the stomach; the man doubled over, hands pressed to his belly, mouth gaping in silent agony. Matt snatched up the club and leaped to his feet just in time to see two more men charging at him out of the roadside brush.

A furry fury landed on one man's shoulder with all claws out, yowling and spitting. The man shouted in pain and anger and swung his club at the cat, but she had already leaped to the ground. Matt gave his own shout of anger, feinting a kick at the other man, then slashing at him with the club. The mugger blocked with his own stick, and Matt slammed a real kick into his hip. The man spun away with a howl of pain, and Matt called out,

> "As England the silver sea surrounds
> As a moat defends a keep,
> Let a barrier unseen be 'round us,
> High and thick and deep!"

The two men in front of him slammed into something invisible and reeled back, falling. He heard shouts of surprise

and pain behind him and spun about to see two more attackers down. Even in that brief glimpse a pattern struck him:

They all wore turbans and loincloths of midnight-blue.

"He truly is a wizard!" one man bleated.

"You were well warned," said a more severe, more au-
thoritative voice, and an older man in midnight-blue robes
stepped out of the shadows, raised his arms, and chanted a
quick verse. Matt instantly started reciting his own spell, but
halfway through the second line, his words turned to nonsense syllables, and the magician's words registered, something about scattering Matt's thoughts and confusing his
speech. Matt strained to force his tongue and lips to shape
intelligible words, but suddenly couldn't even form a coherent thought.

The attackers saw and started swinging with savage delight. A club cracked on the back of Matt's head. The darkness closed in around the magician's vindictive smile, then
eclipsed even that, and the darkness settled in to stay awhile.

Visiting hours were over, so the darkness had to go away.
Light seeped in, and with it, a jackhammer headache. He
groaned, and a voice answered.

"Awake, are you? Haul him up, then!"

Hands seized Matt's ankles and wrists; strong arms heaved
him up and forward. Matt opened his eyes wide in alarm—
definitely a mistake, for the room reeled about him. Even as
he was jammed onto his knees, his stomach took up heaving
where the arms had left off. He managed to turn to the side
and spew most of it onto the floor, not onto himself.

"A weakling indeed! He could not even keep from fouling
his chamber!" The gloating voice turned mocking. "Why are
you so queasy, wizard? Come, recite a spell that will settle
your stomach and banish the headache!"

Well, since he was being given the chance, why not take it?
Matt had a nasty feeling about the taunting note to the man's
voice, but he went ahead and recited anyway . . .

. . . or tried to. Before he could utter more than a few
words, however, a band of greasy cloth had been tied about
his mouth. He tried to push himself up to his feet, to swing a
fist at the gloating grin. Something tugged at both wrists and

ankles at the same instant, and his hands yanked against each other. His stomach sank even farther as he realized he'd been tied hand and foot, with a rope connecting the two pairs of extremities.

"Can you not enchant us, then?" the voice jeered. "Then your doom has come, fool, and you shall pay with your head!"

A huge man stepped up with a huger scimitar, and Matt's stomach clenched with fear as he realized the man spoke with the utmost seriousness.

A soft hand cupped his chin and yanked his head away from the sight of the sword. The room reeled, his stomach roiled, and he found himself staring into the black-bearded face of the man in the midnight robes. Dimly, he remembered it was the uniform of the priests of Angra Mainyu.

"Thus be it ever to the enemies of our lord Arjasp," the man spat, his eyes glinting with malevolence. "Did you think you would find him here? Are you truly such a fool as to believe him to be a Parsi? He is a Persian of the old, pure blood, come from the hills of Iran! He saw that only through Ahriman could the Persians once again gain empire, and that only empire will bring the final battle between Angra Mainyu and Ahura Mazda!"

Matt gargled something incoherent.

"What does he say, the man so proud of his speech?" the magus mocked. "Could it be that the empire will be Mongolian and Turkish, not Persian? Ah, but who will control the Mongol? Who will seize the government of the Turks? Do you truly believe Tartars can stand against the intrigues of a Persian? Nay, be sure that when Arjasp has beguiled them into conquering the world for us and for Angra Mainyu, he will himself conquer the gur-khan, and Persians shall rule again, but this time in the name of the Prince of Lies, not the Lord of Light!"

Matt glared up at the magus with contempt, thinking that Arjasp was in for a very unpleasant surprise if he thought he would be cozening a bunch of country yokels. If they were anything like the medieval Mongols of his own world, they would be quite capable of meeting the wiliest intrigues with their direct and straightforward spears.

The magus saw and scowled. "Die, fool!" He gestured to the turbaned man next to him, and the executioner swung high his sword.

Matt stared up at the edge glinting in torchlight, his stomach hollow with dread. The magus saw and laughed, gloating at Matt's horror. He hadn't been so terrified since he had first come to Merovence . . .

. . . and before he was knighted. The memory of that ceremony suddenly flashed before him, of the questions firing at him as he sponged himself in a cold bath, the advice intoned as he walked the aisle between rows of knights long dead, of Sir Guy's sword touching his shoulder . . .

And the fear was gone. He glared up at the magus, refusing to stretch his neck for the fatal blow.

The man's face filled with fury. He grabbed a fistful of Matt's hair and yanked his head down to expose his neck to the blade—so Matt was staring at the floor when the meowing voice intoned from the ceiling,

> "Wake up the brain besotted
> And weave the web of Peace!
> Unbind the mouth beknotted,
> And bid brain's turmoil cease!"

Suddenly Matt could talk again—but before he had time to chant a couplet, a furious yowl sounded, then a howl of pain and a curse from the magus. Matt pictured Balkis descending on the man with all claws out, then a sickening vision of the man hurling her from him, and wished with all his heart that he could see something besides the man's ankles. His wish came true—he saw a flash of white twist between those ankles just as the man started to turn. He shouted a Farsi curse as he tripped and fell.

The executioner rumbled anger and swung his scimitar high, then bleated with pain and dropped the weapon, hopping on one foot. The white blur streaked toward a corner with drops of red on its claws.

Then light flared, and a stern voice called out commands in Farsi verse. The magus and his minions cringed away from the brightness, their mouths moving—but no words came out.

Finally Matt was able to get a good look at the chamber. It was dark, windowless, all of stone—someplace underground, at a guess. Torches flickered from brackets on the walls. He saw a rack, a brazier, and various torture instruments, and swiveled to see where the light and the voice had come from.

There stood his teacher, the dastoor, seeming ten feet tall and swollen with power, the mobed and four acolytes around him. Then the meaning of the words struck home:

> "You may not touch this man,
> For he is of Ahura Mazda.
> Whoever seeks to hurt him
> Will have no power of speech."

It sounded a lot better in Farsi, of course, with rhyme and meter, but it boiled down to Matt being a Mazdaist, and he wasn't about to correct the notion as long as Ormuzd's mantle covered him.

The priest of Ahriman turned purple in the face, shouting— but no words emerged from his lips. Matt wondered how long the spell could last and struggled with his own bonds, trying to free a hand, his gag . . .

A white streak flashed again, dashing by Matt just as a roar sounded behind him. One of the blue-turbaned, blue-loinclothed bullies charged after the cat—and fell headlong with a bellow of pain. Matt had a brief glimpse of Balkis pulling her teeth out of the man's calf and her claws out of his ankle before she dodged back behind him again.

Out of the corner of his eye he noticed the priest of Ahriman stepping back into the shadows, as any good coward would—but somehow, the movement worried Matt.

The bullies descended on the dastoor en masse, clubs whirling. He spoke a quick verse, hands darting, fingers pointing to the sticks, and they twisted out of their owners' hands to start swinging at their heads and shoulders. Shouting in anger, the bullies tried to catch their own weapons. One did, and wrestled with it frantically; the others suffered blow after blow before one of them finally thought to pluck a torch from the wall and thrust it at the club.

"Flame is Ahura Mazda's!" the dastoor intoned. "Let it sear his enemies!"

The torch's flames roared up, suddenly four feet high, and bent toward the man who held it as though a strong wind blew. He yelped and dropped it. The flames swelled hugely into a bonfire.

It obliterated the corner shadows, exposing the priest of Ahriman—but it threw an even starker shadow of the rack onto the floor. The priest of Ahriman stepped into that pool of darkness, grinning, and chanted a verse in a language Matt understood but didn't recognize. The bonfire and torches suddenly went out.

With a sinking heart Matt realized what the man had done—retreated into darkness, the realm of his lord, and regained his power of speech.

But the old man's light still filled the chamber, and the bullies still wrestled with their clubs. The dastoor pointed at the priest of Ahriman, chanting. Quickly, the blue-clad wizard snapped a return verse, and nothing happened—except tension in the room increased immensely, as good magic strained against bad.

Matt recognized the feeling, and thought with agony that if he could only speak, he could turn the tide. Even as he thought it, fingers moved at the back of his head and his gag fell away. Matt didn't stop to wonder who or why—he shouted,

> "It is sweet to dance to violins
> When Love and Life are fair:
> To dance to flutes, to dance to lutes
> Is delicate and rare:
> But it is not sweet with nimble feet
> To dance upon the air!"

The blue-clad toughs squalled as their feet slipped out from under them, as though a carpet had been yanked away. Unfortunately, they let go of their clubs as they fell, and the sticks immediately set about beating them again. Two of them struck home on the first try; their owners went limp, and the clubs froze, then fell, only wood again.

The priest of Ahriman turned, dark with fury, and chanted,

> "Squash this Frankish insect—"

Before he could hit the second line, the dastoor snapped,

> "From the shadows came your power,
> Therefore return to dark, and fade!"

The shadows seemed to stretch out to envelop the man. He gave a startled cry as the darkness swallowed him.

The dastoor raised his voice over his opponents' wails.

> "Torches, flame, and fire reach high
> To wash all shadows with your brightness!"

The torches on the walls roared to life again, flames stretching two feet and more. The whole chamber filled with light, washing out the shadows. The cries of the priest of Ahriman faded with them.

Matt shuddered, wondering to what realm the man had gone.

The two toughs still awake saw, and cried out in fear. Panic leant new strength; they shot to their feet and bolted for the door. Unfortunately, Matt was between them and it. He sprang aside in the nick of time, realizing they might be able to call up reinforcements, and called out,

> "There was a Door to which I found no Key;
> There was a Veil past which I could not see;
> Some little Talk awhile of ME and THEE
> There seem'd—and then
> No consciousness in THEE."

The toughs wrenched at the door, then froze, then slumped to the floor, out cold.

Matt breathed a sigh of relief and turned to the dastoor. "Thank you, Honored One, for timely rescue."

"I was pleased to be able to afford it." The dastoor smiled, but his smile faltered and the light about him faded.

The younger priest stepped forward in alarm and caught him as he sagged.

"Thank you," the dastoor said with a gentle smile. He was obviously exhausted, but turned to Matt and said, "Thank also your pet, for she came running to us mewing in fear. We cast a scrying over her recent past and found this temple—she had followed your kidnappers. Then we projected ourselves here, and brought her with us. She has served you well."

"She certainly has." Matt stretched out a hand to Balkis, wondering which projection spell she had used to transport herself back to the Mazdean temple. "She tripped up my enemies, too."

Balkis sniffed his fingers, eyeing him suspiciously at the pun.

Matt stood up, turning his back on one of the acolytes. "If you could untie the ropes, there, it would help a lot." As the young man complied, Matt asked the dastoor, "Who untied my gag?"

"A spirit," the mobed said, wide-eyed.

The dastoor nodded. "It was most strange. A girl in a white robe rose up behind you. A moment later your gag fell away, and she sank down again and disappeared from sight."

"Amazing," Matt agreed, his gaze on Balkis. "I am fortunate indeed to have so bright a spirit on my side."

Balkis sat up straight, preening visibly.

On the other side of the door was a tunnel, lined with stone blocks and floored with flags, slanting up toward the surface. Matt and Balkis decided to walk, leaving the transportation spells to the dastoor and his helpers.

Outside of the daivayasnis' temple was an ordinary village, much like that of the Parsis—only this one was inhabited by Hindus, as Matt could tell from the caste marks and the statues in front of the temple. It was night, so there was no one to see them emerge.

Matt knelt, turned to Balkis, and said, "Thanks. Thank you very much—for saving my life."

"It was nothing." The cat lifted her head arrogantly and flitted her tail. "Any cat would have done the same."

"Any other cat would have hightailed it for the deep brush and paid attention to her own survival," Matt contradicted.

"Well, I have some interest in your survival." For a moment, the mask dropped, and the cat's eyes widened, staring up at him with an adoring and very uncatlike gaze. Then the mask dropped again, and Balkis turned broadside, breaking eye contact. "After all, I have much to learn from you yet—and a long way to travel, I know not where. You, at least, seem to have some notion of our destination."

"I know we need to go north, anyway." Matt stood up. "Want a ride?"

"No, I can walk. North is this way." Balkis padded off into the night.

Matt followed, letting the shock show, now that her back was to him. That one-second-long glance had been enough and had left him thoroughly shaken—but the look was unmistakable, even on a feline face.

Balkis had a crush on him.

Not that unusual in a teenage girl but very disconcerting in a cat. Matt had dealt with it before, as a teaching fellow. It was always difficult to deal with, though, having to make it clear that he wasn't interested without hurting the girl's feelings. He couldn't even plead interspecies incompatibility, since the cat shape was only a disguise. Fortunately, Balkis was going to make it easier for him by putting up a good front and not admitting her interest—he hoped. But what was he going to do if she decided to bare all?

In the morning, they came to a much larger village, a regular town, and Matt came through the gates as just one more peasant among many. They found the bazaar, where he pulled out another synthetic-copper coin and swapped it for a throw rug. He bought a few samples of fruit and some Hindu fast food with another copper and shared them with Balkis, who was at least interested in the ghi. Then he found a plot of trees and grass near the temple of Vishnu the Preserver, hoping it would deter any would-be kidnappers, and took turns sleeping and standing watch with Balkis-cat.

"You could have slept on the bare grass," the cat sniffed. "Why spend good money on a rug?"

"In the first place, who said it was good money?"

"You should know—you made it yourself. And the second place?"

"In the second place, you'll see what else I can do with a rug after I've had some sleep. Good night." Matt stuffed a pile of dead leaves under the carpet for a pillow, then lay down and fell asleep far more quickly than he'd thought he would.

"Should we not speed out of the gates before they close for the night?" Balkis demanded.

"No need." Matt was hunting among the debris under the trees and came up with a couple of bird feathers.

Balkis watched him weaving them into the fringe of the rug and said, "If you had wanted feathers, I could have fetched you many."

"Thanks, but I wanted them without the bird attached." Matt made flying motions with his hands and recited,

> "Up in the air, sky-high, sky-high!
> Even though it's often scary,
> Swift through the sky,
> Ever so high,
> We'll commence our journey airy!"

The rug trembled, then began to rise from the ground.

Matt thrust it down with a hand, holding it against its own inclination to rise. "Down, boy! Lie low!"

The carpet still struggled to rise.

"That's right, I have to do it with verse, don't I?" Matt said sourly.

> "Now the throw rug's task is o'er;
> 'Til I call, its flight is past;
> Not yet to fly, not yet to soar,
> Lands the voyager at last."

The rug subsided, settling back onto the ground.

"Okay, climb aboard," Matt told Balkis. "We need to make up for lost time."

The cat shrank away. "You do not mean that we shall fly!"

"You've always wanted to surprise the birds when they tried to wing away from you, didn't you?"

The cat's eyes gleamed. She sprang onto the carpet and settled herself in the middle. "Why do you wait?"

"Only for me to climb aboard." Matt settled down behind her and repeated the elevating verse. The rug stirred and rose, and somehow, without Matt realizing the transition, he found Balkis inside the circle of his knees, forepaws on his calf, staring outward and trembling. Matt winced. "Velvet paws, if you don't mind."

"Oh, if you really must." Balkis was doing her best to sound disgusted, but her mew still shook.

Matt reflected that she must have spent a great deal of time as a cat for its behavior to come so naturally to her. He wondered if the same traits would show in her human form, too, and realized that he had rarely seen her so. He was far more used to seeing her as a cat and made a mental note to be careful not to address her as a kitten when she was in girl-form. An offer to pet her might have drastic consequences.

The carpet rose, slipping to and fro in the evening breeze. Matt recited,

> "Spiraling higher in a widening gyre,
> The carpet seeks out a thermal to ride,
> Rising to bear it aloft ne'er to tire,
> In its own windy element normal to bide."

He wondered if it really meant anything, but the rug seemed to have no problem. It rose in expanding circles, absolutely thriving on Matt's nonsense verse. He decided to call it postmodernism and let it go at that.

Balkis stared down as the carpet banked, claws stabbing into Matt's robe. He gritted his teeth and bore the pain, glad the cloth was thick and understanding her fear—he had a lot of it, himself. Flying in a nice, safe jet was one thing. Even flying wedged between the backplates of a dragon was okay. But sitting on a tilting, rocking piece of fabric without even a seat belt was something else entirely.

When he judged they were high enough, he chanted,

"Go to the left—that's right, go left!
I had a good gag, so I left!
I want to go north, so I left!
I want to go north, so turn left!"

"Monotonous, that," Balkis mewed disdainfully, only a slight tremor left in her voice.

"I know," Matt said, "but you'd be surprised how far it took some people."

"How far will it take us?" the cat asked.

The carpet veered away from the thermal, levelled off, and sailed through the night.

"Until we start getting sleepy," Matt answered. "Then I think we'd better find a nice sheer-sided mountain with a flat top and camp for the day."

"A sound plan," Balkis admitted, but for a moment, the adoration shone from her eyes—only a moment, quickly masked under a haughty feline stare, but enough to chill Matt with apprehension. Sheer good manners and feline pride might prevent her from declaring her feelings—but if they didn't, how was he going to let her down gently?

A substitute single, of course. Matt decided to be on the lookout for something handsome, masculine, and nearer Balkis' own age—but should it be a man or a tom?

They sailed over the mountains of the Hindu Kush as night fell. The rug had to climb pretty high to clear their tops, and Matt shivered in his low-country light-cotton robes. Balkis, on the other hand, simply fluffed out her fur and was fine. Matt considered shape-changing himself, then remembered what he'd been thinking about a handsome young tomcat and sheered away from the idea. Of course, he could become a Pekingese, but he wasn't up for a cat-and-dog fight at several thousand feet of altitude. Some other species—say, a fawn or a raccoon . . . Then he remembered that at his age, he wouldn't show up as a fawn but as a passing buck and that cats didn't generally get on too well with raccoons. With a sigh, he gave it up for the moment.

Down they dove into Afghanistan, sailing on through the gloaming.

"Were we not going to camp for the night?" Balkis asked.

"What are you worried about?" Matt asked. "You can still see."

"Yes, but I am anxious because you cannot. Where is this flat-topped mountain of yours?"

"Should be any minute now—the foothills of the Himalayas . . . There!" Matt pointed off to their right.

Balkis looked, with night vision considerably better than his own, and said, "That would seem to have a flat top and sides too sheer for even a chamois."

Matt noted the European word and regretfully decided that being back in Central Asia hadn't jogged Balkis' memory. Still, this was only southern Central Asia, and with only a cat's brain for storage, she might not have all that much memory accessible. He sang,

> "Look ahead! Look astern!
> Look the weather in the lee!
> Watch high, watch low, and so soared we!
> I see a peak to windward,
> With a parking place at hand!
> Fly low, then glide, and slide to land!"

The rug slowed, slanted downward, then coasted to the center of the plateau and settled as gently as a feather.

Balkis sprang off, stumbled, and righted herself with offended dignity. "This contraption has stolen my footing!"

"No, you just readjusted to a constantly moving surface." Matt stood up, feeling his legs protest at having been immobile for so long. "You'll find you'll get your land legs back in no time at all."

Balkis took a few suspicious steps and decided she was stable. "I shall hunt dinner then" she said, and trotted off.

"Hey, come back!" Matt called. "This plateau is barren—that's what I like about it! Nothing to bother us!"

"But also nothing to eat." Balkis turned back to him with a glare. "Will you magic up a hot supper, wizard?"

Matt frowned, shaking his head. "Don't like to use a spell for so mundane a purpose—too much chance of tipping off

Arjasp or his minions to our whereabouts. It's chancy enough using a magical flying rug."

"Then where are these birds you promised me we would catch on the wing?"

"Well . . . um . . ." Matt looked up at the twilit sky, hoping to spot an early owl or a late hawk. Sure enough, a spot moved against the wash of gray.

Balkis followed his gaze, tail twitching. "Let us rise to chase it!"

"Well, I really wanted to stretch my legs a little longer, but I suppose a bird in the sky is worth two in the nest." Matt folded himself back onto the carpet with a sigh. "Jump aboard."

Balkis did, and Matt thought for a second, then chanted,

> "Carpet, go where I bid you!
> To each direction that I speak.
> Never think that I would kid you.
> Move instantly each turn to seek."

"Can you compel by such single verses?" Balkis' voice was heavy with doubt.

"Only one way to find out," Matt said. "Up, carpet, but slowly, then gather speed as you follow that bird!"

The carpet drifted up from the plateau, then sailed into the evening sky, going faster and faster as it rose toward the dot above.

"I see wings." Balkis tensed.

"Yes, and I see a tail." Matt frowned. "We can't be going *that* fast—the wind would be blowing us flat!"

"It grows larger still," Balkis reported.

"Much too much larger!" Matt stared in disbelief as the bird descended to fill half the sky. "That's no early owl— that's a late roc!"

The golden-brown feathers swung low enough to fill all the rest of the sky, and a bass scream made the whole world shake as talons the size of semitrailers closed about the carpet, the cat, and the man.

CHAPTER 11

Balkis yowled, claws hooking—into the carpet, fortunately, not into Matt. "Wizard, save us!"

"Not in the best position to chant a spell," Matt grunted with a talon pressing through the carpet around his waist.

"There must be something your magic can do!"

Matt racked his brains and came to the startling conclusion that a bird that size wouldn't be out that late of its own accord—the land was cooling off, and the thermals were turning to glacials. What was there to glide on?

"Hey, up there!" Matt called. "What's a nice bird like you doing out on a night like this?"

A huge croaking caw reverberated around them.

Matt frowned. "I couldn't understand that. Could you try a falsetto?"

There was a moment's pause; then the caw sounded again, but in a much higher pitch—the bottom few notes of the basso clef—slow and slurring, but understandable. "I have come to destroy the enemies of the wind!"

Balkis froze, eyes wide in the gloom. "It can talk!"

Matt nodded. "I thought it might."

"How? Never have I heard a bird speak before—and believe me, there are some who would have begged for mercy!"

Matt shrugged. "No matter how wide the wingspan, a raptor that size couldn't fly by itself—too much mass. That means all that's keeping it in the sky is magic, and if it's a magical creature, it might have other powers."

"Such as speech!" The cat's eyes were wide and fearful, remembering the score birdom had to settle with catdom.

"Speech indeed." Matt nodded. "And if it can understand speech, it can be persuaded." He called out to the bird, "We're not enemies of the wind! We need it the same as you do! We were riding it, too!"

There was a minute's pause, during which Matt held his breath. Then the deep, deep voice croaked, "The old man said you were enemies of all the elements!"

"Old man?" Matt asked. "Long blue robe? Soft tapering blue hat with a rounded top?"

"Aye." Doubt shadowed the huge voice.

"We're enemies of him, not of the elements."

"He could not lie," the roc said, sounding puzzled. "He said he was a priest."

"And so he is," Matt called back, "but the god he serves is Ahriman, the Prince of Deceivers. For Arjasp, lying is worship."

The giant bird was silent for a while. Balkis glanced up anxiously at Matt. He gave her what he hoped was a reassuring smile, crossed his fingers, and reviewed a transportation spell.

Finally the roc spoke. "He said you worshiped the god who was the enemy of his."

"I worship the One God who is Lord of All," Matt called back. "But He is not the enemy of Ahriman. The enemy of Ahriman is Ahura Mazda."

"Who is this Ahura Mazda?" The bird's voice was a threatening rumble.

"He is the Lord of Light, and he battles Ahriman through all of time for control of the world and all its creatures. People can help Ahura Mazda by good thoughts, good words, and good deeds, but in the end Ahura Mazda is destined to win."

"Why does not the God you worship destroy this Ahriman?"

"Because He loves not only Ahura Mazda, he loves Ahriman, too," Matt called back.

"He could at least chain his enemy where Ahriman could do no harm. Why does He not?"

"Because He lets people choose," Matt answered, "choose whether they want to be good or want to be evil. Otherwise we'd all be puppets, and there wouldn't be much point to our lives."

"Point? What point could there be?" the bird challenged.

"Why should insignificant mites like you exist at all? Why does your God let you walk the earth to plague ones such as myself? What point is there in your presence?"

"Existence is what we make of it—Heaven, Nirvana, eternal peace and the overwhelming ecstasy of joy, the deep and everlasting friendship of kindred spirits—call it what you will, our souls can grow until they achieve it, as long as we have the choice."

"But the blue priest said that Ahriman would triumph!"

"Only temporarily," Matt assured the creature. "Even if he wins, Ahura Mazda will start taking everything back right away. That's what Arjasp claims to be working for, at least."

"That is not what he told me!"

"As I said, he lied."

The bird was silent for minutes this time. Balkis began to relax, but her claws stayed out. Matt felt the same way—as though the Sword of Damocles was hanging over his head, suspended by a thread. Unfortunately, in this case, he was the one hanging, and could fall at any second. He suspected that the roc could drop him and hold onto the rug. He wondered if he could recite a verse before he hit the ground.

"What proof have you that the blue priest lied?" the roc finally demanded.

"That we were flying on the wind," Matt answered instantly. "If we had been its enemies, would we have trusted it?"

"There is some truth in that," the bird allowed. "But if you do not hate all the elements, tell me their names and their virtues!"

Matt was very glad the dastoor had coached him. "Earth, sky, wind, water, and fire! Earth endures, sky gives life, water cleanses, wind gives us breath, and fire purifies!"

"You know them well," the roc admitted. "I believe you—the blue priest lied. You shall live."

Matt sagged with relief, amazed that he had persuaded the creature so easily—any college freshman would have thought up more flaws in his argument than the roc had. He thoroughly believed everything he'd said, of course, and in this universe it was undeniably true, virtually natural law—but that didn't mean he'd made it sound convincing. He was sure

Arjasp could have come up with a hundred reasons to support his lies, and made them all sound much more credible—even in the few minutes Matt had seen him, he'd had an amazing amount of charisma; fanatics often did.

But Arjasp wasn't here, and he was. Charismatic leaders had to be physically present to make their spellbinding effective. Distance always weakened them, giving common sense a chance to work. That was why dictators and religious demagogues needed mass meetings as well as mass media.

"I will aid your cause against this liar," the bird said, with the weight of a considered decision. "Where shall I take you?"

"Bid him let us go, and we shall fly on your rug!" Balkis urged.

For the first time, Matt let himself look down. The mountaintops of the Hindu Kush had disappeared, and the tree-dotted plain below was zipping past at an amazing speed, making the lone river seem to undulate as they swooped along its bed. "This bird is much faster than the rug," he told Balkis. "As long as it's on our side, we might as well take advantage of it."

He had never heard a cat moan before.

"Do you know where Samarkand is?" he called up to the roc.

"That collection of nests where the caravans stop?" The bird sounded disapproving. "I know it well—its roofs make the taking of camels quite difficult."

Matt had a vision of the roc swooping out of the sky onto a luckless caravan and plucking a camel in each claw, then soaring off into the wilderness to eat them, loads and all. The silk probably didn't taste too good, but the spices must have more than made up for it. "Yes, take us there," he called. "Let's see if the gur-khan has conquered it yet."

"What is this gherkin?" the roc asked.

"Arjasp's top general," Matt told it. "He leads the hordes that conquer ordinary people for Arjasp to sacrifice to his god."

"Arjasp told me the two-legs joined him because of the truth he spoke!"

"More likely because of the swords, spears, and arrows of his soldiers," Matt said darkly. "That one we *can* prove beyond doubt. Fly over Samarkand, and if you see an army around its walls, or barbarians patrolling the city, you'll know I'm right."

"And if I see neither?"

"Then we land and warn them, and if you still doubt me, we can fly east to Baghdad and Damascus and Jerusalem, until you can finally see the horde darkening the plain. If you don't believe me, go look for yourself."

"I do believe you," the bird rumbled, "or I would not take you to Samarkand."

He banked, and Balkis' claws dug into the carpet again. Matt smiled down at her, about to say something reassuring, then saw the look on the feline face and changed to sympathy. "What's the matter?"

"That name, Samarkand!" Balkis hissed. "I have heard it before, I am sure of it."

Matt gazed at her while implications riffled through his mind. When he had sorted them out a little, he said, "Maybe the caravan that brought you to Russia took a longer route than we thought."

Or perhaps, he thought to himself, baby Balkis had heard people talking about more things than feeding times and colic.

Jimena and Ramon strolled along the castle walls, pausing to chat briefly with each sentry. When they completed their round, they stopped to gaze out over the city below, a patchwork of roofs of tile, slate, and thatch slanting down to the river that ran under the town wall, between half a mile of docks and water stairs, and out under the wall again. Beyond, fields of green and gold formed a crazy quilt to a line of distant hills circling Bordestang's valley.

"It is so lovely here," Ramon said, "clean and unspoiled, and with so much room!"

"So much better than New Jersey," Mama agreed. "We had good neighbors there, Ramon, but there are good people here, too."

"And it is nice to be a lord and lady," Ramon said, giving his wife a grin. "Yes, it is a good life to which our son has brought us."

"It is indeed." Mama rested her head against his shoulder, then stiffened. "What comes?"

Ramon frowned, following her gaze, and saw a smudge on the bright green of the distant hills. "What indeed?"

"Oh, for a telescope!" Jimena said, and caught his hand. "Quickly, husband! To our laboratory, and the bowl of ink! If we do not have the instruments of our home universe, we shall have to manage with the magic of this!"

The pool of ink stayed obstinately dark. Saul looked up and shook his head in frustration. "Nothing, Lady Mantrell. Absolutely nothing. If he's anywhere near a pool or puddle, he's blithely ignoring me and not looking down. And he's certainly not pouring his own bowlful and trying to contact *me*."

"So you cannot communicate with him, no." Jimena bit her lip. "And my own scrying shows no trace of him. In what magical sinkhole is he, that our spells cannot find him?"

"Probably his own," Saul opined. "He's traveling in some pretty dangerous territory, out east where the horde is. He very easily may have cast a spell to shield him from magical spying."

"Well, I cannot complain," Jimena sighed. "When he was small, I always told him to be careful in his travels—to cross at the lights, and not speak to strangers."

"I don't think he has too much choice about the strangers now," Saul said, "and I'll bet he'd love to see a traffic light."

Footsteps drummed in the hallway and a fist thudded on the door. "Lady Mantrell! Witch Doctor! Lord Mantrell calls! The dukes attack!"

Jimena was on her feet and halfway to the door, calling, "Ramon has the north wall. You take the east and half the south, and I'll take the west and the other half!"

"Sure, if you get there first!" Saul was out the door right behind her, and matched her step for step up the stairs to the battlements.

There, they each found their soldiers busy pushing over

scaling ladders and squaring off against the few enemies who had managed to get onto the battlements before the ladders fell. Saul came out onto the eastern wall and saw a siege tower rolling toward him. "Captain of the guard!" he called.

The captain, a knight of advanced years who was beginning to move stiffly with age, turned at his call, frowning.

Saul hurried over to him. "Sir Chaliko! Good, it's you! What's the story on that malvoisin?"

"Story?" The old knight frowned. "We have a ready enough cure for it, Witch Doctor."

"Fire arrows?" Saul asked.

The old knight nodded. "We only await its coming into range."

A sergeant called, "The crossbows can reach it now, Sir Knight!"

"Then loose!" Sir Chaliko called.

The sergeant relayed the order, and flaming bolts whizzed through the air to bite deeply into the sides of the boarding tower—and died in puffs of steam.

Sir Chaliko stared. "What witchcraft is this?"

"Water." Saul squinted. "See how the sides sparkle? There's a continuous waterfall on every side!"

"How can that engine carry so much water?" the old knight asked, completely at a loss.

Saul squinted again, trying to see the top of the machine— then froze, staring. "Whatever sort of idiot is that duke using for a magician? The fool has called up an undine just to damp down his siege engine!"

"Amazing!" Sir Chaliko smiled in sheer admiration. "How else could they guard it against fire?"

"I can think of half a dozen ways, and this sure wouldn't be one of them! That amateur can't possibly know what an undine can do if it gets out of control!"

"What?" Sir Chaliko demanded, beginning to catch some of Saul's alarm.

"Drown half the city!" Saul told him. "And in a battle, there's almost no chance that it won't break out of the magician's power!"

"I shall send a sally party out to chop through the tower!" Sir Chaliko turned away.

"No!" Saul reached out and caught his shoulder. "That'll just put the elemental on the ground, where it can really start pouring out the gallons! Worse, its master is almost sure to lose control of it in the fall!"

"Then how shall we guard against the malvoisin?" the old knight asked.

"I'll think of a way," Saul said. "Just give me a minute."

Sir Chaliko turned to gauge the distance between tower and wall—and its speed. "A minute, Witch Doctor. I do not think we shall have much more than that."

The malvoisin rolled closer and closer to them.

"The top, at least!" Sir Chaliko snapped. "We can shoot at the monster itself! Ho, archers! Drop your shafts into the roof of that bad neighbor!"

A flight of fire-arrows arched high and landed on the roof of the tower. A score of puffs of steam rose with a muffled roar.

"We're just making it angry," Saul snapped. "Tell them to hold their fire, Sir Chaliko!"

"Then *do* something, Witch Doctor!"

Saul chanted,

> "Fire seven times tries this,
> An exponent of triumph's bliss.
> So fire shall exponentially
> Really quite intentionally
> And seven to the seventh power
> Assault this undine on its tower!
> If fire should fail as undine's bane,
> To the seventh power 'twill try again!"

Sir Chaliko stared. "Witch Doctor, you chant the oddest spells!"

"Arcane language," Saul said offhandedly. "Seven to the seventh power means seven multiplied by itself seven times."

"Seven times seven times seven times seven times seven times seven times seven times seven?" Sir Chaliko asked.

"Yeah, and if that's not enough, I ended up with a clause to repeat the whole process." Saul watched the tower anxiously. "Let's hope that's—"

With a roar, flames leaped up atop the tower. Something else roared back, and the flames died—almost. Suddenly, they flared high again. Water rose in a wave against the flames, then cascaded down the sides of the tower. The flame lowered, then rose again. The undine bellowed, and the tower turned into a torrent.

"It is in pain!" Sir Chaliko cried. "Agony!"

"I don't think so," Saul said slowly. "I don't think water can feel pain. But it sure is angry."

The flames rose and fell, rose and fell, as the water tumbled forth in an unending cataract. The tower still rolled forward, then lurched and stopped, tilting at an angle.

"You have stopped it!" Sir Chaliko cried.

"Not me," Saul said, "the undine. All that water has turned the ground into a bog."

Sure enough, the tower's wheels were buried in mud. The soldiers inside shouted in panic and jumped for their lives.

So did the undine.

Down it fell, a huge amorphous shining mass, a giant iridescent bubble still issuing torrents of water—but the flames fell with it. The firefall followed the elemental and, roaring, the undine began to roll toward the moat.

"Witch Doctor!" Sir Chaliko cried in a panic. "We cannot have that monster in our moat!"

"Why not?" Saul grinned. "I'd love to see an enemy try to fill in that ditch now!"

"But it will flood the castle!"

"How?" Saul asked practically. "Water seeks its own level, after all. It can't climb higher than the moat's banks—it'll only overflow. Hey, we may be the only castle in Europe to be surrounded by a waterfall!"

"Will it not wash away the very hill?"

"If there's any sign of that, we can find a spell to send the creature back where it came from," Saul assured the knight. "Maybe I can make it evaporate."

The undine tumbled into the moat and, finally, the fire died.

"Amazingly done!" Sir Chaliko said, awed. "But why did you not simply call up a salamander, a fire elemental?"

"How would I have banished it when it had taken care of the undine?" Saul replied.

"I had not thought of that," Sir Chaliko said slowly.

On the south wall, Sir Gilbert faced the forces of the Duke of Orlentin, with only Padraig, an Irish apprentice wizard, to support his soldiers. Sir Gilbert watched as a huge boulder arced through the air to crash against the wall while the teenager made frantic gestures, chanting in Gaelic.

"It struck with somewhat less force," Sir Gilbert admitted. "Can you not make that catapult to break, lad?"

The boy shook his head, wiping his brow, strain in every line of his face. "I do not know enough magic for that, Sir Gilbert—but if you could bid your archers loose a dozen fire-arrows, I could guide them all to the engine without fail."

"We shall do what we can," Sir Gilbert sighed, and called to the archers.

Twelve arrows sailed high in an arch. Padraig chanted feverishly in Gaelic and, slowly, the flight pulled together, forming one coherent ball of flame—but as it fell toward the catapult, the fire went out, and only a clutch of smoking shafts struck the engine.

"A plague on it!" Sir Gilbert cried. "What befell you, Padraig?"

"There is a sorcerer countering my spells!" Padraig wailed.

Sir Gilbert frowned. "Then you must outsmart him."

"Outsmart him? How?" the teenager protested. "As soon as he knows what I intend, the duke's sorcerer will . . ." His voice trailed off as his eyes widened.

He looked so comical that Sir Gilbert grinned even in the midst of danger. "What have you thought of, boy? A magical ambush?"

"Of a sort!" Padraig pushed up the sleeves of the robe that, like the office of battle-wizard, was too big for him. He raised his arms, chanting in Gaelic again.

On the field, the duke's men turned the huge crank, and the tongue of the catapult pulled back and back—and broke with a crack like the boom of a cannon.

"Well done!" Gilbert cried. "How did you that, lad?"

"I turned its core to peat." Padraig grinned. "Whatever the duke's sorcerer may be, he's never seen an Irish bog!"

On the north wall, Ramon confronted the troops of the Duke of Soutrenne, but the huge wagon that rolled toward him was roofed with armor plates that protected its passengers from arrows, stones, and anything else the defenders might throw at them—even, to some extent, boiling oil or steaming water.

"What menace rides within, that they shield it so well?" asked the captain of the north wall, face creased with worry.

"I do not know, Sir Brock," Ramon said, "but whatever it is, I do not think we should let it come any closer."

"Certainly we should not! It rolls without oxen to pull it, or to push it, either. How can my archers stop a thing like that?"

"They cannot." Ramon grinned. "But what magic can propel, more magic can repulse. Let me attempt its halting, Sir Brock."

> "Echo pomposity—
> Banish velocity!
> Surfeit of synergy
> Kinetic energy!
> At bottom or top,
> Revolution must stop!"

The war-wagon rolled to a halt.

Sir Brock stared. "Can you stay them so easily as that, Lord Mantrell?"

"Easily indeed," Ramon told him. "Our lord duke has invested his money in his army, not his wizard. He has a journeyman at best, perhaps only an apprentice."

The war-wagon began to move again, though slowly.

"A journeyman," Sir Brock deduced.

"It would seem so. I must give him a more lasting denial." Papa raised his hands again, thinking of them as antennae cupped to beam magic toward the wagon, and recited,

> "Have you heard of the wonderful war machine
> That was built with such a logical sheen

That it ran twenty hours between
The time between building and falling apart?
Nineteen hours since it's start,
Fifty-nine minutes in part,
Sixty seconds till it falls . . ."

He counted the seconds off softly by a major American river. With five seconds left he called,

"No longer it hauls!"

The pop of something wooden giving way reached them even on the battlements. The war-wagon still moved, but a crack as loud as a gunshot made it list to starboard. Then another report sounded, and another and another. As they watched, the wheels fell off, the axles broke, and the armor plates fell from the roof, exposing a skeleton of heavy beams. From the highest swung a huge iron-headed battering ram.

Sir Brock looked as though he couldn't believe his eyes. "Surely they did not think to crack a six-foot-thick wall with that!"

"They did not." Ramon scowled. "But our wall contains the postern gate, Sir Knight."

"What did they think to do—bridge the moat?"

"I suspect they did," Ramon answered. "When this battle is done, Sir Brock, send men out to bring that engine inside. I think you will find that the wagon-bed is really a very stout affair of planks and beams, and is only laid within the frame, not nailed or pegged. A dozen men will be able to shoot it out across the moat, and it will be strong enough to hold that ram as it rolls."

Sir Brock squinted, trying to see the ram more clearly. "I don't doubt it. Is there anything more we can do to confound their plans?"

"Perhaps." Ramon grinned and recited,

"Ninety times without stumbling,
Swing to, swing fro!
Its life's seconds numbering,
Swing to, swing fro!

Then shoot far, and farther swings forsake,
When the ram's ropes break!"

The ram began to swing. Wider and wider it swung, until the soldiers near it shouted with alarm and began to crowd away.

CHAPTER 12

"The frame is beginning to tremble!" Sir Brock cried with delight.

The trembles turned into shaking and quaking, the beams jerking and jolting as each swing of the ram became harder and harder.

"If it keeps that up," Sir Brock cried, "the ram will break loose from the—"

They could hear the double snapping all the way up to the top of the battlements. The ram shot back into the center of its own army, trailing broken tethers. The jolt of breaking was enough to bring the framework crashing down on the wagon-bed.

"As you guessed," Sir Brock said, "the wagon-bed is strong enough to hold the ram—or its roof, at least."

Daunted by the magical collapse of their secret weapon, the soldiers began to retreat, but the knights roared at them, flailing with the flats of their swords, and the soldiers turned to go back toward the castle, very reluctantly.

"Archers, draw them a line!" Sir Brock called. "Loose!"

Crossbow bolts and clothyard arrows rained down a yard in front of the duke's soldiers. A few missed, striking feet or legs. Their owners howled with pain and fell. Their luckier comrades retreated, and most of the knights let them go—but the duke himself rode out, roaring with anger and swinging a mace at his luckless infantry.

"Perkin! Your arbalest!" Sir Brock called.

Perkin looked up in surprise, then ran to hand his crossbow to his commander. Sir Brock took the cocked and loaded instrument, sighted, and pulled the trigger.

* * *

Samarkand was a collection of white blocks and towering minarets, adorned with mosaics, and geometrical patterns in colored brick, which made it appear bedecked with jewels. Matt caught his breath as he looked down on the fabled city, telling himself he must be imagining the aroma of exotic spices—after all, he was five hundred feet above the rooftops. He was tempted to land, since the only life he saw outside the city was a caravan winding toward the gates—but as they flew over the city itself, he saw squads of bald-headed horsemen on small shaggy ponies riding down the streets.

"This space is taken," he called up to the roc. "Let's try Baghdad."

"In the morning," the great bird rumbled. "For now I grow hungry and weary."

"Uh, yes," Matt said. "Definitely time to camp for the night."

The roc flew on a mile or two, then spiraled down to a hilltop. Hovering, he dropped the rug, saying, "I shall come for you in the morning. Sleep well."

"Not with the thought of that coming back for me at daylight." Balkis stared at the winged form dwindling above them.

Suddenly, the roc folded its wings and plummeted toward the ground. They saw it skim the surface, then beat its way back into the air with something in its claws.

"What has it taken?" Balkis asked, wide-eyed.

"I don't think I want to know." Matt turned away, shuddering. "But now I see why the bird left us on our own for the night. I don't think we'd approve of its table manners. Come on, let's scrounge up some kindling and build a fire."

Dawn woke them. They ate a hurried breakfast, then rolled up in the rug, to be ready when the roc came back. They waited an hour, and Matt's patience was beginning to fray when the huge bird appeared. Of course, Matt realized—it had needed to wait for the world to begin heating up, so it would have thermals to ride. It stooped, seized the rug in its claws, and beat its way back into the sky while they were still yelping with shock. By the time the roc reached cruising altitude, though, Matt had recovered enough composure to ask, "Do you have a name?"

"Why do you wish to know?" the roc answered, with instant suspicion.

"Just so I don't have to keep calling you 'Bird,' " Matt said quickly. "Don't worry, I'm not going to use your name to work magic against you. Tell you what, instead of your real name, how about a nickname?"

"What is a 'nickname'?" The suspicion had faded into doubt.

"Something to call you by, that's not your real name. For instance, I met a manticore who dogged my tracks for a while, so I nicknamed him 'Manny.' "

Balkis' head snapped around to stare at him.

"There was a bauchan who tried to adopt me for a while," Matt went on. "His eyes looked like those of a stag, so I called him 'Buckeye.' How about I nickname you 'Rocky'?"

The bird was silent for several wing-beats, then allowed, "That will do. How am I to call you?"

"Just 'Matthew' will do." He didn't mention the cat, hoping the roc had overlooked her.

"Are you not afeard I will work magic against you?"

"Not really. After all, I haven't told you my last name, have I?" Matt hadn't really thought of magical creatures being able to work spells, but if Balkis could do it, why not a roc?

Sir Brock's bolt sped almost too fast for the eye to follow—straight into the shoulder of the duke, who cried out, dropping his mace and clapping a hand over his wound. His horse turned and led the retreat.

Sir Brock handed the crossbow back to its owner, nodding his head in satisfaction.

"It had to be a knight who loosed that bolt, did it not?" Ramon asked, his voice low.

"It did," Sir Brock confirmed. "If Perkin had shot, we would have hanged him for it—that is the law. But a knight wounding a knight will receive only praise."

Ramon forced a smile, very glad that his son had brought him to this world as a nobleman.

                              *   *   *

The tall, graceful minarets thrust upward from the horizon, and Matt's eyes shone. "Baghdad! The fabled city of Haroun Al-Raschid, of Omar Khayyam and the Arabian Nights! I can hardly wait!" He tilted his head back and called up, "I think I'm going to want to land here, if you don't mind!"

"Should you not wait to see the city from a closer distance?" Rocky asked.

"Closer?" Matt looked down and forward—and saw mosques, palaces, the awnings of the bazaar, only half a mile away. "Hey, this bird moves really fast!" He frowned. "But how come there are so many horsemen in the streets? And why are they riding in squadrons . . ." His voice trailed off.

Balkis dug her claws into the fabric of the rug, daring to look down. "Those horsemen bear lances and wear pointed helmets, wizard."

Matt stared down at voluminous trousers, long moustaches, and scimitars. They weren't Tartars, probably Turks or Polovtsi—but that was fierce enough.

Matt's heart sank. "They've taken the city after all! Poor Baghdad!" He looked up at the mass of huge feathers above. "Uh, pilot? I'd like to request a change of destination . . ."

They were delayed a short while while the bird refueled—with so many horses in their corral, the barbarians wouldn't miss a couple—but were flying over Tadmur by sundown anyway.

"No army around the city, too many soldiers in the street." Matt's stomach sank.

"The gur-khan has conquered far indeed," Balkis hissed.

"Yes." For the first time, Matt began to really worry. "Let's hope they haven't taken Jerusalem. Rocky, can you fly a bit farther west?"

"In the morning," the bird said firmly, but kept going until it found another high hill on which to park them. Rocky definitely preferred the heights, and Matt wondered if the roc would be able to take off from level ground. He'd never seen the bird begin a flight, after all—Rocky always picked them up by pouncing.

The journey-rations the villagers gave them had begun

to run low, so Balkis supplemented their diet with a little hunting of her own. When she came back to curl up on his stomach, she kneaded it first, as cats do to a prospective resting place, then looked up at Matt with a frown. "You are far more tense than usual, and I have been careful to keep my claws in. What troubles you?"

"The fate of Jerusalem," Matt told her frankly. "It's the Holy City of three religions, and if the horde has conquered it, they'll have weakened the forces of Good very badly."

"And thereby increased the power of Evil?"

Matt nodded. "I hope we find the city in the hands of the godly."

"Jews, Christians, or Muslims?"

"That's right," Matt said. "Purr a little, will you? Maybe that will help me sleep."

Balkis turned herself around twice to curl up, then tucked her nose between her paws and began to purr as requested. For a moment Matt remembered that it was really a nubile and beautiful teenager curled up on his stomach, then told himself he was being ridiculous—Balkis was at least as much a cat as a woman. Of course, he could have said that about several other teenagers he'd known during his own adolescence, but that was another matter entirely.

In the morning, Rocky picked them up, rug and all, and flew west again. Matt wondered why rocs weren't vegetarians, like so many birds, then remembered that if they were, they would never have had time to do anything but eat. No wonder they needed their calories in as dense a form as possible.

In late afternoon they came to Damascus, and found it surrounded by a churning ring of warriors half a mile deep.

Matt heaved a sigh of relief. "Thank Heaven! The Holy City is still holy!"

"Where can I land here?" Rocky asked, fretting.

"No need," Matt said. "We still have a flying throw rug. Just soar up a mile or so and drop us."

Balkis yowled protest.

Matt overrode her. "That will give us plenty of time to unroll and start flying before we're anywhere near the ground. Thanks for the ride, Rocky."

"You are welcome," the roc boomed. "This will make a great tale to tell my nestlings, when next I hatch a batch of eggs."

Matt would have answered, but the roc dropped the rug, and for the next few minutes he had his hands full reciting flying spells and trying to dig Balkis' claws out of his arm. By the time he was again settled cross-legged, with Balkis peering out over his ankles, the bird was only a speck in the eastern sky, leaving Matt to marvel over the only mother he'd ever known with the nickname of "Rocky."

Matt circled the biggest building he could find, on the theory that it would be either the most important mosque—Jerusalem being currently in Muslim hands—or the local palace. Sure enough, guards on the walls raised the alarm, and archers came running out to shoot at him. Matt wished for the Western clothing he had lost to the pirates, but went on spiraling down to the courtyard, chanting,

> "You shoot your arrows into the air.
> They fall to earth, I know not where,
> Without impaling fabric or flesh
> As we descend without a care."

The arrows leaped up, then turned and darted down, some without reaching the rug, some after arching high overhead. Balkis followed the highest with her gaze. "Was that a long shot?"

"No, Longfellow," Matt said. "Oh! You mean the arrow? Yes, a long shot indeed, and it's lucky for us it didn't pay off."

Balkis peeked over the edge. "Have you a verse for spearmen?"

"Probably, but I'll see if I can't lance the boil of suspicion." Matt stood up as the rug settled to the ground, his hands up high, and tried the first Arabic phrase he had learned. *"Salaam aleikum!"* Peace be with you.

The spearman with the biggest turban froze in the act of stabbing and frowned suspiciously. He spoke in Arabic, but the translation spell gave Matt his meaning. "What are you?"

Unfortunately, the spell only worked one way. "Frank," Matt said, hoping the word was the same in both languages. "Magic."

"That you have magic, we can easily see!" the big-turbaned man said—probably the captain of the guard. "And yes, you have the pale skin of a Frank. But why are you robed as a Guebre?"

Guebre? What was a Guebre?

A Zoroastrian, obviously. After all, if they dressed like Parsis . . . "I have recently come from their land."

The guardsman frowned. "What? Speak in Arabic! I cannot understand you!"

Matt sighed—no help for it but to make the translation spell work both ways.

"What you've heard when I have spake,
You shall for your language take . . ."

The spear jabbed his ribs. "No spells!"

Matt's mouth hung open in alarm. Without the spell he wouldn't be able to make himself understood.

A meowing voice recited,

"What you hear's not what I say . . ."

A quick glance down showed the cat with her head lowered so the guard wouldn't see her mouth moving.

The guard looked around, not thinking to look down, on the edge of mayhem. "Are you a voice-thrower?"

Balkis meowed on,

"You hear but do not listen,
In your mind, let my words glisten—"

She broke off, stumped for a rhyme that would close the verse with the first line.

The guard set his spear against Matt's throat. "How are you making these sourceless sounds, sorcerer? Reply!"

Inspiration struck Matt. If the guard couldn't understand,

how would the man know that he wasn't answering? Completing the spell Balkis had last spoken, he said, with an ingratiating smile,

> "Let translation work each way!"

Balkis breathed a sigh of relief; the verse was whole.

The guardsman glanced down in surprise, noticing her for the first time, but apparently deciding she was no bother. He looked up to twitch his spear, glaring at Matt. "Tell me your name and business without your magic, or you will lose your life!"

It was only a prick, but it raised a cold sweat. "All right, all right! No need to be so huffy!"

"I assure you there is great need, with our caliph's life at stake!" The guardsman's lips curved into a harsh smile. "So you can speak Arabic after all!"

Matt stared, realizing that the man had understood what he'd said. He reminded himself to give Balkis an extra sardine, if he could find one. "What's a Guebre?"

"A fire-worshiper." The guardsman frowned. "How can you wear their robes and not know how they are called?"

"Because the people who gave me these robes are called Parsis," Matt explained. "They're much farther east than your Guebres, but they're of the same faith—Mazdaeans, worshipers of Ahura Mazda and followers of the prophet Zoroaster. We were captured by minions of the gur-khan's high priest, Arjasp, and the Mazdaeans saved us."

The guard stared. "You know the name of the gur-khan's high priest?"

"We do now," Matt said. "As I told you, we had a run-in with his thugs."

The captain of the guard frowned. "Who are you, Frank?"

"Matthew Mantrell, Lord Wizard of Merovence," Matt told him, "here in answer to the Caliph's letter to Queen Alisande."

"The Frankish queen's husband?" The captain of the guard lowered his spear, staring in horror as he realized who he'd been threatening.

* * *

On the west wall, Jimena faced the Duke of Gurundibyr and a long snaking tunnel of hardened leather that wove its way up the slope to the wall, where the men inside would start digging away at the foundations, possibly even planting a charge of some magical explosive to bring the stones down.

"How would you have us fight that mining engine, Lady Mantrell?" asked Sir Orin, captain of the troops on her wall.

"Will arrows pierce that armor?" Jimena asked.

"Let us see," Sir Orin said. He turned to his archers and called, "Spit me that worm! Loose!"

Bows thrummed, and arrows sailed down to thud into the tunnel for half its length.

Sir Orin shook his head. "See how high the feathers stand, my lady! The heads have pierced that armor and stuck in it. Perhaps a sally party might chop it up—or perhaps not, too."

"Then we shall have to summon a greater force." Jimena drew her wand, waved it at the heavens, and chanted,

> "Like the eagle of the rock,
> Who in his beak a serpent held,
> And showed the Aztecs where to build,
> Let some great raptor, taking stock,
> Think this leather worm his size
> And pounce upon it where it lies!"

A shadow darkened all the castle and most of the army around it. Men looked up, then recoiled, arms up to protect their heads, cursing and crying out in terror.

Jimena looked up, too, and saw a hawk shape silhouetted against the sky, already covering half the vault and growing bigger.

"Lady, what have you done?" Sir Orin called in fear.

The first blast of wind from those huge wings struck, and he held fast to a merlon to steady himself. Jimena stumbled, and he stretched out the other hand to steady her.

"I—I may have summoned more than I knew," Jimena admitted, staring upward wide-eyed.

Then the feathers of the bird's belly covered the whole sky, and claws the size of wagons reached down and clamped around the tunnel. Up the bird rose, shaking men out of the timber and leather contraption as it went. Before it was twenty feet in the air, the empty structure crumpled in the huge talons and fell back to earth in scraps.

Soldiers howled and ran about, trying to dodge, for some of those scraps were ten feet long and a foot wide.

"Cheat!" a huge basso voice bellowed. "Where is the food you promised me? This was nothing but a decoy!"

"What horrendous noises it makes!" Sir Orin groaned, still holding fast to the merlon. "It is like the thunder!"

"It is speech," Jimena exclaimed in wonder. "The huge bird is talking!"

"What language could it be?"

"Arabic," Jimena answered. "At least, it is close enough to that of the Mahdi's Moors that I can make it out." She shouted up to the gargantuan hawk, "Your pardon, O Mighty One! I had not thought so great a creature as you would answer my little plea!"

"There is something familiar about your speech," the vast avian rumbled.

"Familiar?" Jimena stared up at it blankly. What could be familiar, when she had never seen anything like this before?

Then she pulled her wits together; what mattered was to keep the bird talking. "I marvel that your speech is of a pitch high enough for folk as small as we to understand!"

"A wizard far to the east taught me to speak in so high and thready a voice as this, so that you grubs can hear it as words," the monster boomed.

Grubs? Jimena had to get its mind off food! "This wizard . . . was he brown-haired, a little taller than this man beside me?"

"He was! Now I know the sound of your accent, of your manner! It is like his!"

"Then you have seen my son!" Jimena cried. "Tell me, is he well?"

"Well, and making the airways unsafe by shooting about on a flying carpet," the roc answered. "I left him at Jerusalem. He gave me a nickname—Rocky!"

Jimena winced. "Yes, that would be my Matthew."

"But he did not yank me out of my sky and halfway across the world with a spell!" the giant bird thundered. "He did not promise me food!"

"Oh, as to that, there is a village a few hundred miles to the northwest that is plagued with a giant worm growing in the village well," Mama answered.

"The Laidly Worm!" Sir Orin gasped in shock.

"The villagers are worried that it will escape," Jimena explained to Rocky, "for it is already forty feet long, and still growing."

"A toothsome morsel! If it is as good a meal as you say, I shall feast and go my way!" Rocky rumbled. "If it is not, I shall come back and take whatever lives! Farewell, mother of mayhem!" Then with wing-beats that made the castle shake, the great bird lifted up and away.

As she diminished in the sky, light flooded in where her shadow had been, showing the armies of all three dukes streaming away from the castle and toward the hills, overcome by superstitious fear. Their lords rode before all of them, leading as good lords should.

"Praise Heaven!" Jimena's face glowed as she watched the rout. "We are saved, and the siege is lifted!"

"But the bird, our rescuer!" Sir Orin protested. "That 'worm' she seeks is a dragon, nay, something worse, if report holds true. All that will save the feathered one is the worm's youth—it has not yet grown wings! Have you sent this high hawk to its death?"

"I think not, Sir Orin," Jimena said, perfectly composed. "At the worst, though, I have set one problem to cure another."

A crafty look came over Sir Orin's face. "Do you intend, then, for the bird to die?"

"I do not," Jimena said. "If the worm is a threat of any kind, it is far more likely to give Rocky indigestion than wounds." She shook her head. "Rocky indeed! How like my son!"

"The bird's anger lessened when you spoke of him," Sir Orin pointed out. "Can the Lord Wizard have aided us even at so great a distance?"

"It would seem so, though I doubt he intended it," Jimena said.

Then strong arms swept her up in an embrace that crushed the breath from her lungs. "*Mi corazon*, I feared so when I saw that huge bird plummet toward your wall! Thank Heaven you are safe!" Ramon set her down, gazing deeply into her eyes. "But how did you send the monster away?"

"My dear, it was I who summoned it." Jimena stepped a little away from her husband, tucking dislodged hairs back into place.

"You summoned it?" Ramon stared, then smiled. "But of course! It dispersed the enemy! How, though, could you be sure of controlling it?"

"Well, I had not thought it would be quite so large," Jimena admitted, "but I did know where I could find a morsel that would tempt it away from us."

"The Laidly Worm," Sir Orin said grimly.

"What a stroke of genius—and what a morsel!" Then Ramon frowned. "But if curing the cure was so readily done, does it not seem to you that the disease itself was too easily dealt with?"

"The dukes, you mean?" Jimena frowned, too. "At least our daughter-in-law will know whom to chastise upon her return! But yes, I think you have the right of it, Ramon—they were scarcely determined."

"Or depending too much upon magical siege engines," Sir Orin put in.

"Well said." Ramon turned to the knight. "But why would they depend on magic when their sorcerers were so inept?"

"Could it be they expected aid which did not come?" Jimena asked.

Both men turned to her, eyes widening. "That would explain it," Sir Orin said, "but why would a sorcerer promise them a victory he would not give?"

"He has weakened the queen by turning her vassals against her," Ramon said thoughtfully, "and the fact that they needed little tempting does not lessen the offense."

"The sorcerer's true objective, then, was not to win this castle?"

"Now that you mention it, that would have been most foolhardy," Jimena answered. Her brow knit in thought. "Still, if it was not, then what was?"

"Their true objective, you mean?" Ramon frowned, too.

"Weakening her by turning three dukes against her?" Sir

Orin shook his head. "Surely that could not be enough of a goal to warrant so broad an attack."

"The children!" Jimena stiffened, staring in horror. "While we have been distracted with this charade of an assault, neither of us has been guarding our grandchildren!"

Even as his face echoed her alarm, Ramon objected, "But they have at least one nurse always in attendance, and guards at their door!"

"What use is that against an experienced sorcerer?" Jimena snapped, and turned on her heel, catching up her gown to give her freedom to run. "Come, Ramon! We must be sure of their safety!"

CHAPTER 13

The guards at the door scarcely had time to snap to attention before Jimena burst past them and into the nursery. She stopped dead in her tracks, and Ramon almost slammed into her. Even as he skidded to a halt he saw her hand go to her lips and heard her long, keening, mournful cry. Staring at the room over her head, he saw the princess' cradle, the prince's little bed, the bright toys scattered over the floor, and the jolly pictures painted on the wall—but no grandchildren. The nursery was bare.

The captain of the Caliph's guard bowed to Matt. "Forgive this unworthy one, O Esteemed One!"

"Forgive you for what?" Now it was Matt who stared. "For doing your job well? For protecting your ruler to the best of your ability? That calls for praise, not forgiveness!"

The guard straightened up, incredulous and wary. "I had heard the Franks were without mercy."

"Propaganda." Matt waved the idea away. "Atrocity stories. The gur-khan's high priest worships the Prince of Lies, worthy soldier. We must all be wary of rumors from now on. Do you suppose you could tell the Caliph I'm here?"

"At once, effendi!" The captain turned to bark an order to a subordinate, and the guard ran back into the palace. Then the captain half bowed, extending an arm toward the doorway. "Will you come in out of the sun?"

"That would be nice, thanks." Matt stopped to roll up the rug and tuck it under one arm. A ten-pound weight hit his shoulder, shifting as he straightened; a furry tail brushed one ear, whiskers the other. He went where the nice man pointed, managing not to show his wariness.

176

They came into a tall antechamber of pale stone. After the glare of the morning sun outside, it seemed dim and very cool.

"May we offer you refreshment, honored guest?" the captain asked.

Before Matt could answer, the messenger-guard came back. "The Caliph will see the noble emissary on the instant!"

A majordomo came huffing behind him. "This way, my lord, if you please!" He turned and went back the way he had come, through a lancet doorway. Matt followed, wishing he could have changed into something more suitable for meeting a caliph, but he hadn't had a chance to replace his luggage, and Cardmember Services was a long way away.

The majordomo led him not to the throne room, but to a smaller audience chamber, where he bowed Matt to a seat. "The Caliph will join you in a matter of minutes, my lord." He reached out. "If I may take the animal—"

Balkis arched her back and hissed.

"Sorry, but she's part of my wizardry," Matt explained.

The majordomo withdrew his hands but looked uncertain. "I have heard that Frankish witches have spirits with the forms of animals, but I did not think a wizard would."

"You thought rightly," Matt told him. "Balkis isn't an ordinary cat, but she's definitely mortal. Nine lives, maybe, but mortal at the end of them."

The majordomo still looked doubtful, but he let the issue, if not the cat, drop. "As you will, my lord." He stepped back against the wall and lapsed into silence, like the rest of the room decorations—including the two swordsmen who stood against either wall, arms folded, with their right hands near the hilts of the scimitars in their belts.

Matt didn't mind—no matter how urgent his message or lofty his station, protocol demanded that the Caliph keep him waiting at least five minutes. A similar protocol demanded the presence of guards, even though they weren't apt to be of much use against a wizard. At least, to judge by the uneasy glances they gave him, *they* thought they couldn't do much. Matt, of course, knew that either of them could chop off his head before he could finish a quatrain, but they obviously didn't, and that was all right with him.

In the same way, it didn't trouble him that the majordomo hadn't ordered refreshment; it would undercut the Caliph's dignity to come in and find his guest sipping a sherbet.

Other than the human furniture, the room held a large, ornate chair with a low table between it and the less imposing, but still luxurious, chair opposite. The walls were screens, intricately carved in geometric patterns, and the one wide window was swathed in silk. The chamber was simply decorated, but gave the unmistakable impression of wealth, and the power that went with it.

The inner door opened and the Caliph came in.

Matt rose and touched fingers to forehead, lips, and breast as he bowed—not too low, of course. "Long life to the Caliph, and consternation to his enemies!"

"Long life to you, Lord Wizard." The Caliph too saluted with fingers to forehead, lips, and breast, though without much of a bow.

Matt straightened, and for a few seconds they studied one another, estimating strengths and weaknesses. Matt saw a tall Arab with an arched nose, probing eyes, and an elegantly trimmed beard and moustache. His robes were of satin and silk, and the pin that held the plume in his turban glowed with the light of a ruby.

The Caliph smiled and sat. "You are welcome, Lord Wizard. May I hope that Her Majesty follows with her army?"

"She is certainly on the way." Matt remained standing, again as protocol demanded. "Though with so many men, she must travel much more slowly than I."

"Of course. Then she has sent you as her ambassador?"

"Actually, no," Matt said, "though I'm sure she would be glad to know I am here." Very glad, since it would mean he was alive. "I came ahead to learn as much as I could about our mutual enemy."

The Caliph frowned. "There is little we can tell you, other than that they are vast in numbers and ruthless, slaying and destroying all who resist them—with the assistance of sorcery."

"And that they are not one people, but many? Yes, we were grateful for that much information in your message. Actually,

I was surprised to learn that you hadn't had trouble with Turks before this."

"There have been some who have come into my domain to settle and farm over the last few hundred years, but not many," the Caliph said, "and several troupes have become Muslims and enlisted in our armies, but nothing more, till now." He frowned. "Why should they have troubled us Arabs before this gur-khan absorbed them into his horde?"

"Oh, population pressure, maybe." Matt remembered that the Turks of his world had conquered the Arabian empire at the end of the Dark Ages, had indeed been the cause of the First Crusade. Here, though, something seemed to have stopped them. There had been no Crusades, and the Arabs still ruled the Islamic world. He wondered what could have stopped such a juggernaut as Seljuk and his Turks.

Of course, he couldn't explain that to the Caliph. "I have already been to the east, and have learned something more."

The Caliph stiffened, eyes wide. "Speak, then!"

"Their leader is a Mongol, and his title is 'gur-khan'— 'Great King,' in our terms. The source of his power is a renegade Zoroastrian priest named Arjasp."

"Oh, is it indeed," the Caliph said between his teeth. "In what way a renegade?"

Matt hesitated, then asked, "You number Zoroastrians— Guebres—among your own subjects, do you not, O Light of Wisdom?"

"Yes, I do," the Caliph said impatiently, "and be done with such fulsome phrases; call me only 'lord,' even as I shall call you."

"I shall, O Lord," Matt agreed. "Then you know that your Guebres worship Ahura Mazda, the God of Light?"

"Yes, and they honor Him in the sun, and in fire, since both are luminous. What of it?"

"This Arjasp has betrayed them. He has forsworn Ahura Mazda and worships Angra Mainyu, their god of darkness and deceit."

"Shaitan!" the majordomo cried, then clapped a hand over his mouth.

The Caliph's breath hissed in. "Even as you say, faithful

servant. This Angra Mainyu, or Ahriman, as they also call him, is surely Shaitan by another name."

Matt chose his words with care. "Then is it not also possible, O Lord, that Angra Mainyu is only their name for Allah?"

The Caliph frowned, but said, "I will admit the possibility, though if it is true, they are in error about many aspects of His nature."

"That may be," Matt agreed, "but surely He is too vast for any human mind to conceive of entirely, and devotion to the One God is of far more importance than the incompleteness of their understanding—or ours."

The majordomo started to argue, affronted, but remembered himself and caught his tongue in time.

The Caliph frowned in thought. Matt guessed he was trying to decide whether to interpret "ours" as referring to the Christians' lack of understanding of the nature of Allah, or to both Christians and Muslims failing to fully understand the one God. He apparently decided to take Matt's words as referring to the fallibility of Christians, because he said, "Surely devotion to God is more important than human blindness."

"Faith can move mountains," Matt agreed, "and the Parsi high priest with whom I spoke was as angry at Arjasp as either of us—but feared him, too."

"There is sense in that, if not bravery."

"Oh, he was brave enough to rescue me from one of Arjasp's lesser priests when they captured me," Matt said dryly.

All the Arabs stared, and Balkis moved restlessly, claws digging into Matt's shoulder. He tried to ignore her indignation at not getting the credit she deserved. Sometimes it was better to keep a card up his sleeve, and Balkis was proving to be an ace.

The Caliph asked, "How could they capture a wizard?"

"Same way you can capture a king's champion," Matt told him, "hit him from five directions at once without any warning. It's cowardly, but it works."

"I can see that it would." The Caliph had a thoughtful look, and the majordomo was looking cagey.

Matt decided to give himself the magical equivalent of a bubble dome, and to keep it there at all times. "Of course," he said, "catching a wizard and keeping him are two different things—and you really don't want to be around when he decides to get even."

The majordomo looked apprehensive and guilty, but the Caliph merely looked interested. "And what happened to this minor priest of Ahriman when the high priest of Ahura Mazda came upon him?"

"The dastoor buried him in shadow," Matt said, "then washed the whole chamber in bright light. We heard his screams, but they faded with the shadows."

The guards almost managed to suppress their shudders, but the majordomo didn't. The Caliph only looked grave. "A fitting end. Have you learned, then, how to deal with these barbarians?"

"Oh, yes," Matt assured him. "The dastoor taught me a few verses."

"Then perhaps you can aid where my own wizards have proved lacking," the Caliph said. "They have experience only in dealing with sorcerers who gain their power from Shaitan."

"I wouldn't expect your holy men to be terribly bothered by Satanic verses," Matt agreed, "but it would be more difficult for them to counter spells oriented toward Ahriman. Drawing on a different aspect of the Prince of Lies changes the proportions of intentions and effects."

The Caliph frowned. "This is wizard's talk."

Matt tried to find a clearer way of saying it. "It's a matter of finding the right aspect ratio— Never mind. I haven't actually seen the barbarians fight, but if I do, maybe I can get an angle on them—a way to defeat them, that is."

"Come, then." The Caliph rose in one fluid motion. "Sunset approaches, and the barbarians will attack in the dusk."

"They attack at night?" Matt stared, then gave himself a shake. "No, of course they attack at night, if they so much as pay lip service to Ahriman. Certainly, lord. Let us see their battle order."

Jimena, who could stand before an army without a tremble or a tear, clapped a hand over her mouth to smother her own wailing. With eyes wide and tragic, she stared at the devastated nursery.

Ramon gathered her into his arms and, over her head, gave the first useless orders. "Search the palace and the grounds, Sir Orin. Only a fool of a kidnapper would keep close to home, but he or she may not yet have been able to escape."

Sir Orin's face was pale with shock, but he gave a small bow and turned away.

"The nursemaids." Jimena swallowed her tears, recovering some shreds of composure. "They may have seen something, heard something. Ask them all."

Sir Gilbert snapped to attention, struck his breastplate in salute, and turned away.

"Saul." Jimena raised a trembling hand to beckon to the Witch Doctor. "Search magically. There may be some trace. How else but by sorcery could the children have been stolen from a castle under siege?"

"Yeah, sure." But Saul came into the room, not away, and offered his arm. "You'd better come to the solar and sit down, though, Lady Mantrell. We need all your wits, and you're not going to recover your strength standing up."

Jimena accepted his arm and, between the two men, stumbled out of the nursery, down the hall, and into her daughter-in-law's solar. The sheer normality of the room, the comfort of tapestries and polished wood, and the warmth of the sunlight that bathed the chamber, restored her even as she sat.

"Tea," Saul said to the guard at the door.

The man hurried away to find a servant. The tea would be herbal—trade with the Far East had come to a sudden standstill—but it would be reviving nonetheless. Saul poured a brandy to hold Jimena until it came. Then he poured two more for Ramon and himself.

Jimena sipped, swallowed, and her complexion turned a shade less pale. "What do we do now?" she asked. "Wait for a ransom demand?"

"This is not New Jersey," Ramon said with gentle reproof.

"Still, she may have a point," Saul said. "Why would they kidnap the prince and princess, except to hold them as hostages?"

Ramon nodded, mouth tightening. "So the ransom will be in deeds, not in gold."

Sir Gilbert came back, ushering three noblewomen before

him. They came into the solar, wide-eyed and trembling, and lined up before Jimena.

She understood immediately. "Don't be afraid; I don't blame any of you." Then she frowned, looking about. "Where is Lady Violette? This is her time to sit with the children."

"We cannot find her, milady," said Lady Eldori. She was the eldest nursemaid, a woman in her late thirties.

"Cannot find her?" Jimena stared. "Has she been stolen away, too?"

"Or was it she who did the stealing?" Ramon asked, his face darkening.

A huge explosion sounded, muffled by distance and masonry, and the floor trembled, the walls vibrated. One tapestry slipped from its hooks and came tumbling down.

Jimena stared. "What *now*?"

"If that is a demand for a ransom, it is rather more forceful than it needs to be." Ramon started for the door.

Voices called, coming nearer. The door guard blanched and stepped in. "Lord and lady! The wall! We are beset!"

They ran.

Up the twisting stairs, out onto the battlements, as the castle shuddered at another blow. There, though, they jolted to a halt, staring.

She towered above the ramparts, very high above the ramparts, with a killer figure and blood in her eye, beautiful in her rage, raising a boulder in her fist to aim at the wall. "Summon him, I say!" Her voice was thunder, making the stones shake. "Where is this craven, this churl, this limb of Shaitan? Hale him forth to answer me, or I shall demolish your castle!"

"Spare us, O Fairest of the Djinn!" the captain of the guard pleaded.

"Yes, spare us, Princess Lakshmi, I beg of you!" Ramon cried. "Of which limb of Satan do you speak?"

"Your son, wizard, and do not think to cozen me with your handsome face and fair words! I speak of Matthew Mantrell! Bring him forth to me on the instant, or all your lives are forfeit!"

Infantry marched before them, clearing a way through the people who thronged the boulevard, salaaming and acclaiming the Caliph. He rode on a white mare, Matt following him on a brown, side by side with a suspicious-looking man with the indefinable aura of a wizard.

Matt tried for professional rapport. "What spells have you tried against these unbelievers?"

"Everything we can think of," the wizard snapped, and turned away, glowering.

Matt sighed and reined in his horse as the Caliph did, then dismounted and followed him up the steps to the parapet on the city wall. Somewhere along the way he had lost Balkis. He told himself not to worry, that she was as adept at survival as he was, if not more so—but he couldn't help a trace of anxiety all the same.

Outside the city, drums began to throb—not the rattle of snare drums, but the deep grumbling of tympani. They climbed the wall to see a dark mass surging toward them in the deepening dusk. The parapet too was dark, with only an occasional torch to relieve the gloom.

"You learned that light on the wall only blinded you to what your enemy was doing, eh?" Matt asked.

The Caliph looked up in surprise. "Even so, Lord Wizard. Have you fought at night before?"

"Not against an army," Matt said, "but hand-to-hand was bad enough."

Several people glanced at him, startled, the Muslim wizard among them, and Matt realized they had heard about his battle with the evil giant. The wizard quickly looked away, mouth thinning, but the others eyed Matt warily—the fact that he hadn't boasted about it outright made him even more formidable.

Matt didn't tell them that he knew about eyes adapting to darkness from junior high school science, or that the giant would have crushed him if a stronger titan, Colmain, hadn't come to his rescue.

On the other hand, it had been his magic that waked Colmain . . . both giants, in fact . . .

The mass of barbarians rolled closer and closer. Along the wall captains cried, "Nock arrows! Draw!"

Suddenly, the darkness at the base of the wall seemed to become deeper, totally lightless for a space of fifty feet out, embracing the front ranks of the barbarians. They disappeared into it.

"First spell, wizard!" the Muslim magus snapped. "How shall you counter it?"

Scaling ladders slammed against the parapet, and with bloodcurdling shrieks the barbarians came swarming out of the darkness at the foot of the wall.

"Light!" a captain cried, and soldiers lit fire-arrows. "Loose!"

The flaming arrows lanced down into the dark cloud. For a minute or so they gave enough light to show stocky silhouettes moving toward the bases of the ladders; then the darkness seemed to fold in on them and they were gone.

But the light had lasted long enough for the archers to take aim. "Loose!" the captain cried again, and hundreds of arrows lanced half the Tartars. They fell backward cursing, and knocked other dozens off as they plunged.

The other half came howling over the wall.

CHAPTER 14

The Muslim soldiers met them with scimitars and shields, and for a few hectic minutes it was slash and parry. More and more barbarians crowded onto the parapet, ganging up on the Muslim soldiers three to one.

Matt couldn't understand how the defenders had ever lasted a single night of such slaughter. Time to think about it later; for now, he chanted,

> "Not by eastern windows only
> When it is needed, comes the light,
> In shadow globes now wax, not slowly,
> So where we look, the dark's made bright."

Light blossomed inside the gloom at the foot of the wall—blossomed, brightened, and swelled, seeming to shove the darkness back physically. The barbarians stood in a merciless glare, waiting their turns at the ladders.

The few Muslim bowmen who were free of enemy soldiers shouted with glee and started picking off individual targets. Turks, Manchus, and Kazakhs screamed and died.

But the glare didn't stop there. It shot upward in rays, illuminating the whole of the top of the wall, showing the Muslims their enemies as clearly as by daylight. Afghans and Khitans faltered, looking about them nonplussed, and Arab swords ran them through. The barbarians turned back to the business of slaughter with shouts of vengeance, but a third of them had fallen.

Vast voices roared in rage, and huge shapes rose from the back of the army, humanlike forms but with staring eyes, tusks for teeth, and arms knobbed and burled with muscle.

186

There were two of them, but three more came plummeting from the skies.

"Djinn!" the soldiers wailed, cowering away.

"Worse—afrits!" the Arab wizard cried.

The barbarians laughed with delight and swung their swords. Some Arab soldiers woke from supernatural dread in time to parry; some did not.

"Not that much of a problem!" Matt raised his arms. "I'll just command them back into their lamps and rings!"

"Lamps?" The Arab turned to stare at him. "These are no creatures propelled by sorcerers' wishes, foolish Frank— they are wild afrits, far more powerful and dangerous than any djinni, and they have come of their own will, not that of others!"

"Converts!" Matt groaned. "Arjasp persuaded them to back his play!" Then he brightened. "But if they aren't captives, they can be soon enough!" He started a verse.

As one, the afrits all cupped their hands and windmilled their arms. Fog gathered in their cupped palms, thickened, and solidified into huge boulders which the great humanoids hurled at the city.

Matt dropped the spell-in-progress in favor of a more immediate need.

> "The afrits' angry glare
> Made their stones burst in air,
> Giving proof in the night
> That their boss was not there!"

The hurtling boulders exploded like gargantuan grenades. Silicate shrapnel sprayed the barbarians. Men howled in pain and fell. The Arabs ducked down behind their wall, and most of the fragments went whizzing over them. A few men cried out in pain as a shard struck here and there on the parapet; more cried out from the city below; but most of the dead and wounded lay among the men for whom the afrits fought.

Matt went back to his first verse.

> "These afrits need a shell of quiet
> With rations of immortal diet

In a flask of meditation,
Not poured out as a libation,
But bottled for all time's duration!"

With a howl of surprize and anger, one of the afrits went shooting toward the city. The Arab soldiers ducked involuntarily as it shot overhead—then down toward them, where an empty water bottle lay against the wall. The soldiers near it dove for cover, but the afrit shot tail-first, bellowing with pain and anger, into the neck of the bottle. It roared a curse that made all the Arabs blanche, and for once, Matt was sorry he understood the language—the afrit had promised a lingering and painful death for the presumptuous mortal who dared to imprison it.

"Drive a cork in that bottle and cover it with melted wax!" Matt told the Arab wizard. "Then trace the Seal of Solomon onto that wax and chant a spell to make it hold till the end of time!"

"The end of time?" The Arab stared. "What nonsense!"

"Not really," Matt said. "Would you rather have that afrit come shooting out looking for revenge?"

The wizard shuddered and hurried away.

Matt looked up and saw the other afrits, howling for vengeance, winding up their windmill swings again. Quickly, he repeated the bottling verse, but he only spat the first two lines before the afrits all howled with rage and sprang into the air, dropping their half-formed missiles. They shot up into the sky, going faster and faster, dwindling into tiny dots, then disappearing. Matt wondered about escape velocity and what this universe's people would find if they ever developed space travel.

"They are fled!" The wizard was beside him again, staring at the stars above.

Matt nodded. "They recognized the reference and didn't want to get themselves into a jam by being jarred."

"Don't you mean bottled?" the Arab asked, puzzled.

"Bottle, jar, lamp, ring—I'll stuff them into whatever's close to hand." Matt wiped his brow, then stared at his hand, amazed to see it was shaking. "You know, I think those afrits scared me more than I knew."

"Only because when you saw them, you did not stop to think," the Arab wizard said with a knowing smile.

Gongs began beating on the plain below, and the barbarians took up an angry and determined chant that gathered strength and volume as they marched toward the walls again.

Matt stiffened. "What now?"

"Surely it will be only soldiers' boasts!" the wizard protested. Then fog billowed in over the parapets.

Men shouted in alarm and anger—but all men, not the Arabs alone. High-pitched voices cried out in Arabic to kneel, and all the Muslim soldiers did just that. The barbarians' flailing blades hissed over the Arab soldiers' heads and bit into other nomads. They shouted with pain and dismay.

The barbarian sorcerer had outsmarted himself, and Matt was tempted to leave bad enough alone. But he knew the Central Asians were shrewd, and would realize soon enough where their foes were. Matt called out,

"Some beams of light on Arab soldiers fall,
Strike through and make a lucid interval,
Barbarian's mist of night can't forestall rays,
His rising fogs will fall without delay."

The fog thinned and dissolved, leaving a sheen of moisture on every blade; the Arab burnooses hung thick and heavy. But the Muslims could see their targets now; they shouted their war-cries as they sprang to their feet, felling another third of the attackers with their Damascus blades.

The archers, no longer beset by invaders, went back to shooting unhorsed barbarians at the base of the wall. Realizing that their concealment was gone, the barbarians scattered, leaving their scaling ladders behind—and as quickly as it had begun, the assault was over. Here and there, Arab soldiers finished off a last barbarian or two and threw their corpses down for their fellows to gather.

"Well done, my soldiers!" the Caliph cried. "Well have you struck blows for Islam this day!"

The soldiers cheered, but the Caliph turned to a sharif and said, "They may come back—they may always come back. Bid all our men to stay vigilant."

The captain nodded and turned away to carry the word. Soon lieutenants were going among the soldiers, relaying the command.

The Caliph turned to another sharif. "See that the fallen are taken away for burial and the wounded tended. Call for more arrows and have all archers restock their quivers."

The man nodded and hurried away.

"Are these uncouth sorcerers so easy for you to defeat, then?" said a voice at Matt's side. Turning, he saw the Arab wizard, face hard with hostility.

"They are truly unlettered barbarians," Matt said in as agreeable a tone as he could muster, "and to defeat them, one need only memorize spells from written books."

The Arab stared, startled by the thought. Then his eyes narrowed again. "But these verses you have recited, they all pit light against darkness."

"Ahriman's servants work by the concealment of night and the confusion of fog," Matt told him. "There will be others, when they seek to work by lies and clouding of the facts, by illusion and partial honesty, and we only need appeal to truth to make itself shown—but their spells are pretty basic, yes, and not hard to defeat at all, once you know how they're founded."

The wizard frowned. "Then what force is there in these barbarians, that we should fear them?"

"Not much," Matt answered. "Most of their impact comes from having so very many warriors, all of whom can ride swiftly, and from sheer, brutal violence and total lack of mercy to any city that dares resist them."

"Well, our caliph has spared the cities that, at least," the wizard said, "since he has defended them with his army, and given them no choice to fight or not to fight themselves."

"A wise policy." Matt nodded. "But their sorcerers aren't really doing much at all."

"Then the power of their Satan-inspired verses is one of their illusions?"

"Just gossip," Matt confirmed, "just rumor—and a rather nasty sort, too, not really lies, just gross exaggeration. Partial truth can be more effective than an outright falsehood."

"So the tale of their strength has grown as it passed from one careless mouth to another," the wizard inferred.

Matt nodded. "Their spells are very weak, really—nothing to trouble any of the faithful for more than a minute. They only have power if you believe they do."

"But the afrits?" the wizard asked, face lined with concern. "What magic has it taken to bind them to the service of these monstrous invaders?"

"Only the charms of a silver tongue, I'm afraid," Matt said, "plus the afrits' natural cruelty. They enjoy making people suffer, so of course they'd be inclined to believe anything Arjasp told them about the worship of Ahriman—probably that the Prince of Lies would give them even more power to torment their victims."

"Can he do so?" the wizard asked, staring.

"I said he was the Prince of Lies, didn't I? Hey, these afrits are powerful enough as it is!" Matt shook his head. "Don't worry about the barbarians' verses, O Wise One—the monsters out of your own legends are a lot more dangerous than the spells of their shamans."

A trumpet blew. The Arab wizard turned toward the western gate, staring. "What comes?"

Voices cried out in jubilation, drowned by the clash of arms, the howls of battle-cries, and the screams of the dying. Soldiers ran to pull the twelve-foot bar from the gates; other soldiers hauled them wide open.

"The fools!" the wizard cried. "Will they welcome an army into their midst?"

Through the gate pounded a huge white horse bearing on its back a figure in gilded armor. It bore a bloodied sword in its right hand, and on the left arm wore a shield quartered with the lilies of Merovence and the double crown of Hardishane. Behind crowded an army of archers with steel helmets and leather cuirasses, and behind them rode a hundred knights.

"This army they will welcome!" Matt told the Arab wizard, "and so will I! If you'll excuse me, I'd like to go say hello to my wife!"

* * *

Jimena stared. "My Matthew? What could he have done to offend you?"

The djinna turned to her in fury. "Are you his wife, then? You seem too old!"

"Old enough to be his mother," Jimena said, with anger of her own. "I am his mother indeed, and quite proud of it!"

"Proud!" Lakshmi cried, and the battlements trembled. "Proud of a kidnapper, of a thief in the night?"

"My son, a kidnapper?" Jimena stared in outrage. "You lie!"

"No, she is mistaken." Ramon held up a hand to forestall his wife. "Matthew is not here, O Fairest of the Djinn. He is gone to the Holy Land, to help in fighting off the forces of Evil that seek to seize all the East. He has been gone more than a month. Why would you think him to be a kidnapper, and of which children?"

Lakshmi still glared at him, but there was uncertainty in her eyes. "No matter where he lies, he could still steal my babes from me!"

"Babes?" Ramon stared. "More than one? How wonderful for yourself and your prince! But Highness, you did not tell us!"

"Your son found out nonetheless! Two babes have I borne, twin darlings, and when I came to their cradle this morning to give them suck, both were gone! Vanished! Their cradle was empty, and who but a wizard could have stolen a child of the djinn from its father's palace?"

"They charge the wall!" a sentry cried.

The night was cool, the stars filled the firmament, mocking the torches that stood along the walls of Damascus—but the shrilling of the barbarian horde drove all peace from their light and brought the Arabs to the walls, to bend their bows and fire at random.

Alisande leaned from her horse to kiss Matt. "If I die in battle," she said, "I shall have that to have lived for!"

"You won't die in battle." Matt fastened her helmet into place. "I want more kisses, a lifetime more. You'll have to come back."

Her eyes flashed with amusement, but not with desire—she knew well that he spoke of more afternoons like the one they had shared that day, not only of the kisses that had adorned it. "Guard me well!" she told him, then turned her horse and spurred toward the eastern gate. With a shout, her knights rode after. Their footmen followed at a run.

The Caliph watched her go, then gave Matt a critical gaze. "How can you let a woman go in your place?"

"It's her place, not mine," Matt corrected. "She's the queen by birth and inheritance. But if you mean why aren't I riding beside her to protect her, the answer is that I could, I'm a knight, but I'm also a wizard, and I can ward her better from the wall." He shrugged. "It galls me, but it's the course of wisdom."

The Caliph smiled. "It seems odd, when you Franks make such goddesses of your women."

"It seems odd to me, too," Matt told him, "but I'm getting used to it . . . There they go!"

The gates swung wide, and the barbarians shouted with joy and surged toward them. Alisande let them cover half the ground before she kicked her charger into motion and thundered toward the invaders, lowering her lance.

The Asians were excellent horsemen who could literally ride rings around the knights—but they were hemmed in by their own men, all crowding toward the open gate. There was scant room to maneuver, and their ponies were much smaller than the Europeans' Clydesdales and Percherons. The knights plowed into them, and the lances did the least damage—they could only skewer one barbarian each—for the great warhorses literally trampled the barbarians underfoot. Those who veered to the side and swung their spears high fell at the hammer-blow of heavy shields; those who came at the knights from the right met blows of heavy swords. Some spears did reach past both shield and sword, but the points only glanced off the European armor.

The "Franks" plowed deep into the mass of barbarians before they ground to a halt, their momentum blunted by the sheer numbers of their opponents. Thousands more barbarians started to close in on them from behind.

Then came the Arab cavalry, as light and maneuverable as the barbarians, their horses taller, their spears as sharp. Their own battle-cry ululated above the barbarians' as their scimitars met the Asians' steel. Here and there a barbarian fell, and

Alisande's infantry were upon him even as he scrambled to his feet. Other infantrymen were experimenting with tactics for separating riders from horses. Two-man teams worked together, one planting his spear-butt to absorb the shock as the horse ran onto the point, the other raising a long shield to protect them both from Tartar blows.

As they did, the knights turned their horses and, hacking with broadsword and battle-axe, carved their way out of the horde in a broad arc. Clear of the press, Alisande turned her juggernaut as squires came running with fresh lances. Couching the huge spears, the knights followed their queen in another smashing charge into the barbarian line.

There was this to be said against the horde's encircling the city—they couldn't get out of the way of the knights.

Atop the wall, Matt was sweating profusely, chanting himself hoarse as he countered first a spell to soften the ground under the knights' feet, another to make their armor rust, a third to weaken their horses, a fourth to make their lances overly heavy, and a fifth and a sixth and a seventh. The Arab wizard gestured and chanted beside him, equally frazzled.

There was a lull of a few minutes as the knights regrouped for another charge and no more Asian spells were in evidence. Matt lowered his arms and panted, "Any of these spells terribly strong?"

"Not a one," the Arab wheezed. "Elementary, every one of them, even clumsy. But there are so *many* of them!"

Incredibly, the barbarians began to retreat from the city so the horde could break into smaller, more maneuverable groups.

"Now!" Matt called. "Multiplication spell! Make it look as though there're a hundred knights for every real one!"

He and the Arab chanted in tandem, and suddenly the city was surrounded by a ring of European knights charging down at the separate clumps of barbarian cavalry. If anyone had read the coats of arms on those knights' shields, of course, they would have realized that there were a hundred of each—but the Asians weren't skilled in Western heraldry. Deep-toned trumpets blew, and the barbarian host, exhausted, retreated from the walls of Jerusalem.

Alisande drew up and turned her equally exhausted

knights back toward the walls of the city and the gate that opened before them—but their illusion clones rode on, chasing the barbarians over the hills and far away.

Jimena watched her husband out of the corner of her eye, feeling the first seed of suspicion sprout within her, a seed that could grow into a choking vine named "jealousy." Of course, she had heard Matt's story about the luscious djinna Lakshmi, who had saved him in his travels between this world and New Jersey—but seeing her was quite another matter, and Ramon's courtly flattery didn't help at all.

"I am amazed that even Matthew could conjure a djinn child from its cradle," Ramon said. "I am sure he would not, but those who oppose him might. Tell me the manner of it."

"The manner? There was no manner! I washed them and let them play in a sea of cushions while I left the chamber to hang the washcloths on their rack. I could not have been gone a minute, surely only seconds, but when I returned, they were gone!" Tears filled the huge eyes, and Lakshmi pulled from her bodice a slipper the size of a small boat. "Only this remained, this tiny slipper that I had myself embroidered with such care! All else was gone, trousers, vests, and slippers all—and the children with them!"

"Oh, you poor dear!" Jimena cried, her heart aching with sympathy for a soul who shared her own plight but felt it even more sharply, being not grandmother, but mother.

"And you thought of Matthew," Ramon said gravely.

"Of course I thought of your son! Is he not the mightiest wizard of the West?"

Jimena stared, amazed. Was Matthew really so skilled?

"Who else would have magic strong enough to steal away djinn, even such small ones?"

"Not even Matthew, I should think," Ramon said. "He is not Solomon, after all."

"Who else!" Lakshmi's face distorted with anger, turning dark. "Who else in all the West?"

Jimena knew the anger for the other side of fear and cried, "You poor child! I know how frantic you must be, for my own grandchildren have only now been stolen away! Oh, let us share our grief, not rant at one another!"

"Your grandchildren?" The blood drained from Lakshmi's face as she turned to stare at the little figure on the battlements. "Matthew's babes? *His* offspring stolen?"

"His, and Queen Alisande's," Jimena confirmed. "A little boy five years of age, and a princess who has only learned to walk within this last month."

"Can he think that I stole his children away?" Lakshmi gasped. "Can he have done this to me to retaliate?"

"He does not know of his children's abduction, for he is halfway around the world fighting barbarians and evil magic! Surely he is too deeply enmeshed in protecting the West from a barbarian horde to have reason to kidnap children! Besides, the little ones are precious to Matthew, all of them, not his alone! He would never do such a thing!" Jimena took a breath and held out her hands, beseeching, tears in her eyes. "Princess of djinn, will you not help us to recover our lost babes? Then perhaps we can aid you in regaining your own! We must strive together, not against one another!"

Lakshmi wavered, the uncertainty in her eyes metamorphosing into longing for another woman to share her pain—but she could not give in so easily. "How can I trust you? Or you!" She turned back to Ramon. Then comprehension dawned in her eyes. "If she is Matthew's mother, she is your wife!"

"That is my great good fortune," Ramon acknowledged, "and she my greatest blessing." He caught Jimena's hand. "Lakshmi, Marid and princess of djinn, may I introduce my wife, the Lady Jimena Mantrell? Jimena, this is the Princess Lakshmi, who aided Matthew and myself so greatly in Ibile, and without whom we might not have come home to you."

Jimena curtsied. "I am honored, Your Highness."

But Lakshmi only darted a guilty glance at her, then back at Ramon. "Your wife? But she is not old, is not . . ." She ran out of words.

Just as well, for her guilt fanned the coals of Jimena's suspicions into white-hot flames. Did the djinna feel guilty about what she had done with Ramon, or what she had only wished to do?

CHAPTER 15

Ramon threw in a discreet reminder. "But your husband, the Prince Marudin—why has he not come to interrogate Matthew with you? How is it we have been spared his wrath, which, when coupled with yours, would certainly have leveled this castle in minutes?"

Lakshmi stared at him, stricken, for a long minute. Then she bowed her face into her hands, blasting a wail like a tornado siren that shot up the scale and diminished in volume as she herself shrank, stepping down onto the battlements and diminishing to mortal size to bury her head against Ramon's chest. Her shoulders shook and her whole body shuddered as she wept out her rage and grief.

Ramon folded his arms around her more or less automatically and stared over her head at his wife in shock and alarm.

All Jimena's jealousy vanished on the instant, for if Lakshmi had been Ramon's lover, he would certainly have known how to give the comfort she needed. Jimena gave him a small smile and a nod of encouragement, pantomiming holding a baby and patting its back.

Ramon nodded his comprehension and tightened his arms about the weeping woman. Djinna or not, centuries old or not, she was a beginning mother who needed comfort and reassurance, and he gave what he could. It also occurred to him to wonder where her parents were.

The storm of tears passed, and Lakshmi pushed against Ramon's chest, moving away a little. Ramon pulled out a handkerchief and dabbed at her cheeks, then let her take it. Jimena stepped forward, and Ramon, knowing his cue after a quarter century of marriage, stepped back.

Jimena embraced the taller woman with scarcely a second's

lapse in hugs. "Poor child, what tragedy is this that has be-fallen you? Has your husband played the rogue and vanished in the night?"

"No, never!" Lakshmi cried in indignation. "Marudin loves me! I have bound him to me by love—" She blushed a moment. "—of many sorts. He would never leave me of his own will!"

"Then of whose will has he left you?" Jimena looked straight into her eyes.

Lakshmi bowed her head, and the tears gushed again.

Jimena held on, patting her back, crooning, and wondering if djinn babies needed to be burped.

When the worst of the storm had passed, Jimena pressed gently, "Come now, we must know! What vile creature has stolen your husband away, and by what power?"

"By the power of the lamp that once held him!" Lakshmi said, with a hiccup.

"But Matthew dissolved that spell!" Ramon exclaimed.

"He did, but another sorcerer has found a way to weave a new spell around the same lamp." Lakshmi began a fresh tor-rent of tears.

Jimena held on and gave what comfort she could. "You poor child, to have your husband abducted, then your chil-dren, too! I can see why you thought of Matthew, for who could know better how to reweave a spell than he who had un-raveled it? But since we know he did not, tell me—what mon-ster has made you the target of such malice?"

At last the tears slackened, and Lakshmi drew back. "Some vile Eastern sorcerer. More than that I know not, save that his skin is that of any Arab or Persian, and he wears a long robe of midnight-blue and a tapering hat with a rounded tip. Oh, and white whiskers and hair."

"There is not much there for us to work with." Ramon frowned. "Where has this sorcerer taken him?"

"To these very barbarians whom you say your son has gone to fight! I have followed, I have espied from on high, I have seen Marudin boil forth from his lamp to smite his old masters the Arabs!"

"Would he not enjoy such revenge?" Ramon asked.

"He would not! Through centuries of serving Muslims, he

became convinced of the truth of Islam, and had himself come to the worship of Allah! No, I am sure that every muscle within him rebels at the notion of attacking the sultan's troops, of fighting against the Faith—but the compulsion of the lamp-spell leaves him no choice."

"Then his new master is not a Muslim," Jimena inferred.

"He is a vile sorcerer who serves some corrupted pagan god!"

"Then Prince Marudin most surely acts against the dictates of his conscience." Jimena's eyes lost focus. "That would require a powerful spell indeed—but its hold would be tenuous."

"How did this sorcerer discover Marudin's lamp?" Ramon asked.

"How?" Lakshmi threw up her hands in exasperation. "How did he ensorcel my husband? How did he steal my—" Her voice choked off, her eyes widening. "How did he steal my babes?" she whispered.

Then the tears poured forth again, and she embraced Jimena. "Oh, forgive me, forgive my rash indictment of your son! Of course the sorcerer who stole my Marudin would also have stolen my babes! For what purpose I cannot guess—but surely the same villain stole all three, and I was very wrong to blame Matthew!"

"He would be the first to pardon you," Jimena assured her, "and the first to attempt to find and rescue your children." She looked up at her husband.

Ramon nodded.

"And if he would do it, so shall we!" Jimena said stoutly.

The tears stopped. Lakshmi stepped back, staring in amazement. "Could you truly? After I have raged at you and battered your castle, could you truly help me find my babes?"

"We can try," Ramon told her.

Jimena nodded. "I must stay here as castellan, but Ramon shall search—and, I think, so will Saul. Be of good heart, my dear. If wit and wisdom can find them, we shall have them back."

"And your prince with them," Ramon affirmed.

Jimena looked up at him with an expression that said, Are you sure?

Ramon shrugged. "Why not attempt the impossible twice? Besides, if Matthew and Alisande fight the horde, we must weaken the barbarians in any way we can, and surely freeing Prince Marudin to fight as his heart dictates will weaken them most amazingly."

"But how can you manage this?" Lakshmi protested.

"We must learn more before we can try," Ramon told her. "Try to remember, Princess Lakshmi—try as hard as you can. When you came into the nursery and found your children gone, was there—"

Wind hissed and kicked up a dust-devil right there on the battlements, where there was no sand and little enough dust.

" 'Ware!" Lakshmi pushed Ramon and Jimena back and stepped between them and the shoulder-high whirlwind. "It is no eddy of air, but a sprite come from the desert! Spirit, it is a princess of the Marid who commands! Show yourself, say why you have come—but if you seek to do harm, I shall dissolve you into the air from which you were born!"

The dust-devil coalesced instantly into a humanlike form, but one covered with rough hair and a hump like a camel's. Its eyes were small and unwinking, glistening with the cover of a nictating membrane; its lower face pushed out into a muzzle with nostrils that opened and closed and long, thin lips that moved and wriggled like a camel's preparing to spit.

Princess Lakshmi held up a palm and recited an Arabic verse in a tone that threatened doom. The mobile lips stilled, and the sprite swallowed.

Jimena wondered what the princess had threatened.

"Speak!" Lakshmi commanded. "How come you to know of this place, let alone appear on these battlements?"

"I am commanded hither." The voice was like the hiss of windblown sand over rock, rasping, eroding.

"Who is he that has commanded you?"

"A magus with silver hair and beard, cloaked all in midnight-blue," the dust-devil answered, and volunteered no more.

Lakshmi's eyes narrowed, offended by his obstinacy. "Why has he bid you come?"

"To bear his word to that man and woman behind you." The dust-devil pointed, and Jimena fought the urge to flinch. She glared at the slight creature with a face of stone.

But its words rasped against her granite. "That the queen and her wizard must withdraw from the defense of the city, or their children shall never again on earth be seen."

Lakshmi's face contorted with rage. She stepped forward, lifting a hand, and the dust-devil flinched away, eyes wide in shock. It spun about, pivoting faster and faster until its form blurred into a whirlwind again.

"Stay!" Lakshmi snapped.

The whirlwind hopped up into the air.

Lakshmi snapped her arm out straight, forefinger pointing at the dust-devil. It halted in midair, spinning and hissing but going nowhere.

"They are not here," the princess told the spirit. "They are in the East, fighting the horde."

"They must be in the city of which the spirit spoke," Ramon said, "or its master would not have demanded they withdraw."

"Even so!" Lakshmi said. "Go to that city, spirit, and give your message to the queen and her Lord Wizard. But beware the wizard's magic, for he knows nothing of his children's kidnapping and may be enraged."

"Enraged forsooth!" the rasping voice said from the whirling form. "Can his magic harm a spirit?"

"It can and has! Speak, O Tool of the Wicked! Where are my own babes?"

"Yours?" The spirit sounded shocked.

"Even so! He who has taken the queen's children has taken mine also! Where are they?"

"I know nothing of the babes of a Marid." The dust-devil sounded thoroughly shaken. "I know not where the queen's babes are hid! Spare me, Highness—I know naught!"

"Save what you were commanded to say," Lakshmi said sourly. "Enough, then! Begone!"

She waved a hand, and the dust-devil leaped high, as though she had batted it away. Its hum rose in pitch to a shriek, and it winked out.

The battlements were silent for a minute or so. Then Ramon said, "Now we know what ransom is demanded."

"And who has captured your grandchildren!" Lakshmi agreed. "Can you find them from that?"

"I doubt it," Ramon said, "the more so because we know who ordered the kidnapping done, but not who actually carried it out—and we certainly do not know the destination to which the kidnapper took the children."

"It is so." Lakshmi's face puckered again. "Nor do we know where my own babes were taken . . ."

"Oh, do not weep, do not!" Jimena took Lakshmi in her arms again. "We know more than we did, and we shall learn what we need!" She held the taller woman close and turned to Ramon. "Speak with Saul! Find these robbers, and quickly!"

Ramon nodded and beckoned to the Witch Doctor. They went back into the tower, talking earnestly.

Lakshmi lifted her head, wiping her eyes. "Where do they go?"

"To their workroom," Jimena told her. "Be of good heart, Princess—you have three very powerful wizards to aid you, and what the vision of the djinn cannot discover, the science of magicians shall."

The Caliph was conducting his royal guest and new ally on a tour of the battlements of Damascus when a shout of joy rose from the western wall. "Muslims! An army of Muslims!"

"What army is this?" The Caliph turned to Alisande, inclining his head. "Your Majesty, shall we go to see?"

Alisande smiled at his eagerness. "At once, my lord. Set the pace."

Without armor, clad only in flowing silken robes, she was easily able to match the Caliph's stride. Matt hurried along behind, thinking that if his stint as a galley slave had done nothing else, it had gotten him back into shape.

As they rounded the southwest corner they saw the army. It darkened the plain in a huge wedge of horses and camels, the soldiers so numerous that it seemed they must surely equal the horde. At their head, beneath a canopy held by four riders and astride a snow-white mare, rode a slender young man in the bright robes of the Rif.

"It is Tafas!" Alisande exclaimed. "It is Tafas bin Daoud! The Moors have come to the relief of Damascus!"

"Thanks be unto Allah!" the Caliph intoned, then called, "Throw wide the gates, for these are allies!"

"Surely now we can drive the horde back to Baghdad, my lord," Alisande said, "perhaps even recapture it!"

The Caliph nodded. "It may be, it may indeed be. With your knights to smash a gap in the barbarians' line, and Tafas' lightly armored riders to counter their horsemen and widen that breach, we may well resist their numbers and greed."

Then the dust-devil boiled up from the stones of the parapet, where there was little or no dust at all.

The Arab soldiers fell back with oaths, making signs against evil. Alisande took a step backward, too, hand going to the sword that was never far from her side, and Matt called up an all-purpose verse for banishing evil spirits. What came to his lips, though, was:

> "Stay rotation, stop your storm!
> Spirit, stand and show your form!"

The whirling sand abruptly ceased, grains falling to the stone in a fine hissing rain, and the sprite within jolted to a halt so abruptly that it staggered, barely managing to keep its feet. It recovered and turned slowly, regarding each of the humans with a gaze so malevolent that Alisande's sword whisked out. The rasping voice demanded, "Who has dared to interfere with my motion?"

"I have!" Matt stepped forward, fists on hips. "Shall I call up a storm to drench and dissolve you, or chant a spell to suck you into a bottle and cork it?"

The spirit's eyes widened; it shrank away. "You cannot!"

Matt began a singsong chant:

> "Let mist rise from bog and fen,
> Gather clouds beyond our ken—"

"I shall obey!" the dust-devil cried. "What would you have of me?"

The Caliph stared, then transferred that stare to Matt.

"Truth," Matt replied. "Who sent you?"

"A magus all in midnight-blue, with silver hair and beard."

"His name?" Matt demanded.

The dust-devil gave him a nasty grin, recovering some of

its confidence. "What magus would give a name whereby to wreak ill upon him?"

"One who lies," Matt retorted, "one who knows how to keep his true name secret. So he gave you no name at all, and you obeyed him without asking. What magic had he wrought to make you fear him so?"

The dust-devil turned wide-eyed and began to tremble. "Another dust-devil, like to me! He conjured it up, and made it cease to exist with a single gesture, only a couplet of song!"

Matt frowned. "You are of the elements of air and earth. To make one of you cease utterly, he must have wrapped it in a cloud of steam."

The wide eyes stretched to take up half the spirk's face. "How did you know!"

"I am a wizard as powerful as he," Matt said, "and shall banish you as utterly unless you speak truth. Why did the magus send you here?"

"To—To bear a message," the dust-devil stammered.

"Speak, then!"

The dust-devil cowered, but spoke in a trembling tone. "Your children are stolen away! You shall never see them again unless the queen turns her army about and withdraws from the defense of this city at once, and you with her!" Its voice rose to a wail. "Blame me not! It is not I who stole your babes! I only speak what I have been given to say!"

Matt's eyes widened, and the stare he gave the dust-devil would have been enough to set a brave man trembling—but the fury that blazed forth from Alisande cast his in the shade. She didn't speak a word, but stepped closer to the dust-devil, sword rising. Its cold iron might not have hurt an Arab spirit the way it would have burned a European, but the spirk cowered away from her rage and the wizard behind her, gibbering nonsense.

It was the Caliph who spoke, who made some sense of the message. "Who did kidnap the children?"

"I know not!" the dust-devil howled. "I know only that the blue magus commanded me to tell you of it! I know not where they are!"

"So," the Caliph said heavily, "the high priest of Ahriman will stoop to any means to win his war, the more evil the better." He turned to Alisande. "We know who we fight. There is no profit in slaying this impudent creature—it bore nothing but the message."

"There is no profit in keeping it with us, either," Alisande said through stiff lips. "Husband, banish me this spirk!"

The dust-devil didn't wait. With a moan that rose into a howl, it began to pirouette, spinning faster and faster until its form blurred into a funnel-cloud again. With a bound, it rose into the air, sailed out over the wall, and sank to the ground, humming and skittering toward the Moorish army.

Tafas' chief wizard chanted a verse and pointed a wand at the dust-devil. A huge fat spark exploded at its rim. The funnel-cloud bounced high, shrieking, and went skipping and hopping away from the army, away from Damascus, and over the horizon.

The Caliph turned a somber face to Alisande and Matt, to find the queen pale, rigid, but composed, and her husband hunched and seething, his face dark with anger.

"How then, Majesty and Lord Wizard?" the Caliph asked. "How shall we deal with this news?"

"I cannot chance my children's lives, my lord," Alisande said through stiff lips. "I deeply regret, but I must leave your side, and all my army with me."

"We will be safe in Damascus," the Caliph assured her, "now that Emir Tafas has joined us."

"But that doesn't get us our children back," Matt said, "and giving in to kidnappers only encourages them to try again."

Alisande whirled to him, staring as though he had betrayed her. "You do not mean to stay!"

"Of course not," Matt said. "On the other hand, the message didn't say how fast you had to return to Merovence, and you don't *have* to load everybody back aboard ship. You could just march your army around the Mediterranean."

"And be nearby if the horde attacks Byzantium?" Alisande asked bitterly. "I would only receive another demand that I forgo the battle!"

"Yes, but if, in the meantime, I have managed to find the kids and rescue them, you'd still be close enough to turn back and join the attack on Damascus."

Alisande stared at him for a long minute. Then, slowly, she began to smile, the light of battle kindling in her eyes.

"This is a grievous risk," the Caliph said doubtfully. "Do you truly think you can save your babes?"

"If any man can, he can—and he is right that we dare not leave them hostages to a man so evil," Alisande told him. "Belike Arjasp will slay them anyway, when he has done with his conquering."

"Even so," the Caliph said, "it is nevertheless quite dangerous. Do you not wish them to have every minute of life they can?"

"I certainly do," Matt said, "and the only way they're going to live to grow up is if I go find them and bring them out by my magic."

"It will take great wizardry indeed," Alisande said with a catch in her voice, "if the magus succeeded in stealing them from your mother and father, and the Witch Doctor, too!"

"Mighty magic, or a traitor in their midst," Matt said darkly. "Never underestimate the power of human greed, or good old-fashioned violence."

"Simple solutions are often the best," the Caliph agreed.

"Nonetheless, whatever watchers Arjasp has sent, they will have to see Her Majesty's army ride away," Matt said, "and me with them. Of course, they probably won't mind if I go off on my own."

A sudden weight struck his shoulder, and purring buzzed in his ear.

In spite of himself, Matt looked up at the white cat with a smile. "Well, not entirely alone. What's the matter, Balkis? Don't like people mistreating kittens, even if they are human?"

Balkis answered with a very emphatic yowl.

CHAPTER 16

Jimena and Ramon led Lakshmi back to the solar from which her attack had drawn them. The peace and harmony of the room seemed to calm the djinna instantly, the sun streaming in the tall windows onto the warm, polished woodwork and furniture and brightening the colors in the tapestries. Jimena showed her to a chair, told the guard to send for some of the coffee Tafas bin Daoud had been sending them, then summoned Lady Eldori.

"I do not understand," Lakshmi protested. "What good can come of what this woman may *not* remember?"

"We deal with an enemy that is prince of negatives," Jimena told her. She realized that, to Lakshmi, anything that didn't relate directly to the finding of her own twins must seem a waste of time. She patted the younger woman's hand. "Patience, my dear. Whoever kidnapped your children may have kidnapped Matthew's, too. It is worth trying to pick up the trail here."

"Would it not be better to trace them by the slipper?" Lakshmi touched her bodice, as though reassuring herself the little garment was still where she'd left it.

"It would be as good," Jimena conceded, "but not better. Where do you find the beginning of a circle, my dear?"

"Why . . ." Lakshmi gazed off into space a moment, thinking. "Anywhere!"

"Exactly." Jimena nodded, settling back in her hourglass chair. "And Lady Eldori will start us as well as your babe's bootie. Come in, milady!"

Lady Eldori entered with furtive glances at Lakshmi. Ramon rose in respect.

"Please sit, my lord," Lady Eldori said automatically. She

glanced at Lakshmi and tilted her chin up with a sniff of scorn for the scantiness of the guest's attire.

Jimena said, "Lady Eldori, may I present the Princess Lakshmi."

Lady Eldori stared, then, flustered, dropped a curtsy. "Your Highness! My pardon for not recognizing your exalted station!"

"Granted," Lakshmi said, amused.

With a nervous glance at her, Lady Eldori turned to her mistress. "What further help can I be, Lady Mantrell?"

"Only to repeat what you spoke before our interruption, milady," Jimena said. "Whose turn was it to care for the prince and princess when the castle was under attack?"

"The Lady Violette's, as I said—and she is not here."

"Have you searched while we dealt with the disturbance?"

The disturbance, sitting next to her, blushed.

"We have, milady." Lady Eldori lifted her chin again. "She is not to be found."

Jimena frowned. "Nowhere within the castle?"

"Nowhere at all." Lady Eldori's voice was heavy with censure. "Not in her apartments, nor in the nursery, nor anywhere that we can find."

"So the children's nursemaid has disappeared with them?" Lakshmi asked, wide-eyed.

"I would not have put it that way, Your Highness," Lady Eldori said, "but that is the gist of it, yes."

Lakshmi turned to Jimena, frowning. "Why would the kidnapper take the nursemaid also?"

"Perhaps because she clasped the children to her," Jimena suggested.

"There is a less pleasant possibility," Ramon said in a somber tone.

All three women turned to him, bracing themselves. "What is that, my husband?" Jimena asked.

"It may be that Lady Violette is herself the kidnapper," Ramon said.

Jimena and Lady Eldori stared, taken aback, but Lakshmi's eyes narrowed. "I should have seen that."

"But . . . but why would a lady-in-waiting steal her own charges?" Lady Eldori protested.

Ramon shrugged. "As I remember, she is young and unwed.

Perhaps a handsome gentleman played upon her affections—
or a less handsome one upon her greed."

A shadow crossed Lady Eldori's face. "She had a great
fondness for fine gowns and other luxuries . . ."

"And a yearning for freedom?" Ramon suggested. "Life
within these castle walls might seem confining to a young
woman still in her teens. The promise of money and the
freedom to enjoy the pleasures it could buy might persuade
her."

"She is young and foolish," Lady Eldori snapped. "Such
fripperies might move her indeed."

Storm clouds gathered in Lakshmi's face.

To avert the blast, Jimena said quickly, "Let us discover
where she has gone, then—and trust we shall find her alive."

Lakshmi spun to her, appalled. "I had not stopped to think . . .
but of course . . ."

"That Lady Violette might have died in defense of her
charges, and her body hidden so that we should waste time
searching for her?" Jimena nodded. "Still, do not be too
quick to pity her, Highness—we may yet find her alive, well,
and enjoying the fruits of her treachery."

Lakshmi's face hardened. "We may indeed! Bring me
some article that belonged to this woman—clothing, or a ker-
chief, or something else that touched her body."

Lady Eldori stared in confusion, but Ramon only ob-
served, eyes kindling with interest, and Jimena turned to the
lady-in-waiting and nodded. "Find something of the sort,
Lady Eldori, and bring it to us, if it pleases you."

"It will most assuredly please me!" Lady Eldori bustled
out the door.

She was back in two minutes with a handkerchief, and pre-
sented it to Lakshmi with a curtsy. "Will this do, Highness?"

Lakshmi sniffed the square of linen, then nodded. "It has
still her scent, and has not been laundered since last she used
it. It will do admirably." She turned to Jimena. "May I see the
nursery?"

"Of course." Jimena rose and led the way.

The emptiness of the room still tugged at her heart, and at
Lakshmi's, too, to judge by the tears that filled her eyes. But she
blinked them away and waved a hand over the handkerchief,

fingers writhing in intricate gestures, and chanted a verse in Arabic.

Footprints glowed, brightening slowly on the floor and the carpet.

Lady Eldori gasped. Ramon and Jimena blinked, and wished they understood Arabic.

"Let us see where she has gone." Lakshmi paced the footprint-trail from the doorway. The marks of the noble nursemaid's shoes went in and out the door several times and here and there about the chamber, as anyone's caring for small children would. Lakshmi picked up a brightly colored ball and gestured over it, reciting her spell, and tiny footprints glowed, too, here and there about the chamber. Finally, though, the lady's trail led to one set of small footprints, which ceased, then to the other, which also ceased.

"Here she picked them up." Ramon pointed.

"And there she went with them." Lakshmi traced the path to the door, her face grim.

"She did steal them!" Lady Eldori went pale, and Jimena, looking at her, could see she hadn't really believed in the possibility until then.

"Follow," Lakshmi snapped, and paced alongside the footprints as they left the room.

Ramon and Jimena came after. With professional curiosity, Ramon murmured, "How can she know these footprints are only a few hours old? Surely Lady Violette has come and gone from that chamber a thousand times!"

"No doubt the spell limited the trail to that duration," Jimena answered. "Perhaps Lakshmi commanded only the most recent footprints to show."

Ramon nodded and followed.

Down the stairs they went, out the door and into the courtyard. When the trail led to the postern gate, Ramon called for horses and a dozen soldiers.

Accompanied by the small troop, they rode out of the castle and down into the city. Jimena reflected that it must have been only courtesy that kept Lakshmi riding by their side when she could have drifted like smoke over the trail far faster than they rode. She seemed quite at home on horseback, though her mount wasn't anywhere nearly so calm—it rolled its eyes and fought the bit, wanting to run from the very creature it carried.

"Animals always know when magic is about," Jimena commented.

"Their instincts are sure," Ramon agreed, and wondered about the stray cat who had visited the castle so recently. Had she left because of the taint of magic about Matt's person?

The footprints sprang into light a dozen yards before Lakshmi and died out a dozen yards behind. She followed them unerringly, right down the main street of the town. The sergeant of their troupe pushed his horse to the fore, riding ahead and calling, "Make way! For Lord and Lady Mantrell, make way! For the Princess Lakshmi, make way!"

The townsfolk cleared the road with amazing speed.

"They all know we are wizards," Jimena said with a smile, "and wish to have as little to do with magic as possible."

"I would feel the same way, if I were not the magician," Ramon said. "Our honor guard cannot be feeling too sanguine themselves, escorting a creature so capricious and powerful as a Marid."

"Yet they perform their duties faithfully." Jimena bestowed smiles on two or three of the guards. They looked back with surprise, then turned forward and bore their pikes with greater determination. Jimena turned the smile on Ramon. "A little gratitude is never wasted."

"Especially from a beautiful woman," Ramon agreed.

"Your nursemaid certainly showed no shyness in her going," Lakshmi said.

Looking ahead, Jimena saw the footprints going in the door of Bordestang's grandest inn. "No, not a bit of shyness, nor of shame." She frowned and rode with her face set.

They dismounted at the inn door. One of the guards held the reins of all the party while the others followed their lord and lady through the portal, Lakshmi leading.

Inside, all was merriment and the music of viols and hautboys.

The tables of the common room had been folded back against the walls and the benches set against them. A score of well-dressed couples paced through the figures of a dance, laughing and chatting as they moved. A glance at broadcloth, fine wool, and linen showed them to be gentry—squires and their dames, burghers and their wives, with here and there a knight and his lady. The glowing footprints vanished in the throng.

Jimena, however, only had to look closely at the laughing, chattering throng before she saw a familiar young face above a velvet dress, laughing, batting her eyelashes at each of the young men in her square, and replying to their flirtations with sallies of her own.

"There!" Jimena snapped.

"I see her," the sergeant said, and strode into the center of the dance. Couples broke apart as he strode toward them, their exclamations of anger dying as they saw his livery and the half-dozen guards behind him. Lady Violette too looked up, frowning at the sudden ending of her dance—then saw the grim-faced soldiers and screamed.

The male dancers at once pressed forward, shouting at the sergeant, but one elbowed his way to the front, the sword at his hip proclaiming him a knight. "Why do you disrupt our merriment, Sergeant?"

"This lady's presence is required by the castellan, Sir Knight," the sergeant replied evenly, sure in his duty.

Lady Violette turned pale. "It was not I! I had no choice! He made me do it!"

Lakshmi strode straight through the throng, eyes blazing, and dancers and soldiers alike stepped quickly aside for her.

Jimena hurried to catch up, dreading what the angry djinna might do. "I think we might obtain more information if I question her, Your Highness."

"Well, if you must." Lakshmi stepped aside, but her glare would have stripped paint.

"Now, my dear," Jimena said to Lady Violette, striving for gentleness, "I must tell you that this young woman beside me is a princess of the djinn, whose children have only this morning been kidnapped."

Lady Violette screamed and fainted dead away.

"None of that!" Lakshmi snapped, and twisted her hand in a gesture as she rapped out a staccato couplet.

Lady Violette turned a fall into a stagger and looked about her wild-eyed, disoriented by what had proved to be merely a moment's dizziness. Then she saw the djinna's anger and Jimena's sympathetic smile, and moaned.

"Pluck her purse and search it," Lakshmi snapped.

The sergeant drew a dagger. Lady Violette screamed, but he only cut the strings of her purse and took it from her belt, then upended it over his palm. A stream of gold coins cascaded down, overflowing his cupped hand and piling up on the floor.

"Who gave you that?" the djinna snapped.

"He!" Lady Violette cried, tears streaming down her cheeks. "He who compelled me to bring him the babes!"

"I pity you," Lakshmi sneered, "if the prospect of gold is a compulsion."

"Tell us who he was, my dear," Jimena said, much more gently.

"I do not know! He gave me no name, only promised me gold if I would bring the babes to the postern, and a lingering, agonized death if I did not!"

"He knew the weak link in the chains that protected your grandchildren, surely enough," Lakshmi said, with total condemnation.

Lady Violette flushed but could say nothing.

"Tell us his appearance," Jimena urged.

"He was in his middle years, with black hair and beard, and wore a robe of midnight-blue, with a hat that was sort of a cone, bulge-sided and rounded at the top! More than that I cannot tell you!"

"And you brought the children to the postern gate, where you gave them to him?" Ramon asked, choking on his own anger.

"I did! Oh, blame me not, for who would have protected me from him?"

"Lady Mantrell or I!" Ramon snapped. "Then he bade you flee?"

"He did, for he said my head would roll when you learned of this! Oh, spare my life, I beg of you!" Lady Violette sank to her knees, sobbing.

"Spare her? Why?" Lakshmi demanded. "She felt not the slightest remorse until we caught her—indeed, she was so eager to spend her guilt-gold that she could not even wait till she had passed from the town! She has nothing more to tell us. Shall I kill her quickly, or slowly?" She caught Lady Violette's hair and yanked her face upward, drawing a dagger from her bodice.

The male dancers shouted and thrust forward, drawing their own weapons. The soldiers readied themselves to hold off the dancers, but Lakshmi gave them only one dark look, and they bowled away backward in a wave.

The sergeant's parade-ground voice rose above the din. "Beware! She is a princess of the Marids, the most powerful of the djinn! Seek not to oppose her will!"

"Yes, but your will need not be quite so apposite, Your Highness," Jimena said quickly. "Lady Violette kidnapped Queen Alisande's children, after all, not your own. It is for the queen to judge her."

Lakshmi glared down at the cowering woman for a minute, then said, "You are right. She is for the Queen's Justice." She let go of the woman's hair.

Lady Violette fell, sobbing with relief.

"Do not be too merciful," the djinna snapped. "She did not think her crime very great, or she would not have stopped at so near an inn. She is a silly, vain, and foolish thing, and as such is a ready tool for evil. She feels not an ounce of remorse for her deed, but only for being caught."

"That is all true, I doubt not." Jimena bent a sorrowful gaze on the teenager. "I fear you must dwell in the dungeon, poor child, until Her Majesty returns. Still, we shall give you the most comfortable cell that we have."

"No, n-o-o-o-o," Lady Violette moaned as the soldiers dragged her to her feet. "Not the dungeon!"

"Be glad you still have your life!" Lakshmi snapped, and turned on her heel to follow Jimena. She caught up with her quickly and demanded, "How could you be so gentle with so vile a traitor?"

"Why, because I had you to rage at her and revile her," Jimena said as though it were obvious, and hurried out the door. "Come, Your Highness! Let us ride back to the postern door without delay! Perhaps there is still some trail to be found there, though if a sorcerer is the true kidnapper, I suspect he will have covered his tracks far too well."

"A sorcerer?" Lakshmi frowned as they mounted. Then her face cleared. "Of course! Midnight-blue robes, a conical hat—he would be a magician, would he not? Had his robes been white, I would have thought him to be a magus indeed, one of the priests of Ahura Mazda or Agni, before the prophet Zoroaster reformed the religion of the Persians."

"One of the magi?" Jimena exclaimed, staring.

"Perhaps he is," Ramon said, frowning, "but has not yet heard of Zoroaster. Tell me, who was their god of evil? Angra Mainyu, was it not?"

"Angra Mainyu, yes." Lakshmi nodded. "The older djinn have told us tales of this demon, and the fools who did his work whether they knew it or not. Ahriman, they call him now."

"It is surely a coincidence," Jimena said as they started riding back up to the castle, "but I have a very bad feeling about it."

Saul saw them coming and met them at the portcullis. "Did you find her?" Then he saw Lady Violette surrounded by guards, and relaxed a little. "At least she's still alive."

"Yes, through Lady Mantrell's foolish mercy," Lakshmi snapped.

"See her to her dungeon," Jimena called to the sergeant, then held out a hand to the Witch Doctor. "Come, Saul! We must hurry to the postern."

"Why?" Saul asked, but he was already in midair, leaping up behind her onto the horse's back.

"Because the man to whom Lady Violette gave the children was waiting for her there! We may still find his trail!"

But at the postern, Lakshmi could only shake her head in frustration. "I have nothing that belonged to the man, nothing he had touched. I cannot cast a spell to make his trail appear."

"And his footprints only go to the water." Saul frowned, following the indentations in the perpetually damp ground.

"Why bother?" Lakshmi demanded. "If we cannot follow—"

"Perhaps we can." Jimena laid a hand on her arm. "Saul never does things without reason. Watch him."

The Witch Doctor stopped at the bank and pointed to a gouge in the earth. "A boat's bow did that. He had a dinghy waiting with an oarsman in it."

Lakshmi stepped up beside him, frowning. "How can you tell there was an accomplice? Have you the Second Sight?"

"No, just logic." Saul gestured at the gouge. "It's too small for him to have pulled the boat up high enough to keep it from drifting away, and there's nothing near to tie it to."

"There is also no mark of an anchor," Jimena said, studying the ground.

Saul nodded. "The castle has a couple of boats it uses for fishing, doesn't it?"

"You mean he fled in the castle's own skiff?" Lakshmi was beginning to look outraged again.

"He could have," Saul agreed. "After all, if you're going to bribe one person on the inside, why not two?"

"Because that yields twice the likelihood that one will talk before the deed is done," Ramon answered.

Saul nodded. "Much easier to bring your own boat and carry it away with you."

"Or sink it," Ramon said, "when you're done."

"That's it!" Saul turned away from the water. "Race you to the drawbridge."

"Why bother?" Lakshmi spread her arms to gather them all in as she swelled to forty feet high. Saul shouted a protest, kicking, but Jimena and Ramon hung on, stifling protests, as the djinna calmly stepped across the moat and set them down as she shrank to human size.

"Well, I have to admit that saved time." Saul wiped his brow with a shaky hand, then looked down at the bank. At once, he saw the tracks. "There! Two horses—one for the kidnapper and one for an accomplice!"

"Then the boat should be—" Ramon leaned, gazing down into the water, then pointed. "—there!"

Saul waded in before Lakshmi could pull another one of her growing pangs, reached down under the surface and heaved. One side of a small skiff came up, then rolled over so the whole boat floated upside down. Saul fished, found the painter—the rope tied to its bow—and waded ashore, pulling the rowboat with him. As it came up onto the bank, Ramon flipped it over, then leaned his weight against the painter. Jimena joined in, and the whole craft slid up onto the grass.

"Now I have something they have touched!" Lakshmi purred, and stepped forward.

"Will not the water have washed all trace of them from it?" Jimena asked.

"Their actual touch perhaps—the oils from their skin and any fibers their clothing may have left—but not the fact that they have touched its wood." Lakshmi passed her hands over the boat in an intricate pattern, chanting a verse in Arabic.

Footprints glowed into sight on the boat's bottom, semicircles on its seats; the ends of the oars glowed from the touch of the rower's hands. Still chanting, Lakshmi continued her gestures over the horses' hoofprints. They too began to glow.

"Couldn't she have just recited her spell over the horses' traces in the first place?" Saul asked.

Jimena shook her head. "The principle of contagion, Saul. The horses are living beings themselves, and she had no trace of them to use as a magical lever. True, the kidnappers had touched the horses, but Lakshmi had nothing the horses themselves had touched."

"Except the earth." Saul nodded. "And that's a thirdhand touch, once too far removed."

"Follow!" Lakshmi commanded, and set off, following the prints of the horses. Saul and the Mantrells followed, (marveling at the durability of the djinna's delicate-looking slippers).

The tracks sprang to life in front of Lakshmi and faded behind her, leading them down the talus slope and across a field to the rough, unplowable land around a watercourse lined with trees and thick with undergrowth. The djinna pressed canes and shrubs aside—and saw the tracks end. "It cannot be!"

Saul shouldered up beside her, frowning, and agreed. "The

ground's damp enough that the horses would have left ordinary prints. How'd the sorcerer pull *this* disappearing act?"

"He did not," Lakshmi said, thin-lipped. "He left this plane."

CHAPTER 17

Ramon stared. "You mean he went to another world?"

"Not a world," Lakshmi said. "I doubt an underling could have that much power. He has gone *between* worlds, the quicker to transport himself to his master."

Saul turned away, cursing.

Jimena stared after him. "It is not like him to give up so easily."

Ramon touched her arm, frowning. "He has not. He searches for something."

"There!" Saul pointed.

Spreading between two trees, a huge spiderweb reflected sunlight.

Lakshmi paled. "You do not mean to call upon the Spider King!"

Saul nodded. "This is just the kind of stunt that would appeal to his mordant sense of humor. Keep dinner warm for me." He stepped forward, directly into the spiderweb. For a moment his outline wavered, then it disappeared.

"Let us follow!" Jimena stepped forward.

"I dare not!" Lakshmi paled. "The Spider King is a spirit who could confound even a Marid!"

"He transported you before," Ramon pointed out, "to our world."

"He did not! I did that myself, following Matthew!"

"Who was taken there by the Spider King," Ramon said, with appreciation of the irony, "who would therefore resent your intrusion on his domain. Well, I shall follow Saul, if I may."

Jimena called out in alarm, but Ramon was already stepping toward the spiderweb.

He bounced off.

He bounced hard enough to knock him down. He sat on the ground, staring up in disbelief. "I knew spider silk was strong, but not so strong as *that*!"

"I think you are being denied passage," Jimena said with relief. She stepped forward, groping toward the web—and saw it begin to glitter with sunlight, a glitter that seemed to fill her eyes, wrapping about her. Dazzled and confused, she blundered forward—and disappeared.

Ramon cried out, leaping to his feet and charging after her, but again he bounced off the web and stood, fists clenched, raging and cursing in American English.

Lakshmi frowned, wondering about the meanings of the foreign words, though she thought she could tell the essence of them. She stepped forward, touching his arm. Ramon whirled to her, face contorted with anger, then saw her and forced himself to calm. "Your pardon, Princess."

"Given," she said. "It would seem neither of us shall follow, Lord Mantrell—I by my choice, and you by the Spider King's."

"If ever I meet him, I shall have bitter words to say about this," Ramon said, his eyes turning glacial.

"Calm your soul," the djinna advised. "The Spider King is shrewd as well as intelligent, and very, very knowledgeable. If anyone understands what we are fighting, it is he—and if he let the Witch Doctor and the Spellbinder go, it is because they alone have the talents to forestall this rogue priest. We would burden them."

"How could we?" Ramon asked, frowning.

"Why, by lumbering them with concerns for our safety," Lakshmi said. "Let them go, my lord, and trust to their own powers. After all, the Spider King does."

The dazzle slackened, the dizziness passed, and Jimena looked about her in astonishment. She stood in a landscape shrouded by fog so thick that she could see nothing but grayness, though here and there a bare, dark, and dripping branch reached out of the gray wall like a skeletal hand. She shuddered and looked down to find that even the ground was hidden, so thick was the mist.

But here and there a hoofprint glowed, burning away the mist enough to show the bare and barren ground about it.

Fear paralyzed her for a minute, but Jimena called to mind the faces of her grandchildren and stepped forward to brave the fog, following the glowing hoofprints.

She had gone about ten minutes, and knew not how much distance, before the shouting broke out ahead. She stared a moment, then caught up her long brocade skirts and hurried forward, though still with a wary eye on the trail of hoofprints.

The mist parted enough to show her Saul, standing rigid with his fists clenched and face red, shouting verses at a mounted man in midnight-blue robes who chanted in a sonorous tone, gestures weaving complicated patterns as he tried to outshout the Witch Doctor.

Jimena stopped, watching, mind clicking into analytical mode as she waited for the effects of the spells, and for the sorcerer's companion to show himself.

There he was, sitting his horse a yard or two beyond his master, a darkness within the fog—no doubt also wearing the midnight color of Ahriman. His gestures, though, did not mirror those of the sorcerer, and his voice was a low mutter droning between the sorcerer's words.

Saul's final phrase jumped out clearly at her: ". . . with a scorpion!"

The sorcerer's form fluxed, flowed, and gelled. He had a shell for a face, with yard-long antennae atop a man's body—if you didn't count the pincers where his hands had been, or the tail he had suddenly grown, complete with stinger. His companion blanched and sidestepped his horse away, spell forgotten, but the sorcerer, not realizing anything had happened, finished his gestures with his pincers and chanted the last few words in a high-pitched rasping voice.

The mist thickened, formed into snakes, and swarmed up Saul's legs, intertwining with one another and tightening. He fell with a shout, and more snakes started on his arms.

Jimena said quickly,

"From mist you come, to mist you go.
Every wise man told us so,
That as you were when you began,
So shall you be when the race you've ran."

The snakes dissolved; Saul's thrashing arm shoved him halfway back to his feet. He gave a single wild glance about him, saw Jimena, grinned, and scrambled to his feet.

"My lord, you are transformed!" the sorcerer's assistant cried.

The scorpion-sorcerer astride the horse looked down at himself in astonishment. He shrilled in anger, lashing his tail. It lashed far enough to come into his eyesight. He froze, staring at it, then turned his horse with a vengeful chittering and thrust the stinger at Saul.

Saul leaped aside in the nick of time. "Uh, maybe this wasn't such a good idea after all."

The stinger stabbed again. Saul dodged, barely evading it, leaping toward the horse's head—and the sorcerer swung a pincer and caught his neck from behind. Saul howled with pain, then shouted,

> "He welcomes little errors in
> With gently smiling jaws.
> How cheerfully he seems to grin,
> How neatly spreads his claws!"

The sorcerer's pincer suddenly sagged open, as though it had no strength left. He chittered angrily, but seemed to have lost the pattern of words.

His assistant, however, had recovered, gesturing and intoning a verse. He finished with a flourish, and something huge and dark flapped out of the mist to wrap itself around Saul, whose voice gargled off in mid-verse.

Jimena spread her hands, chanting,

> "How doth the careless flutt'ring moth
> Rest from her dancing game?
> Her body swells, her wings absorb,
> Returning to whence they came."

The wings shriveled, the central body absorbing them as the creature turned into a giant caterpillar, its mouth probing for Saul. He shoved it away with an oath, then intoned,

"Oak, ash, or thorn,
Sprout branches and grow taller
With delicious leaves newborn
To attract a hungry crawler!"

Sure enough, a shoot shot and grew, developing into a sapling that budded and opened abundant leaves.

With both hands, Saul forced the creature's head around. "Look! Dinner! Yummy!"

The caterpillar dropped off him and hurried over to the sapling, as much as a caterpillar can hurry. It climbed up, munching as it went, until its whole length clung to the stout sprout.

Saul chanted,

"If it should live to see
The last leaf upon the tree
In the spring,
Let it spin its silk of gold
And its own cocoon uphold.
Let it swing!"

Then he turned away and forgot the giant larvum. It munched away, busy with its own defoliation campaign.

But the sorcerer's apprentice had been busy while he'd had Saul distracted with the insect kingdom, and he had his master almost back to human status. The tail with its stinger was gone, as were the pincers and all of the exoskeleton except the head—which chittered angrily, as though to chide the henchman for not giving him back the power of speech. All things considered, the apprentice should have started from the top and worked his way down, but the habits of subordination took their toll.

That left Jimena free to take her time. She crafted the verse slowly, remembering how she'd come into this weird place and weaving explicit instructions. As she did, a multitude of spiders came scuttling out of the mist and up the legs of the sorcerer's horse to its rider, where they began to spin busily.

The sorcerer, intent upon regaining human form, didn't notice what was happening right under his nose. Of course, at the moment, he didn't have a nose, but his assistant was working on it.

The spiders, however, had been working on the assistant, too.

The mist deepened about the sorcerer's head, then dissipated, showing his face as it had been before Saul had begun work. "Aha!" he shouted triumphantly.

Jimena too shouted her final instruction to the arachnids: ". . . and pull your webbing tight!"

Spider silk wrenched fast, binding both men's arms tight to their bodies in gray tubes. They cried out in shock, then tried to lash their arms free—but all they succeeded in doing was weaving their bodies about so sharply that they fell from their horses. The animals whinnied and went.

Both men tried to scramble to their feet, but Jimena shouted another command, and the horde of spiders went busily to work casting loops about the men's legs. They toppled again, swearing in languages Jimena didn't know, and lay helpless on the ground.

Saul stepped over beside her, watching the little spinners do their work. "Quite a sight, milady. Never knew you were an entomologist."

"More of an etymologist, really," Jimena told him, "but any boy's mother becomes far better acquainted with spiders than she wishes to be."

The sorcerer stopped struggling and started shouting—rhythmical shouting, with rhymes thrown in.

Quickly, Saul called out,

> "The apple that struck Newton's cranial
> He forgot in delight mathematic.
> Since to him it was incidental,
> Let me borrow two for a fanatic."

Something round and solid filled each of Saul's hands. He glanced down at them and was glad the caterpillar hadn't seen it first.

As he lay on the ground, the sorcerer ranted on in his own language, leaving Saul no doubt that if he ever finished, this would be a spell to end all spells—or at least to end him. So

Saul stepped up beside the man, waited until his mouth was open its widest, then leaned down and jammed the apple in between his teeth. The sorcerer stared, stunned. Then his face darkened and he began to gargle sounds that probably would have been dire curses, if he could have managed a few consonants.

Saul turned to the assistant, who looked up at him with wide eyes. Tossing the other apple in the air, the Witch Doctor asked, "Need one?"

The man swallowed heavily, shook his head and clamped his mouth shut.

Saul strolled back to Jimena. "I think we've caught them, Lady Mantrell."

"Yes, we have." Jimena frowned as visions of torture rose up in her mind. She shoved them aside by sheer willpower. "But what shall we do with them?"

"Why, question them, of course." Saul turned back to the assistant. "Ready to answer a few questions, fella? Or would you prefer the fruit course?"

The caterpillar, having run out of leaves, raised its snout, weaving about, centering on the aroma of apple.

"On second thought," Saul said, "your boss might be on the menu himself—unless you decide to talk."

The assistant swallowed and shook his head. "I will speak," he said with a very thick accent.

The sorcerer shouted with alarm.

"Hey, it could be worse." Saul looked down, met the sorcerer's eyes and narrowed his own, gazing directly into the pupils. "A lot worse. Believe me." His voice sank low. "Oh, you really had better believe me. It could get very, very bad indeed."

The coldness of his tone froze the sorcerer, whose own gaze became murderous, but Saul called up his reserves of outrage, and the man had to look away. Then the sorcerer saw the caterpillar peeling itself off the stalk and squalled in alarm.

Of the apprentice, Saul demanded, "Where are the children?"

"I know not!" he protested. "As soon as we had come within this mist, my master chanted a verse that transported them back to him who sent us! They may be with him, or he may already have hidden them!"

Jimena gave a cry of alarm, quickly muffled by her hands.

"Oh, very nice," Saul said, with complete sarcasm. "No blame, no shame—you just followed orders. What is this master of yours?"

He meant to add "animal, vegetable, or mineral?" but before he could, the assistant asked, "You do not know?" in amazement.

A cagey look came into his master's eyes, and Saul knew he had better tread very carefully—and quickly, since the caterpillar was already treading in its own way.

"I can guess," Saul said. "Confirm it for me." He tossed the apple again. "Of course, if you don't want to talk, there's no reason to leave your mouth free."

"He is a priest," the assistant said quickly, "a high priest."

Saul froze for a moment. Then he said slowly, "Which means your boss here is one of the lower-ranking, run-of-the-mill priests, and you're his apprentice?"

"Acolyte!" the assistant snapped, suddenly brave in vanity. "I am his acolyte, for he is a priest of Ahriman!"

Saul stared. Then he said, slowly and carefully, "There ain't no such thing."

"No," Jimena agreed. "The Zoroastrians were monotheists. Ormuzd was their only god. Ahriman was a demon."

"*Is* a demon!" the assistant snapped.

So did Saul. "You want mercy?" He strode up right next to the man and held up the apple, his knuckles white. "You want us to go easy on you, spare you torture, maybe even get you out of here before the immature moth arrives? You come here and steal our prince and princess, you suborn their nurse and carry off a couple of perfectly innocent babies, and on top of all that you have the gall to tell us this demon of yours actually exists? And your boss is so deep into devil worship he actually calls himself a priest?"

The assistant tried to shrink away within his bindings and wailed, "It is not he who calls himself such, but Arjasp who has declared him so!"

The sorcerer gargled in outrage and threat.

Saul froze, looking down at the apprentice as though measuring him for a coffin. "Who," he demanded, "is Arjasp?"

"He is the high priest of Ahriman! It is he who had the genius to realize that Ahriman is a god, not a demon only! The genius to begin the worship of the Dark God! It is Arjasp who has given the gur-khan his victories!"

The sorcerer groaned.

Saul stood very still, mind working at express speed, considering alternatives and realizing the need to be very, very careful. Finally he said, "So Arjasp is a magus?"

The sorcerer howled protest.

Saul turned to him, then glanced at Jimena to make sure she was on guard. She gave him a small nod, so he stepped over, pried the apple out of the sorcerer's mouth, and tossed it to the caterpillar. "Was there something you meant to say?"

"Arjasp is no magus!" the sorcerer ranted. "Accursed be the magi, who led their people only to doom and degradation! Who lost them their empire and found them only a small piece of the world in which to hide, and that pestilential with heat and humidity! Nay, Arjasp is not one of those craven priests!"

He seemed to be overlooking the fact that if any priests had helped the ancient Persians win their empire, it must have been those same magi. Thinking as deviously as he could, Saul shrugged and said, "So this barbarian from the steppes is an improvement?"

"Arjasp is no barbarian!" the sorcerer exclaimed indignantly. "He is a true son of the old Persians, come from the purity of the mountains to lead the remnants of that noble race to triumph—and with them, we who are so enlightened as to join thcm! He has gathered a score of different peoples to the worship of Angra Mainyu, and the Dark God shall lead us to victory, aye, to dominion over all the world!"

"Oh. So that's why he needs to send you to steal babies and run his other little cowardly errands?"

"Arjasp is no coward!" The sorcerer's body convulsed with anger; he actually managed to sit up. "He is courageous and mighty! The power of Ahriman is great within him! If he stays in the center of Asia, there is no cowardice in it, but only the need to continually inspire the gur-khan and the chiefs of all the peoples, and to assure that all work together to hold the conquered lands in subjugation and teach them the worship of Ahriman while the hordes press toward the West to conquer more and more of the world! He shall retake the lands the Arabs stole from his fathers, he shall triumph in every corner of the world, and Ahriman shall have dominion over all!"

He made it sound as though the barbarians had already overrun China and India. Saul devoutly hoped not. "And you? What are you going to get for being his errand boy?"

The sorcerer gave him a nasty grin. "I shall be vizier to the chieftain given governance of a conquered province—shall we say, Merovence?"

"Not when he finds out how you bungled it."

The sorcerer, realizing Saul's intention, opened his mouth for a scream of outrage—and Saul pushed the other apple in, to hold his teeth apart.

Jimena began to mutter to herself:

> "Out of the mist you came riding
> Because your master had told you do so,
> To bribe and to steal
> And ignore all appeal . . ."

While she was chanting, the sorcerer gargled in fury. Saul, grinning, shoved his toes under the man's hip, pried and lifted, and rolled him, howling, to jar against his assistant. Then he spread his hands and chanted,

> " 'Twill not avail you to shout,
> 'Twill not avail you to hack.
> When your master sent you my way,
> You had nowhere to come but out,
> Now you've nowhere to go to but back.
> Get thee hence, get thee gone, get away!"

But priest and acolyte, mouths free now, had been chanting in unison; they turned translucent, then solid again. The priest grinned, stabbed a finger at Saul and began intoning another verse in his native tongue.

Jimena called out the last line of her verse:

"So back into mist you shall go!"

Still howling, the sorcerous duo turned into mist and blew away, joining the vapor around them.

Saul turned and came grimly back to Jimena. "Thanks for the save."

"What would you have done here without me?" she asked simply.

Saul nodded. "Yeah, it was smarter to gang up on them."

Jimena looked puzzled. "Two against two?"

"That's what I meant. Sounds like we're up against worse than we knew, milady."

"Yes." Jimena shivered. "Let us return to our own place and time, Saul, while we discuss this. I feel strangely vulnerable here."

"Not strange at all," Saul said. He looked around. "Which way did we come in?"

A giant spiderweb spread into sparkling life against the mist.

"I think we are being given a hint," Jimena said.

"Seems so." Saul proferred his arm. "Milady, shall we walk?"

Jimena took his arm, and together they stepped into the spiderweb.

The caterpillar, having finished the apple, started to follow them. The six-inch spider eyed it hungrily.

CHAPTER 18

Jimena staggered, but steadied herself on Saul's arm. A moment later he stumbled, and she had to steady him.

Then Ramon was sweeping her up in his arms, pressing her close. "*Mi corazon!* I was so anxious!"

"That is good to hear." Jimena let herself rest in his embrace for a few minutes; after the strangeness of that void between worlds, it was very reassuring.

Saul, however, felt otherwise. "No danger, Mr. Mantrell— no danger at all. Well, yes, there were dangers," he corrected himself, "but nothing she couldn't handle easily."

"With your aid, of course, Saul." Jimena stepped a little away from Ramon, touching her hair back into place. "It might be more correct, my dear, to say that Saul dealt with the kidnappers while I stood guard over him."

"Kidnappers?" Ramon's eyes fired. "There were more than one?"

Jimena nodded. "Two, a sorcerer and his assistant."

"The sorcerer claimed he was a priest of Angra Mainyu," Saul amplified.

"The evil principle of the Zoroastrians?" Lakshmi cried in surprise. "I knew them when I was a child—but while I slept the ages away in my bottle, the Arabs conquered their people! Where had this so-called priest heard of Angra Mainyu?"

"From his master, whose name is Arjasp," Jimena said. "Judging by what the kidnapper said about him, I would gather he is a renegade magus."

"A priest of Ahura Mazda who has turned against his god?" Lakshmi stared, flabbergasted.

Ramon asked his wife, "How do you deduce that, my love?"

"Partly because the kidnapper said he came from the northern mountains," Jimena said, "and there are still a few communities of Zoroastrians there in the hills of Persia."

Saul nodded. "The kidnapper said Arjasp was a true son of the old Persians who had decided Angra Mainyu wasn't just a demon, but an actual god, and converted a bunch of Central Asian tribes to his worship by promising they would conquer the world."

"Which, of course, they are likely to do by sheer numbers, if all their tribes and nations fight as one." Ramon's face darkened. "And you think he was one of the magi who went rogue?"

"I do," said Jimena. "Who else would know enough about Angra Mainyu to concoct a counterreligion centering around him? And who else would know the old magic to teach his priests?"

"Or be able to invent a twisted version of it," Saul agreed.

"Yes, I see." Ramon nodded, "After all, 'magi' is the root word of 'magic,' is it not?"

"Last time I read the dictionary, yes," Saul said. "But he's no dumb-dumb—not our boy Arjasp, no siree! Him go out on campaign and risk his neck? No way! He's staying out there in the middle of Asia, flattering the gur-khan and coordinating the conquests!"

Ramon managed a small smile. "After all, if your fate in the afterlife was to be the eternal victim of an evil god, would you chance death?"

"Not a bit," Saul affirmed.

"I suspect Arjasp has persuaded himself that Angra Mainyu will make him a prince over the underworld," Jimena said darkly.

"People's capacity for self-deception sometimes amazes me," Saul agreed, "particularly mine."

"Even the princes of the demons live in eternal torment," Lakshmi said darkly.

Saul couldn't help wondering if she was talking from personal acquaintance.

Jimena clasped Ramon's arm. "So if we wish to have the

children back, it seems we must confront the evil genius of the horde directly."

Ramon paled for a second, then reddened with anger. "Indeed we must! But one of us must stay here, as castellan."

"I had forgotten that," Jimena admitted.

"Lady Mantrell ought to go," Saul said stoutly.

Jimena blinked, surprised that this opinionated young man had spoken for her instead of her husband. "What is the matter, Saul? Do you fear I cannot protect Bordestang by myself?"

"Oh, you've proved that well enough," Saul said, "when Mister—excuse me, Lord—Mantrell went off with Matt to help King Rinaldo. Now it's his turn to be castellan."

"Thank you for your confidence," Ramon said dryly. "But equal opportunity is not the only reason you choose Lady Mantrell as a traveling partner, is it?"

"Frankly, no," Saul said, and frank he was, with a disarming self-honesty. "In spite of all my efforts, I'm a sexist at heart, and I can't help believing that women are better with babies than men."

"So you think my wife will be more apt to find the children than I." Ramon kept his voice carefully neutral.

"I agree," said Lakshmi. "This is women's work. Come with us, Lady Mantrell."

"Don't pay any attention to her." Saul jerked his head toward the djinna. "She's a sexist, too, a product of a patriarchal culture."

"Sexist! Fool, do you dare bait a djinna?" Lakshmi shot up to twelve feet, glaring down at Saul.

Saul raised both hands. "All right, all right! After all, you're arguing my side of the point. Idle down, lady!"

"I am not a lady—I am a princess!"

Saul sighed. "Y'know, for traveling companions, we're not exactly getting off to a good start."

"We are not getting off to *any* start! Will we argue all year about the manner of our going?"

Ramon spoke up before Saul could. "I think you are right, Saul—it had better be Jimena who accompanies you."

Jimena took Ramon's pack from his hand and stretched up

for a lingering kiss, then clasped his hand between both of her own and gave him a smile full of promise. "Endure in patience till I come home, my husband."

"Don't be too long about it," Ramon said gruffly, but his eyes filled with anxiety and, already, with longing.

A few minutes later he watched the diminishing figure in the sky that was Lakshmi carrying her traveling companions through the air. Beside him Sir Gilbert said, "Do not be offended, my lord. Seeing how attractive the princess is, I think our Saul may have wanted a chaperone."

"Or a witness his wife would trust, to assure her he has been faithful during his travels." Ramon nodded. "Yes. That would also explain why he is not terribly cordial to Princess Lakshmi."

Lakshmi set the two of them down, and Saul staggered, the landscape tilting around him. "That's . . . much more comfortable than tourist class," he said, "but I think I still prefer jets." Then the landscape stabilized and he caught his breath. "Wow! Is that the Mediterranean?"

Below them, a mountainside covered with evergreens fell away to a strip of tan and green. Beyond it, a sheet of blue rose to the sky. "How far away is that horizon—a hundred miles?" Saul asked.

"What lies to the west matters not," Lakshmi said impatiently. "Turn toward the east, and your enemies."

Turning, Saul looked out over the world, or so it seemed. The land stretched away to a horizon just as distant as the ocean's rim. "Where are we? The hills of Lebanon?"

"We are, and those evergreens are its fabled cedars," Lakshmi told him. "Here the East begins, as far as you benighted Franks are concerned. If our kidnappers' master is in Central Asia, this should be a good vantage point to begin our search."

"What do you mean, 'benighted'?" Saul returned. "Matt may be a knight, but I'm quite content to be a wizard only, thank you."

"Cease playing with words and seek out the children!"

"Oh, all right," Saul huffed, "but playing with words is

what wizards do. You're right, though—if there's anything to see, we should be able to see it from here—if we have one whale of a telescope."

Lakshmi scowled down at him. "What manner of spell is that?"

Saul opened his mouth to tell her a telescope was an object, not a spell, then remembered duplicating the effect magically. "One that lets you see something clearly from a great distance."

"How great?"

Saul thought of the huge instrument at Mount Palomar and pictures of the planets. "Very great."

"Then conjure it up! But how will you know where to point it?"

"Ah." Saul nodded ruefully. "That's the hitch."

"It is indeed," said Jimena. "How are we to discover traces of these kidnappers?"

Lakshmi asked, "You did not bring a scrap of their clothing or anything they had touched, did you?"

"No." Saul flushed. "I should have thought of that."

"You were thinking of protecting yourself, and tricking them into telling more than they knew they were saying," Jimena told him.

"I don't suppose you can find a sight of Arjasp across a couple of thousand miles of steppe, without something to remember him by?" Saul asked.

Lakshmi stared, astounded. "What sort of spell could work thus?"

"None I know," Saul sighed.

"Perhaps if we had a hair of his beard . . ."

"Remind me to talk to his barber," Saul said sourly. "Since I can't, what else can we use for a starting point?"

All three were quiet, thinking.

"Highness," said Jimena, "may I see your child's slipper?"

Both of them stared at her blankly. Then Saul grinned. "Of course!"

"I see!" Lakshmi cried. "Since whoever kidnapped my babes, stole yours also, the slipper may lead us to the thief's master!"

"It does seem likely," Jimena said. "May I have the slipper, Highness?"

"Of course." Lakshmi shrank down to human size and handed over the pointed bootie.

Jimena frowned, passing her hand over it and chanting a verse in Spanish. A blue glow began on the sole and spread upward around the slipper. It lightened; forms seemed to dance within it, fuzzy at first, then beginning to clear . . .

Abruptly, the image died. Lakshmi cried out in grief and anger.

"A block?" Saul asked.

Jimena nodded. "Someone or something has detected my spell and cancelled it with a counterspell. I shall have to neutralize it." She began to chant again.

"How can she forestall such a spell?" Lakshmi asked.

"She can make it turn back on itself, tie it in a sort of knot of energy," Saul explained. "That's her special talent—binding other people's spells so they can't work."

"So that is why folk call her the Spellbinder!"

"So does Ramon," Saul said, "but I think he has a different reason."

Jimena held the slipper in both hands, staring at it as she chanted. Strain began to show in arms and shoulders, as though the weight of the tiny shoe were becoming greater and greater, the effort raising the dew of perspiration upon her brow.

With a sudden notion of what would happen, Saul stepped toward her—but all he saw was her body freezing, her gaze turning vacant.

Lakshmi saw, too, and cried, "What has happened?"

"Her spirit has gone adventuring," Saul said, his voice flat and crisp. "Touch her with a fingertip and pour your own power into her, if you can!"

"We must follow!"

"How?" Saul asked.

Lakshmi gave no answer, so he touched Jimena's hand with his forefinger and concentrated on lending her his strength.

> "As I gather magical power
> And send it coursing through me,

Thus I send it on to you,
Though to what use, beshrew me!"

Jimena found herself once again in the realm of mist. Cold
gray fog surrounded her, above, below, before, behind. She
felt its tendrils chilling her face, saw nothing but grayness.
The cold seeped in beneath her robe, beneath her skin,
reaching inward, iciness reaching for her heart.

But warmth spread from her hands, up her arms and into
her chest. She looked down and saw that the glow around the
slipper had become rosy. She frowned at it a moment, wondering how so small an object could generate so much heat—
and why it would.

A heavy sound came to her, muffled by the fog, but coming
again and again, regular, doubled, grace notes—footsteps.
But they were footsteps of something huge and very heavy,
growing louder, coming closer, and she looked up in alarm as
the fog began to move, to billow, to open into a tunnel before her.

It came into sight dimly, dark against the gray of the
mist, growing clearer as it came closer, an obscene pallid
shape with tentacles writhing from its scalp, a leering grin
splitting its face with shark's teeth, huge goggling eyes
glowing in the gloom. Spindly legs carried it forward on
huge flat feet, foot-wide hands reaching out from the ends
of sticklike arms as long as the creature was tall. "Come," it
crooned, "you who seek to merge your magic with me!
Come within, join with me, become a part of me, be absorbed in me!"

In a rush of understanding, Jimena knew the creature for
what it was—a parody of love, an embodiment of the destructive aspects of desire. The love with which Lakshmi had fashioned this tiny shoe drew the monster as a shivering beggar
would come to even the smallest of fires.

A beggar who sought to eat that fire, to have its warmth
within him.

She understood, too, that her own anxiety for her grandchildren was another such magnet—but she also understood
the power that love could give anyone who sought to harm
them.

"Avaunt, thing of emptiness!" she cried, to give it fair warning, but the monster only came closer, slobbering and crooning in a mockery of lovers' kisses and murmurs, cold flabby hands reaching for Jimena's warmth, and she chanted, with grim conviction,

"Unlike the wise thrush, who
Sings each song twice through,
To be sure he'll recapture
The first careless rapture,
And hold it close, giving
His love to his living
Sweetheart entire—
But you, selfish thing,
To whom love is a liar,
And destruction entire
Who only finds leisure
For your own selfish pleasure
And seeks those whose giving
You drink for your living,
And cripple and block
Love from its true lover
Now shall you go,
And never recover,
But be gone entirely
Disintegrate gyre-ly.
Destructive love I now banish!
This monster shall vanish!"

The broad hands and long, boneless fingers reached closer and closer, touching her cheek and drawing all the warmth out, chilling her to the bone, touching also the little slipper . . .

And snatching away, crooning turning to screaming, the huge weal of a burn on the skin of its palm, the other hand coming quickly to cradle the first as the monster hooted and howled. But the burn spread, turning the whole hand bright red, the whole arm bright red, the whole monster swelling and reddening and whirling in a widening helix until it burst with an explosion that hurled Jimena back into the cold clinging fog, back into a dizzying, churning kaleidoscope of black and white that gained color and fitted together like pieces of a puzzle. Raucous calling filled her ears, and against it a man's voice rose in angry song:

> "Where y' goin', y' flyin' ferlie?
> Stay away from our true girlie!
> Ken ye not that we've joined battle?
> Be knocked aside as with a pattle!"

Somehow, she was looking upward, seeing Saul towering over her, and some strange leather-winged creature with four legs and long sharp claws, with a face half reptilian, half human, trying to reach past him toward herself. Saul batted each grasping talon aside, though his hands dripped blood from half a dozen wounds.

But Lakshmi towered above them all, swelling huger and huger, shouting orders in Arabic which the creature ignored. At last a huge feminine hand reached down, wrapped about the hovering monster, wrapped and enveloped as the djinna's voice thundered its commands. Something popped, and a wisp of smoke drifted up from her fist. Then it opened, showing only a darkening where something had turned to powder, darkened dust that drifted away on the wind as the djinna shrank to human size, her voice rising in pitch as she seized Saul's hand in both of hers, commanding, "Hold still!"

"It's all right!" Saul protested. "Just a few scratches, I'll be—"

"Dead!" Lakshmi snapped. "I know not that monster, but I know its kind! There was poison in those talons, and I must draw it out or you will die!" So saying, she pressed her lips against the first of the scratches on Saul's hand.

His face went blank with surprise, then lit with delight that intensified to ecstasy. Lakshmi turned her head to spit out the contaminated blood, and Saul came out of his trance long enough to look down and say, "Don't tell on me, Lady Mantrell." Then Lakshmi's lips pressed to the next wound, and the idiotic smile of rapture lit Saul's face again.

"I will preserve your confidence." Jimena smiled, amused. Then she realized that if Saul was looking down at her, she must be below him. She pushed herself up on one elbow, felt around, and realized she was lying on the rock of the mountaintop. How had she fallen, she wondered, and why?

Well, Saul would tell her as soon as he was able—and as soon as Princess Lakshmi was done with her healing. Jimena didn't even wonder how the djinna could suck out poison that had already begun to percolate through Saul's veins, or why it would not harm her—she knew that magical creatures, such as the djinn, had inborn powers mortals could only hope to achieve through long study and practice.

While she waited, though, she picked herself up off the ground—and stumbled. She found a boulder and sat, amazed at her own weakness. She realized she must have spent a great deal of energy fighting the monster of mockery in her trance.

She looked down and was surprised to see the little slipper still in her hand.

"All right, all right, I'm cured!" Saul protested, but not very strongly.

Lakshmi eyed him narrowly, then nodded. "You are. For once, you are right."

Saul bridled. "Whaddaya mean, 'for once'? Why, I'll have you know that—" He broke off, eyes widening.

Lakshmi watched him, amused.

"You're right," Saul admitted. "You not only cured the poison, you cured the cure."

"Not difficult, with a man of such vanity," Lakshmi assured him.

"Vanity? Who, me? The original blue-jean-and-chambray kid? Well, maybe not original," Saul qualified, "but—"

"But that is not the quality of which you are vain," Lakshmi finished for him.

Saul gave her a glare, but the habit of introspection was too strong in him. "Well, maybe," he grumbled. Then he turned to Jimena, the quarrel instantly forgotten. "Are you all right, Lady Mantrell?"

"Perfectly, I assure you, Saul." Jimena summoned the energy for a smile. "Only very tired."

"No wonder, the kind of effort that spell-breaking must have taken!"

"You have spent some, too, it would seem," Jimena said. "What happened? Here, I mean."

"Here?" Saul shrugged. "You chanted a verse, and a blue glow sprang up around the little slipper. Then your eyes went vacant, and I knew your spirit had gone off to untie the blocking spell. But that winged monstrosity came diving out of the sky, and I had to fight it off."

"It was surely a tool of the sorcerer who set the spell-block," Lakshmi said, "come to weaken you by attacking your body. If it could have slain you, your spirit would have wandered wherever it had gone forever."

Jimena shuddered. "I thank you most surely for protecting me!"

"It was my honor to do so," Lakshmi said.

"Mine, too," Saul agreed. "I thought the fight would end when the little slipper's blue aura blew up. That was when you fell, and I was too busy fighting the bat-wing to catch you. Lakshmi had started growing, but she shrank down fast enough to keep you from hitting the ground hard. Then she cried out and reached for the smoking slipper, but she yanked her hands away and blew on her fingers."

Lakshmi nodded. "It was so hot! How can it still be whole?"

"The heat was of magic resolved," Jimena said. "Two spells strained against each other until both broke."

"But if your spell did break . . ."

"That was its purpose," Jimena explained to the djinna. "Now we can renew our tracking—and this time the trail of magic should lead us toward the children."

"You sure you're up to it?" Saul asked with concern. "Maybe you ought to rest."

"For all we know, the babies are being taken farther and farther away from us as we speak." Jimena came to her feet with an effort, then staggered and reached out for support. "Though perhaps, Saul, it should be you who casts the spell this time."

"Yeah, sure." Saul transferred her arm to Lakshmi and took the little slipper. He held it in both hands as she had, frowning, concentrating, then recited,

> "Children we seek, and need to view.
> We know them well, as family tend to do.

Show of this slipper's foot a guiding trace—
From us to them, a path that we may face."

His eyes widened as a line of glowing golden dots appeared, starting at the slipper, running down the outside seam of his jeans, and spearing out toward the northeast, more dots appearing, more and more, until they were lost in the distance. "Well, how about that!"

"About what, Saul?" Jimena frowned, following the direction of his gaze.

"What indeed?" Lakshmi asked, puzzled, also looking where Saul looked.

"Follow the dotted line!"

"What dotted line?"

Saul stared from one to the other. "You mean you don't see it?"

"We see nothing," Lakshmi said.

Jimena nodded. "What is it?"

"A line of golden dots, heading off toward the northeast until it disappears."

"But only he can see it?" Lakshmi asked, turning to Jimena.

"It would seem so," Jimena said. "After all, he is viewing something magical, something that is not there as an object everyone can see and feel. Since he is the one who cast the spell, he is the only one who sees it."

"A strange effect." Lakshmi looked off toward the northeast. "It did not happen thus when we tracked your babes from the castle."

"True," said Jimena, "but in that case, we were merely bringing out actual footprints that were physically there. Saul has conjured up a trail that is magical only, made by the slipper at one end and the child who wore it at the other." She bit her lip in anxiety. "Pray Heaven the trail that leads to your children will lead to ours also!"

"I shall pray," Lakshmi assured her, "though to Allah, not to your Heaven."

"We can use any help we can get," Saul said, "which reminds me—let's check out Damascus and see how the Caliph is doing. Better to know the political climate before we find ourselves in the middle of it."

"There is sense in that," Jimena admitted, but her impatience at the delay showed clearly in her face.

Saul turned to Lakshmi. "I hate to impose, Princess, but could we hitch another ride? I don't really think we should take the time to walk."

CHAPTER 19

They saw the spires of Damascus on the horizon, but they saw the army marching toward them first.

Saul stared. "Armor and Percherons? That's our people! They're going the wrong way!"

"We must discover the reason," Jimena called above the wind. "Princess, can you set us down behind a hill, so that we not afright their horses?"

"Or their infantry," Saul muttered.

"Is this delay necessary?" Lakshmi demanded.

"I fear it is," Jimena replied. "Alisande would not be returning if Arjasp and his wizards had not wrought some new deviousness. We must learn what."

"I suppose we must," the djinna grumbled, and sank downward toward a brush-covered hill. Just before its top cut off sight, Saul could make out men pointing toward them and horses rearing.

His boots touched earth; he took a shaky step or two, caught his balance, and breathed a sigh of relief. "This may take a little longer than we thought, Princess. They saw you, and some of them panicked."

Lakshmi instantly shrank down to human size. "Will not Matthew reassure them?"

"Yes, but it takes a while to reassure a skittish horse." Saul didn't mention the horsemen.

They strolled out from behind the hill to the road and waited. In ten minutes they saw the cloud of dust; in fifteen they could see lances and pennons rising before it. Fifteen minutes after that, Alisande saw them and reined in, raising her hand to stop her troops. Sergeants bawled orders and the army came to a halt.

By that time Alisande was down from her horse and embracing Jimena, with Matt grinning only a step behind. "Milady! How wonderful to see you! But how came you hither?"

"By Djinna Air." Saul nodded toward Lakshmi. Thinking how to break the bad news gently, he went on, "You and Princess Lakshmi have something in common, Your Majesty."

But before he could continue, Matt said, "A messenger told us about Kaprin and Alice."

"My dears, I am so sorry," said Jimena, tears welling in her eyes, "and I can only beg your forgiveness for my lack of vigilance."

"Lack of superpowers!" Saul snorted. "They were kidnapped while we were fighting off an attack on the castle, Your Majesty."

"How'd it happen?" Matt demanded, face grim.

"An inside job," Saul told him. "The real kidnapper bribed the youngest and most frustrated of the noble nurses to bring the kids to the postern gate during the battle." His mouth tightened with self-disgust. "Sorry, man. We should have seen it was a diversion."

"Why?" Matt asked. "I wouldn't have."

But Alisande picked up on what Saul had said. "In common?" She turned to Lakshmi. "Is your husband missing?"

"He, too," Lakshmi said, "but at least I know where he is."

"How often have I wished I knew as much about Matthew!" Alisande said with as much sympathy as she could muster.

Matt tried a sheepish grin.

"My dear," Jimena said gently, "the problem is greater than a wayward husband."

Matt jumped to the conclusion faster than Alisande; after all, he'd had more practice. "Her children, too?" He turned to Lakshmi. "You didn't send us a birth announcement!"

Lakshmi looked disconcerted. "I had not thought . . . our lives had diverged . . ."

"Well, they just joined again!"

Alisande turned to them with a stony visage carved into lines of incipient mayhem. "How may we find where they have gone?"

"We're on the trail now," Saul said.

"The nurse's tracks led to a man robed in dark blue who took the children and rode into the night," Jimena said.

"Then we traced my children magically, through my son's slipper," Lakshmi said. "Their trail led Saul and your mother to fight a magus in a land of mist between worlds."

"Magus?" Matt jumped on it. "Any connection to Arjasp?"

"One of his junior priests," Saul confirmed, "attended by an acolyte. We seem to be dealing with a home-grown brand of demon worship here. Arjasp made the whole thing up."

"But the demon may be nonetheless real for all of that," Lakshmi said.

"Yeah, I know." Matt forced himself to the question he dreaded. "Why the kidnapping? Any other ransom demands yet?"

Saul frowned. "That's why you're riding west, is it? It was a ransom demand."

"We're complying, for the time being," Matt said.

Lakshmi stared in horror. "You will not imperil the children!"

"I won't, but Arjasp will. At best, after this war is over, he'll keep them hostages all their lives."

"And at worst?" Lakshmi asked with foreboding.

"I think we all know that."

The little group was silent awhile, looking at one another helplessly.

Matt spoke first. "After all, the messenger didn't say I couldn't try to find the kids."

"Sure," Saul said with a mirthless grin. "Easiest way to set a trap for you."

"I might return the favor. After all, did your magus and his helper say anything about my not trying to track down Arjasp?"

"Nothing," Jimena confirmed. "But did not the Caliph take offense at your leaving?"

"He understood our dilemma instantly," Matt said, "and was all sympathy—nervous at the thought of facing the horde without our help, but since we had hung around long enough for Tafas to catch up, he wasn't exactly left in the lurch."

"Therefore we left the city together," Alisande said, "but did not plan to remain so."

"We hadn't planned to split up quite so soon," Matt said, "but since you folk are here, we might as well."

Alisande nodded. "I shall ride west with my army."

"But nobody said she had to hurry," Matt pointed out. "Armies march notoriously slowly, and here in strange territory, European soldiers might come down with all sorts of minor ailments that wouldn't do them any real harm but would force them to go at a snail's pace."

That coaxed a tiny smile from Alisande. "Verily, it is so. Why, even a knight might be prey to such illnesses. I would not be surprised if, in a week's time, a quarter of my force had to be hauled in horse-drawn wagons."

"Ox-drawn," Matt offered. "Oxen go more slowly. Gee, and it'll take forever to find wagons and teams to buy when you're already on the road."

"Hey, I wouldn't play games with these guys," Saul said nervously.

"Oh, I think we have some leeway." Jimena smiled, amused. "After all, our enemies will rejoice in our ill fortune, will they not?"

Matt was sure they would—which left him wondering why Arjasp hadn't demanded that he stop tracking him, especially since the renegade magus had already tried to trap him twice, and failed. Was Arjasp really that sure of the next snare?

They made the arrangements quickly and prepared to set off again.

"I appreciate your staying with Alisande," Matt told his mother as he helped Saul into his own doublet. "Thank you, too, Saul, for wearing my outfit."

"Nobody said I couldn't," Saul returned, "any more than they said your going home was part of the ransom. So what if I decide to wear your dress-up clothes for a while? It's not as though I were carrying your shield with your coat of arms."

"And if Arjasp and his boys have the mistaken impression that I'm with Alisande for the next week, is that our fault?"

"Definitely not!" Saul said. "Of course, the trick won't work any longer than the first magical probe, or scrying by a spy who knows your face."

"Sure, but why should they take that close a look?" Matt

countered. "They'll probably scry the whole army, maybe zoom in for a close-up of the head of the column, but when they see a woman with long blond hair under her crown, and someone my size and build in a doublet and hose beside her, why should they check the details?"

"I suppose a brief glance might make Arjasp and his boys overconfident," Saul allowed, "maybe enough so they won't check to make sure it's really you riding at her right hand."

"Can't hurt to try." But Matt felt his stomach sink and tried not to think what Arjasp might do in a rage. He consoled himself with the idea that the sorcerer would try to parley first, send a message telling him to turn back. "At any rate, it might buy us some time."

"Even an hour or two would help at this point." But Saul eyed Matt doubtfully. "You sure you know what you're getting into, man?"

"As much as I ever did."

"That's what I meant."

"Hey, there shouldn't be more than a few thousand guards left behind to protect Arjasp," Matt told him. "I've got that much going for me."

"Sure, what's a thousand or three against one?" Saul said airily, and shuddered. "Did I ever talk to you about your sense of proportion?"

"Only during that art history class. After all, the vast majority of the horde will be out conquering. They'll probably have left the walking wounded as home guard."

"Hey, man, from what they say about these people, I'm not even sure I'd want to tangle with an octogenarian."

"Yeah, but these don't have tentacles."

"Look," Saul said, "I know you want to make sure Alisande is safe, but she feels the same way about you. Couldn't you maybe take one of us with you just as a sort of good-luck charm?"

"Or a chaperone." Jimena eyed Lakshmi with misgiving.

"There is certainly no need for your concern," the djinna said huffily. "He is nothing compared to my Marudin."

"Your husband is a most handsome male," Jimena agreed. "Not as handsome as my Ramon, of course . . ."

Lakshmi started to argue, but Matt said quickly, "Isn't that the way every spouse should think about a mate? Besides, folks, I'm scarcely going without protection."

"Sure, a djinna who's distracted about her children and her husband," Saul said with skepticism, "and a little white cat. That's real great odds against a few thousand bloodthirsty nomads, yeah."

"But they're octogenarians," Matt reminded, "and my little cat is fairly bursting with the enthusiasm of youth."

"Hidden talents, huh?" Saul shook his head, but gave a sigh and slapped Matt on the shoulder. "Good luck, man." He cocked an eye at Lakshmi. "Don't drop him, okay, Highness?"

"Drop you!" Lakshmi seethed. "What sort of fumble-fingered nanny does he think I am?"

"Saul just worries too much." Matt gave an uneasy glance at the landscape far below, so far below that it seemed to be moving slowly. Balkis watched it wide-eyed, peering out from the collar of Matt's shirt—even more secure than a seat belt, and secure she seemed indeed, without a worry in the world. In fact, she even closed her eyes and, purring, dropped off to sleep.

Matt envied the cat's nonchalance—one flight, and she took it as routine. Not that he had anything to worry about, being snuggled tightly against a firm and beautifully curved bosom. Once again he wondered why it stirred not the slightest trace of desire in him—possibly because it was bigger than he was. "By the way, Highness, where are we heading? In particular, I mean, not just east."

"To Baghdad," Lakshmi answered. "If the gossip of the Muslim army is true, the horde still holds that city. Surely they will have my Marudin at the front of battle!"

"And you're hoping I can free him from their compulsion-spell."

"At the very least, you should be able to shield me from falling victim to the same spell myself," Lakshmi replied. "I could not venture so close as to aid him before, but with a mortal wizard to ward me, I can chance it. Besides, you can free him, can you not?"

"Unless they've come up with a spell that's completely different from anything I've ever dealt with, yes," Matt said slowly. "But surely they know that!"

Lakshmi frowned, and her huge voice echoed about him. "You think they will not have him at the front, then?"

"I wouldn't," Matt said, "especially since they're planning several different fronts. It would make more sense to station Marudin's current master at the frontier of China or India, where they've never even heard of djinn."

Far above him, Lakshmi's face darkened. "Let us hope you are wrong."

"I'll try to keep a freedom spell ready." Matt looked away from the brewing anger in her face, and saw far below him a long curve of dots facing a sort of M-shape of other dots. "Princess! Can we go down for a closer look?"

Lakshmi lowered her gaze. "I can see quite well from here. It is the Caliph's picket line retreating from a vanguard of the horde."

"The *Muslim* army's retreating? I thought that with Tafas' army to back them up, they might actually be able to drive the barbarians back."

"I had hoped as much myself." Lakshmi studied the battle. "Could this be some mere stratagem?"

"Of course!" Matt clapped with delight. "Arjasp's generals expect to be able to start winning again, now that Alisande and her army are retreating. The Caliph doesn't want to disappoint them."

Lakshmi frowned. "You mean that he bade his men retreat to raise false hopes in the barbarians?"

"Exactly! Let them think they're winning, then hit them with the reserves from both flanks." Uneasily, Matt remembered that Genghis Khan had pioneered the tactic—but Genghis wasn't here, maybe never would be born in this universe. "Even so, it makes you want to go down there and help out."

"No!" Lakshmi thundered. "We go to Baghdad and must not be baited into delay! After all, if we can free Marudin from barbarian bondage, we will weaken Arjasp and strengthen the Caliph in a single stroke!"

From the air Baghdad was a veritable anthill, with double lines of dots streaming through all its gates—merchants, other travelers, and farmers trooping in to sell produce and filing back out with empty carts and full pockets.

"Shouldn't be any trouble getting in," Matt said. "All we have to do is join one of those lines and walk past the guards."

"Easy enough for you," Lakshmi said, frowning, "for you are dressed in traveling clothes—but mine are far too fine for the road."

"All you need is a veil." Matt pointed downward. "See? All the women are wrapped from head to toe in one big piece of dark fabric, with only the eyes showing."

Lakshmi looked down, frowning. "It is so. And in the bazaar . . . let me see . . . We shall land."

Matt couldn't help a shout of alarm as his body shot downward and his stomach tried to stay up. Balkis woke up, sensed the motion, and dug in her claws with a yowl. "Ease off!" Matt shouted, to both djinna and cat. "We don't need to get down there *that* fast!"

The acceleration did ease off. Lakshmi snapped, "Your pardon. I am impatient."

"We're going to have to walk the last quarter mile anyway," Matt protested.

They landed in a grove. Lakshmi set Matt down and started shrinking. In minutes she was human-sized again. "Give me a coin!" she demanded.

Matt handed her a piece of silver. "Not a bad rate, considering that air fare is going up."

Lakshmi took the coin and made several passes over it with her other hand, fingers writhing in symbolic gestures as she chanted, frowning down at it with great concentration. Matt started to ask what she was doing, then caught himself—if she needed concentration for this spell, the last thing he should do was interrupt.

The coin winked in her palm, reflecting sunlight—then was gone. A second later a length of dark fabric fell out of thin air across Lakshmi's hand. A small flask followed it, then a swathe of brown fabric, a smaller square of white cloth, and, finally, a sort of rope headband.

Matt stared, then gave himself a shake. "Y'know, if that catches on, it's going to revolutionize shopping!"

"It is even as you say," Lakshmi confirmed. "These garments have disappeared from a booth in the bazaar, and your coin has appeared in their place." She inspected her purchases, then added, "The merchant had far the best of the bargain."

"I'm not arguing." Matt held up the brown garment and found a lighter ivory-colored tunic of cotton within it. He started dressing. "What's in the bottle?"

"Walnut juice," Lakshmi said, "to stain your face and hands."

Matt sighed and remembered his days in college theatricals.

Fifteen minutes later a man in Arab dress stepped onto the roadway between another traveler and a farm-cart. A woman stepped out beside him, decently veiled, presumably his wife. Long-lashed eyes looked out from the veil, taking in her surroundings in quick glances. Lakshmi muttered through the cloth, "I marvel that your mortal women allow this!"

"Not my women," Matt protested. "We Europeans like to see each other's faces—but I don't think the women here have much choice about it. After all, they don't have your magic spells, and it's a violent world."

The eyes above the veil narrowed. "Perhaps I should do something about that."

"Perhaps you should," Matt agreed, "after we get your children and your husband back. For now, let's just get inside that city and see if we can find any trace of them."

The guards were collecting an entry fee at the gate. Fortunately, Matt had made a little money in India, so they didn't have Alisande's likeness to upset them. They strolled on through, and Matt promptly forgot about his mission, looking about him, enthralled by the graceful minarets, the ivory palace in the distance, and the squalor by the roadside. "Baghdad! The city of the Arabian Nights! Haroun-al-Raschid, Omar Khayyam, Haji the poet!"

"It is a place of stenches and sin." Lakshmi wrinkled her nose. "I shall never cease to be amazed that your kind choose to coop themselves up in places such as this when they could have the freedom of open skies and the cleanliness of the desert."

"It has something to do with making a living," Matt said, "and with having something to do in your free time."

Lakshmi looked about her, fairly radiating nervousness. "How shall we begin to discover Marudin's whereabouts?"

"Well, there's a good place." Matt stopped and nodded toward an alley they were passing. At its far end was a little courtyard with women gathered about the low wall of a well, chatting and laughing. "Mingle with those women, get into the conversation, and try and turn it toward things magical, especially ones that come out of lamps and bottles."

"I?" Lakshmi turned to glare at him. "Why not yourself?"

"Not a member of the club," Matt explained. "Wrong gender. Sure, I could go in there, but I'd be even more of an outsider than you, and the women would clam up in a second. Besides, in this part of the world, women don't talk to strange men."

"A good rule anywhere, I should think." Lakshmi's tone was tart, and her glance directed the comment unquestionably toward Matt himself.

Matt smiled and took it philosophically—after all, by the standards of this world, he was indeed strange. Maybe his own universe's, too.

Lakshmi gave a sound of disgust, then held out her hand. "Another coin!"

Matt handed it over without asking, reminding himself that the trip was still amazingly cheap.

Lakshmi stared at the coin, muttering and gesturing over it. It flashed and disappeared; an instant later she held a water jug. "I shall learn what I can." She turned away toward the well.

Matt watched her go, admiring the sway of her walk that no veil could hide, and envying the ease with which she could use magic for casual ends. If he tried that, magical alarms would clamor all over the city wherever there was a sorcerer or a priest of Ahriman. Lakshmi, though, was a magical creature, and spells were as natural to her as walking was to him. The sorcerers might note the presence of one of the djinn, but no more. In fact, they would probably assume it was one of their own.

Matt turned back to the stalls and rugs of the peddlers that lined the street, reminding him of New York even though none of them featured young men making three cards dance like the thimbles in a shell game. He fingered fabrics, hefted rugs, and squeezed fruit, not replying to the vendors' hard-sell spiels but getting a feel for the local dialect. He found the booth from which Lakshmi had conjured her veil—he could tell by the silver coin lying between two other lengths of fabric—and bought one of them just to call the merchant's attention to the transformation. At first the merchant scowled at discovering one of his wares missing, then positively beamed when he saw the price it had fetched.

The veil slung over his shoulder like a serape, Matt strolled along the line of booths, enjoying a brief moment of relaxation. The shopkeepers might be enmeshed in the toils of commerce, but he felt a holiday air about the bazaar, as though he were a tourist on vacation. He glanced over at a display of carvings—and felt a jolt that froze his head in place.

CHAPTER 20

Matt found himself staring at a slender stick of ebony about fifteen inches long inlaid with gilded astrological symbols. The gold was chipped here and there, the wood looked dusty and brittle, but the stick itself fairly screamed at him to pay attention.

"Ah, I see the sir is interested in this ancient artifact." The merchant lifted the stick and held it out on his palms. "Rare it is, a relic found in the ruins of Ninevah. So excellent a ware should be worth its weight in gold—but I shall sell it to the sir for a mere ounce of silver."

With a thump, Balkis landed on the ledge, purring and staring in fascination at the stick.

"Wondered where you'd gotten to," Matt muttered. "So it called to you, too, huh?"

"Begone, foolish feline!" The merchant waved a hand at the little white cat. "Be off with you to find a fish head!"

Balkis, ordinarily the most circumspect of cats, laid her ears back and hissed. The merchant's face darkened, and the waving hand balled into a fist.

"Oh, she's not all that much trouble." Matt picked up the little cat, who stayed frozen in her crouch, and set her on his shoulder. "Easy enough to get her out of the way. An ounce of silver, you say? It doesn't look all that fine to me. How about half an ounce?"

Claws dug into his shoulder. Matt winced and tried to ignore them. Didn't the silly kitten understand that if he didn't haggle, he'd look suspicious?

Yes. Of course she understood that. But something about this trinket made her abandon her usual caution.

The shopkeeper's eyes lit with greed, but he said, "Only

half? Sir, that could not be a fraction of its worth! Only think, the Emperor of Assyria might once have held this very scepter! Nine-tenths of an ounce, perhaps."

Matt upped his offer to six-tenths. The vendor launched into loud lamentation of how such a price would impoverish him, taking bread from the mouths of his children and leaving his wife only her single threadbare veil for the marketing. Matt listened with interest—after all, his area of study was comparative literature, and the man's fiction techniques fascinated him. Finally, though, he saw Lakshmi returning from the well, so he boosted his offer to three-quarters of an ounce.

The merchant pounced on it and shoved the stick into Matt's hand before he could change his mind.

Matt froze, eyes widening as he felt the power of the ebony stick tingling through his hand and up his arm. The merchant studied his face, beginning to think that perhaps he had settled for too little, so Matt fumbled another Indian coin out of his purse and pressed it into the man's hand. "Here you go. Keep the change." He suspected there wouldn't be any, but didn't want to have to wait around to discuss the issue. He hurried back to Lakshmi with the stick in his hand.

"What is that?" she asked.

"An excuse to loiter without seeming suspicious," Matt told her. "Learn anything?"

"Well, the women have at least paid close attention to their conquerors," Lakshmi told him, "and to the sorcerers and priests of Ahriman most of all, since they seem to be able to hold the soldiers in check if they wish."

"All Mongol tribesmen?" Matt asked.

"Nay. From what the women say, they seem to be a hodge-podge of tribal magicians of every nation between Persia and China. There are even some taller men who wear clothes like those carved on the walls of the ruins of the ancient cities in Persia, but who speak a language like the merchants who come from India."

"Antique Persians?" Matt felt excitement kindle. "They would be Aryans from the hills, still speaking the ancient Aveston language! If what I've heard about Arjasp is true, he was one of them!"

"Interesting." Lakshmi's tone held a promise of slow death. "There was even an Arab among these field sorcerers—an old man with a huge ring."

"A ring?" Matt pounced on it. "Who lives in it?"

"My thought exactly," Lakshmi said, "and I asked for all they knew about the man, but there was not much—only that he stays inside the city, leaving the other sorcerers to go out with the army."

"Sounds like the local high priest," Matt said. "Where's he live?"

"He dwells in the mosque, which the invaders have defiled and turned to their own purposes. It is in my mind that we confront the man and learn what he knows."

"Yes, that could be very profitable," Matt agreed. "Unfortunately, it could also be very dangerous."

"Are you afraid?" Lakshmi demanded.

"Frankly, yes," Matt said, "but that's not going to stop me. In fact, I'd say there's no time like the present. Which way to the mosque?"

Lakshmi caught his sleeve in alarm. "Now? In the middle of the day?"

"When better?" Matt countered. "By their religion, midday should be the time when Ahura Mazda is strongest, since the sun is pouring down light."

"And Ahriman should be at his weakest." Lakshmi frowned beneath her veil, nodding. "Then, too, most of the army are miles from the city, marching to strike again at Damascus."

"Which means the guard on this old Arab will be weaker now than when the city is crammed with soldiers." Matt nodded. "Feel like a little sightseeing, Princess? I should think the central mosque would be a wonder to behold."

"Let us see it," Lakshmi agreed. She set down her water jug and walked off toward the minaret. Matt hurried to follow.

The mosque really was a wonder, faced with alabaster, its arches graceful, the geometric patterns of its tiles breathtaking in their beauty, the guards muscular, scowling, and stationed every thirty feet. Matt made loud noises like a hick from the sticks, totally overawed.

"The wonders of the East are breathtaking for a Frank, are they not?" Lakshmi's tone was condescending.

"Sure are," Matt said, "and the more I ooh and ahh, the less of a threat they'll think I am. Sound impressed, Princess."

Lakshmi stared at him in surprise, then turned back to stare at the mosque. "How tall it is! How pale its stones! Why, never could there have been such a wonder back home in Besuki!"

The nearest guard heard her and struggled to hide a complacent smile. He seemed to relax just the slightest bit.

They walked on around the mosque, exclaiming with wonder and delight, lulling the sentries' suspicions past amusement and into boredom. Suddenly, though, Lakshmi froze, eyes wide in surprise, then shadowed by fear.

Instantly, Matt lowered his tone. "What is it? What's happened?"

"He knows I am here," Lakshmi answered, her own voice hushed and strained. "He knows what I am—and he has set his ring to enslave me! I can feel its power, pulling at me, burdening me, seeking to compel me to obey!"

Matt thought quickly, then said, "Well, you don't want to keep him waiting, do you?"

Lakshmi whirled, staring at him, appalled. "Do you wish to see me enslaved? More, do you wish to have to do battle with me when that old impostor has me in thrall?"

"Not at all," Matt said. "After all, I only told you to answer his summons—I didn't say what you should do once you get there."

"And will you shield me from the power of his ring?" Lakshmi challenged, but the mere mention of the talisman was enough to give her eyes a faraway look.

"Of course," Matt said, "if I need to. But instead of the ring capturing you, why don't you go capture the ring?"

The faraway gaze turned thoughtful.

"Go get it," Matt urged, "and don't let anything stand in your way. If anybody tries to come between you and the ring, eliminate them!"

In a trance, Lakshmi turned and glided toward the entrance to the desecrated mosque.

Balkis gave a meow of protest.

"Don't worry, she'll be okay—if we do our jobs right." Matt pried the cat off his shoulder and set her down behind a stone curb in the foundation, then laid the wand beside her. "If this works like other magic wands I've seen, it will use any spell you give it—but it'll concentrate the effects into a small area, not much larger than two or three people. When I say 'concentrate,' I mean it'll make it stronger, too—much stronger—and I suspect this little wand will add a kick of its own. Keep an eye on us and help if we need it." He laid the veil beside the wand and added, as an afterthought, "You might need this, too. Call it a disguise."

Balkis gave a plaintive mew.

"Hey, you wanted the wand, didn't you?" Matt stood up. "Don't take any chances. Wait until you have a clear shot, snap your spell out, and run! Got that?"

Balkis gave a confirming trill, but she looked doubtful.

"Hopefully you won't have to," Matt said, "but if it frightens you, just find a nice safe place and stay hidden."

"And what shall I do if you do not come back?" Balkis demanded.

It gave Matt a start—she'd been speaking cat so long, he'd forgotten she was bilingual. "Same as you've been doing—make friends with the local spirits and keep going. I'm pretty sure we'll be back, though." He turned and hurried to catch up with Lakshmi.

He didn't quite make it. As the djinna came through the portal, a huge hulking guard with a long beard and a hooked nose turned to glower at her. He wore a tall turban, a short open vest over a bare chest with bulging muscles, and loose billowing trousers pegged down to pointed slippers. The guard decided she didn't have the look of an abject worshiper and stepped forward to bar her way.

It was a bad mistake. Lakshmi had already been under the influence of the ring when Matt told her to eliminate anyone who came between her and it, so she took his words literally. She gave the man a glare and he slumped, unconscious. Lakshmi stepped over his body and glided onward into the mosque.

Matt followed, stomach sinking at the ease with which the djinna had disposed of a merely human adversary.

Several of them. Other guards saw what had happened to their fellow and came running to avenge him, shouting with anger. Lakshmi glared at them, turning her head slowly, eyes burning with anger at the audacity of the mere mortals who dared to bar her from the ring that was calling, calling . . .

The guards jolted as rigid as though they had run into a wall, then slumped to the floor, limp. Matt snatched a scimitar from one and tried to keep up with Lakshmi. He took one quick glance behind and saw a woman coming through the door, veil wrapped about her from head to foot. She had drawn a fold of her white gown over her head so that it shaded her eyes, and the dark brown veil made an inverted V over the center of her face, disguising the youthful appearance of her eyes. Matt couldn't see the wand, but he was sure it was under the veil in her hand.

A quick glance only; then Matt turned back to Lakshmi and discovered the djinna had gone farther than he'd thought. She glided zombielike toward the ring, and the old man who wore it.

Four guards stood by him, two before and two behind. He wore the tall bulging-then-tapering hat and robe of his priesthood, midnight-blue. His hair and beard were long and white, his eyebrows bushy and gray, his eyes a faded brown. He sat at the focal point of the mosque's dome in a throne whose gilding glistened with newness, his elbow propped on one arm to hold up the huge emerald ring that decorated his palsied fist.

"Princess!" Matt shouted. "Close your eyes!"

"Begone, dog!" one guard snarled as he advanced toward Matt, scimitar swinging high. Another guard was only a step behind him.

Matt met the scimitar with his own. Steel rang against steel, and the other two guards came running, just as Matt had hoped. He backed and sidestepped, parrying madly, keeping the first guard between himself and the other three. That wouldn't last long, but it wouldn't need to—if his words had penetrated Lakshmi's daze, and she had heard him and closed her eyes.

If she hadn't, she'd be the old man's next weapon, and the guards' scimitars wouldn't matter.

One thing at least was working: the guards were so intent on Matt that they didn't see the small black-and-white cat trotting past them with the stick in her mouth.

Black and white?

The old man was grinning now, beckoning and crooning, "Look at my pretty jewel, Princess. Look upon it, look into it, deeply into it."

Lakshmi drifted closer and closer, eyes growing wider and wider, pupils shrinking, fixed on the gem.

The guard swung; Matt leaped back, but another guard stepped in from the side, slashing. Matt ducked under the blade, but the knuckle guard struck his head, and he reeled backward, the room swimming about him. He fought to hold his scimitar up, hoping desperately.

Then the old man screamed. Matt's vision cleared enough to show the guard pivoting away from him in alarm.

A young woman stood beside the priest, wearing a black veil and white under-robe, chanting in Allustrian. She held a wand near the old man's elbow, and he howled in pain, arm limp, grasping the injured funny bone with his other hand.

The other three guards had whirled to see what was the matter, too. The fourth remembered the strange man barely in time; he snarled and turned back, cutting wildly at Matt, who parried, then swung high. The guard's scimitar leaped up to parry, and Matt pivoted in to slam a fist into his belly. The man folded, eyes bulging, but still managing to keep his sword up. Matt beat it down, kicked his feet out from under him, and gave him a punch with his hilt for good luck.

Balkis yanked the ring off the priest's finger and cried, "Look, O Princess! See what I have found!"

Lakshmi looked, and was instantly spellbound.

The old man shouted a curse and reached for the ring, but his arm merely flopped, the nerves stunned. He pushed himself up from the throne to reach with his left hand, but Balkis stepped away, ring still held high, and as the priest tried to push himself out of his seat with both hands, his right hand gave way. He fell back into his throne, cursing.

The guards ran to help him.

Balkis chanted a spell, shouting the last line as a command. Lakshmi's head snapped back, her eyes clearing. Then Balkis called out,

> "With justice let this priest be served.
> Treat him as he has deserved!"

Matt stepped forward, crying out in protest, but Lakshmi had no such scruples. She raised a hand, the three guards leaped between her and their master, and flame leaped from Lakshmi's fingers. The guards turned to cinders so quickly that they didn't even have time to cry out. Then the djinna advanced on the priest of Ahriman, eyes narrowed to slits, hands gesturing.

The old man shrank back in his throne and pointed at her, howling a verse in Arabic. It might have made for interesting study, but Matt didn't really pay attention—he leaped forward, scooped Balkis up in his arms and ran for the door.

CHAPTER 21

"What are you doing?" Balkis cried, thrashing about in his arms. "She will need our help against his magic!"

"Not anymore she won't!" Matt made it through the portal before the screaming started. He bolted across the square, then set Balkis down in the shadow of a marble-fronted building, but it wasn't far enough—she could still hear the screams, hoarse and ragged. She clapped her hands over her ears and sat trembling.

"Only what he deserved," Matt reminded her. "You couldn't know how many people he had butchered, how many he had weakened as the horde charged down, how many he had tortured."

But Balkis clasped her head, still trembling.

Matt had to bring her out of it. He knelt as the screams faded and said, voice low but insistent, "Prince Marudin. While you have the ring, recite the spell! Free the prince, wherever he is, and you'll weaken the horde enough so that they might retreat!"

"Do you really think so?" Balkis held out the ring on a trembling finger and began to recite once again in Allustrian—obviously one of the spells Idris had taught her. Matt doubted it had been invented solely for djinn, and wondered what kind of compulsions to obedience Idris had dealt with.

He caught the gist of the spell and could only admire the crafting of the verse—lines of alternating meters with an intricate rhyme scheme, ending in an imperative. No wonder it had freed Lakshmi from the sorcerer's power . . . but bound her to Balkis' spell, with deadly results.

Matt leaned closer. "Lakshmi, too! Command the ring to free Lakshmi, too!"

"I have," Balkis gasped. "I should have before."

"Believe me," Matt said with total sincerity, "it wouldn't have made the slightest difference."

Balkis looked up at him with naked, vulnerable gratitude, then looked beyond him, horrified. "She comes!"

Matt turned to look. Lakshmi came striding across the square, long black veil whipping about her legs, angry eyes staring out above the cloth.

"It's done!" Matt held up his hands to slow her down. "Princess, he's dust! You've had a revenge you didn't need!"

"Any who seek to enthrall the djinn merit revenge!" Lakshmi snapped. She looked past him and saw the little cat, now black and white, cowering in a corner of the marble. Instantly Lakshmi's rage evaporated, and she knelt, reaching out a hand and crooning. "Ah, poor mite! Did I so afright you, then? Surely I had not meant to do so! Do not pity that old monster, for he suffered only what he had given, and that much only by his own magic come back upon him, for I turned around the spells that he had cast on others, so that they struck him. Nay, poor child, come hither, for I owe you only gratitude, never harm!"

Balkis began to relax. She stepped forward, nose twitching warily to sniff the djinna's hand.

"Yes, I owe you my freedom, sweet child," Lakshmi said, voice soft as velvet. "Never would I seek to harm you. Your enemies perhaps, as I have smitten my own, but never you!"

"I told her that last command she gave you didn't make any difference," Matt said, "that if she'd freed you to do as you wished, you'd have done just as you did."

"Be sure of it." But there was no anger in Lakshmi's voice, only gentle reassurance. "He gained what he had given, no more. Indeed, left to my own devices, I should have done far worse."

Balkis thawed enough to step forward, rubbing her head against the princess' hand. Lakshmi murmured with pleasure, stroking the black and white fur, then rubbing gently behind the ears. Balkis raised her head, eyes closing for a minute of pleasure, and Matt knew the two had made friends again.

Lakshmi took up the cat's paw, studying the emerald on her foreleg with a frown. "I cannot take it from you, though dearly I wish I could."

"Really?" Matt stepped up to look more closely. "Why not?"

"See how its band has tightened to fit her—it knows it is hers now. Never shall she be separated from this gem while she lives, unless she comes across a magic greater than her own."

"But the old priest's magic must have been greater than hers!"

"You gave her a wand," Lakshmi reminded him. "There is great power of magic within her, and the wand strengthened it tenfold. Nay, now the ring is hers by right, and I can think of few I should trust with it more." She gave Balkis a rather bleak smile. "Or will you, too, seek to command me, little cat?"

"Never!" Balkis mewed indignantly.

Lakshmi laughed. "I believe you, as I would believe few mortals—but then, you are somewhat more than mortal yourself, are you not?"

Balkis gave a mew of doubt.

"Be sure that you are." Lakshmi reached down to stroke the cat. "A thousand thanks for this fair rescue, sweet one! Three wishes shall be yours when this turmoil is done—three wishes and more, if I can free my Marudin!"

"He may be free already," Matt said. "While we were waiting for you, she chanted a spell to give him his liberty, no matter where he was."

"Let us hope the ring had so much power as that," Lakshmi said fervently. "If indeed it has, we shall be ever in your debt, little cat."

Balkis looked up wide-eyed. Then her look turned calculating.

Lakshmi laughed and scooped her up to hold opposite her face. "Aye, think what you can do with such a friendship, think of the wishes for which you shall ask, ponder long and carefully—for once a wish has come true, you shall have to live with it."

Matt found that even a cat's face could develop a thoughtful frown.

"Come, now!" Lakshmi said, all business again. "Let us take to the sky and see what effect this action has wrought upon the battle we passed on our way hither! If the horde was winning because of the magic of its sorcerers, then the slaying of this dotard should have turned the tide in the Caliph's favor!" She began to grow, catching up Matt as she went.

In minutes they were high above the battlefield, and sure enough, the horde was retreating. The Caliph's troops followed, but cautiously, wary that the barbarians might turn their own tactic upon them—retreating at full speed, waiting until the defenders had broken ranks to pursue, letting them get close, then suddenly turning on them and cutting them to shreds. Knowing that, the Muslims advanced without breaking their battle line.

"I see him!" Lakshmi cried. "Marudin! He rises above the battle, he fights for the Caliph!"

Sure enough, Matt could see a huge turban growing huger as it both rose and swelled, with a burgeoning set of shoulders beneath it. Prince Marudin rose high, scooping boulders from thin air and hurling them against his erstwhile masters.

"I must go to help him! Down, you two, where it is safe!" Lakshmi dove back toward the city. Matt cried out, then clung for dear life. So did Balkis—sinking her claws into Matt and yowling every foot of the way.

Lakshmi shrank as she descended, so that it seemed to be only a normal-sized woman who set them down in a back alley, then leaped into the sky again.

"Impetuous, isn't she?" Matt tried to hide his shaking by kneeling down and holding out a hand to Balkis. "Care to ride for the first few blocks?"

Balkis spat and raised a claw.

"I know—I wouldn't trust anybody's arms after a trip like that, either." Matt rose again, leaned against a wall for a minute, then started down the alley toward the little square at its end.

There were women around the well, but their water jars were mere excuses—they were all chatting with excitement about having seen a djinna descending toward the city, disappearing, then flying away from it. There was speculation about Lakshmi being a weapon of the Caliph in the battle the barbarians were even then fighting, some guesses as to why she might have come otherwise, more guesses as to why she would have left so quickly, but no real information. Matt kept walking, but glanced back—Balkis was just coming out of the alley, with seemingly lofty indifference to the world of mere humans, but Matt was sure that if the women mentioned anything about the missing children, the cat would know it in an instant.

He crossed the square and went up the opposite alley; Lakshmi had dropped them at the western gate, so as long as he headed east, he should come closer to the city's center. As he reached the end he heard an attack-yowl and turned back to see a young woman in black veil and white under-robe seem to sprout from the pavement. A huge tomcat let out a caterwaul of dismay and sprinted for cover. Balkis allowed herself a small smile of satisfaction as she shrank back into the form of a cat.

Matt came to an actual street, not another mere alley, and followed it north until he came to another street that met it at something resembling a right angle. He turned east again and kept going. There was gossip and speculation all around him—from porters carrying loads, merchants engaged in heated discussion on street corners, women walking along chatting with one another. The topic was the battle, and that the djinna must have been a sign that it was coming closer to the city. Speculation was rife—what would the barbarians do if they lost? Would they take revenge on the citizens? Or would they ride out the eastern gate and never be seen again? The consensus was that they would barricade themselves within the city and defend it against the Caliph's siege.

No one mentioned two small kidnapped children, or anything that would give the barbarians leverage against the djinn.

Every now and again Matt glanced back and saw the little black and white cat trotting along, weaving her way between people's feet, ears pricked up, listening with interest. He was quite sure he had the right cat—you didn't see too many felines with an emerald ring around one foreleg. The sight was reassuring, but Matt doubted she'd learn anything he hadn't.

Suddenly, the cat picked up its pace, running to catch Matt's leg with a claw. "Ouch!" he said, looking down, but Balkis ducked into an alley and looked back to meow at him. Matt took the hint and stepped after her, but the little cat ducked behind a mound of trash and began to grow. Fur became cloth, and her body stretched in some very odd ways. Matt turned his back, feeling queasy and watching the street.

"I have had a thought."

Matt looked down at the black-veiled teenager, marveling at the way she had arranged the extra cloth in the white robe to veil her head as well as her body—probably just as well, considering that the veil was rather translucent. "I'm interested. What thought?"

"That this ring is tied to djinn." Balkis held up her right fist. "Perhaps it can show us the path to a djinni."

"You mean a very small djinni?" Matt felt a burst of excitement. "It's worth a try. Got a spell handy?"

"I do not know one," Balkis confessed.

"Let's see what I can do." Matt stared at the ring as he searched his memory, and came up with:

> "Where ask is have, where seek is find,
> Where knock is open wide,
> Where someone lost our search abides—
> There point! You to them this spell shall bind!"

"Of course, it's tuned to you now," Matt explained. "Probably doesn't do any good for me to recite it."

"As you say." Balkis stared at the emerald and recited the verse. When she was done, she said, "It grew warm as I spoke, but now it cools."

Matt wondered about crystal matrices and computers. "It was absorbing the spell and adding a new . . . call it a sensitivity. Try it for direction. Tell it who you're looking for. Why don't you start with Prince Marudin? At least we know which direction he's in."

"It will do for a test," Balkis said, doubt in her voice. "Ring, show me where Prince Marudin flies!" She turned slowly toward the west. The ring began to glow, brighter and brighter as it came to line up with the western gate. Then, as Balkis continued turning, the glow faded.

"It works!" An idea lodged in Matt's mind. "Try the same thing with Lakshmi."

"But we know she fights beside her prince!" Balkis objected.

"Yes, but in finding her, it might become sensitized to the two of them, and when you combine them . . ."

"Which their children have!" Balkis nodded. "I begin to understand why I was sent to you. Ring, waken your inner light when you are nearest the Princess Lakshmi!" She began to turn backward. Again the ring glowed most brightly when it pointed due west, then faded as she went on to the north.

"We can't program it any better than that," Matt said. "Try for the kids now."

"Program?" Balkis looked up, alert and hungry for knowledge.

"Telling it what to do," Matt explained. "Try."

"Ring, glow when you discover the direction in which the children of Princess Lakshmi and Prince Marudin lie!" Balkis commanded, and held the ring out at arm's length as she turned again. It began to glow as she neared north, glowed more and more brightly until, when she pointed it toward the northeast, it glowed so brightly that Matt marveled it didn't burn her finger—but she seemed to feel nothing, only kept turning. The glow started to dim, and died away by the time she pointed due east.

"Northeast," Matt said, musing. "Well, that's what we had guessed—but it helps to have it confirmed."

"It helps mightily to know they are still alive!" Balkis said fervently.

Matt looked down at her, surprised, and saw a very real dread there in her eyes—one she hadn't dared recognize until she had proven it baseless.

"Yes," Matt said slowly, "that is good to know." Suddenly, he wished the ring were sensitive to his own kids. He had never let himself consider the possibility that they might be dead, but he knew the reputations of kidnappers. As soon as he had some time alone, he'd have to try a scry.

"What lies in the northeast?" Balkis asked.

Matt shrugged. "The Mongols' homeland, and Arjasp."

"Nay, there is more than that." Balkis frowned. "There must be, for I feel it pulling at me when the ring glows brightest."

Matt stared down at her, wondering, and was about to offer an idea when a crash sounded in the distance. They turned, staring down the broad avenue, and saw that the western gate had boomed open, spilling barbarian horsemen into the city from which they had ventured to attack the Arabs.

"They are routed!" Balkis cried. "The Caliph has won!"

"That is good," Matt said. "But this isn't a good time for a pretty girl to be watching, veiled or not. How about stepping back into the side street?"

"Wisely thought." Balkis retreated behind the corner of the wall, and Matt stepped over between the street and the girl. A minute later a black-and-white cat strolled out between his ankles, tail twitching as she watched the warriors come trotting down the broad avenue. As they passed, Matt caught snatches of conversation, liberally interspersed with cursing.

"That traitorous djinni!" one warrior brayed. "How dare he turn upon us in the thick of battle!"

"It was the djinna who bewitched him!"

"Nay," cried a third soldier, "for he turned upon us ere she came!"

"Flay the sorcerers!" bawled a fourth as his foam-flecked pony rode by Matt. "They made him turn upon us! They called the djinna to aid him!"

"Cannot our own sorcerers hold the Arab magicians at bay?" howled a fifth. "Let them practice their spells upon one another!"

"Nay!" cried a sixth. "Let us practice our archery and our lancing upon them!"

"I don't like that kind of talk," Matt told Balkis. "Once they start shooting magicians, who knows where they'll stop?"

Balkis mewed agreement.

Then came a barbarian on a tall horse, far taller than the
Mongolian ponies, though his features were those of the
khans. His armor was gorgeous, his helmet chased with
gold, and his temper absolutely foul. "I shall have their
heads!" he bellowed. "What sort of incompetent sorcerers
has the high priest given me, that they cannot keep control of
their own djinn—nay, even with the very lamp that held
him!"

"At least they kept the five lesser spirits leashed," called
a younger and somewhat less splendidly costumed man beside him.

"Only five!" the general roared. "Only five minor djinn
against two Marids! How can they think to preserve us from
such might?"

A man in midnight-blue robes rode behind him, protesting,
"It is a spell beyond our ken, O Khan! Only the Arab priest
himself could counter it!"

Then they were gone, riding on down the street, but Matt felt
claws in his calf. "Ouch!" He looked down, ready to scold—
and saw the emerald glowing, a glow that faded even as he
watched. Balkis looked up at him and meowed impatiently.

Matt took the hint and lifted her up to his shoulder. She set
the leg with the ring under his headcloth to hide it and said
into his ear so that no one else would hear, "It glowed when
that sorcerer passed! Can he be a spirit disguised?"

"Possible," Matt said slowly, "but it probably just means
that he still controls five djinn."

"If that is his specialty," Balkis said, "perhaps he knows
where to find two very small djinni."

"He might at that," Matt said, following her thought about
Lakshmi's children. "Excellent idea, Balkis. Let's just saunter
along after that crew." He strolled down the street, not seeming
to hurry, but actually eating up the ground at a very good pace.
He was impressed with Balkis' intelligence. Obviously she had
more going for her than a saturation in magic.

"Perhaps they are bound to the mosque," Balkis offered.

"I was kind of thinking that, too," Matt said. "After all, if
they're going to blame it on the old high priest, they'll want to
chew him out right away."

"And they will find him dead."

"Should be an interesting sight," Matt said. "Let's go have a look."

They arrived minutes too late—the general and his aides were boiling back out of the mosque, faces gray. "Slain!" one cried.

"I have rarely seen so many wounds in one man," cried another.

"Aye, even in battle." The general shuddered. "And his guards burned to cinders! What can have happened here?"

"Magic," said his chief aide, his face grim. "Magic far stronger than his—but how can such be possible?"

They were silent, considering the question. Then one warrior offered, "Ahriman is displeased with us."

"As well he might be, for this loss in battle!" But the general now looked frightened.

"Shall we abandon the city?" another aide asked. "We can slay all its people as offerings to Ahriman before we go."

"There is not that much time, if we are to retreat," the general said, scowling, "and if we are to stay, we shall need the services of the people. Let them live; we shall hold them hostage in case the Caliph besieges us."

"But should we stay or go?"

"Our sorcerer has not come out," the general said grimly. "No doubt he seeks to placate Ahriman, to learn what the god wishes of us. Let us wait to hear his answer."

Matt stepped back into the shadow of an alley and told Balkis, "That means we have to take him out the back way, if there is one."

"And make one if there is not," the cat agreed.

Matt lifted her off his shoulder and down to the ground. "You stay here while I go in and bring him out." He slipped the wand out from under his robe. "Use this if I don't."

"Use it yourself," the cat snapped. "If you would not beard the high priest without me to help, you should not dare his minion!"

Matt sighed. "Everybody's gotta get in on the act. Okay, we saunter around to the back of the mosque as though we're going home. Ready?"

"Lead on," Balkis replied.

Matt stepped out and strolled down the street, hoping the officers would be so involved in trying to fix blame that they wouldn't see him.

Behind him, he heard a shout.

CHAPTER 22

Matt kept on walking. Boots clattered on the cobbles behind him. A heavy hand landed on his shoulder and spun him about. "You, Arab! What are you doing here?"

It was one of the aides, and two more were coming up behind him, leaving the rest of the party to stare anxiously at the archway. Matt gave the man his best idiot's smile. "I came to worship, effendi."

"Did you now!" The Tartar stared at him narrow-eyed, searching his face for a sign of malice. Apparently he was a better horseman than an intriguer, for he pushed Matt away with a grunt. "Well, there will be no more praying this day! Away with you now!"

"Don't let him go so easily," his mate objected. "We could do with a little fun."

Matt went cold inside.

"Aye, an Arab like the ones who beat us today!" The third aide spun Matt about and slammed a fist into his belly. Matt doubled over, pain making him limp, as the man stepped aside for another, who straightened Matt with an uppercut. Matt saw stars, heard a roaring in his ears, felt the blow to his chest, then heard the howl of pain. When the stars cleared, he realized he was leaning against the wall of the mosque, and the man who had hit him was still howling, shaking a hand that was beginning to blister with an ugly burn. His comrades stepped in, faces stormy, to finish the job, but one thought surfaced through Matt's sea of pain. He reached into the robes over his breast and drew forth the wand, crying,

"Befriend me!
Defend me!"

The wand spat sparks, a fountain of sparks that set the Tartars' clothes on fire. Matt stood staring, mind beginning to work again as he watched the men hopping about howling, swatting at burning patches of cloth in a sort of dance.

"Quickly! Follow!" said a mewing voice.

Mind triumphed over matter, or at least pain, and Matt remembered who spoke with meows. He turned and stumbled after Balkis.

At the back of the mosque the cat stopped by a small door, barely large enough for Matt, and said, "I have found it—but can you open it?"

"I think so." Matt jabbed the wand into the keyhole. They heard a muffled explosion, then silence broken only by the howls of burning Tartars. Matt pulled the wand out—and the door swung open.

"Quickly!" Balkis urged. "Those Tartars will come for you soon, and their burns will bring them with rage!"

"They'll be in hot pursuit," Matt agreed, and stepped through the doorway. He pulled the panel shut behind him and groped down the darkness of a passageway. Behind him, he heard angry shouts and boots clattering on pavement; then the noises faded.

"Quickly!" Balkis' voice hissed ahead of him. "Why are you so slow?"

"Some of us can't see in the dark," Matt grunted. He felt doorways to either side of him as he moved on down the passage and wondered what behind-the-scenes facilities he was passing—wondered also if they were original, or a conqueror's additions.

Then he could see light in the archway at the end, and stepped out into the vast open space of the mosque.

He was behind the old Arab's throne, in an excellent position to see the junior sorcerer's face where the man knelt over his master, sprinkling powders and chanting verses. Matt's hair tried to stand on end, for he understood the words the man was saying. He was trying to bring the dead back to life, to summon the soul that was already gone.

And it came. Air thickened above the corpse, and the old Arab's face appeared. The junior sorcerer took one look and flinched away, screaming, hands raised to block the vision from his sight.

Matt wondered what could be so horrible. Then the vision became completely clear, and he saw the flames that wreathed the head.

"Look upon me, Gasim, as you wished to do," the hollow voice bade the junior sorcerer. "See the torment with which Ahriman rewards his followers!" Suddenly the head tilted back and an unearthly scream ripped from its mouth. "I . . . I shall not, my master!" the ghost gasped. "I shall speak no truth, I shall . . . shall . . ."

"Who . . . who has brought you to this pass?" Gasim cried.

Matt knew what was coming. He pulled out the wand and ran toward the man.

The ghost materialized an arm and hand, spearing out at an impossibly backward angle at Matt. "They did!"

Gasim looked up, face working in fear and anger. He raised his hands and began to chant.

"I shall take the younger!" Balkis stood beside him in human form. She pulled the wand from Matt's hand and pointed it toward the living man, chanting a quick verse in Allustrian. Matt heard the man shout, but he didn't stop to look, only turned to the ghostly face, trying to ignore the hollow eyes and the grimace of pain as he shouted,

> "The day doth daw,
> The cock doth craw,
> The channering worm doth chide.
> 'Gin you must be back to your place,
> In sair pain ye maun bide."

The face screamed again, leaning back—and back, and back, till it was only a line of darkness, then gone.

Matt whirled around to see Gasim flat on his back, arms wrapped about his chest, legs crossed, lips working but making no sound. Balkis stood over him, brandishing the wand like a club. "What shall we do with him?"

"Get him out of here before those Tartars get curious about the screaming!"

Even as he said it, five stocky shapes darkened the doorway.

They saw only a man, a girl, and their own sorcerer lying supine. Scimitars hissed out, and they came on at the run.

Matt grabbed Balkis' wrist with his free hand. "Quick! Get a hand on that sorcerer!" He swirled the wand to draw an imaginary circle around the three of them, chanting,

> "Oh, to be in a brook's grove now,
> Where the lowest branch and the brushwood sheaf
> 'Round the elm tree bole are all in leaf,
> While the chaffinch sings on the orchard bough!"

The mosque started to grow dim around them. The shouts of the Tartars came closer and louder, but so did the roaring in Matt's ears. A hand seemed to touch his arm, then instantly let go, and he thought he heard a scream fading into the distance but couldn't be sure. The whole world appeared to heave and tilt, and so did his stomach, but he managed to choke it down.

Then things steadied, sunlight enveloped him, he heard something chirping nearby, and he staggered, then caught himself.

Balkis didn't. She overbalanced and fell into the mud beside the brook.

Matt dropped to a knee and helped her up. "Sorry. That's the roughest ride I've had yet. Must have been the aura of sorcery in the place." Then he broke off, staring, and bit his lip to keep from laughing, for though her veil was clean, Balkis had fallen with her face in the mud.

She wiped it off with both hands. "Faugh! What manner of place is this?"

"Oh, a really pretty place, once we're here." Matt's knees suddenly went weak; he sat down. "The brook makes very pretty music, too. It's just that it has muddy patches here and there."

Balkis looked around her and saw the beauty of the mountain wall rising a hundred yards away across a meadow filled with wildflowers. Matt thought of mentioning that she still had mud on her nose and around her mouth to her chin, but just then she breathed out a sigh that turned into a shudder.

"Yes. It is pretty, very. And so clean, after the sink of depravity into which the barbarians have made of that city!"

"We have not!"

They turned to look. The barbarian sorcerer was struggling to sit up. "We shall purge, cleanse the earth of unbelievers! We shall conquer all, and thus put an end to these silly wars! We shall put an end to the fairy-tale notions of any god but Ahriman, and extirpate their foolish notions of right and wrong!"

Matt stared at him. "You don't really believe any of that!"

"Wh-What?" Gasim's voice faltered as he tried to make the question a demand. "How can you argue with Ahriman?"

"How can you believe him?" Matt retorted. "Don't you know he's the Prince of Lies?"

"That is a vile rumor put about by his enemies!"

"You just saw somebody who knows firsthand how badly Ahriman lied to him," Matt said grimly. "Arjasp told him Ahriman would give him eternal luxury for his service, didn't he?"

"So he will!"

"Sure, the luxury of central heating," Matt said with full sarcasm, "only the old priest gets to be in the center of the heat."

"A vile lie!"

"It was a vile lie indeed, to promise him pleasure and give him pain—and when he tried to tell you the truth about it, he found out that no matter how bad the pain was, it could get worse. It could always get worse."

"An illusion you conjured up," Gasim accused, but he wouldn't meet Matt's eyes.

"No, you did the conjuring," Matt reminded him. "Is it my fault that you got what you asked for?"

"It must be your fault!" Gasim cried. "You must have sent a glamour instead of a true summoning! How you did it, I know not—but you must have!"

"I didn't," Matt said sternly, "and you know it. Think, Gasim—it's not too late. Your boss put himself into Ahriman's power. He declared himself to be the Liar's man, to do the Destroyer's work. You don't have to let that happen. You can turn away from the Prince of Lies, turn to Ahura Mazda. Ahriman has no power over you unless you give it to him."

Uncertainty shadowed Gasim's eyes; for a moment his face was gaunt with fear. Then he summoned bluster to drown his doubts. "It is you who speak untruths! Your power that you wish me to accept! Ahriman will blast you, will fry you, will turn you to ashes!" He lifted his hands to start spell-casting. "And I shall begin it! I shall seal you into a prison that shall endure a thousand years!"

Balkis snatched the wand from Matt and leveled it at Gasim. She started to chant in Allustrian.

But Matt didn't want a charred corpse, he wanted information. "Prison? Don't make me laugh! Either of us has more than enough magic to break out of any prison you could think up! Don't we, lass?"

Balkis broke off her chant to stare up at him as though he were mad—but she saw the calculating look in his eye and said, "Aye. Why, we can summon a djinna, and any of the djinn could break from a prison wrought by Ahriman's magic."

It was a great thought, and Matt picked up on it instantly. "Yeah! Any of the djinn, even a baby! After all, any prison of Ahriman's must be just another one of his lies, a mere illusion!"

"It is you who lie, ignorant warlock!" Gasim dropped back out of hysterics into vindictiveness. "Why, even now we hold two djinn children in a prison wrought by Arjasp's magic!"

"A prison for djinn?" Matt scoffed. "Maybe in a city, maybe in Persia where there are cities thousands of years old—but in Tartary, far out in the midst of the central plains, where their idea of a city is a collection of tents?"

Gasim blanched. "How did you know where the babies are?"

"We didn't." Matt grinned. "It was just a guess. But we do know now. How about the two mortal babies with them?"

"What about them?" Gasim frowned.

Matt's spirits soared—Pay dirt! But he kept his poker face on. "Oh, sure! Sure you've got four full-sized babies in there together! And what's keeping the kids alive? They have a prison spacious enough for a wet nurse, too?"

"Fool!" the sorcerer spat. "Do you think we would risk the death of such valuable hostages?"

Matt almost went limp with relief, but he forced himself to

stay upright and sarcastic. "Why not? You're going to kill them anyway. Their parents will never let Evil conquer the world just to save their babies."

Doubt flickered in the sorcerer's eyes, but he said, "If their parents do not go back to their homeland as they promised, we will slay one of the infants. We will not have to slay the boy."

The thought of his baby daughter dead turned Matt's stomach so much he almost collapsed then and there— almost. "So you're keeping them alive by magic."

"Of course," Gasim said, his sneer comfortably back in place. "Do you really need to have this explained, foolish one? The prison itself provides for them." Then Gasim frowned, suddenly realizing they had stayed on the topic for an unusual amount of time. "Why are you so concerned with these babes?"

"It could be simple professional curiosity," Matt hedged.

"Or it could be because he is the father of two of them," Balkis snapped, "and the djinna we can summon is the mother of the other two."

Gasim's face convulsed with terror, but as quickly turned back into a sneer. "Oh, verily! A princess of the Marid will come at your beck and call!"

"So he knows which djinn babies they are, too," Matt said softly.

"You are too patient," Balkis snapped. "Let us find a quicker way to learn all he knows." She lifted the wand.

Gasim cringed away, but started gesturing and rattling out an Arabic verse.

Matt laid a hand on Balkis' arm. "No, I think it'll be more speedy to let him meet the worried mother."

> "Marid princess, attend and hear us,
> For we do hold a foe who may be
> One who knows of your sweet babies.
> But who won't tell—he doesn't fear us!"

Gasim broke off his verse as a whirlwind sprang up to tower over him. He cringed, covering his head with his arms. The whirlwind shrank down to the size of a dust-devil, its

winds slowing until its dust dropped away, revealing Lakshmi, human-sized, slowing in her final pirouette. The sorcerer cried out in terror, trying to scramble away.

Lakshmi jumped to conclusions and advanced on him,
blood in her eye.

"No!" Matt cried. "He can't tell you much if he's in
pieces!"

"True," Lakshmi said, "but if he knows aught of my children, be sure he shall speak." She darted forward, zagging
when Gasim zigged, and held him up by the back of his collar.
Gasim writhed, his neckline digging into his windpipe, his
face turning an interesting shade of mauve.

"All he knows is hearsay," Matt said quickly. "Right,
Balkis? . . . Balkis?" He looked about, in a sudden panic because the girl had disappeared. Then he thought to look
down, and sure enough, there sat a small black-and-white cat
with a brown nose and chin. Matt remembered the mud and
was sure who she was. "Great! So you'll have to take it all on
my word!"

"I trust you," Lakshmi said, "now." She regarded the wriggling sorcerer. "What does he know?"

"Uh, you'll never hear it if he chokes to death."

Lakshmi turned to him, frowning. "But he cannot utter
spells if his throat is pinched!"

"True, but he can't breathe, either," Matt pointed out. "Let
him down and ask him, okay? You can always kill him later, if
you don't like his answers."

"I will like the truth!" Lakshmi dropped the man into a
pitiful heap. "Or, more to the point, I will accept the truth
whether I like it or not, and let him live!"

Gasim rolled to his knees, groveling. "Spare me, O Fairest
of the Fair! I abjure Ahriman and all his lies! From this moment forth I shall speak only truth, and devote myself to
Ahura Mazda all my days!"

Rumbling sounded all about them, and the ground trembled.
Matt fell, but Lakshmi dropped to her knees, digging her
hands down through the grass into the soil, and chanted a
verse in Arabic—a long verse, but the longer it went on, the
less the ground shook. When the earthquake stopped, the
djinna came to her feet again, dusting her hands. "That was

partly magic and partly prayer—to Allah, the Source and Creator of all. Your conception of Ahura Mazda is but an imperfect understanding of the One God. Still, through the mirror of your Lord of Light, you do look upon the True God. If you seek safety from Shaitan—no matter that you call him Ahriman—if you seek safety, I say, surrender yourself to Allah, and testify that there is no god but God, and that Mohammed is His prophet!"

"I . . . I will surrender, as you say," Gasim gasped, staring up at her in awe.

Lakshmi's severity seemed to lessen a bit. "Then you shall be safe from the Prince of Lies and his works. Tell me now, unworthy one, what you know of my children."

"I . . . only know what I have heard from the high priest of Ahriman, here in Baghdad, O Marid," Gasim babbled. "The babes are hidden away together, in a place known only to Arjasp the high priest. That is all my master told me!"

Lakshmi was silent for minutes, and Gasim began to tremble again. At last the djinna reached out and prodded him with a toe, none too gently. "Would we learn more if we gave him a bit of pain?"

"No!" yelped the former sorcerer. "I have foresworn Ahriman and his lying ways!"

"I don't think he did know anything more," Matt agreed. "He was too quick to boast. If he'd had anything else to bargain with, he would have used it then."

Lakshmi glowered down at the miserable ball of a man. He glanced up, saw her expression, gasped, and buried his face again.

"I think I shall let him live," the djinna said, "but I cannot speak for my husband. Go, man, and go quickly, as far from this place as you can!"

"I—I go, Princess!" Gasim scrambled to his feet and backed away, bowing. "Ever shall I acclaim your mercy! Ever shall I pray that you prosper! Ever shall I—"

"Ever shall you go, and speak of the mercy of Allah wherever you find yourself!" Lakshmi snapped. "Begone!"

Gasim gulped down his last thank-you and fled.

Lakshmi watched him go. "How long do you think his conversion will last?"

"Ordinarily, I would have said until he made it back into the city, and among the barbarians again," Matt said judiciously, "but considering the fright you gave him, I have a notion he'll bypass Baghdad and keep on going until he comes to a mosque that hasn't been desecrated. I think this is one conversion that will last, Princess."

"Will he be able to stop wandering?" asked a mewing voice.

Lakshmi looked down. "Are you there, little friend?" She considered. "Perhaps not. I may have cursed him with lifelong fleeing. If so, he may count himself lightly punished." She looked more closely at the little cat and frowned. "What has happened to your face?"

The cat stared back at her. "I do not know. What has?"

"Just a little accident," Matt explained to Balkis. "You didn't get all the mud off. It's a problem that has a very simple solution, the next time you change back to a human."

"What solution is that?" Balkis demanded.

"Soap and water." Matt turned to Lakshmi. "Maybe we should tell your husband about this?"

"Aye, at once!" Lakshmi said. "Then off we shall go, to Kharakhorum. Come!" She caught Matt with her right arm and Balkis with her left as she swelled, growing huge, tucking them both against her bosom and springing into the sky.

"Oh-h-h-h-h . . . here we go again!" Matt wailed.

Balkis simply curled up in the crook of Lakshmi's arm and stared down, watching the landscape rush by, fascinated all over again.

Half an hour later the bosom against which Matt was cuddled was significantly harder, and it was Marudin's bulging arm that held him. Balkis had elected to stay with Lakshmi, and Matt was rather grateful not to have to endure her claws.

"I shall be forever in your debt for discovering the whereabouts of my children, mortal man," Marudin's voice rumbled.

"My pleasure," Matt called back. "Just remember, we haven't found them yet. We're only a little closer, that's all."

"I shall remember," Prince Marudin promised.

A huge bellow sounded all about them. Marudin rocked,

then spun; the world went whirling past them, and Matt found himself falling, the djinni's arm gone. He looked up and saw the jagged peaks of the Hindu Kush Mountains, thousands of feet below but racing up at him. He howled for help, but the wind tore his words away as he fell and kept falling.

CHAPTER 23

A huge hand slid into his field of view, horny palm up and wide enough to park a truck. Matt squirmed, trying to writhe away from it, but the huge palm followed him. He smacked into it and saw stars again. He just had time for the crazy thought that he should qualify as an astronomer when his body sent his brain the message that it was one big ache—but his brain forgot that message in panic as huge fingers closed over him and the whole world rang with a very nasty laugh.

His stomach could tell he was going up; then the fingers opened to show him the ugliest face he'd ever seen. Huge eyes bulged beneath a grimy turban with scarcely any forehead separating them. The nose would have looked nice making furrows in a field, and the grinning mouth was mostly notable because of the two huge tusks where lower eyeteeth should have been, tusks that stabbed upward and a jaw that sank downward, opening a maw like the back of a garbage truck, both in size and smell. The hand holding Matt swung him toward that mouth . . .

"Unhand him!" cried Lakshmi's voice, and slender fingers slipped between mouth and man to catch Matt as he slid. The djinna's fist closed about him, swinging him aside, but he could see between her knuckles as she backhanded the ugly djinn with her right. He flipped backward and kept flipping as Lakshmi tucked Matt against her bosom, as usual, and dove earthward with Balkis sinking her claws into Matt and yowling every inch of the way.

Lakshmi swung down for a landing somewhat rougher than customary, telling them, "It is a monster of an afrit, and an unbeliever, one who still worships only himself and has not come to believe in Allah. But he knows not what he has

284

set upon. We shall put him to rights soon enough." Then she shot back up into the sky.

Watching, Matt saw that Prince Marudin and the afrit had squared off against each other and were trading blows— boulders, fireballs, thunderbolts, all conjured from nowhere. But the afrit was clearly getting the worst of it—each of Marudin's blows sent him reeling backward in the sky, sometimes flipping toes over turban, whereas Marudin advanced upright and steadily.

Then Lakshmi hit the afrit, and hit him hard.

He was just finishing a flip caused by a giant toadstool. Lakshmi caught him by the heels and began to swing him around. The creature bawled with terror as she swung him faster and faster, a virtual blur, and it must have been his own imagination, Matt thought, but he could have sworn the afrit was beginning to come apart in the middle.

Marudin floated nearby, watching judiciously. Just as it seemed the afrit was about to be subdivided, he pronounced, "Enough."

Lakshmi let go, and the afrit went flying, to slam spread-eagled against a mountainside. Marudin and Lakshmi were instantly upon him, materializing bronze spikes and hurling them to strike deep into the rock at either side of wrist and ankle, pinning the afrit in place.

Prince Marudin wiped a hand across a bleeding mouth, and the wound healed. "How shall we punish this fool of an unbeliever, my love?"

"For the audacity of attacking two Marids?" Lakshmi answered. "Shred his essence and scatter it to the winds! Let him be a century putting himself back together, if he can."

"A good thought." Marudin drifted closer to the rock, hands out to shred.

"Punish me not at all!" the afrit bleated. "I had no choice in what I did! I am set here by a magic greater than my own, to stop all who may seek to pass the Hindu Kush!"

"No, wait." Lakshmi reached out to stay her husband's hand. "I have suffered such a fate myself. If 'tis true, 'tis not his fault."

Marudin frowned, drifting in to inspect the afrit closely.

His nose wrinkled. "It is true; I smell the stench of foul magicks even here!"

"Who stationed you so?" Lakshmi demanded.

"A mortal clad all in dark blue," the afrit told them. "He bound me by the power of a ring!"

Lakshmi frowned. "Was he old or young?"

"Old, very old! White hair and beard!"

"Was he Hindu, Arab, Persian, or Afghan?"

"An Arab, most clearly!"

"I think he is dead," Lakshmi informed the afrit. "At least, one such sorcerer is gone to his doom." She turned to Marudin. "Let us leave him here; he will work his way loose soon enough. We shall bid the wizard free him from his binding to these mountains."

"But what shall protect me from more of these mortals' spells?" the afrit protested.

"Islam," Lakshmi replied, "surrender to Allah. Become a believer, and the minions of the Prince of Lies shall lose all magical power over you." She turned away and dove down toward the earth.

Marudin lingered long enough to say, "Never again be such a fool as to attack a Marid." Then he followed his wife.

They shrank to human size as they landed, to find Matt bemused and awed.

Balkis, on the other hand, had found a pool of water in the rocks, fed by the last rain, and was washing her face—in human form.

"What make you of this, Lord Wizard?" Lakshmi demanded.

"A narrow escape," Matt said fervently. "I'm just glad I was traveling with you two."

"That, of course," Lakshmi said impatiently, "though you should have known we would never let you come to harm."

"Oh, I do! It's just a little hard to remember when you're in free fall."

"Be mindful of my debt to you, when next you fear," Marudin advised. "What say you of this afrit, though? Why was he set here to stop all who sought to cross these mountains?"

"Isn't it obvious?" Matt asked, surprised. "Arjasp is afraid of magic workers coming anywhere near his barbarians."

"So I thought, too," Lakshmi said with grim satisfaction.

"We go not only toward our children, but also toward the center of these invaders—the throne, and the power behind it."

"It also tells us that Arjasp isn't all that sure he can win against us," Matt said. "At the very least, this gives him warning we're coming."

"How can he know that it is we who come?"

Matt shrugged, and Balkis said, "He knows it is folk whose magic can match his own. Who else could it be?"

"Very true." Matt looked down at the teenager. "Though to be honest, I don't think he knows about you."

Balkis stared at him in alarm. "Do not think that I can do more than I can!"

"We shall not," Lakshmi promised her, "but I take his point: that sometimes even a small magic may win a battle, if it is sent at the right time and place, and the enemy knows nothing of it."

But Balkis still looked scared. At least, being in human form, her fur wasn't standing on end.

Back in the air, with the Hindu Kush unreeling below them again, Lakshmi confided, "I expected fretting and anxiety mixed in with the joys of parenthood, but never such as this!"

"I know what you mean," Matt sighed. " 'He who hath a wife and babes, gives hostages to Fortune.' "

Balkis looked up sharply. "Is that where the babies are? With Fortune?"

"Uh . . . well, not literally," Matt tried to explain. "The first part is a metaphor, you see—ascribing the characteristics of one thing to another. The second part is a personification, pretending 'Fortune' is a person, not a thing, and—"

"Nonsense!" Lakshmi declared. "If you can ascribe it, then Fortune can indeed be a person, not a pretense! Does she not govern all our lives? Or at least weight them heavily. Nay, let us go and find her!" She raised her voice. "Marudin! A new trail! Follow!"

"Don't be so literal!" Matt cried. "Fortune's a concept, not a person!"

But Lakshmi said, "Not in this world. Let us go to find this Fortune." Again she called out, "Husband, aid me!"

Then she spun into a whirlwind, chanting a verse in Arabic,

voice rising higher and higher. Nearby, Marudin's voice underscored hers with the same words.

"No, wait!" Matt protested. "It was only a figure of speech, a—" Then he broke off, clamping his jaws shut against nausea.

Djinn and djinna chanted, and the world whirled about Matt and Balkis. They were lost inside a multicolored tornado. Balkis, becoming a cat again, yowled and sank in her claws. Matt was glad he'd thought to wrap his robe about his arm this time. Then all he could think of was trying to hold down his last meal as the tornado churned about him, rising, rising interminably . . .

. . . then suddenly fell. The whirling slowed and stopped, the scenery steadied around them, and Matt was glad somebody had taken the overdrive off the merry-go-round. Even more slowly, his stomach stopped churning and settled back into place.

Even through his queasiness, habit and caution made him survey his surroundings. They were mostly a blank, gray, curving wall, though as he turned farther, he saw stalactites and stalagmites, some joining to form pinch-wasted pillars. At least he knew he was in a cave.

Then he heard the singing.

"I think I'd better get down," he whispered to Lakshmi.

"Can you stand?" she asked.

"Only one way to find out."

Lakshmi let him down by shrinking down to human size, spilling him out of her arms as she went. Balkis abandoned ship, took a few wobbling steps that grew steadier with every paw-padding, and prowled ahead toward the light that came through the assortment of stone icicles and columns ahead of them. Matt tried to follow, but stumbled. Lakshmi caught his elbow and held him up; someone else caught his other elbow. He looked up, surprised, to see Prince Marudin smiling down at him. Matt tried to grin back, took another step, and within ten paces was walking unaided.

As quietly as they could, they followed the sound of singing and the light.

The contralto was singing in several minor keys, which made things interesting if painful to hear. Matt reminded himself that scales and modes were cultural variables and tip-toed ahead, following a curve in the cave. As he came around it, he stopped, staring in astonishment.

The cave opened out into a large chamber, perhaps thirty feet by sixty. An older woman with a head of wild, light-colored curls stepped forward to a multitude of spinning disks fixed to the wall. She stopped half a dozen of them, drew out darts, then set them each spinning again. She backed away, surveying the collection. The whole wall was filled with such disks, all spinning, though Matt couldn't make out the markings on them. With a nod of satisfaction, the woman raised a dart and sighted along it. She was perhaps in her fifties, and heavy enough to have a double chin and jowls. She wore a great deal too much makeup, cheeks very obviously rouged, eyelashes even more obviously false. Her frowzy hair was so bright a yellow that it seemed to owe more to chemistry than to Nature, and the way the curls were coming undone and straggling spoke of a similar debt to curling papers and irons. She wore cloth draped in a style that might have been Greek or Roman, but might also have been a hodgepodge of ancient fashions, and her singing was some-times tuneless, sometimes wordless, sometimes bewitching in its loveliness, sometimes filled with poetry and wonder, sometimes completely empty.

The beldame hurled the dart. It struck one of the disks with so sharp a sound that it was clearly going to stay. She clapped her hands, exclaiming with delight, then picked up another dart and sighted for another throw.

"Can this be the dame herself?" Lakshmi hissed in disbelief.

"It can," Matt said with resignation. "Fortune isn't what it used to be, you know."

When she had thrown all the darts, Fortune strode over to the disks to inspect her handiwork more closely. She nodded, chuckling, pleased with the results, then suddenly frowned and clucked her tongue, shaking her head. With a shrug and a sigh, she started choosing darts to pull out and darts to leave in—but as her hand touched one that had lodged in a rather small disk, she looked, then looked again and stared, mouth dropping open. She shut it with a snap and whirled, setting her hands on her hips and staring directly at Matt. "How dare you seek to spy out the workings of Fortune!"

"I have to," Matt said. "I'm in politics." He frowned and stepped out from the maze of stalactites. "How could you tell I was here just by looking at your targets?"

"You are one of the folk in this complex!" Fortune pointed to the little wheel. "I could see that a chance remark had made you come visit me!"

A chance remark? Well, yes, he supposed that line from Shakespeare fitted that description.

"How did you think to find me?" the dame demanded.

"We did not think," Lakshmi said, "only acted."

The beldame frowned in thought, then nodded. "That is a way to find me, yes—in fact, you'll find little else by such deeds, save perhaps Doom and Disaster."

Matt shuddered. "I'd rather not make their acquaintances, if you don't mind."

"Would you not?" Fortune asked in surprise. "But you have come close to them so often."

Matt shuddered; she confirmed what he had suspected. "Uh, any ideas on how to avoid their company?"

"Do you truly wish to?" Fortune's gaze strayed, becoming misty-eyed and nostalgic. "The dear lads! We were so close once—still are, really . . . Well!" She turned back to Matt, and to the moment. "Avoid them? Then avoid me! Or build a stout hedge between yourself and myself, if you can!"

"If," Matt said with a shiver. "How do you recommend I do that?"

"Oh . . . become a boon companion of Prudence and Forethought." Fortune made a face at the mere thought of the two. "A dull pair indeed! You know the ways—save money and goods; invest wisely in the present so that you may build a fortune in the future; make friends, doing favors for one another, so many friends that you become a community . . ."

"Find security," Matt summarized, then bit his tongue. "Sorry. I didn't mean to mention your enemy."

"Oh, Security is no enemy of mine." Fortune dismissed the remark with a wave. "Indeed, Security is not a person, but a sort of castle you mortal folk seek to build, and I have the most delightful time trying to knock it apart, which I sometimes can.

Of course, those who become bosom friends with Prudence have her strength to buttress their walls, and though I can shake their castles, I can knock down very few of them . . ."

"But you have pulverized mine," Lakshmi said, face darkening, "shattered my walls and stolen my children! Where are they, rapacious one? Tell, or we shall measure the power of the djinn 'gainst those of Chance!"

"No, not Chance." Fortune shook her head with certainty. "You would not want to meet him; he lives in a cavern nearby, and has the teeth of a shark and the tentacles of an octopus; even I cannot stand against him, and you? Or any creature of the waking world? No, no, poor lass! Do not so much as think of it!"

Lakshmi's head snapped back in shock; then her eyes brimmed with tears. "Where are they, then? If 'tis you who have sundered them from me, then 'tis you who can tell me where they are! Do, I pray thee, or I shall have to confront this Chance of whom you speak."

"Not Chance, never Chance, never." Fortune came fluttering toward her, arms out to embrace. "Poor dear, poor bereaved lass!" She folded the unwilling djinna into her arms. "Courage, though, for you have regained the husband who was stolen from you already. Ah, if I could tell you where your babes are, I would, but even I know only that Arjasp has spirited them away to Central Asia, and there hidden them—but where I cannot say, for 'twas done with Shrewdness and Care, whose cloaks shield all from even my eyes!"

She released Lakshmi, plucking a handkerchief from her bosom and offering it. Lakshmi took it and dabbed at her eyes, pleading, "Tell me, then, since you can see what is to be—will my babes still be in that same hiding place when I find Arjasp?"

"You will not find him—he will find you, for he summons you through your little ones," Fortune said regretfully. "As to seeing the future, no, I cannot. I have some role in making it, but I cannot see it, for I throw my darts blindly and know not where they will land until I hear them bite into my targets—and it will be some time yet ere I throw the darts for the balance of your quest. I cannot even yet say whether you will come to Arjasp's court with your companions." At the concluding word, her gaze drifted and her eyes filled; she took another handkerchief from her bosom and pressed it to her nose as she sniffled. "Companions! Ah, would I could have some! 'Tis a lonely life, you know, being Fortune."

"Surely there must be some among those whom you have blessed who would be delighted to visit with you, at least!" Lakshmi protested.

"Few." The tears were running freely now. "Those whom I have most favored believe in me least—and even those who do, have not the magic to come to me. You, now, you have the magic, but I may not favor you, for my wheels spin and the darts land where they will, so in a few weeks time you, too, may hate me!"

"Surely you could take better aim," Lakshmi argued.

"I can take aim, yes." Fortune nodded. "Sometimes that aim holds true. But there are sudden gusts through my cave, from the cavern next to mine—the Winds of Chance—and no matter how carefully I choose, Chance may deflect my darts whenever he wishes."

"Try, at least," Matt urged. "If we aren't too sunk in gloom at the end of our quest—" He let the sentence hang while he gave Lakshmi a questioning glance; she nodded. Matt turned back to Fortune and finished the sentence. "—we'll stop and visit on our way back, if we're not too glum to be good company."

"You will? Oh, bless you, my friends!" The tears dried on the instant, and Fortune seized a throw rug from its place between two stalactites. She gave it a shake, letting it float to the ground. "Come, let us share a bite and a sip before we part!"

The rug landed in place, revealing a silver service laid out for tea, with small trays of tempting biscuits and sandwiches—cucumber, cheese and tomato, and chicken salad. Fortune glanced up at them and misinterpreted their amazement. She clapped her hand over her mouth, then took it away to say, "Oh, my! I had forgotten! Arabian, not English!" She seized the rug, gave it a shake. It snapped in a wave, and when it settled, the service had changed to a small brass pot with a wooden handle protruding from its side, brazen demitasses, and a collection of small brass plates holding little squares of Turkish Delight and baba-au-rhum.

Lakshmi gave a glad cry, and Matt closed his eyes as he inhaled the fragrance—but Balkis shied away, eyeing the service warily.

"Do you not like it?" Fortune asked anxiously.

"Love it!" Matt dropped down cross-legged next to the rug. "You just got yourself a guest!"

Fortune smiled with relief and sat gracefully across from him—and Matt realized that she must have lost twenty pounds at least, her gown seemed to have stabilized along classical Greek lines, and her frowzy curls had settled into a neat coiffure. She poured, asking, "What do you think of the weather over the Hindu Kush?"

"Over it is fine," Matt said. "On it is another matter. The southern slopes seem to be getting a lot of rain, which is fine for India, but the Afghans could probably use a bit more moisture on the northern side."

"Ah, the poor Afghans!" Fortune sighed, handing a cup to Lakshmi. "Try as I may to hurl my dart toward rain for them, Chance always blows it aside!"

"They survive, though," Matt said. "A very hardy people. And how has the weather been in Baluchistan this year?"

So it went, a very pleasant half hour, but when they were done and Fortune was lifting the rug to shake the service away, Matt asked, somewhat tentatively, "I don't suppose you could tell me if my children are with Lakshmi's?"

CHAPTER 24

"You did not know?" Fortune looked up in surprise. "I had thought that was why you traveled with her! Yes, most certainly all four children are together! After all, both pair were stolen at Arjasp's behest."

Lakshmi stared a moment, then turned to Matt. "So it would seem that the Lady Jimena was right, wizard, and our two quests are one."

"It would seem so, yes." Matt almost sagged with relief. "Thank Heaven! At least we know where they are now—and, uh, thank you, too, Dame Fortune." Matt had always trusted his mother's insights.

"But I thought you knew." Lakshmi still frowned at him, puzzled. "You said that they were hostages to Fortune."

"Oh, not to me!" Fortune protested. "To Arjasp, yes, but never to me!" Abruptly, though, she reconsidered, turning away, brow puckered in thought. "Well, yes, I suppose you might say that if you have not built your castle of Security high enough or strong enough, I could knock it over quite easily with a throw of a dart—and since it takes a much bigger castle for a family than for a single person, it is that much harder to build it strong enough to resist me. Therefore those who are married and who are parents must do as Fortune dictates, for their castles are too weak to resist me . . . Yes, I see. In that sense, your babies are hostages to me—but they will be all your life! For now, the only one who holds them hostage is Arjasp."

"What do we have to do to get them back?" Matt asked. "Arjasp only required that Alisande leave the Caliph, and she's done that. Me, I'm trying to track them down, but is that enough?"

"It will be now, yes!" Fortune nodded vigorously. "You have made friends with Fortune, wizard, so you need only keep working, keep striving, and sooner or later some of my darts will favor you."

"Maybe we could speed that up a little," Matt said with a slow smile. "How about a game of darts?"

But Fortune only smiled on him with fond pity. "Poor lad, you challenged me to that game the day you were born!"

"Oh?" Matt asked, giving her a leery eye. "How's my score?"

"Like those of most." Fortune shrugged. "You have won some and lost some, and won one great score, though it took a great deal of hard work to consolidate what I had sent you—but overall, you are winning."

"Well, I can't complain," Matt said slowly. "I married a queen, and I have two children whom I love. Seems they're always in peril, though, and that my winnings are very temporary."

"Everyone's are, everyone's are!" Fortune nodded vigorously. "There are one or two who have built enough Security to be safe from my worst darts, but they are rare, rare."

"And I'm not one of them," Matt said with a sinking heart.

"You have insisted on true, passionate love, or nothing," Fortune reminded him. "If you had found nothing, Security would be quite easy to build—but you found true love, and thus set yourself high, where you are exposed to more darts than most. But you have built a different kind of Security, too, not only wealth of belongings, but friends. Indeed, you have helped some people so much that you have become necessary to them—and if they have need of you, they will help you when you have need, and fight to defend you when you are attacked."

"I haven't—" But Matt broke off, thinking of Sir Guy, King Rinaldo, Frisson, Sir Gilbert . . . Could all those people he had helped have come to depend on him?

Yes. They could.

"You see, your true security is other people." Fortune smiled upon him. "The more of them who need you, the more who will aid you in your hour of need, even as you have helped this djinna, and she has helped you—so that now you aid one another again."

Matt and Lakshmi looked at one another as though seeing each other for the first time.

"You, however, have not challenged me," Fortune said to Balkis. "Come, assume your true form! I know you for what you are; there are no secrets from Fortune."

Matt looked away, not wanting a queasy stomach after all those Middle Eastern sweets. When he turned back, Balkis stood in human form, glaring out from under her veil at Fortune. "How do all others challenge you at birth, but I did not?"

"Because your mother took your challenge upon her." A tear formed at the corner of Fortune's eye. "Poor woman, she died for it." Balkis looked stricken, and Fortune stared. "You did not know? Poor child, I did not mean to speak so brusquely then! But yes, she died, but before she did, she set you adrift in a basket, begging the water-spirits to care for you—and so they did, and entrusted you to the dryads, who laid a geas upon you that would compel all magical creatures to treat you kindly."

Lakshmi gave Balkis a sidelong look, reevaluating their relationship.

"So you are one of the few of whom it can be said that you bear a charmed life." Fortune stepped forward, holding out a dart. "Come, take it! You shall see that you cannot throw it amiss."

Warily and with every doubt showing, Balkis took the dart.

"Step up to the line, now." Fortune took her by the elbows and led her into position. "There, now! Throw!"

Still hesitant, Balkis drew her arm back, then hurled the dart. It bit deep into wood, and Fortune bustled over to inspect the wheel in which it had landed. She nodded briskly. "Even as I foretold! You have determined where the three of you will go next." She turned, smiling broadly as though at some inner joke. "Go, then! Off to find your children, parents—and child, off to discover your destiny!"

Balkis still looked wary, but Matt was glad of a way out. He caught her hand and started to turn away—but a pang of sympathy kept him from turning his back on Fortune. "You could, you know . . . if you wanted . . . come with us . . ."

Lakshmi looked alarmed, and Balkis shrank down into a

ball, but Fortune backed away in sheer terror. "Go . . . out? Out of this cavern, you mean? Oh, no, I could not! I dare not, all manner of things might come at me out there, Heaven alone knows what monsters await! Go out? No, never, nay!"

Her voice ended in a scream; she backed up against a wall of rough stone, arms spread wide, fingers clutching at its niches and crevices.

"Okay, okay, it was just a suggestion! An invitation, I mean!" Matt knew a case of agoraphobia when he saw one, even if he'd never seen one before. "Don't worry, nobody's going to make you come with us. You're safe, you can stay here."

"Can I?" Fortune thawed a bit, at least enough to bring her arms down. "I can remain in my cavern, then? But, oh, I miss the outdoors, the wide sky and the rolling plains!" Tears gathered in her eyes. "I so long to see them again—but I dare not."

"You used to live out in the open?" Matt asked, surprised.

"Oh, aye! The herding folk, they thought me a goddess, and every tribe had a hearth for me in their camps. But they ceased, yes, gobbled up by those same barbarians who even now threaten the Caliph, or settled down by a river-fork and built themselves cities, then forgot me. There was no more hearth for Fortune, no more meal-cakes or puddings assured, so I hid myself away here, yes, and made myself wheels to spin, through which I could watch the endless pageant of humankind." She stepped away from the wall, eyes damp with reminiscence. "You are a wonderful species, you know, combining wisdom and folly, courage and cowardice, nobility and vulgarity, and all steps in between." She took a deep breath, let it out in a sigh as she shook herself—spilling her coiffure into frowzy curls and gaining a dozen pounds again—and said regretfully, "No thank you, my friends. I shall stay here."

"As you wish," Lakshmi said, with a smile of sympathy. "We shall try our best to visit again, when we return."

"Yes, do!" Fortune nodded vigorously. "I shall look forward to it. But now, good-bye!" She stepped over to the wall of wheels, stopped one particular disk from its spinning, and stabbed a dart into it without even letting go. A huge blast of wind caught the companions, and Lakshmi barely had time to

catch Matt and Balkis to her breast before she was whirling
about and about in the wind, and the world turned into a kaleidoscope of churning colors again.

When the Technicolor tornado stopped spinning, Matt
looked up and saw down. He was rushing head first toward
the sharpened peaks of the Hindu Kush Mountains again.

"Yikes!" Matt shouted. "This is no improvement! At least
when we left, we were flying level!"

"Oh, be not such a babe!" Lakshmi snapped, disregarding
how she was holding him. Her flight path began to curve and
she called out to her husband, "Marudin! Fly due north!"

The djinni only nodded, lifting his head and, thereby, his
torso, then the rest of his body, swooping in a great curve and
steadying on his new heading.

The mountainside swung from in front of Matt's forehead
down to under his chest, and "before" suddenly became
"below" again. His stomach tried to stick by its preconcep-
tions and stay where it had been, but he choked down the
nausea, accepting it gladly as the lesser of two evils.

He gave the new heading ten minutes or so while he developed the shakes and let them run down, leaving his body limp
as spaghetti. Then he called up to Lakshmi, "Any idea where
we're going?"

"To find this Arjasp's capital," she told him, "or should I
call it a mere headquarters?"

Matt thought it over. "Considering most of his warriors are
nomads, we're probably looking for a collection of tents large
enough to be a small city. The direct route seems a little haz-
ardous to me, though."

"Filled with hazards? What do you mean?" Lakshmi
demanded.

"He knows we're going to be looking for him," Matt explained, "or at the very least, ought to be suspecting it and be
on the watch for it. He'll have spies on the lookout, maybe
even wizards scrying."

"You think he will see us coming, and prepare to defend
against our magic." Lakshmi turned thoughtful. "Still, we
must go where he is. How do you suggest we mislead him?"

"Let him think we're looking for another destination. Land
at some city that's on the way, if you can find one."

"Of course—there is Samarkand." Lakshmi nodded, no longer uncertain. "We shall stop there and visit. Certainly some there will know where this Arjasp's city can be found, and perhaps we can contrive some sort of disguise."

"Maybe we can." But Matt wasn't thinking about the disguise—he was fired with the wonder of it all. Samarkand! One of the fabled cities of the East, rich with the trade of the Silk Road, the caravan route across Central Asia, and he was actually going to see it!

They landed on a hill overlooking the city. It glistened in the morning sun as though it were made all of ivory—cubes of ivory, boxes of ivory, domes of ivory decorated with gold.

Some of those were the bulging and pointed domes of mosques, but others were the half-globe shapes of Christian churches. There were several minarets, but also several steeples, too, and Matt was sure he saw the tiers of a pagoda and the beehive shape of a Buddhist stupa.

"Samarkand!" Matt breathed. "The crossroads of Asia, and it sure looks like it!" He turned to his companions. "Come on, let's get down there and visit!"

"There is a small matter of disguise," Lakshmi pointed out.

"What disguise?" Matt asked. "I'm still dressed as a Persian."

"Indeed!" Lakshmi said archly. "And are Marudin and I to go into that city dressed as we are?"

"Why not?" Matt countered. "You can't be the first Arabs they've seen. If you're worried about the proprieties, don't be—this is Samarkand, not Tehran. Even Muslim women don't have to wear the complete veil here."

"Indeed," Lakshmi said dryly. "What of these spies you spoke of?"

That gave Matt pause.

"She speaks truth," Marudin said. "Surely Arjasp knows that djinn can shrink or grow to any size we wish. His spies will have been told to look for an Arab man and woman clad as a Mameluke and a dancing girl."

"As well as a Frank," said Lakshmi, "but you are right in that you are well enough disguised, and Balkis has always her own guise with her."

Balkis meowed confirmation. Looking down, Matt saw

she was pussyfooting around again. Absently, he reached
down, holding his palm horizontal, and she flowed under it
back and forth for automatic petting. "She's got the best disguise of any of us," he agreed. "Arjasp probably can't keep up
with her shifts in color and markings. But as to you two . . .
Let's see, I suppose I could pass for a merchant; we could
claim I'm carrying semiprecious stones in my robe . . ." He
patted the wand in his sash. "You could, too, Princess, and
Marudin could be our bodyguard. Persian robes all around—
okay?"

"That 'okay' is certainly one of the strangest words in your
language," Lakshmi complained, "but I take its meaning in
this case: 'Is it acceptable?' "

"Close enough," Matt said. "Is it?"

For answer, Lakshmi made a gesture as though drawing a
curtain over herself, and as her hand passed downward, her
bolero jacket became a yellow robe, her harem pants turned
into the ankle-length skirt of a light blue under-robe, her slippers became stout boots, and a turban sprouted from her long
silky tresses. Marudin gave himself a similar gesture and
stood forth in a costume matching hers, except that he wore a
yellow shirt and trousers with a crimson sash instead of a
dress and a sky-blue robe over them.

Matt stood back and eyed them critically. "Okay, I guess
we'll pass. Let's . . . uh, join the traffic into the city." He had
almost said "Let's hit the road," but then remembered that
Lakshmi might take him literally.

They passed through the gate, and Matt inhaled the rich
aromas of cinnamon, cardamom, cloves, and others he couldn't
identify. "Certainly are spice traders here. Well, let's have a
look around, folks."

The "look around" lasted two hours. Even the djinn seemed
amazed at the richness and variety of their surroundings. Far
Eastern architecture stood side by side with Persian and Indian. The bazaar held booth after booth filled with silken cloth
and Chinese carvings; Indian puppeteers acted out stories
from the Mahabharata, and the turbans and caftans of Western Asia mingled freely with the trousers and tunics of the
steppe barbarians, the pyjamas and saris of India, and the

silken robes of China. Booths of lath and canvas stood in the shadows of buildings of alabaster trimmed with gilt and archways decorated with tiles in geometric designs.

The djinn wandered through the town, amazed by its opulence and its poverty both. Matt had to explain who those yellow-skinned, slant-eyed people were, then guess at the differences between Mongols and Chinese. He was able to tell a Turk from a Russian and did, but had difficulty explaining the people of mixed strains, of whom there seemed to be many—people who'd had both Chinese and Turkish parents, like the great Chinese poet Li Po, or Turkish and Mongol forbearers, like Tamurlane, or any of the other rich varieties of people he saw. He was able to identify Hindu traders and distinguish them from Sikh guards, and his recent experiences in India made him able to tell the difference between a Parsi trader and his Guebre cousin, but there were others that put him completely at a loss.

Finally Lakshmi said, "I am wearied, wizard, and dazed with so much looking. We must rest."

"Museum fatigue," Matt identified. "Okay, let's try to find some nice, quiet little residential square where somebody has a booth selling sherbets."

They took to the twisting alleyways, Balkis padding silently along, now in front, now behind, nose twitching at the wealth of scents and, no doubt, trying to find the track of a mouse that hadn't been overlaid with curry. In a few minutes they came out into just such a small, quiet court as Matt had hoped for, one whose quiet was broken only by the merry calls of children at play and the more subdued cry of a sherbet vendor. It was surrounded by dwellings with large patches of stucco missing—and on the side across from the alleyway, a building whose cross over a double door proclaimed it to be a church.

But what a church! Its architecture was definitely Asian, not European. Matt stared. "What kind of Christians worship in there?"

"Go in and find out, Frank," Marudin sighed as he sat down cross-legged in the shade. "But before you do, buy us sherbets, will you not?"

"Me?" Matt fought righteous indignation. "What makes me the waiter here?"

"Because you have coins," Marudin explained, "whereas we should have to conjure some up, and by your leave, we are rather wearied."

"Wearied from having carried you across half a continent," Lakshmi said pointedly.

"Okay, you win." Matt strolled over to the booth and bought three sherbets with his smallest silver coin, and by the grin on the vendor's face, he had obviously overpaid again. He brought them back to the djinn couple, ate a few spoon-fuls of his own, then set it down next to Balkis' nose and turned away to go to church.

The interior was dim and cool, the decorations unfamiliar and Asiatic, but there was a cross over a stone table that was recognizably an altar, and racks of votive candles that might as easily have come from a Chinese temple as from a Catho-lic church. There were no pews, but Matt knelt anyway and said a few silent prayers of thanks for their safety, and for suc-cess in rescuing the children. As he was climbing to his feet again, he saw a man with a gray beard come out by the altar. The man glanced at him, then turned and stared.

So did Matt. The tall hat and dark robe looked suspiciously like those of a priest of Ahriman!

Then Matt blinked, clearing away the illusion. There was a resemblance, yes, but that hat was a cylinder, not a cone with a rounded top, and the long beard looked very familiar. Matt had a sudden memory of a Coptic bishop he had seen on a television documentary. He relaxed—somewhat.

The priest came toward him, puzzled and with an energy that belied his gray hairs. "Good day, Christian."

He spoke a dialect Matt had never heard before, but his translation spell was still working. He hoped it would still work in reverse, and said, "Good day, Reverend Sir. I am not familiar with your sect. Can you tell me what manner of Christian church this is?"

"Ah." The priest relaxed, smiling, as though Matt's words had removed his own question. "Ours is the sect founded by Bishop Nestorius, young man."

"Nestorians!" That explained a lot. Matt had heard that the

Nestorian brand of Christianity was widely spread through Asia, though scattered—that there had even been some churches in China, though most of them were in Central Asia.

"And yourself?"

Matt thought fast, not wanting to give any more clues to his identity than he had to. "I learned my religion from a Christian who came from the Far West, reverend."

"Ah! A Frank! Then your sect are those who follow the Bishop of Rome." The priest nodded. "I have heard of them. Distant and fabled lands, they are. I have seen one or two Franks in the marketplace, but I have never met one before." He frowned, looking more closely at Matt. "You have not the Frankish look, though."

"I have traveled widely," Matt said vaguely. "Tell me, reverend—are there many of your churches in these lands?"

"Some," the priest said, "not many—at least, not this far south. Most of us dwell in the kingdom to the north, where a priest of our own faith rules the land."

"A Christian priest-king?" Matt stared, then caught himself. "Your pardon, reverend. The only Christian priest I've heard of who rules a land is the Pope, whose holdings are small and who never calls himself a king. Who is he who rules this northern land, then?"

"He is called Prester John," the priest said.

CHAPTER 25

Prester John! That explained a lot. He had heard the name, the Oriental Christian king who had been the hope of Europe during the Crusades. Someone had supposedly carried a letter from Prester John to the Emperor of Byzantium, but since he hadn't been able to find Byzantium, he had thoughtfully copied the missive several times and sent on the copies—and other hands had copied the copy, then copied copies of the copy, all of which passed from hand to hand and pen to pen until the emperor finally got the message, along with most of the rest of Europe.

Of course, whether the word the emperor read was the message Prester John had sent was a very open question, since with each copying, the letter had grown, and so had the glory of Prester John and the wonders of his kingdom, claiming that he ruled a land filled with marvels and led an invincible army that, being Christian, would surely attack the Turkish conquerors of the Holy Land from the East, catching them between Prester John's forces and the Crusaders in the West, assuring a Christian victory. Never mind what kind of Christian—any kind was better than the Muslim Turks.

"Prester" was another form of the word "presbyter," the stewards of the early Church. Over the centuries, in the East, it had apparently come to mean "priest," and John, in the finest Oriental tradition, was a priest-king.

All of that was fable, of course, drawn from the deeds of a Mongol prince who had battled a Persian sultan and won. Word of his victory had spread to the West, but become somewhat distorted in the process, so that from having Nestorian Christians in his army—along with Buddhists, animists, and Muslims—he had become himself a Christian, a priest, and a king. When Europeans first heard of the conquests of Genghis Khan, they had been delighted, thinking that at last Prester John had come to rescue the Holy Land from the Muslims. They had been sadly disappointed.

That, however, had been in Matt's home universe, where Prester John was only a fable. Now Matt lived in a universe of fantasy in which trolls and manticores were real, and Prester John was apparently fact, not rumor.

"What . . . what is Prester John's kingdom like?" Matt asked.

"A land of peace and plenty," the priest told him, "where the rivers teem with fish and the crops never fail. The people are industrious and cheerful, living as the early Christians did, with love toward one another and living so closely by Christ's precepts that there is little friction between them."

"But that's not the case with their barbarian neighbors."

"Not at all," the old priest said sadly, "and therefore does Prester John maintain an army that cannot be beaten—or could not, until this accursed Arjasp and his gur-khan began their apocalyptic ride."

"They conquered Prester John?" Matt asked in surprise.

"We know not," the old priest sighed. "No word has come from the North since first the gur-khan began his conquests, for the caravans had to find routes that kept them away from the fighting."

"Which means that even if Prester John is alive and well, his kingdom is suffering a major recession," Matt said thoughtfully.

"Perhaps, but they would scarcely be starving." The old priest smiled. "His granaries are reputed to be as high as mountains, and his supplies enough to last for seven years."

"Are they really?" Matt recognized a literary convention when he heard one. "What about Prester John himself? Is he as splendid as his kingdom?"

"He is said to be heir to the sanctity and wisdom of Saint John the Evangelist, he who wrote the fourth gospel and the Book of Revelations."

"Which is why he's called John?"

The old man smiled. "Perhaps. He is also heir to the crozier of St. Thomas, the evangelist to the Indies and, therefore, the first bishop of the East. Prester John is also said to be descended from the magi, those same wise men who came to kneel before Baby Jesus in His manger."

"Magi!" Matt's eyes opened wide. "A Christian descendant of Zoroastrian priests?"

"Why not?" the old priest asked. "Surely gazing upon the infant Christ would have been enough to inspire them with Christian faith."

"But the gur-khan's wizard Arjasp is preaching a very twisted form of Zoroastrianism—instead of worshiping Ahura Mazda, the Lord of Light, he's worshiping Angra Mainyu—Ahriman—the Prince of Lies!"

The old priest's smile faded. "So I have heard."

"That would make him the natural first target for Arjasp!" Matt dropped his gaze, frowning, thinking. "Either the first or the last—if they thought John's army was invincible, they might have decided to wait until they had conquered everything else before coming after him."

"That is possible." The old priest began to tremble. "Woe for the Elder, if he is beset by enemies on all sides!"

"Yes, he might need a little help." Matt looked back up at the priest. "Thank you for your information, reverend. It will be a very helpful guide on the rest of my journey."

"Yes," the priest said somberly, "to avoid the battleground to the north."

"Yes," Matt said, "or to seek it."

He turned away, but the old man cried, "Stop!"

Matt turned back, reining in his impatience. "There isn't really time to spare."

"Better here than in a Tartar cage." The old priest came closer, peering into his face. "Do you truly mean to go among the Mongols?"

"If I have to," Matt said, "yes."

"Then take these talismans." The priest took two lumps of incense from the candle rack beside him and pressed them into Matt's hand. "They came from Prester John's kingdom—perhaps they will bring the land itself to favor you."

Matt looked down at the incense, mind racing, realizing that the priest could be right. He sniffed the incense and recoiled—

the smoke might be sweet, but the resin itself was sharp and pungent. Nonetheless, he said, "Thank you, reverend."

"I do it gladly. Resume your journey, then, and take the blessing of a priest with you." The priest recited a short verse in a Latin dialect, then said, "Go with God!"

Matt bowed his head and turned away again.

He strode out of the temple and back to his companions. "Sudden change in plans," he told them. "We still head due north, but we're not trying to find Kharakhorum anymore."

"Then where do we fly?" asked Marudin as he and Lakshmi both came to their feet.

"Prester John's capital city," Matt said. "He's supposed to have an unbeatable army. He could be a big help against Arjasp."

"Directly north, where Arjasp's headquarters lie?" Lakshmi stared. "How can he have escaped war with the horde?"

"And if he has fought, what if he has been conquered?" Marudin asked.

"Then Arjasp will have taken over John's city," Matt said, "and it will be the natural place for him to have hidden the kids! Let's go!"

It wasn't hard to tell when they came to Prester John's kingdom. They flew over a mountain range that Matt was sure had never existed in his own world, especially since it was right-angled, the two arms running almost exactly north and east. The eastward arm dropped very quickly into foothills, then sank to a plateau bordered by a glittering river that descended from the mountains. Flying low, they were shocked to see that the river was made of stones, millions of boulders of all sizes, rolling onward as a current. On the southern side of that river was desert; but the northern side was lush with plant life, cut into a patchwork of green and golden crops interspersed with groves of trees. Through them all ran many streams, both marking the boundaries of fields and watering them. In the distance gleamed spires of ivory and gold—but as they crossed the peaks of the mountain range, Balkis' ring blazed.

"Look!" she cried. "It glows!"

"Glows? It's nearly blinding!" Matt shielded his eyes and

called out, "We're a little conspicuous, Princess! Maybe we ought to land and pretend to be ordinary travelers again."

"The caution is wise, but I crave speed!" Nonetheless, Lakshmi·began her descent. "Does that ring speak of djinn who guard our enemy, or of my children?"

"Either way," Matt said, "I think we'll be better able to deal with them on the ground." He remembered the last nosedive brought on by the attack of the border-guarding afrit, and shuddered.

By the time they landed, Lakshmi and Marudin were back to normal human size. Lakshmi set them down, and Balkis, in human form, drew her gauzy veil about her and shivered. "I had not thought 'twould be so cold!"

"We have come to the North, child. Even of a summer's evening, it will be chill." Lakshmi slipped off her yellow robe and wrapped it about Balkis' shoulders. "Take this, and be warm."

"I thank you." Balkis looked up in surprise. "But what of you?"

"Djinn do not feel the cold." Lakshmi smiled. "We are creatures of the warm South, and bear its heat with us. How else do you think I could race through the chill winds of the upper air with only this skimpy vest for a garment?"

"I had not thought," Balkis admitted, and hugged the coat more closely around her. "I thank you for your kindness."

With a pang of guilt, Matt realized he hadn't considered the problem, either. The warmth of Lakshmi's bosom had protected him from the chill of high altitude so well that he'd forgotten the air was supposed to be cold up there.

"Well, let us find a road." Lakshmi and Marudin stepped off with the certainty of those who remembered the terrain from an aerial view. They had landed in a grove by a stream, and she followed the water as the easiest way of moving under the trees.

Matt followed, then looked back to see Balkis moving very slowly, looking about her, dazed. He went back for her, concerned. "What's the matter?"

"It all seems so ... familiar," Balkis said, her voice dreamy, "as though I had been here before, moved by this very stream under these very trees."

"Déjà vu," Matt explained. "It's a trick your brain plays, bouncing back your sensory impressions a split second after they've come in. Sure, you've been here before—about half a second ago."

"Is it truly that?" Balkis wondered, but she let him lead her at a faster pace.

They caught up with Lakshmi and Marudin. Together they walked through the woods, exclaiming over the beauty of the flowers on the bushes set against emerald leaves. They inhaled exotic perfumes and listened, charmed, to the music of the brook—but Balkis moved like an automaton, directed by Matt's grasp, looking about her with a gaze vacant and entranced. The azure sky seemed to burst upon them as they came out of the grove and stepped onto the road with a golden field to their left and trees heavy with fruit to their right. As Matt turned to ask Lakshmi how far she thought the city would be, barbarians burst from the trees.

They were ugly little men with long, pointed moustaches, bald heads ridged with scar tissue, and shaggy ponies under their bowed legs—but they also held sharp swords and screamed like demons as they charged down upon the party.

A sword cleaved into Marudin's left arm, but he caught its owner's wrist with his right hand and yanked the man out of his saddle, then tossed him under the hooves of the next rider's mount. Another slashed at Lakshmi, slicing deep into her turban; she rid herself of it with a toss of her head and grew amazingly, catching the little man around the neck as his horse charged by.

Matt shouted in alarm and leaped in front of Balkis, who blinked, waking from her trance, but another barbarian dashed behind her, slashing at her, the yellow coat tangling about his sword. Balkis came fully awake with a shout like a spitting cat and turned to meet the man with fingernails hooked like claws as he turned his horse to ride back—but Lakshmi picked up one of his companions and hurled both horse and rider. The two men fell in a shouting tangle, too mixed up with their horses to see who had landed on top and who on bottom.

A warrior charged at Matt, howling, curved sword slashing down. Matt sidestepped, reaching for his sword. His hand closed on the wand instead, and the barbarian swerved to track him. In despair, Matt swung up the only weapon he had.

The sword struck it and sparks fountained. The rider shouted in pain and slumped forward onto his horse's neck, unconscious and smoking—but the hilt of the sword struck Matt, sending him spinning. So secure was the rider's seat that the horse galloped a dozen yards before the rider fell.

Matt scrambled to his feet, hand pressed to his aching side, looking about the field frantically—but all he saw was a dirt road running between a field and some trees, with half a dozen Mongols lying on it, unconscious or dead. Several of the horses were, too; the others were still running.

Marudin pressed a hand to his left shoulder, chanting a charm, and when he took his hand away, the flesh was so smooth Matt would never have known he'd been wounded. Lakshmi stood over the fallen men, fuming and cursing in Arabic. Matt hurried to Balkis. "Are you all right?"

"I—I seem to be." She looked up at him, eyes shining with gratitude.

For what? He hadn't protected her. But she was trembling, and he gathered her in, pressing her head into his shoulder and letting the storm of tears break.

As it slackened, he looked up and saw Lakshmi watching him closely, frowning. Well, she could watch all she wanted—he was only comforting a child. Still, he winked at her and nodded. The djinna returned the nod and stepped up to take Balkis from him with an arm around the shoulders, saying, "There now, it has passed, and no worse than toms fighting over a puss! Poor lass, your new yellow coat cut short and ragged. There, there, it is over, and nothing more to fear."

"Thanks," Matt said to Marudin, his voice shaky.

"My pleasure." The djinni prodded the nearest Mongol with his toe. "What offal are these, to fall upon innocent travelers so!"

"Bandits, I expect. Odd, when this land is supposed to be peaceful and prosperous." Matt looked down at the horsemen, then noticed they were all dressed in the same colors. "Your Highness—I think these were soldiers."

Marudin stared, then gave a judicious nod. "They have that look. But why soldiers without a battle?"

"A patrol," Matt said, "to bring in anybody who looks like a threat. They must have seen us coming in for a landing."

Marudin frowned, looking about him. "I see no one who might have witnessed this struggle." He turned back, waving a hand over the Mongols. Coruscating lights seemed to run over their bodies; their forms glimmered and faded away.

Matt stared. "What did you do with them?"

"Sent them to the nearest battle-line, where a few more dead will not be noticed," Marudin said. "These barbarians seem always to have some strife going on somewhere—in this case, far to the east."

"The east? What, are they attacking China, too?"

"It would seem so," Marudin said grimly. "Is there no end to their greed?"

"I think not," Matt said slowly, "and if they're foolish enough to fight a war on two fronts, they deserve what they get." He pursed his lips, thinking. "As you said, probably nobody saw us—but it won't pay us to hang around, either. I still want to take a look at that city."

"I, too," Marudin said.

"Indeed," Lakshmi agreed. "Perhaps we will learn why there were Mongol soldiers riding through Prester John's kingdom!"

They found out even before they entered the city gates, for the soldiers who guarded them were Mongols, watching every traveler with vigilance and suspicion. Matt felt his skin prickle as he went between them, feeling as though they could see the wand beneath his cloak—he'd had the forethought to hide his sword a hundred yards back down the road, as soon as he'd seen the Mongol guards. Lakshmi wore another yellow robe and carried a calico cat—no longer just black and white, but with yellow splotches here and there, especially in a ragged band across her shoulders and back.

As they came through the gate, Matt breathed a sigh of relief. "I think that tells us why there was a Mongol patrol on the road."

"On the road, and in this city." Lakshmi nodded her head at a troop of stocky, bandy-legged men riding by on shaggy ponies. "The folk of the town have a different look entirely."

"Yes, they do." Matt looked about him thoughtfully, studying the civilians. Their skin tone was tan, almost golden, and there was only a hint of a tilt to their eyes. They had heart-shaped faces where the Mongols' were round, and their lips were thicker. Both had high cheekbones, but Mongols had black eyes where some of the citizens had brown, sometimes flecked with gold, and larger than those of the soldiers. Some of the local men wore beards, though most were clean shaven. Dark brown hair was the rule, but here and there he saw light brown and even dark red. He knew that if the Mongols had let their hair grow, it would have been black.

There was something about the look of the locals that tickled Matt's memory. He tried to place the odd feeling of familiarity but had to give it up. He could only note that their physical blending of East, West, and South made them a very attractive people.

So were the buildings they had made. Matt lifted his gaze to the architecture. It was even more wonderful than that of Samarkand. The buildings were taller, with many windows, shutters open now, roofs tiled to channel rain and pitched to shed snow. They were every color of the rainbow, mostly pastels but some in full, rich hues. Most of the color seemed to be worked into the plaster that covered them, but many were tiled in geometric patterns. Some were even decorated with mosaics of tall, peaceful-looking people with halos, magnificent bulls and slender deer, white tigers and black panthers, graceful cranes and fish whose scales fairly glowed in the sunlight. The streets were broad and paved with cobblestones, baked with an ochre glaze that made them appear golden.

If there had been a battle, it left no sign.

He could make out one minaret and the dome of a mosque, and five steeples.

"Why do we linger?" Lakshmi said impatiently. "Either the Mongols have conquered, and your Prester John is dead or fled—or the barbarians are his hirelings, and he awaits us in the palace."

Matt felt a chill. "How can he be waiting for us? He doesn't even know we're coming."

"I had not meant it in that fashion," she snapped.

"No, but it's a point well-taken anyway," Matt said. "We're not the only ones who know magic. Let's go cautiously, friends."

"Well enough, but let us go indeed!"

"That big building must be the palace." Matt nodded toward a distant edifice that towered over the tile roofs of lesser buildings. It glowed royal-blue in the afternoon sun with the gloss of tiles, thousands of tiles. At a rough guess, taking distance into account, it was two hundred feet wide and fifty high. Scores of windows reflected light, which meant they were filled with actual glass, not just parchment or horn.

"Wants plenty of room for guests, I suppose," Matt said.

"Let us hope that we shall not be among them," Lakshmi said darkly.

The street they were on curved, and after thirty yards or so Matt realized that it was an arc, probably a piece of a circle. He kept going until he found a broad avenue that intersected it at an angle close enough to ninety degrees so that he could look down it and see all the way to the palace itself. Other streets intersected it, and as they walked down the avenue, they could see that the side streets also curved. "I think the city is laid out as a series of rings," Matt said, "and each avenue is a radius from the center to the rim."

"But the rim is the wall," Marudin asked, "and the palace is the center?"

"That's my guess."

"We could have known," Lakshmi huffed, "if we had flown over it."

"Yeah, but we're supposed to be incognito," Matt said. "Can't surprise them much if we make that kind of an appearance, can we?"

"Why not?" she said archly. "I doubt not that they already know we are here."

"Hope not." Matt looked around the pavement. "Anyone seen Balkis?"

"Aye, at the last corner," Marudin said, "but she was gone at the corner before that. She comes and goes."

"She explores, as any good cat would," Lakshmi said, "and

there cannot be too much danger here, or she would stay close
by us."

"Yeah, but what's dangerous for us and what's dangerous
for a cat are two different things." However, Matt remembered how Balkis had rid herself of the last importunate tom
and didn't worry too much.

Finally they came to the palace—or rather to the immense
circular plaza that surrounded it. They stood at the southwest
corner, so Matt could see that the building was half as deep as
it was long, and set on a small hill, with a broad staircase
leading up to it. He hoped he wouldn't have to climb up there
very often—there were a hundred steps at least. As he
watched, though, he saw horsemen riding down a ramp from
the back, and decided to try the servants' entrance if he
needed to get in.

The front steps seemed to be largely taken up by shamans
and sorcerers.

At least, Matt assumed they were sorcerers, by the zodiacal
signs and alchemical symbols embroidered onto their robes.
There were also a fair number of Ahriman's priests, to judge
by the dark blue robes and bulge-cone hats. It bothered him
that some of the men were both priests and sorcerers. The
shamans were easier to identify—they were still dressed as
plainsmen in furs and leather, faces painted or masked with
ornate, terrifying leather creations, adorned with feathers and
beads. If shamans they were, they were dressed for business.

"I don't think Prester John lives here anymore," Matt said
slowly.

"Stand aside!" Lakshmi laid a hand on his arm, pulling
him out of the way as a squadron of Polovtsi warriors came
stamping their way behind a gaudily caparisoned officer.

Matt stepped lightly and quickly to his right.

So did the officer. Matt sidestepped again, and the officer
swerved again. Matt decided not to try for the charm and
faced the music, or at least the officer.

The barbarian marched up within five feet of him and
stamped to a halt; his squadron did, too. "You are not the
mere merchants you seem," he accused. Translation spell or
not, his Persian had an atrocious accent.

"Uh, just tourists," Matt ad-libbed, hoping the spell

wouldn't give him such a horrible lilt. "Wanna see the sights, you know—and that castle sure is a big building."

"Do not play the fool!" the officer snapped. "You will come with us!"

"You hoped not to be a guest—but I think we have been invited," Marudin said.

CHAPTER 26

Matt glanced at him and noticed the soldiers had spread out to encircle their little group. Speaking Merovencian, he said, "Why not? We can leave whenever we want to, can't we?"

"If they keep us together, yes," Lakshmi told him.

"I'll stick to you like glue." Matt glanced surreptitiously at the ground and was glad not to see a little calico cat. "Thanks for your kind invitation, hetman. I was wondering where we were going to sleep tonight."

Not that they had time for sleep, of course. After the steps, all hundred of them—with Marudin grumbling under his breath about less taxing modes of transportation, and Matt hissing at him not to say that nasty word "tax"—they were ushered down a series of corridors until they stepped into a room elaborately decorated with frescoes and mosaics showing scenes of heroes fighting monsters, and furnished with Chinese lacquer, Russian inlays, and Persian carpets. The hetman brought them before a barbarian seated cross-legged on top of a desk, leafing thoughtfully through the piles of documents around him. He was such a perfect picture of uncouth ignorance of civilized ways that Matt had to suppress a laugh—until the man looked up and met his eyes. Then the laugh stopped, for the eyes were hard, piercing, and shrewd. Matt realized that this was going to be no easy match, that he would have to talk his best to keep this plainsrider from seeing through him.

"I am Tarik, governor of this city," the official said. "Who are you?"

Matt decided ignorance was the best excuse. He spread his

hands, looking lost and shaking his head. "I don't under-stand," he said in Merovencian.

Lakshmi and Marudin looked just as lost, but without having to fake it. Matt thought it interesting that they, who knew so many languages, hadn't learned Mongol—even Marudin, who had unwillingly been in their service.

Tarik, irked, beckoned a secretary from a desk. The heart-shaped face and golden skin told Matt he was looking at a local, not a conqueror. Again, that sense of familiarity haunted him, but refused identification.

The secretary's hunched posture and subservient bow said quite eloquently that he was one of the conquered. "What do you wish, Excellency?"

"Tell me what language this outlander speaks," Tarik commanded.

The secretary turned to Matt—and the quiet competence of his gaze made Matt suspect that he was determined to make the subservience temporary. "Hail, outlander!" he said in Hindi.

Matt shrugged and shook his head, and the secretary tried Persian, Russian, and several other languages that Matt didn't recognize. When the man hit on Arabic and Lakshmi and Marudin looked up in surprise, Matt decided he had stretched the ruse about as far as it would go. "Hail, Honored Sir," he said, with a small bow.

"Be welcome in Maracanda," the secretary said with re-lief, then turned to Tarik. "They are Arabs, Excellency."

"Very good," said Tarik. "Ask them why they have come."

The secretary turned back to them. "I am Cheruk, secre-tary to Tarik, the Mongol who sits on the table governing this province." He managed to keep the contempt out of his voice, but Matt saw it in his eyes. "What brings you to Maracanda?"

"A wandering minstrel I," Matt ad-libbed, "scratching out a living along the caravan routes by singing for my supper, and seeking to exchange songs for stories and news—but I have seen no caravans since Samarkand, and there were no Mongols in this city when my father brought me here as a boy. What has happened?"

Marudin stared, but Lakshmi gave him an elbow in the ribs. Cheruk noticed and asked, "What of your companions?"

"They are jewel merchants," Matt explained.

"We have no jewels," Marudin interrupted. "Bandits fell upon us, and I gave them my diamonds and emeralds so that they would not take my wife."

"Commendable, I'm sure." But Cheruk's look said he didn't believe it for a minute. He turned back to Matt. "If you are a minstrel, where is your instrument?"

"Oh . . . uh . . . the bandits took it," Matt said lamely.

"What do they say?" Tarik asked.

"That the small one is a minstrel, and the tall one a gem merchant." Cheruk turned back to his master. "Bandits took the jewels but left him his wife, and took the minstrel's instrument, too."

"Perhaps we can find him another," Tarik said.

Matt's stomach sank. He might have been able to fake on a guitar, but he'd have been lost on anything else.

"What does he seek here?" the governor continued.

"Money for his singing, and new songs and news," Cheruk said. "His companions must live off what he can bring, I suppose."

Marudin and Lakshmi were frowning, unable to follow the dialogue in Mongol, so Matt frowned, too, with apprehension.

"They may ply their trades in the bazaar," Tarik decided. "What news have they of the lands through which they have traveled?"

By the time Cheruk was done repeating the question, Matt had decided what the governor wanted to hear. "The citizens are happy with the peace and prosperity the gur-khan's governors have brought, and would not seek freedom if they could."

"That is not true," Cheruk said evenly. "Have no fear, none others of these can speak your language. Tell me truly what happens."

Matt stared a moment, then shifted gears. "Actually, the people of Samarkand are going about warily, and the women are hiding their faces whenever a squadron of barbarians passes, so the Persian veil is becoming very popular. The caravans have had to find a southern route."

"We have noticed their absence here," Cheruk said grimly.

"You didn't answer my question," Matt pointed out. "What happened here in Maracanda?"

"The armies of the Great Khan conquered us," the secretary replied, "some fifteen years ago—your father must have left with you shortly before the Mongols attacked."

"Only the Mongols?" Matt asked in surprise.

"Only them," Cheruk confirmed. "We were the first city they attacked, since our armies had always held the wild tribes at bay."

That explained why the Turks hadn't reached the Arabian empire. "But this time they had magic your wizards didn't know," Matt said grimly.

Cheruk looked at him more closely. "You truly must be a minstrel, to have gathered so much news as that. Yes, we fought their forces to a standstill, so they used evil magic far more sophisticated than anything their shamans had ever wrought, summoning monsters who chewed our soldiers to bits until our officers ordered a retreat that became blind, fleeing panic. Perhaps if we had won, the Mongols would not have been able to sway so many other barbarians to join them, and would not now be overrunning all of Asia."

"Perhaps," Matt said thoughtfully.

"What is this conversation?" Tarik demanded.

"He has told me that the people of the empire rejoice in the gur-khan's rule, Excellency," Cheruk reported, "for it has brought them peace and prosperity. In turn, he asked why Maracanda is not as it was when he visited here as a child."

Tarik sniffed. "He should know the answer to that, if he has seen our garrisons in other cities. Tell him that we conquered, and that the false priest John slunk away to the wilderness, where he has hidden so well that our troops cannot find him—or may be dead, for all we know."

Sorrow wrenched Cheruk's features, but he fought it off even as he turned to Matt. "When the Mongols conquered, our king, Prester John, gathered the remnants of his troops and fled to the mountains. We hope he is well and will come back to free us, but we have heard no word of him, nor have the many search parties the governor has sent to quarter the slopes, seeking him."

"And they presumably have scouts who are excellent

trackers." Matt thought it over, then asked, "What of their sorcerers? Surely they must have sought John with magic."

Cheruk stiffened, but said, "You guess aright—they have sought, and have found naught."

"Then John must still be alive, and shielding his army with his own magic," Matt said, "for if he were dead, the sorcerers would surely have scried out his body."

Cheruk's eyes fired. "There is truth in what you say, and I thank you for hope. I would guess you are more than a wandering minstrel. Now speak more to me, so that I may tell Tarik you have given me more news."

Matt thought it over, then said, "Tell him that your armies attacked the Caliph of Baghdad and that he had to retreat to Damascus, but that an army of Franks and another of Moors came to his rescue. Their wizards fought the barbarians' sorcerers and won, and the horde had to retreat to Baghdad. We know nothing more recent. Will that do?"

"Quite well." Cheruk fought to hide his delight at the news and had managed to achieve another deadpan expression when he turned back to relay the information to Tarik.

"Couriers have told me that already," the governor replied testily. "Tell him that our setback in Damascus is only temporary, and that our eventual victory will prove that the Christian God is weaker than Angra Mainyu and all the gods of all our plains-dwelling peoples—as might be expected of one against a hundred. Tell him also that if John the Priest has survived, he is living like a wild animal, not even raiding our outposts or trying to win back his capital—which is well for him, for if he tries, he is doomed to defeat."

Cheruk turned back to relay the message with a face of stone, obviously thinking that Tarik was rubbing it in to make sure he knew he was ground down. Matt, though, recognized an attempt to use the media for propaganda, even if the medium in question was only a wandering minstrel.

"Dwell in hope," Matt said quietly. "I think your Prester John lives, and is only awaiting his moment. When he thinks he has a chance of success, he will attack."

"Yes, but how can he hope for victory against such as these, and their demons?" Cheruk asked, defeat in every line of his body.

"Enough!" Tarik waved a hand, turning away. "Put them to work reinforcing the walls. At day's end, if they have any energy left, they can ply their trade in the bazaar."

The soldiers instantly surrounded the companions again. Cheruk said, his tone apologetic, "He sends you to forced labor. You may yet have some chance to sing and trade in the evenings, though."

"We also might escape," Matt told him. "So might you—and all your people with you."

Cheruk was erasing another look of surprise and hope as the soldiers came between him and the trio. They hustled the companions out of the chamber, through corridor after corridor, and out of the palace.

As they came out into the street, though, they heard a meowing voice by the doorway chant,

> "By djinn and John and Grecian Fates,
> Take these strangers to the gates!
> By cats and khans and Presters old,
> Clear the way for . . . for . . ."

Matt realized that the spell must have been an improvised verse, not a memorized one, because Balkis was having trouble with the last line, as usual—no talent for rhymes. He helped her out gladly, calling out the words that finished her verse: "Clear the way for captives bold!"

"Who are you talking to?" the hetman demanded, but a meowing voice echoed eagerly,

> "Clear the way for captives bold!"

The hetman went glassy-eyed.

Marudin's fist poised over a guard's head, but he frowned at the man's suddenly vacant gaze and withheld his hand.

"Uh, I think it'll work better if we use them for camouflage, Princess." Delicately, Matt disengaged Lakshmi's fingers from the collar of the soldier she was holding in the air. The man landed with a thump, but stayed upright and started walking with his mates, all following the hetman.

"What has plagued them?" Lakshmi looked about her even as she hurried to match her steps to theirs.

"Balkis pinch-hitting for us," Matt explained.

The squadron marched them straight down the avenue that led directly away from the steps. Citizens scrambled out of their way; carts and wagons swerved over to the side. Fifteen minutes later the hetman stamped to a halt just inside the gate. The guards outside looked up, startled, and were about to start asking questions. So were Marudin and Lakshmi, but Matt grabbed their arms and lurched out from among the soldiers, pulling them stumbling with him.

"What do you think you are doing?" Lakshmi demanded, righting herself.

"Yeah, what do you think you're doing, turning down the best songs of the year?" Matt shook a fist at the stone-faced hetman. "You can tell that governor of yours that I've been thrown out of better places than this! Come on, friends." He turned about and marched off with wounded dignity. Lakshmi and Marudin followed, comprehension dawning.

Ten feet down the road Matt looked back and saw the squadron beginning to come out of their daze, asking questions of the hetman, who was shaking his head, palm pressed to his temple, looking about him as though waking from a dream, which he more or less was.

"A little faster," Matt snapped. "We don't want to become a topic of conversation!"

They dove into the outbound stream of traffic. A dozen paces later Matt looked back, but the hetman had only formed up his squadron and was leading them back into the city. Matt didn't blame him for not wanting to raise the hue and cry—he wouldn't want to be caught sleeping on the job, either.

"I think we're safe for the moment," he said, then felt something furry rub against his ankles. He staggered but kept his balance. "Thanks, Balkis. I'd been wondering how we were going to get out of that one without letting everybody know what we are."

"You are welcome," the cat mewed. "Perhaps next time you go into a mouse hole, you should make sure you know how you'll get out."

"Yeah, well, I wasn't planning to go into the palace," Matt told her. He looked up and saw a grove of trees. "Let's go in where it's green and quiet, folks."

"Wherefore?" Marudin asked, but Lakshmi took his arm and purred, "Do you truly need a reason to step aside with me?"

Marudin beamed down at her. "Never, sweeting! But I would rather not bring company."

" 'Fraid it's got to be a community project, folks," Matt said. "I need to talk this over and make some sense out of it."

Just as they came to the leaves, though, a distant voice shouted, "Stop in the name of Arjasp!"

Matt looked back and saw Turkish warriors riding toward the city with a blue-robed priest in their middle. He groaned. "I thought Arjasp might be able to sense that someone was working unauthorized magic. Let's move a little faster, folks!"

Fortunately, the Turks were so intent on getting to the city that they didn't stop to examine the flora. They passed the grove at a canter and certainly weren't looking upward behind them. All they would have seen was a double whirlwind rising from the trees and blowing away toward the west, but the priest might have known what that meant. Looking down, Matt had the satisfaction of watching the patrol ride to and fro, searching and baffled, then turning back to ride intently toward the city, sure that their quarry had not yet escaped.

"Where now, wizard?" Lakshmi asked.

"To the mountains," Matt told her. "Where else would you look for guerrillas?"

Of course, he had to explain what guerrillas were, then had to try to persuade the djinn that Prester John was living like a bandit and trying to harry the conquerors, but without success.

Lakshmi flatly refused to believe it. "This king is, from what you say, much like a caliph," she said, "and no caliph would make his stronghold among brambles!"

"She speaks truly," Marudin seconded. "Perhaps in your country, Frank, a caliph can lose pomp and circumstance without losing dignity and strength—but believe me, in the East no one would follow a ruler who had fallen to living in a tent in a forest!"

Matt bridled. "Got any better ideas?"

"Seek a city," Lakshmi said, "perhaps one lost in the desert or the wilderness, but a city nonetheless."

She did. With Matt and cat in her arms, she and Marudin quartered the mountains, then the desert beyond—and sure enough, a hundred miles out in the wasteland on a dusty, eroded track that might have been a caravan route twenty years earlier, they found a walled city whose houses had weathered to seem much like the sand around them, but whose walls still stood firm. Looking down from a hundred feet, they saw only a few civilians in the streets, but the great central square around the fortress was filled with soldiers dressed more or less as the civilians had been in Maracanda, though all in the same colors and with the same insignia embroidered on their chests.

"Okay, you win, Princess," Matt grumped. "Let's try the front door and see if they send us around to the back."

Civilians and soldiers alike had already noticed their aerial visitors and were pointing up at them, exclaiming, so Lakshmi took the chance of landing fifty yards from the gate—but she kept her arms around Matt and Balkis, ready to take off again if anybody shot an arrow, as did Marudin, who landed a few feet away. No one threw anything, though, and no squadron of cavalry came charging out, though there did seem to be a lot of running to and fro along the walls. Finally the gates opened and a gorgeously clad man stepped forward, surrounded by soldiers, but with the heart-shaped face and golden skin tone of Maracanda. He wore a purple turban with a spray of peacock plumes held by a jeweled broach, and a cloak and robe of purple satin over tunic and trousers of the same material. His sash was scarlet, and so were his boots. "Welcome, O Djinn! And who is your servant?"

Lakshmi started to answer, then caught herself and said, as though spitting tacks, "They will hearken better to a man's voice. Speak to them, my love."

"I think they would listen to a princess of the Marid," Marudin said easily. "Speak for us, love." But he swelled up a little, hulking behind her with arms crossed, smiling wickedly at the emissary.

Lakshmi stepped forward and said, "I am Lakshmi,

Princess of the Marid. This is my husband, the Marid Prince Marudin, and my friends: the magician Balkis"—who had now returned to human form—"and Matthew Lord Mantrell, wizard and husband to Her Majesty Alisande, Queen of Merovence. He comes as her emissary."

Court functionary or not, the emissary looked impressed. "Why have you come?"

"We seek the renowned king known as Prester John."

"Come in, then, if you dare," said the functionary, "for you have found him."

CHAPTER 27

"Found him?" Matt stared, then felt a wave of unreality sweep over him. "Really found him at last?"

"Prester John awaits you," the functionary confirmed.

Matt felt the thrill of victory.

"However, be warned," the emissary cautioned, "that they who enter this city may not leave it."

Matt felt the agony of defeat.

"I shall chance it," Lakshmi said dryly.

The emissary bowed, turned, and led the way. Soldiers fell in on either side of them, and the citizens and off-duty soldiers lined the street, pointing and discussing the strangers in excited tones.

"We seem to be the biggest thing that has happened here in a long time," Matt said. "Must be a pretty dead town."

"Let us wish it a few more weeks of life," Lakshmi said.

Matt glanced at Balkis, concerned. "Any more déjà vu?"

"None," the teenager said, looking about her with a frown. "There is something familiar about the people, but not the city."

Then they were climbing the road to the fortress and walking between files of soldiers through a gateway whose open portals were oak, a foot thick and twelve feet high. Matt had to remind himself that he was a knight, and that knights weren't afraid, as he walked into the fortress of a mythical king whose name was synonymous with mystery, magic, and might.

They entered into a courtyard whose walls gleamed with whitewash over plaster, where soldiers were practicing with wooden weapons. There was a certain lack of verve about their drill, blows perfunctory, very obviously going through the motions.

"Low morale," Matt muttered to Lakshmi.

The djinna nodded. "They are not yet in despair, but neither are they far from it."

The soldiers stopped to stare as they paraded across the courtyard, four people in outlandish but common clothing led by a gorgeously clad courtier and surrounded by half a dozen soldiers, and Matt was sure the rankers were wondering what was so important about these strangers.

The Eastern castle was rather different in architectural style from its Western counterparts, but the necessities of defense dictated a certain similarity, even as the army forts of the American West resembled the early wooden strongholds of the Britannic chieftains. There may not have been a keep or donjon, but one wall of the fortress was much thicker than the others, and the functionary led them up a broad but short flight of stairs and in through another pair of stout oaken doors, but only eight feet high and three inches thick.

Inside, soldiers lounged, leaning on their spears, but straightened up amazingly when the courtier came in sight. They kept their eyes resolutely to the front, but Matt could see the curiosity in them.

He was amazed at the contrast of the interior with the exterior. Outside was harsh, blocky, and glaring white; inside was luxurious. Turkish carpets covered the granite floor and carved wooden screens hid the stones of the walls. Spouted lamps burned in sconces and on tables, making Matt edgy, expecting djinnis to jump out of them, until he remembered that he had two djinn with him.

The courtier led them down a broad, short hall toward two more massive doors, no doubt the Great Hall or Throne Room or some such, but turned aside at the last minute and faced two guards who stood at either side of a very ordinary-looking door. One of them bowed, then opened the door and stepped in. He stepped back out a second later and held the door wide.

They came into a chamber filled with light from three large windows that looked out into the courtyard. It was more or less rectangular, only about thirty feet by twenty, with a guard every six feet. They stood in front of tapestries and mosaics. The floor was covered with a single huge carpet with an intricate, stylized floral design. The furniture was limited to two nests of cushions around a low table in one corner opposite the windows, four Chinese-style chairs around a higher table in another, and in the center, directly in front of the windows, a large table with a man behind it, parchment and ink in hand, scanning other parchments. Matt felt a surge of disappointment, for he seemed quite ordinary.

Then the man looked up, his eyes singling out Matt before anyone spoke, and Matt stared, electrified. Even seated, the man seemed taller than he, radiating such an aura of power, of wisdom and authority, that he appeared altogether magical, and every inch a king. There was no doubt that this was Prester John.

Matt felt pinned to the spot by those eyes. They were alert, piercing, and gave the impression that their owner saw everything, even Matt's innermost thoughts. He wore a neatly trimmed black moustache and beard, flowing black hair, a tall golden crown studded with gems, and an ornate golden robe embroidered with black dragons down either side. Beneath it he wore a tunic of royal-blue. As he stood and came around the table, Matt could see trousers of the same color and red Persian slippers. His face was heart-shaped, golden-toned, and high-cheekboned, like those of most of his people. But his brown eyes were larger, his nose straighter and more prominent, and his lips not quite as full.

The courtier dropped to one knee, bowing his head and shoulders, then gestured angrily at his charges to imitate him. Balkis curtsied, but Marudin and Lakshmi stiffened and only inclined their heads—they, too, were royalty, after all, and djinn, not mere mortals.

Matt, however, was mortal. He bowed, though not very low.

"Do not insist, chamberlain," Prester John said in mellow tones. "This man is, after all, the highest lord in his own kingdom."

Matt guessed that a messenger had overheard the introductions at the gate and run ahead with the news.

The chamberlain rose, every line of his body expressing indignation, but he only said, "Profound, wise, and merciful monarch, may I introduce into your exalted presence Matthew Lord Mantrell, Prince Consort and emissary of the queen of the barbaric land of Merovence."

Matt bridled at the term "barbaric," but managed to hold his tongue.

The wise and merciful monarch's eyes glistened with amusement, but he kept a straight face and said, "You may."

The chamberlain turned to the companions and said frostily, "Bow to His Supreme and Royal Majesty, Prester John, King of the Christians!"

Again Matt inclined his head and shoulders, though Balkis dropped another curtsy and stayed there with a faraway gaze, entranced.

John glanced at her, then back to Matt. "And your servants?"

"Not my servants, but my companions, and in some ways, of higher rank than I." Matt turned to the djinn. "May I present Lakshmi, Princess of the Marids, and her husband, Prince Marudin."

John's eyes widened, as did those of the chamberlain and all the guards, and Matt heard a distinct chorus of indrawn breaths.

"Can this be true?" asked the monarch. "Can you truly be djinn?"

"We can, and we are," Lakshmi said, with a glance of ill-concealed contempt for the chamberlain.

"Then may the saints be praised!" John said fervently. "We have prayed that the kings of the West would ride to our aid, but we never guessed they would bring djinn, too."

Matt stared. "*You* were hoping we were going to come rescue *you*?"

"Why, yes," John said, mildly puzzled. "Is that so odd?"

Matt smiled. "Only because in the West we're used to the idea of you coming to save us from the Turks."

John stared, then laughed, a rich if rueful sound. "Perhaps before the gur-khan swept in off the steppe with his horde, you would have been right to expect this. Now, though?" He shrugged eloquently and swept a hand at the chamber around him. "You see our reduced circumstances."

"I wouldn't have called them reduced if I hadn't seen your

palace in Maracanda," Matt said. "Since I have, though, I can only say that I see what you mean."

John's gaze sharpened again. "You have been in Maracanda? For what purpose?"

"Seeking you," Matt said simply.

"And you managed to escape?"

"Well, they didn't know who we really were," Matt explained.

"How did you hide your identities from Arjasp and his sorcerous priests?" John asked. "And how did you evade their prisons and their corvees?"

"Well, the djinn are magical, of course," Matt explained, "and I have a bit of magical knowledge myself."

"He is Lord Wizard of Merovence," Lakshmi said.

John's eyebrows rose.

"And this is my pupil." Matt turned to Balkis, didn't see her, then looked down and saw she was still deep in her curtsy. "She has a fair amount of magic in her own right."

"Companions in magic, all four!" John turned to Balkis and reached down, taking her hand and lifting. "I had thought this one was your guide through our kingdom, that you had met her here and hired her."

Like an automaton, Balkis rose, gazing with disbelief into John's eyes.

The comment seemed odd to Matt. "No, she's been with us since we left Merovence."

"Then she alone of your party is not a prince, a princess, or a lord."

"Why yes, I suppose that's true," Matt said in surprise. Now that he thought of it, he did have something in common with the Marids—other than missing children, of course.

"Still, if she is your pupil, we must talk as near-equals." John drew Balkis with him as he swept away to the chairs in the corner. He gestured for them to sit and said to a guard, "Coffee."

Matt tried not to drool, and wondered why, halfway to China, they hadn't been offered tea. He put it down to John's having a better knowledge of the West than he'd expected—at least, what was West to him, though it was the Near East to Matt. "I am surprised that you can spare such luxuries when you and your people must be hard-pressed, Majesty."

John smiled with irony. "That, at least, Arjasp had not expected—that this old city would have a granary that never emptied and a bazaar whose stalls were always replenished during the night."

"Really!" Matt said. "I assume you had magic enough to make all that happen?"

"Only in reviving old spells that the ancients had placed here long ago," his host replied. "There is a legend of a prince who did great favors for one of the Marid, freeing him from the prison a greedy sorcerer had made for him. In gratitude, the Marid summoned spirits and bade them supply this city forever more."

Matt heard a sharp intake of breath and turned to see Marudin's eyes burning. He didn't ask, but he had a sudden suspicion who the Marid in question had been. Lakshmi had once mentioned something about Prince Marudin having spent most of his thousand-year life in thrall to one sorcerer or another, or in suspended animation in his lamp, until Matt had set him free. The prince liked Matt. A lot.

"You say that was one thing Arjasp hadn't thought of," Matt said slowly. "Does that mean he chased you to this city deliberately?"

"Not by choice, no." John's face hardened with memory. "I am sure he would have preferred to see his gur-khan slay me and all my army. They swept in off the steppe without warning and did not begin their unholy howling until they heard my own sentries raising the alarm. Then horrible monsters descended from the skies while others even more terrible clambered up our walls. Our sentries could not stand against them. A fireball burned our gate to ashes in seconds, and the barbarians rode in, howling like demons and laying about them with their swords. My soldiers did what they could to protect the people, but many of them died, and those who lived did so only because they retreated to the gate and out." His face had become a rigid mask. "I led them in their retreat."

Several of the guards made involuntary noises in their throats, but caught themselves, though their spears trembled.

John glanced up, annoyed, and admitted, "Well, true enough that I led from behind, staying between my troops and the monsters until we were clear of the city, holding them at bay with such spells as I could muster—but I rode to the head of the column as quickly as I could, for I knew that there would be no peace for us in our own land, but that the conquerors might not choose to follow through the mountain passes, where we could stop them by throwing rocks down upon them. Sure enough, they hesitated—long enough for me to lead the remnant of my army out into the desert, to this city, for only I knew of its existence, since it had long stood emptied of people. We set to repairing its defenses as quickly as we could, and by the time the gur-khan had ridden around the mountains and surrounded us, he saw our walls would be impregnable. He summoned up his monsters again, but I was ready for them now, and called up the spirits of the ancestors of this town to battle them. At last Arjasp set demons to pen us in and left, sure that we could no longer interfere with his plans." He admitted it with bitterness. "For the last fifteen years we have only proved him right. Every time we sally forth, demons of gruesome and horrible aspect appear from the very ground itself and fall upon us. It is all we can do to win back to the city alive."

"But we didn't see any demons on our way in," Matt objected.

"Oh, be sure you would not! They will let as many as wish come in to join us—but will tear to pieces any who seek to leave."

"I suppose that makes sense," Matt said, frowning, "if Arjasp didn't know you had unlimited rations. Since he didn't, he probably expected you all to starve to death within a fortnight."

"So did we," John said grimly. "But after a week's time the stewards came to me and reported that no matter how much grain they drew out of a granary during the day, it was full again the next morning—and no matter how much meat, dried fish, and dried fruit were taken from the other stores, they too were full again by morn. Even the heaps of fresh fruit were high again each and every dawn. I set my wizards to watching the night, but they could see nothing. At last I myself took up the vigil, and saw blurs so fast I could scarcely distinguish them—but I knew the form of the whirlwind, and thus discovered what passed in the night. Each evening we gather, every household, to thank our benefactors, and hope that they hear."

"I shall be sure of it," Prince Marudin told him.

"So of course Arjasp is plenty willing for his demons to let people in," Matt said. "He thinks that every extra mouth will just eat up your limited stock of provisions that much faster—and he knows you're too charitable to turn away any refugee."

"Even so," Prester John agreed. "I fear his spies may have told him we still live, though. Any day, his demons may turn upon any who come near."

Matt shuddered. "Glad we made it in before the deadline. But how did Arjasp know to hit you first? Were you such an obvious threat?"

John's smile was hard. "There has been a Prester John in Maracanda to hold back the barbarians for five hundred years; I am the twenty-fifth by that title and name. The first, the founder of my line, led a small band of Christians, fleeing from the Muslims in search of freedom to worship as they pleased. They found this valley, farmed, and prospered. Then came famine, and they had food when their neighbors had none. The first Prester John insisted that his folk act with Christian charity, welcoming people of all nations and sharing food with them, provided they were willing to live in peace with one another. He enforced that peace sternly, for hard labor had made his people hardy and hunting small game had made them doughty archers. Even the Kirghiz and the Kazakhs lived in truce in his country, as did the Turks and the Mongols."

"Warlike peoples all," Matt said, musing. "Didn't he insist they had to become Christians?"

"He did not, for he realized that they who seek baptism only to gain food are likely to fall away when famine ends. Nonetheless, the goodness and charity of his people, combined with their strength, induced many of the immigrants to convert."

"And as time went by with their descendants growing up in a Christian environment, more and more of them converted?"

John nodded. "They did indeed, until we became as you find

us—almost all Christian, but with Muslims and Buddhists and others welcome to come, and to worship as they please."

"I take it the immigrants intermarried with the original pioneers."

"They did," said Prester John, "and taught one another their martial arts. As time went by, we became one hybrid people with the blood of Russians, Persians, Turks, Mongols, and Chinese—indeed, all the peoples of Asia—coursing in our veins, with their combined wisdom in our heads and hearts."

"And their blended prowess in the arts of war in your arms," Matt concluded.

"Indeed," their host confirmed. "The third Prester John established athletic contests in these arts, and the young folk strove to perfect their skills, while those who were mature exercized to keep them at their peak. Late in his reign, when the Mongols and Turks allied against us, the Prester led his armies to a battle that was hard fought but brief, routing the hordes completely."

"And every Prester John since has had to fight off his own attack by barbarians?"

"Yes, and sometimes twice in one reign. If the wild horsemen of the steppes have never penetrated to the West before, you may thank my predecessors. Even my father, in his youth, fought off an alliance of Mongols under a chieftain named Temujin."

Matt's scalp prickled as he recognized the man who had held the title "Genghis Khan," universal ruler, in his own world.

Prester John's face darkened and his head bowed. "I alone have failed in this duty."

"Only temporarily," Matt said briskly. "That does explain why Arjasp realized his gur-khan had to hit you before he attacked anyone else, though."

"Indeed," Prester John said, his expression grim. "Arjasp and his gur-khan seem to have learned from the mistakes of those who attacked and lost before them. They struck first at my capital of Maracanda, as I have told you. Later, fugitives told us that they sacrificed those few of our nobility whom they caught, slew them with ceremony on the altars of their god of deceit and blood. Then the gur-khan left Maracanda and all the kingdom with a strong garrison and rode west to conquer in their tens of thousands, with little to stop them save armies who knew not of their coming."

"Surprise has served them well," Matt said, "and their reputation for being both unbeatable and cruel to their enemies, but merciful to those who surrender, has taken them even farther. Of course, legions of the conquered have been quick to convert to the worship of Ahriman."

"So many will side with them who triumph, no matter who or what they are." Prester John sighed. "I fear that Arjasp plans to conquer all the continent of Asia."

"I don't think he means to stop at the Caucasus or the Bosporus, either," Matt said. "He means to go on and conquer all of Europe, too, clear to the Atlantic."

"And when he has finished," John said grimly, "he will come back to tear this city apart brick by brick and slay us all."

"On top of which, since the demons have let in anyone who was seeking you out, Arjasp will have all his remaining enemies in one place." Matt slapped his knees and stood up to pace. "Your pardon, Majesty, but I don't think we should hang around—any of us."

"Agreed," John said with a smile of weary amusement. "What business brought you to me, after all?"

"Oh, just to ask a little favor," Matt said. "Nothing much, just that you would take your invincible army and attack the barbarians from the rear."

John nodded heavily. "I will gladly, Lord Wizard, but I must first defeat those who have conquered my own kingdom."

"Deal!" Matt declared. "We help you win back your capital, and you attack the barbarians. Of course, I realize you'll have to clear them out of the rest of your kingdom first."

Prester John stared up at Matt as though he were insane, then asked the djinn, "Is he serious?"

"Most serious, I assure you," Lakshmi said grimly. "I have come to realize he is at his most profound when he seems most foolish. But wizard, what of our true mission?"

John was instantly on the alert. "What mission is this?"

"A small matter," Matt said. "Four small matters, actually, and every one a child. Arjasp stole our offspring."

"For hostages!"

"And distractions," Matt said. "The hostage idea hasn't worked too well—it just made me more sneaky than ever. But the distraction is working very well indeed—we're off trying to find our kids instead of fighting barbarians." He turned back to Lakshmi. "But you haven't forgotten, Princess, that the kids are with Arjasp, and Arjasp is in Maracanda."

"Of course!" Lakshmi cried, and Marudin grinned. "Win Maracanda, and we have nearly won the children back."

"Only need to find them," Matt agreed. "Of course, if Arjasp saw the three of us coming, he might kill them—but if he only saw John and his army?"

"Certainly there would be a hundred places for us to hide, if Arjasp were so distracted," Lakshmi agreed.

Prester John frowned. "How, though, can you help me take back my capital if you have no army?"

"By being a wizard who has three companions," Matt told him, "two djinn and one very talented apprentice."

Balkis finally came out of her daze and stared up at him.

They came to the eastern gate accompanied by Prester John and a whole company of cavalry. "I do not see how poor three of you can banish a host of demons," John said for the tenth time.

With weary patience Lakshmi assured him a new way. "It is an old tale I learned from a djinn who lived a thousand years before me, Majesty."

Marudin reddened and looked straight ahead.

"I trust your knowledge, or I would beseech you not to go," John said, but his voice reverberated down the corridors of dread. "Still, if you fail to banish them and are beset, my soldiers and I shall charge out to rescue."

"You would all die in a trice." Lakshmi was still trying to be gentle. "Be of good cheer—you shall not need to. But deeply do we cherish your courage and loyalty."

"Only be sure all your people are ready to march when we win," Marudin reminded him.

"They are summoned and set." Prester John looked back

down the long avenue to the fortress. Every inch was filled with soldiers and civilians, carts and packhorses, wagons and chariots. "They stand at your whim."

"I must go out with you, too!" Balkis insisted, though she was trembling with fear.

"Other way around," Matt told her. "We need to have you watching from the wall to bail us out, just in case we do get in over our heads."

"Fear not, lass," Marudin assured her. "We shall emerge unscathed."

Balkis stopped trembling, but her face was pinched with worry.

"Sorry, Your Majesty, but you can't talk us out of it." Matt turned away from Prester John and called to the porters, "Open the right-hand gate!"

With obvious misgivings, ten soldiers put their shoulders under the huge bar and slid it clear. Two more stepped in and swung the right-hand portal open. Matt marched out with the djinn on either side of him and heard the great valve boom shut behind him.

"I just hope you're right," he told Marudin.

"I assure you, I have seen it," the prince told him testily. "When you behold them, you shall understand."

"Forward, then, to glory!" Lakshmi commanded.

Matt swallowed his heart down out of his throat and matched their pace, striding forward with the sound of his own pulse drowning out the awed and fearful murmur of the people thronging the wall behind him.

They hadn't gone more than three paces before the sand before them began to stir and churn, as far as they could see from east to west and all the way to the desert horizon. Forms rose from the ground itself, and braced though he was, Matt nearly cried out in terror.

CHAPTER 28

They were horned, they were horrid, they were whelked, they were warty. They came in sickening combinations of human and animal parts—and features that came from neither. There were single glaring eyes, dozens of eyes, and any number in between—bulging, dished, compound stalked, large as platters, small as pebbles. There were pointed teeth, shark teeth, viper fangs, chisel teeth, dagger teeth, serrated teeth, and plain strips of whetted steel. There were trumpet snouts braying, wolf muzzles, octopus tentacles, beaks clacking, fur, goat legs, elephant legs, feathers, and fins. There was everything humans have ever seen and much more that they had imagined, all put together in mockeries of anthropoid and animal forms. There were giant insects with human heads, human bodies with scales and insect heads, claws and pincers and mantis-arms and spider legs.

They gibbered and hooted and droned and brayed and howled and shrieked. They marched toward the trio, looking neither to left nor right, grinning with menace—obviously meaning to chase them back inside if they could, though probably hoping the companions would stand their ground so that the demons would have an excuse to tear them apart. They were creatures of nightmare, some that Matt recognized from his own childhood night terrors, and the sight of them evoked that numbing, paralyzing fear all over again. His knees turned to jelly, but Lakshmi's arm clamped about him to hold him up, and he understood in a flash that half the creatures' power was the sheer terror they inspired in anything that saw them.

Anything except djinn, it seemed. "Recite, wizard!" Lakshmi snapped. "It shall take all our power merged to stop *this* horde!"

Matt felt Marudin's hand tighten on his other arm and realized they were all three linked. The prince began the chant they had rehearsed, and he and Lakshmi joined in:

> "The wall is long and tall and wide.
> Let it be with silver dyed—
> A mirror polished clear and bright,
> Reflecting all who stand outside!"

Then just for good measure, Matt threw in,

> "There be fools alive, I wis,
> Silvered o'er, and so is this!"

Matt knew he shouldn't take his eyes off the monsters for a second, but he risked a quick glance back over his shoulder. The white plaster of the city's walls shimmered in the pounding glare of noon, glimmered, clouded, then cleared— to reflect the sunlight back in searing brightness. But it wasn't the light that mattered, it was the reflection of the horde of monsters that faced those walls, walls that had become one gigantic mirror.

A second of unearthly silence held the desert.

Then it broke. The air filled with shrieks and howls of unearthly pitches and tones as the demons saw an army of horrible and twisted forms facing them. They couldn't bear the ugliness, either, and the sheer horror of the sight struck terror into their very cores. As one, they turned and charged away, bellowing in panic, stamping down into the ground and disappearing beneath the sand. Those with wings took to the air and soared away until they were only dots in the sky, then disappeared. In minutes the plain was clear.

Matt stared, dumbfounded, but Lakshmi kept her wits about her. She whirled, beckoning with her whole arm and crying in a voice like a trumpet, "Come now as you promised! They are gone, they are banished, but they may come back before sunset, and they will not be so easily daunted a second time!"

Matt shook himself awake. "That's right—it was the surprise that got them, wasn't it? The shock. They'd seen each other before, but never all together!"

"And did not realize the wall had become a mirror," Marudin confirmed. "They saw an army of monsters marching toward them and were as terrified by the sight as we were. But when they return to whatever power sent them, it will chastise them most severely and send them to confront this city again."

"Come on!" Matt bawled to the city. "This is your one chance, and it may not last long!"

The gates burst open and Prester John came riding out with Balkis beside him on a mount of her own, looking decidedly insecure in her saddle. They rode at the head of a column four horses wide, all that the gates would allow. The priest-king rode up to them and turned his horse aside. An honor guard of several score soldiers drew rein behind and around them while the generals led the procession on past.

"I cannot thank you enough, djinn and wizard!" John said. "Forever shall my people sing your praises!"

"Had you not better lead them, then?" Lakshmi demanded.

John shook his head. "My generals shall suffice for that. It is my place to stay and watch, to be sure the last of my people has left the city. Then may I ride in their wake."

"Commendable," Lakshmi sniffed, "but only if your generals know where to go and how to ride there. Can they lead your army to Maracanda?"

"They can," John assured her, "and are more than enough to counter any barbarian patrols we shall meet on the way."

"Even if you slay such patrols to the last man, you shall have no surprise," Lakshmi warned. "I doubt not Arjasp has spies who will warn him of your coming long hours before you near the city."

"Let them be warned," John said, with a feral grin. "They are only a garrison, after all, not the conquering army that battles in Persia. Even with my forces being only half what they were, they shall still prove more than a match for so few."

"What if they close your own gates upon you?"

"They are indeed my own gates." Prester John touched a long black case hanging from his belt. "I hold the key."

Matt wondered what kind of a key could move a locking bar hundreds of pounds in weight, but decided to wait and see. Not that it mattered—he knew half a dozen spells that could do the job, so long as Arjasp hadn't already detected them and set the counterspell on them—and if Prester John's spell was as old and complex as Matt suspected, it would be like trying to protect a Yale lock by putting it inside a tin can.

"Then hew your way into the city," Lakshmi said, "but if you hack your way to Arjasp, first make him tell where my children are locked. Then remember his crimes!"

"That I swear," Prester John told her. "If we catch the man, we shall see justice done."

"The justice we seek," Marudin said, "is that you give him over to us."

Matt glanced at the djinni's eyes and shuddered.

They rode through the mountain pass and down into John's own kingdom, an army ten thousand strong with two djinn, a wizard, and his apprentice to strengthen it. They could see peasants in the fields freezing at their work to stare, then running to spread the alarm to the villages. Presumably the Mongols picked up on the rumor, for now and again Matt saw a stocky rider on a shaggy pony sitting atop a rise. Whenever John sent a party after such a one, though, he wheeled his pony and disappeared.

Late in the afternoon, as they climbed toward a ridge, a score of horsemen appeared against the darkening sky, filling the road between two outcrops of trees.

Prester John, once more back at the head of his troops, said only, "They have chosen their ground well, and their time."

"Yes," said Lakshmi, "for your folk are wearied with a long day's travel."

"So are they, though," Prester John pointed out. "I doubt not they have scoured the countryside for all who could come quickly. Many of them have ridden a hundred miles this day."

"You have to admire their courage," Matt said. "There can't be more than two dozen of them, but they're still going to try to stop us."

"They are fools," John said simply. "Surely they must know that I will guess they have hundreds more hidden within those woods!" He snapped orders to his men, and companies of horsemen whirled to the left and right, plunging off the roadway to ride through the fields around the woods.

John sighed. "The peasants shall lose their year's labor this day, but fight we must, though it destroys the standing crops." To his general, he said, "Be as merciful as you may. These are brave men who choose to die from loyalty to a falsehood. Let us spare them if we can."

The general nodded heavily, his own face heavy with regret.

"We might be able to make it a little less bloody," Matt said thoughtfully, then slipped the wand out, pointed it at the northern grove, and chanted,

> "Afrit of the Hindu Kush,
> Who sought to bar our Marids' path,
> Leave your station in the evening's hush!
> Come to your master's men with wrath.
> Fright all horsemen whom you see
> And chase them from these verdant trees."

"What have you done?" John cried. "You have set an afrit upon my soldiers!"

"Not yours, no," Matt said. "I told him to come to his master's men, remember."

Shrieks and howls split the air. Horsemen boiled out of the northern grove, riding away in terror any way they could. Some, seeing John's soldiers before them, drew their curved swords, ready to strike down any who stood in their way, but officers barked orders, and the soldiers opened avenues for the fugitives.

A howl of disappointment sounded from the grove, and a horrifying sight came charging out into the roadway. Twice as tall as horse and rider, tusked and bug-eyed, it leaped into the midst of the barbarians. With howls of terror they galloped away. The afrit stood, looking about in consternation and bewilderment. Then it shrugged and dove into the southern grove.

Seconds later Tartars came boiling out of those trees, too, riding hell-bent for leather in any direction except back.

Even Prester John's soldiers needed stern commands to

keep them from fleeing, especially as the monster emerged again, looking about, frustrated and angry. Seeing John's party, he strode down toward them with a roar.

Lakshmi bellowed back as she grew to half again his height and strode to meet him. Marudin was only a step behind her and half a head slower in growing. The afrit took one look at them and disappeared with a howl.

"I told him to come to his master's men," Matt explained. "He assumed he was supposed to protect them, but they didn't know that."

Prester John stared as his officers barked orders and calmed their men, though they themselves looked distinctly spooked. Finally, the king asked, "Are your friends so terrible, then, that one mere look at them is enough to send even an afrit packing?"

"Not their looks, no. But they've met before, you see," Matt explained, "and the afrit found out the hard way that he was no match for two Marids."

John decided that the ridge made a good campsite, and his soldiers filled the groves and the hillside with their tents. The next morning, though, three Mongols came riding up to them carrying a white flag. John frowned, donned his robes of state over his armor, and stepped forth to meet them with twenty men at his back. After the formalities that even the barbarians required, he demanded, "What is your leader's message? If it is anything but surrender, save your speech."

"It is a message not for you, O King, but for your companions, the Frankish wizard and the djinn." The Mongol turned to them, and if there was any fear in him, it was hidden behind a face of stone. "Arjasp, high priest of Ahriman and lord of us all in the gur-khan's absence, commands that you leave this overweening prince on the instant, or he shall destroy your children."

Lakshmi cried out in distress, and Marudin advanced on the Mongol with a snarl. The horseman set a hand on his sword and braced himself, but Prester John held up a hand between the Marid and the Mongol. "Remember the flag of truce."

"I am a Marid!" Marudin snapped. "What care I for the customs of you puny mortals?"

"Have a care for your children, then."

That brought Marudin up short. He stood, hulking and seething, glaring at the messenger with unconcealed loathing.

If the Mongol felt any shame at hiding behind children or at the prospect of slaying them, he showed not a trace of it. His visage was still of stone.

Lakshmi advanced, her face drained of color, her hands crooked to claw.

Matt hurried to catch up, muttering, "The kids. Don't jeopardize the kids."

Lakshmi drew to a halt beside Marudin, seething and flexing her hands. Then she spat, "Begone!"

The Mongol bowed his head, whether in mockery or respect, Matt couldn't tell, then turned his horse and rode away, his companions with him. The farther they went, the faster they rode.

When they were out of sight, Lakshmi bowed her head. Suddenly she seemed to sag, all the fight going out of her, and turned to Marudin. He gathered her in, her head upon his chest, and sobs racked her body.

Prester John stood watching in grave silence, and when the worst of the spasm had passed, he said gravely, "We shall fare mightily without you. I have the key to the city, after all, and we must be a thousand to their one."

"But they have the power of Arjasp's magic, and all his priests!" Lakshmi raised a tear-stained face.

"That will not aid them until we come near the city," Prester John told her, "and I have some magic of my own and spirits to counter his, now that I know the manner of his spells. Still, it would greatly aid my cause if you could find and free your children, so that you are there at the end, within the city, to help me defeat the Priest of Lies."

"Lies!" Lakshmi stared at him, then up to Marudin, fierce with hope again. "The children may not be so much within his power as he makes us to believe!"

"And we may indeed be able to find and free them," Marudin exclaimed, catching her fire.

Prester John nodded. "Then go and seek them."

Doubt made Lakshmi sag again. "But how?" she wailed.

"With this." John lifted Balkis' hand; she looked up at him, startled, but the huge emerald winked in the morning sunlight. "When first I saw this lass, I noticed that her gem always glowed," he said, "but when the afrit appeared, it fairly blazed. Will it glow if you are not near?"

"No," Lakshmi whispered, eyes round.

"Then if you come nigh your children, it shall again light within," John told them. "Ask it, and it shall lead you."

Balkis gave Lakshmi a long, steady look. The djinna came forward and threw her arms around the teenager.

They asked the ring. With a little help from Matt on the final couplet, Balkis remembered her verse commanding the ring to show them where the children were. Then she held the ring out at arm's length and turned from one point of the compass to another—but she had barely started before the gem glowed as she faced due east.

"Toward the city of Maracanda," Prester John breathed. "They are in my capital!"

"Of course!" Matt said. "With such valuable hostages, Arjasp would want them where he could keep tabs on them. They're in his city, under his thumb!"

"I shall slay him," Prince Marudin said, and gathered himself to leap into the air.

"Oh, no!" Matt reached out a restraining hand. "He has probably given standing orders to their guards that if he dies or is captured, they're to slay the children!"

Prince Marudin turned a frown on him. "How can a mortal slay a djinn?"

"I don't know," Matt said, exasperated, "but he can certainly recite a spell that will pull them into a bottle, pop the cork in, wax it with the seal of Solomon or some such, and bury it where it will never be . . ." His voice trailed off and his eyes lost focus.

"Of course!" Lakshmi cried. "Why did I never wonder how he held them?"

"We just assumed that anybody who had enough magic to kidnap a couple of djinn would have enough magic to hold them," Matt said. "Well, he does, all right—the old tried-and-true magic." Matt's pulse quickened with the thrill of victory. "What kind of prison could hold djinn?"

"A bottle or a lamp, of course," Lakshmi said, and Marudin almost managed to suppress a shudder.

"Just an ordinary old bottle?"

"Yes," Marudin said, "quite common—but one with the Seal of Solomon impressed on the wax that holds the cork."

"The Seal of Solomon?" Matt stared. "Stamped on by a devil worshiper? That doesn't quite seem to fit."

All five magic-workers looked at one another for a minute. Finally Prester John said, somewhat tentatively, "Perhaps Arjasp does not limit himself to the magic of Ahriman."

"Good point." Matt pursed his lips in thought. "Sure—he's not particular. He'll use any magic as long as it works. After all, he's not really committed to Ahriman, is he? He's committed to himself!"

Prester John shrugged. "I would guess that any magic can be turned to Ahriman's use. After all, it is only a matter of the symbols one uses, and the intent that shapes them."

"So the seal is a parody of Solomon's," Balkis deduced, "and since the djinn are but babes, it suffices to hold them in their bottle."

"That makes sense." Matt turned to Marudin. "How big a bottle would he need—four feet high?"

"Four inches, rather!" the djinn said with a sardonic smile. "Any size would do. The spell that entraps them shrinks them so that there is room to spare. I doubt not that he has made all four children so small that their prison seems a virtual palace to them!"

"Well, they won't be the first bottle babies the world has seen," Matt mused. "How else do you hold a djinn, except in a lamp or bottle or some other vessel?"

"In a ring," Prince Marudin suggested.

Lakshmi's gaze went to the ring on Balkis' finger.

Matt shook his head. "Can't be in there, or it would be glowing like a coal all the time. Besides, when we found it, it was very far from Arjasp—and he never would have let some other magus get his hands on it. Blast!" Matt struck his fist into his palm. "Now we know where the kids are, we're within a day's ride of them—but if Arjasp sees us coming, he'll project the bottle off someplace where we'll never find it!"

"Do you say we cannot go to steal them back?" Lakshmi asked, her face thunderous.

"That's right," Matt said, and the words tasted like wormwood. "We can't."

"But I can," Balkis said.

CHAPTER 29

The other three turned to stare at her.

"I must go," she insisted. "I cannot leave four kittens—I mean, children—torn away from their mothers."

Matt could see the fear in her eyes, but also the determination. "Are you sure?" he asked. "This isn't really your fight."

"But it is," Balkis said. She passed a hand over her forehead, closing her eyes, and wavered for a moment, as with a passing dizziness. Lakshmi leaped forward to help, but Balkis recovered and waved her off, explaining, "Somehow, deep in my bones, I know it is my battle as well as yours. The fairies told me I came from the East, after all, and the caravans took me from the East into Europe. Whoever set me on my course had probably suffered from this zealot's armies." Her eyes burned with anger. "He robbed me of my life, whether he knew it or not, and the fact that the spirits gave me a new life that was good and rich does not pardon him. He may not know he has hurt me, there may be hundreds of thousands whom he does not know he has hurt, but that is all the more reason to punish him!"

Prester John listened, gaze intent on her face.

"Okay," Matt said. "Just make sure you don't get punished yourself."

"I will not," Balkis assured him, but her voice trembled. Nonetheless, she waved her hand, forearm swooping like the bottom of a curtain in front of her, and the air thickened and clouded about her. Then the small calico cat stepped out of the cloud.

"Come, little one." Lakshmi held down a hand. "Let me send you to the high priest's chamber."

"Take some care," Prester John warned.

"I shall use a spell that will return her to us in half an hour's time." Lakshmi picked up Balkis, set the cat on her palm, and recited a spell. A small whirlwind blew up from her palm, churning two feet high, then died down and disappeared. Her hand was empty.

"Brave kid," Matt said, feeling his stomach go hollow.

Balkis felt the world turn solid, saw the whirlwind about her cease, and stumbled, head still whirling. She fought to steady herself, feeling so vulnerable as to be on the verge of panic. When the floor stopped tilting, she took a step without staggering, and could finally pay some attention to her surroundings.

She stood on a Persian carpet in the center of a very large room. To her right stood a high bed with a golden coverlet. To her left, chairs and tables stood around the room, padded with cushions and inlaid with mother-of-pearl and ivory. More cushions were heaped about the floor surrounding low tables. There was one high table littered with books and pieces of parchment, one huge tome lying open. True to her word, Lakshmi had sent the little cat to Arjasp's private chamber.

Fortunately, he wasn't there at the moment. There wasn't too great a chance that he would be, during the daytime—Arjasp was probably the de facto governor of Maracanda as well as the brains behind the whole barbarian onslaught—but it was still a relief.

Her heart quailed within her, but Balkis forced herself to study the room more closely. Despite the carpet and the cloth-of-gold, it was nowhere nearly as luxuriously furnished as she would have expected. So much the better—there were fewer hiding places. She looked down at the ring on her foreleg.

It was so bright it dazzled her.

She tore her eyes away with a surge of elation—the children were near! Then she began to prowl, letting her natural feline curiosity take its course. She seemed to remember having heard, sometime in the past, about the effects of curiosity upon cats, but ignored it—she wasn't idly inspecting, she was searching.

She searched for most of her half hour, her heart thudding in her breast every minute for fear of detection. She found no

trace of the bottle, though the ring was so bright it rivaled the
sunshine that spilled through the carved screen over the
window. She inspected the lamps closely, but the ring was no
brighter near them than farther from them.

Finally she stood in the center of the room, faced the door,
and turned slowly about, watching the ring for changes in
brightness. She had turned a half-circle when she heard footsteps approaching the door.

Balkis looked about her, heart in her throat, searching for a
hiding place. It was a choice between the piles of cushions
and the bed. She chose the bed.

The cloth-of-gold coverlet came down to the floor. She
scampered under it, feeling well hidden in the gloom—and
the ring flared.

Balkis stared at it a moment; it was so bright that it lit up
the under-bed space so that she could see every knot in the
ropes that held up the mattress. But where was the bottle? The
ring was telling her that the little djinn were nearby, but
where? She padded about under the bed quickly, looking into
every corner, but found no bottle, no lamp, no ring other than
the one she wore. She heard the door open, though her own
heartbeat threatened to drown it out, and looked up at the
mattress in desperation, waiting and dreading to hear a body
lie down on it.

There, hanging from the knotted ropes, hung a brooch with
a huge crystal of rose quartz.

Slow footsteps moved from the door to the desk—she
heard parchment rattle. A rasping, quavering voice said,
"They cannot prevail so without their wizards! Has this self-
proclaimed Mahdi such excellent magicians as to stifle the
best efforts of our best sorcerers?"

"Master, he must have djinn to aid him," a quavering fruity
voice answered. Balkis instantly saw a fat middle-aged man in
her mind's eye, multiple chins trembling at Arjasp's agitation.

"The djinn are banned!" Arjasp ranted. "We have bid them
leave the struggle on pain of the deaths of their children!
Even if they seek the brats, they would have left the sultan's
force!"

"Perhaps they have left lesser members of their kind behind," the aide suggested.

"And who would control them? Again, wizards! I am certain it cannot be the Lord Wizard of Merovence—I did not forbid him to seek his children, so I have no doubt he is attempting to do so! Much good may it do him," Arjasp added as an afterthought, reveling in the notion.

"Perhaps he has left junior sorcerers behind," the aide suggested.

"They could not be so adept as to foil the ones whom I have trained! And now, to make it worse, Prester John has broken out of his prison! We must have protection!"

"Surely our barbarians can hold him back," the aide protested, "and if not, there are the city's walls . . ."

"We shall call the horsemen in, not risk them against his army. They are only a garrison, after all—but all of them manning the city's walls should hold us secure until help can come." A chair scraped, parchment rattled—Arjasp sitting down at the desk. "This Tafas bin Daoud has too many soldiers, and they ride too well! We dare not chance the Caliph using him to chase our horsemen back to their steppes! We must have more warriors."

Balkis heard a pen scratching.

"Take this letter to the general who commands the troops attacking China," Arjasp ordered. "Have him withdraw all but enough to hold the men of Han at the Great Wall! He must bring his force to exterminate Prester John and his army once and for all! Then without delay they can go to the front in Persia, before we lose all we have gained!"

"Excellency, it shall be done!"

"Of course it shall be done!" Arjasp roared. Metal tinkled, and he said, "Give this chain and amulet to the courier who will bear the message! It will protect him from djinn and afrits as he travels."

"Must we forego the conquest of China, then?" the aide asked, voice quavering still.

"No, but we must delay it! Their emperor is so decadent, and his government so rotten, that a fraction of our barbarian army can easily hold them until Prester John has been buried and the Caliph fully defeated. When all is secure in the West, we may turn east again! Then the horde can ride back to finish the conquest of China. Now go and see it done!"

Hurried footsteps padded to the door; it swung open and closed.

The chair scraped, and Arjasp's slower steps scuffed the rug as he paced back and forth, muttering to himself.

Balkis crouched in the ring-lit world under the bed, waiting for him to leave. Then she began to feel a very queer sensation, as though invisible fingers were pulling at her, not up or down or sideways, but in some direction that was neither. Her fur stood on end; she barely managed to keep herself from arching her back and spitting. In the nick of time she realized that she was feeling the pull of the spell that would return her to Lakshmi.

There wasn't a moment to spare. Balkis stood up and began to worry at the brooch with her teeth, trying to pull the pin loose from the rope. The return spell pulled more strongly—but some warding spell of the high priest's began to tug at her, too, and she felt stretched between them with her middle in a void.

The footsteps stopped with an exclamation of surprise. Then they began again, approaching the bed.

Fear pierced Balkis as she realized the tug-of-war between the two spells could tear her apart—and that the tension had alerted Arjasp to a presence within his private chamber. If he saw her, what would he do?

Whatever it was, it would be painful. She worried at the brooch, twisted and tugged.

Old bones creaked as Arjasp knelt by his bed. The bed-skirts lifted, showing a faded but angry blue eye beneath a shaggy white eyebrow next to a blade of nose over a voluminous white moustache and beard. The eye narrowed in anger and Arjasp shouted, "Leave be! Whatever manner of creature you are, let go of that brooch!" A palsied, bony hand reached under the bed, hooked to catch Balkis.

"That's more than half an hour!" Matt cried. "She isn't back yet! What's wrong?"

"Peace, Lord Wizard." Prester John laid a gentle hand on his shoulder. "You are not her father, you know."

"No, but I'm responsible for her. She's only a kid, blast it! I shouldn't have let her go! Lakshmi, what's wrong?"

"Something is fighting my spell, striving to hold her prisoner." Lakshmi's brow was beaded with sweat. "Lend me strength, husband. You also, wizards! We must have her back and dare not delay!"

Matt seized her hand as she reached for Marudin with the other. John tightened his grip on Matt's shoulder.

"All together, now!" Matt started singing,

> "Will ye no' come back again?
> Will ye no' come back again?"

But Prester John interrupted, calling,

> "If ye will not, Mantrell we'll send!"

Matt yelped with dismay as the whirlwind caught him up, spun him around, rotated him to the horizontal, spinning, spinning . . .

Spun. He landed flat-faced on something soft but solid. A skinny hand closed on his wrist, and he wrenched it loose by reflex, snarling. A voice cried out; there was a scrambling, then running footsteps, a creaky old voice calling for guards and assistant sorcerers, and a door opening.

As the surroundings stopped reeling, Matt realized he was under a bed that was lit by a rosy light—and was nose-to-nose with a very frightened Balkis. The cat mewed in astonishment at seeing him—and a brooch fell from her mouth. Matt caught it just as she disappeared.

The little cat squalled with surprise and pain, for she found herself suspended by the forepaws between Prester John and Lakshmi.

"Put her down, quickly!" the djinna said, but the calico cat's form clouded, stretched, and turned into a teenage girl, standing tall and squeezing the hands that held hers in a panic. "We must help him, quickly! The Lord Wizard is in Arjasp's private chamber! The sorcerer is calling for guards and magicians! They shall overwhelm him by sheer numbers, and he will be too stubborn to let go of the brooch so that he can escape!"

"What brooch?" Prester John demanded.

"The brooch that has the kittens in it!" she cried. "That foul Arjasp transported them into a jewel, not a bottle—and he has enchanted it with a spell that held it near him, no matter how hard we pulled away!"

"Be sure Matthew will not let it go if it has his children in it," Lakshmi snapped, "and ours! It is the brooch that has the holding spell?"

"Yes! Enchant it! Make him drop it! Whisk him away!"

"An excellent thought." Lakshmi, still holding Marudin's hand, closed her eyes and chanted in Arabic. When she opened them, she seemed much more relaxed, even smiled.

Balkis looked about her. "He has not come!"

"Of course not," said Lakshmi. "Arjasp would follow such a spell and appear beside us here with all his forces."

"Then where have you sent him?" Balkis asked, eyes round.

Lakshmi smiled. "Do you not remember the Lord Wizard telling us that he who has babes gives hostages to fortune?"

"You have not sent him there!"

"Of course." Lakshmi shrugged. "They seemed to like each other well enough, after all."

The air clouded and developed into streaked and curving colors whirling around a vortex, right there in front of them.

Balkis cried out and ducked behind Lakshmi. Prester John stepped to the fore, but Marudin stepped in front of him, arms out to protect them all.

The color wheel streaked more and more tightly as it turned until it shrank into the contours of a large woman wrapped in a voluminous garment, a fluffy turban, and a look of high indignation. In her arms she held Matt, brooch and all, dripping wet. She dropped him unceremoniously at Lakshmi's feet and jammed her fists on her hips. "Most embarrassing! Have a care where you send your victims, young woman, and when! I have no wish to have unexpected company arrive when I am in the bath—especially when they *arrive* in the bath! I can only say it is well that I use plenty of bubbles!"

"I had never thought." Lakshmi hung her head in repentance— and to hide her smile. "Your pardon, Excellent Dame."

"Well . . . there is no damage done, after all," Fortune said, somewhat mollified. She transferred her gaze to Matt. "Have a care, young man, or I shall send word to your wife, telling her that you come unexpectedly upon poor women in their private moments. Be warned—never involve me in your machinations again, or I shall rig my darts to always land in the wrong squares on your wheel!"

Matt climbed to his feet, all meekness and apology. "I am very, very sorry, Good Dame. I certainly never intended to intrude." He lifted his head a little, cracking a smile. "However, I must say that you do look grand in a towel and turban."

"Well! Such cheek!" said Dame Fortune, clearly flattered. "See that you behave yourself in the future!" She turned about and disappeared, leaving behind only a whirling disk of colors and a mollified but very indignant sniff.

Matt sagged. "I suppose I have to thank you for the rescue, Princess—but it was a bit of a shock."

"You are welcome." Lakshmi snatched the brooch from his hand and frowned, studying it. "How shall we enter here?"

"Isn't the point to bring them out, not go in?" Matt asked.

"I do not trust it," Lakshmi said. "They might be caught between my spell and whatever force holds them."

"Even so!" Balkis said. "I felt stretched between the pull of your spell and Arjasp's wards!"

"So he works that way, huh?" Matt frowned. "That means somebody has to go in and bring them out, all right." He turned to Prester John. "You'd better march on and attack the city, Your Majesty. We're going to have our hands full for a little while."

"If you say it," John said, but he seemed doubtful.

"Be warned," Balkis said. "I overheard Arjasp order a messenger to China, to send troops to aid his forces against your soldiers."

"I regret that we shall not be able to accompany you," Lakshmi said, gaze still intent on the gem, "but we must recover our children first."

"Indeed," John said, decision firming. "I shall see if I can remove this canker that plagues us. May good fortune attend you!"

"After she's dried off," Matt said, with an apprehensive glance at the region of air where the color wheel had been. "Thanks, Majesty. See you in Maracanda."

"In Maracanda," John confirmed. He turned his horse and rode back to his troops.

Matt turned to join Lakshmi in gazing at the gem. "I'll go."

"They are my children," Marudin said. "I shall go."

"We shall all go." Lakshmi held up the brooch. "Gaze into the gem—let it seem to grow to fill all the space about you— let yourself become lost in it."

Matt gazed, feeling as though he were being hypnotized, and heard Lakshmi's voice droning in Arabic. He was just realizing that she was speaking in rhyme and meter when the rosiness of the quartz seemed to envelop him and pull him in.

He found himself trying to walk, but the pink fog about him seemed to be sticky, clinging to him, trying to hold him back. "Are we there yet?" he called.

"Not yet," Lakshmi's voice answered, seeming distant. "Strive, wizard! Press on a little longer!"

Then, abruptly, the mist pulled back, cleared—and Matt saw what had been making it red. Two flames burned brightly before him, each ten feet tall, each with eyes toward its top— narrowed eyes that glared down at them as though seeking to pierce them. The flames began to move toward the companions; at the bottoms they divided and became legs, stamping forward on feet of coals.

"Avaunt!" Lakshmi cried, her voice dropping into a strange accent. "Thou dost stand betwixt me and my babes!"

The fire roared higher and kept on coming.

What happened next was too fast for Matt to follow. All he saw was the two djinn moving in blurs and little bits of flame flying everywhere. He did manage to make out that Marudin was taking the left-hand flame and Lakshmi the right, but not exclusively. He knew he had to do something to help. The only thing that came to mind was,

> "O Rising Sound of the Rain
> That comes on with the speed of a train!

To a parched and thirsty brain
Comes a sudden, needed rain!"

A deluge struck, and a hiss like that of a thousand serpents went up with a cloud of steam.

" 'Nothing succeeds like excess,' " Matt quoted to himself, and called out one more:

"On the djinn let it rain
As it pours on the flames!
Hail this downpour
That's our visitor!"

Sure enough, the stinging drops hardened into half-inch balls of ice. Matt gave it ten minutes, until he saw the last of the flames die down. Then he called out,

"Turn off the tap!
The rain we have lapped!
No need for a flood—
Nip the rain in the bud!"

It wasn't exactly a bud, more like an overblown rose—but the rain slackened. When it lifted, the two djinn were lying, spent and gasping, near two small piles of very dead coals.

Balkis let out a cry and dashed to Lakshmi. Matt thought that was a good idea and went to Marudin. He picked up the djinn's wrist, felt for a pulse, and wondered if djinn had blood—but if they didn't, they certainly had an equivalent, for Marudin's pulse was strong and steady. Matt held a hand in front of his nostrils and felt breath. He scanned the prince anxiously, but didn't see any signs of injury except some red patches that faded even as he watched.

"I can see no wounds," Balkis called anxiously, "yet still she sleeps and does not revive."

"I think that fight took an awful lot out of them," Matt said, thinking as he said it. "Energy, I mean. Also breath—the flames used up all the oxygen, that close to them. That's probably what knocked them out." He sat back on his heels.

"I think they'll revive on their own if we just wait long enough."

"We dare not!" Balkis spun to him, eyes wide. "Surely Arjasp knows we have come into the gem! If he did not see us take it, then surely the fall of these sentries will have told him!"

"You're right." Matt stood up and turned away. "We'll have to let them recover on their own." He gave Balkis a long, steady look. "It's going to be very scary. There might be worse than this."

"Do you think I am afraid?" Balkis stood up, back straight, chin high. "Well, so I am! But I shall press on! Four kittens are in peril!"

"Stout heart." Matt smiled. "And this way, at least the fear won't take you by surprise. Let's go, and hope the djinn catch up with us when we need them." He took her hand and stepped over the piles of coals.

The pink mist closed about them again.

CHAPTER 30

"When shall we become small enough to fit into this gem?" Balkis asked.

"I hate to say it," Matt said, "but I think we already are."

"What!" Balkis' hand yanked tight on his.

Turning toward her, he could barely see her through the mist. "I think this fog all around us is the outer shell of the gem. We're not just tiny, we're almost microscopic."

Balkis only stared at him with wide, dark eyes. Matt turned and started walking again. He felt a slight tug on his hand, then she came with him.

Only a few steps later the mist began to lighten. A few steps after that it thinned, then was gone—and Matt and Balkis stopped, staring at an astounding landscape.

They stood at the top of a rise. Before them, a meadow filled with red, white, and pink flowers fell away to a rose-colored stream. Beyond the water stood a forest of rosebushes grown into trees, with reddish bark and russet leaves filled with dusky pink blossoms. Above them, the sky stretched, pink and translucent.

"It is enchanted," Balkis breathed.

"Literally, I'm afraid," Matt agreed.

But Balkis wasn't listening; she had raised her gaze to the sky. "Surely that cannot be the surface of the gem!"

"I think it is," Matt said. "At least we'll walk in the midst of loveliness. Let's go."

But they were only a few steps down the hill before he stopped again.

"What troubles you?" Balkis asked.

"Those flowers," Matt said, "the red ones."

"What of them?" Balkis looked more closely. "They are only poppies." She frowned. "Why do I know of such?"

"A memory left over from infancy," Matt suggested, "and they're triggering one of mine, from childhood. They remind me of a story I once read." He fished in his pouch and came up with the two lumps of incense the priest had given them in Samarkand. "Hold this under your nose, lass, just in case."

"In case of what?"

"Sleepiness."

"I can scarce credit that," Balkis said.

"I know the feeling," Matt said. "My credit used to be pretty scarce, too. But it can't hurt to try."

Within twenty paces Balkis said in surprise, "I do begin to feel somewhat drowsy!"

"Keep that incense close to the nose," Matt told her.

"But it is so unpleasant a scent, when it is all in a lump like this!"

"That's what we need," Matt told her. Then inspiration struck. "It shouldn't bother you—I've known cats to make much more unpleasant scents."

Balkis bridled instantly. "There is no need, when we are properly cared for!"

"What 'we'?" Matt taunted. "You're a human at the moment."

"Once a cat, always a cat," Balkis insisted. "There will ever be much of the feline in me, and when I am in cat-guise, there will always be much of the woman!"

"Then how come toms don't stay half man?"

"Toms are disgusting! If you wish to blame cats for bad smells, there are your culprits!"

"Yeah, well, at least they do their jobs and catch mice and chase squirrels."

"Do you mean to imply that I do not do my share of work?" Balkis spat. "Must I recite for you all I have done to save you and help find your kittens?"

"No, you don't," Matt said, "and I'm sorry if I've given offense."

Balkis stared, caught flat-footed by the apology. Then she asked, "Why did you make such insults, then?"

"To get us through that field of poppies," Matt said.

Balkis kept staring at him, then whirled to look back and see the broad sweep of flowers behind them.

"It's harder to fall asleep when you're angry," Matt explained.

Balkis turned to him, a touch more respect in her gaze now. "You are devious."

"Shh!" Matt pressed a finger to his lips. "I don't think we should say that word here."

"What? De . . . Why not?" It was the student hungry for knowledge who asked now.

"Because of where the word came from. I'll explain later." Matt had just realized that *devious* might come from *daeva*, the old Persian word for a demon. "Into the woods, okay?"

They went in among the trees and managed a whole four paces before tentacles came snaking out from the roots of the trees to grab their ankles.

"Hold on!" Matt threw an arm around Balkis to keep his feet from being pulled out from under him. She leaned on him, too, managing to stay on her feet. Matt kicked his right foot against the left ankle. Something screeched off in the trees and the tentacles loosened. He kicked his left foot free and snapped the heel against the tentacles on his right foot. A muffled howl sounded off to his right, and the tentacles let go. Matt turned and started tromping on the tentacles holding Balkis. He kicked them off, turned and started them back on the path—and jerked to a stop. He didn't even need to look down; he knew that new tentacles had grabbed their ankles, and he could see many, many more writhing over the forest path ahead.

"We must work magic," Balkis said, her voice trembling.

"Right you are," Matt said. "I don't think a cat would have any better luck with this than a human."

Balkis shivered within his arm.

Matt recited,

> "With service oracular,
> Banish tentacular
> Members like rope

That blindly do grope
To catch and to hold up.
Let them all now be rolled up!"

The tentacles unwrapped from their ankles in a snap and
shot back into the trees like window shades pulled and let go.
Cries of dismay echoed all around.

"Come on." Matt hurried Balkis forward. "Let's get out of
this wood before they learn how to unroll themselves!"

But a dozen steps later Balkis cried out and pointed downward. Looking at the trail, Matt saw the prints of two pairs of
tiny slippers.

"The djinn twins!" he exclaimed with relief.

"But how did they pass that gamut of grasping tentacles?"
Balkis wondered.

"I don't think they did." Matt frowned ahead along the
trail, seeing the little footprints leading away. "I think the
grabbers were positioned here after the children had gone
through. The point was to keep them in, not to catch them."

"But they will do quite well to prevent rescue?"

"Not all that well," Matt said, starting forward again. "Useless against any adult with magic—and no other kind could
have come in here. You watch the trail, lass—I'll watch the
trees."

Balkis shivered again. "I had not thought . . . but of course,
where there was one sort of monster . . ."

"There could be others. Yes." Matt scanned the greenery to
either side. "No sign of any yet, but—"

"There are more!"

"Where?" Matt looked about frantically.

"More footprints, I mean! See! Another trail joins this!"

Looking down, Matt saw that the track forked; another pair
of small footprints had come down the side trail to mingle
with those of the twins'. Both wore round-toed shoes such as
Western babies wore. One pair was the same size as the twins,
but the other was considerably larger.

"A three-year-old and a six-year-old!" Matt went weak
with relief. "My kids! Alive and well!"

"Pray Heaven," Balkis murmured.

They hurried on down the path, but after a few minutes Balkis began to slow.

Matt slackened his pace impatiently. "What's the matter?"

"My . . . loins." Balkis blushed. "There is some . . . irritation . . ."

"Just sweat," Matt said. "Pardon me, perspiration. I hate to be heartless, but please keep going."

"I shall . . . try . . ." But Balkis went slower and slower, turning redder and redder. "It grows quite painful."

"I know it's asking a lot, but . . ." Then Matt began to feel it, a burning in his loins. "What the hey? Excuse me a sec." He stepped into the trees, unlaced, looked, and stared. Then he pulled himself together and went back to the path. "I see what you mean."

"What could it be?"

"If we weren't both adults, I'd say it was—" Matt broke off. As a father, the adventures of watching a child work his way through diapers and training pants into miniature adult wear were very fresh. Facts clicked together, and he exclaimed, "Diaper rash!"

"Nappies?" Balkis asked, wide-eyed. "But I certainly do not wear them!"

"Neither do I, but the hazards of this route aren't geared to adults! They're the kinds of obstacles that children want to avoid, very young children—having to go to sleep when you don't want to, the Monster Under the Bed, and now diaper rash!"

"We must recite another spell," Balkis said.

Matt thought of infections, but also thought of the kinds of childhood monsters that could come out of a woods like this, and found he had nothing with which to meet them. "Don't have much choice, do we? This is one place where we don't want to be slowed down." He tried to remember the commercials he hadn't paid much attention to, back in his own universe when marriage was only an unapproachable goal due to a dearth of the main requirement—i.e., a woman in love with him. One particularly annoying jingle surfaced:

> Take a powder!
> Find it welcome!

Spoil yourself after your shower!
Not for infants is our talcum!

"Okay," he said, "let's go."

Balkis didn't ask, she only forced herself to walk with him, lips pressed thin—but after a few steps a look of surprise washed over her face.

Matt could sympathize. The fluid feeling replacing the earlier friction did kind of take you aback, if you weren't expecting it. "Still a little bit of a rash, but I'm sure it will fade fast."

"It is . . . a most singular sensation," Balkis said, blushing again.

"One I don't remember ever having felt," Matt agreed, "at least not consciously."

They didn't have any more trouble walking, though.

They followed the four steps of small footprints, Balkis watching the ground, Matt watching the forest until, quite suddenly, the trees opened out to reveal a little grotto. A tiny waterfall purled down the center of a series of rocky shelves to chuckle away as a brook. To either side of the tumbling fluid, wildflowers sprang from the rocky shelves. The spring ran through a dusky pink lawn, soft enough to cushion baby feet. Cushions of moss sprouted here and there about the clearing, and a tiny house, perhaps four feet high and ten wide, stood against the rocky wall. The whole was shaded by giant rosebushes, with just enough light from the pink sky overhead to make the whole grotto look comforting and cheerful.

"I could not have crafted a better nursery myself," Balkis said, awed.

But Matt started toward the little house. "Suppose anybody's home?"

He wasn't even halfway there before a naked baby came toddling out, giggling. A six-year-old boy came charging after, waving a diaper and looking very harried. "Nay, nay, little Alley, you'll catch your death of cold!" He managed to catch the toddler and twist the diaper about it, but before he could tie the corners, a little girl came somersaulting out of the house, giggling, and a little boy came running after, crying, "Gimme back! Gimme back!"

The six-year-old dropped the diaper and turned to run, managing to catch the little boy's wrist before he could strike. "Now, now, little Hammy, you know 'tis wrong to hit when you can talk! Sister, give back Hammy's slipper!"

The little girl hid her hands behind her back, turning truculent. "Shan't!"

"But Alice, you must!" the six-year-old cried in despair. " 'Tis not yours!"

Just then little Alley came charging past, waving his diaper and crowing with delight.

The older boy turned away from the incipient fight to chase, crying, "You will drive me out of my mind! Oh, Mama, why can you not come?"

"Will Papa do?" Matt asked.

All the children froze, staring at the intruder. Then with a glad cry, the boy and Alice came running to their father.

Matt knelt and caught them up, holding them close, very close. "There now, we're together again, and we'll go home and find Mama very soon." He loosened the arm around the boy to tousle his hair. "Well done, Kaprin. You've been taking care of your little sister and the twins, huh?"

"Yes, and am almost out of my wits with trying to keep track of all three!" Kaprin said fervently. "Praise Heaven you have come, Papa!" He suddenly jumped away from Matt and turned to run back to his charges, crying, "The twins! What mischief—" Then he broke off, plowing to a halt and staring.

"They've found the world's best toy," Matt assured him.

The twins were laughing and grabbing at a little calico cat who was playing catch-me-if-you-can.

"Can that be Balkis?" Kaprin asked.

"Sure is," Matt said. "She just decided to change clothes, that's all."

"I wish I could," Kaprin sighed. "Two days in the same robes grows wearisome."

"Only two days?" Matt asked in surprise, then turned quickly sympathetic. "Only two days, but it probably seemed like a month to you! How did you feed them, son? And where did you find the clean nappies?"

"There are three bottles in the house with leather teats on top," Kaprin explained. "As soon as a babe sucks one empty, it begins to fill again. Apples grow on the trees, and there is an oven that always has warm bread. There is a pile of clean nappies that never seems to grow smaller. All three have been quite good about using the little chair, but accidents happen."

Matt wondered who would have taken care of the children if one of them hadn't been old enough to manage. Actually, at six, Kaprin *wasn't* old enough, but he had managed anyway. Matt said, his voice low, "I'm very proud of you, son. You've taken care of your sister and the twins excellently."

He could almost see Kaprin expand with the praise—but the boy only said, "The twins must be magical, Papa, for when I chase them and almost catch them, they will disappear from my hands and reappear on the branch of a tree, and if they slip off the branch, they do not fall, but drift to the ground."

"You guessed right," Matt confirmed. "They're baby djinn."

"Djinn?" Kaprin's eyes grew round. "Truly? But who are their parents, Papa?"

"Some friends of mine," Matt said. "They came with us to find the four of you, but they had to fight some monsters who were trying to keep us away from this grove. They won the fight, but it, uh, tired them out horribly, so they're sleeping now."

"Will they come to us?"

Inspiration again. "I've got a better idea. How about we go to them, then we all go back to Mama!"

"Mama! Mama!" Baby Alice cried.

"Yes, darling, yes, we'll go find Mama right away." Matt cuddled his daughter, and she chirruped happily.

"Alley! Hammy!" Kaprin cried. "We go Mama!"

"Mama! Mama!" The twins left off playing with the cat and came running, arms wide.

Matt gathered them in. Out of the corner of his eye he noticed the cat going in through the little door. "Kaprin—would you go into the playhouse and see if my friend is in there?"

"Your friend?" Kaprin looked up in surprise. "Who, Papa?"

"Her name is Balkis, like the cat," Matt said, "and she came along to help me find you . . . Oh, there she comes!"

Kaprin looked up and saw the veil-clad girl coming toward them. "What a pretty lady!"

Matt decided his son was growing up faster than he had realized. "Yes, isn't she? Hold her hand, now, and hold Alley's, too, and I'll hold Hammy's hand while I hug Alice . . . Got Hammy's other hand, Balkis?"

"I have." Balkis smiled, melting at the child's touch.

Matt noticed she had taken the chance to discard the ragged remains of the yellow jacket. "Okay, then, back to Hammy and Alley's mommy . . ."

He was about to improvise something about returning to djinn, but Balkis beat him to it, reciting a verse in Allustrian. Pink mist boiled up from the ground, hiding them from one another. Alice cried out in fright, but the twin djinn only laughed with delight. Kaprin called out, his voice trembling, "Papa, what is happening?"

"It's how the magic works that takes us to Princess Lakshmi," Matt explained.

Then the pink mist lightened, thinned, and pulled away in wisps to make a large sphere around them. At its bottom, Marudin was kneeling, looking very groggy but also very concerned as he held his wife's shoulders in his arm, bracing her half sitting; she was holding one hand to her head.

"Mama! Mama!" cried the djinn twins, and lit into her full speed.

Lakshmi's arms went around them automatically; then her face lit up as she realized what she was holding. She pressed her babies to her and spent a few minutes kissing and murmuring, then looked up at Matt and Balkis, eyes filled with tears. "Thank you, wizards! Thank you with all my heart! I shall never forget you for this!"

"Nor shall I," said Marudin, but he didn't look at them, he had eyes only for his family, and those eyes were glowing. "I thank you from the core of my being, and shall never forget what you have done."

Matt had heard similar words from other and less friendly people. All in all, he liked the parent djinns' version better.

* * *

Lakshmi seemed to have sustained the worst of the fire-fight, so Marudin chanted the spell that took them all to a cave in the mountains that divided the fertile land from the desert. There, he and Matt left Lakshmi to take care of the children—there was no way she would have left them for any reason—and left Balkis to take care of Lakshmi. Riding in the crook of the prince's arm, Matt watched the countryside reel by below until they saw Maracanda with Prester John's army surrounding it. If the barbarians had tried to stop him outside the gates, they had given it up quickly, for they were all inside and manning the walls—perhaps a quarter as many as John had soldiers. Still, the walls were stout, and the Mongols and Turks were fighting bravely—but as Matt and Marudin watched, a hundred of John's men galloped up to the wall, slowly raising their shields until they held them as umbrellas, deflecting the rain of arrows and stones until they stood directly in front of the gates. Some of them fell in the advance, but most lived, protecting their king with their shields.

The barbarians began to roll huge steaming kettles into place.

"They must break through that gate, and quickly, or they will be boiled!" Marudin said.

"John said he had a key . . ." Matt stared. "He did!"

The gates flew inward, and John led his vanguard through. A third of them fell to Mongol arrows. The other two-thirds rode bravely against two hundred Turks—but the rest of John's army came on at the gallop.

They boiled into the city and overwhelmed the Turks quickly. Then they rode on, leaving a circle of captives bound and kneeling, surrounded by a guard of John's men.

They rode on toward the palace—but as they neared it, a circle of fire roared up around it almost as high as its roofs.

"They shall have more difficulty in winning the palace than in gaining the city!" Marudin predicted.

"Yeah, Arjasp is pulling out all the magical stops." Matt frowned.

"We must aid Prester John!"

"Nice thought." Matt was developing an idea. "Say, Prince

Marudin—you don't suppose Arjasp took the time to transport his brooch back to him, do you?"

Marudin looked down at him in surprise, then grinned. "Why should we doubt it?"

"It's worth a try," Matt said.

Marudin recited an Arabic verse. As the pink mist closed about them he said in disgust, "I never thought I would seek to send myself back inside a prison!"

"Yes," Matt said, "but this time we have the key." He recited,

> "Reversal's prime as paradox!
> Inverse laws give all the shocks.
> Jail, surrender what's inside!
> Shut your shell with us outside!"

He took a step through the mist—and found himself falling.

CHAPTER 31

Matt barely managed to choke off a shout of surprise and fright. He was falling toward huge blocks of granite—but they were growing smaller even as he fell. He managed to swing his feet below him, landed in a crouch, and stood up slowly, realizing that he was growing as he straightened.

Beside him, Marudin touched down, then began to grow, too.

Matt looked about him. The first thing he saw was the brooch, hanging by a chain in front of a stone wall. He looked down and saw stone flags, an open window, stone walls curving in a circle, and shelves upon shelves of books and jars. In the center of the room was a huge ring of sand, and to one side stood a long table cluttered with retorts, alembics, bell jars, and other alchemical apparatus.

He was in Arjasp's laboratory, where the renegade magus worked his most serious magic.

Arjasp was at the table now, flipping pages in a huge old tome and muttering to himself as he tried to find a spell that would stop Prester John.

"Don't bother," Matt told him. "You've lost this one already."

Arjasp looked up at him and turned deathly pale, which contrasted nicely with his midnight-blue robes. In fact, his face almost faded into the long white beard and longer white hair.

Matt seized the initiative while he had it. He also seized his wand, pointing it at the renegade magus and chanting,

> "I've thrown my gage,
> The battle's joined.
> Pay sorcerers in their own coin.
> Send this fell mage

To his own cage.
To princely lies he hitched his coach—
Now let him lie within his brooch!"

As soon as he began to chant, Arjasp spat out a verse—but Marudin shouted him down, bellowing a counterverse in Arabic. Arjasp tried another in a voice more frantic, which rose into a scream as he suddenly shot across the room toward the brooch, shrinking as he went. His voice rose in pitch past a shriek to a whine, then an oppression on the ears as he shrank to the size of a fly and plunged into the pink surface.

Matt wiped away sweat with a trembling hand. "Thanks for the protection, Marudin."

"My pleasure," said the prince, gloating at revenge.

Matt glanced at him and shuddered, looking away. "Do you suppose we can find a jeweler who can cut the Seal of Solomon into that quartz?"

"It should be simplicity itself," Marudin assured him, "and if you cannot, be assured that I can."

"Oh?" Matt looked up in surprise. "You know what the seal looks like?"

Marudin turned to him with a sardonic smile. "Wizard, if anyone knows that seal, I do!"

Come to think of it, it had been a pretty dumb question.

The reunion with Alisande was touching and brief. The children did most of the touching, to the point at which they had to be pried loose when it was time for Mama to go—and it had to be brief because Mama was raging to go back to join the Caliph's forces and get in her licks of revenge on the barbarians. Her knights were just as eager, but by the time they got to Damascus, Tafas and the Caliph had chased the barbarians back to Baghdad, and by the time they reached Baghdad, the allies had chased the steppe-horsemen halfway to Maracanda. They were nearing the city's walls when the Caliph caught up with them.

It was quite a sight, and Matt was aloft with Marudin and Lakshmi to direct his magic wherever it was needed. The barbarian sorcerers were putting up some resistance, but their power was tremendously weakened—apparently Arjasp had been their source, or conduit, if he actually had managed to tap the energy of the Prince of Lies.

The battle-line turned gradually into a bow as Tafas and Alisande outflanked the barbarians and started pushing in. The bow bent farther and farther, but the barbarians managed a counterattack, and the bow developed recurves. The recurves deepened, and for half an hour it looked as though the barbarians might actually manage to hold their ground.

Then troops came riding around the city walls to take the barbarians in the rear, troops with Prester John at their head.

Matt stared down. "He sure finished off Arjasp's reinforcements from the east fast!"

"He caught them at a pass in the Tien Shan Mountains." Lakshmi, quite happy with Balkis as babysitter, had left her cave and gone east to see if her help had been needed. She shrugged. "It was brief and bloody, but most of the barbarians had the good sense to surrender."

"And Prester John marched his army halfway across Asia in a month." Matt shook his head in admiration.

Below on the plain, the bow's center crumbled, the recurves fell apart, and the barbarians surrendered.

"Their strength was only in their magic," Prince Marudin said, shaking his head in wonder.

"Not entirely." Matt remembered Genghis Khan's conquests in his own world. "If they had met our armies one at a time, we would have fallen to them piecemeal."

Marudin nodded. "But when all the armies of Islam and Christendom joined together, they could not hold against us."

Matt shrugged. "The Mongols are excellent horsemen, but so are the Arabs. Okay, so several light cavalry can chop one European knight to pieces, but nothing can stand against fifty of them charging in a body. Then too, Arjasp made the classic mistake of fighting a war on two fronts. Which reminds me, we'll have to tell Prester John to go back and check for garrisons along the Great Wall."

The monarchs met with reserve and wariness that quickly turned into temporary friendship as they sat together to judge Arjasp's field-sorcerers and priests of Ahriman. They were unanimous in agreeing that the only ones of his temples that could stay open were those that had not advocated treason against the local government, and since all of them had, the priests were given a simple choice: repent and return to farming under close military supervision, or die. Most saw a great deal of virtue in following the plow.

The sorcerers and shamans were another matter. The sorcerers, threatened with death and a face-to-face meeting with the Prince of Lies, decided on conversion and denunciation of their former profession. The shamans were quick to admit their mistake in having believed Arjasp's claims. Convinced of the sincerity of their devotion to their totems, Prester John sent them back to their peoples, only requiring that they leave with him the talismans Arjasp had given them. Tafas, the Caliph, and Alisande were content to follow his lead in the matter, since shamans were outside their experience.

When the tribunal was over, Matt and Balkis drew Prester John aside and pressed a small leather-bound trunk into his hands.

"What is this?" he asked, frowning.

"Leather bound around a silver box," Matt told him. "Inside the silver box is a brooch with a huge crystal of rose quartz carved with the Seal of Solomon, and inside the crystal is Arjasp."

Prester John smiled slowly. "The Seal of Solomon? Then he cannot come out!"

"I did sort of have that in mind," Matt admitted. "Of course, if you want him out—for, say, a military tribunal or some other sort of trial—I suppose you could pry it out of its setting and loose him out the back."

"We could at that." John turned the brooch over and saw the seal engraved on the back of the metal as well. "Of course, it might be kinder to leave him within, especially since he is secure as long as the stone remains set."

"To leave him within for eternity?" Balkis protested. "Surely that is too harsh a punishment for anyone!"

"It would be more harsh to execute him, and let him confront the demon he has worshiped," John said grimly. "Be easy in your heart, young one—his fate is not so harsh as you might imagine."

"Ask Prince Marudin about it," Matt advised. "He's gone through it, sometimes for centuries at a time."

She did, and Marudin told her, "A crystal, lamp, or bottle with a spell that can hold a djinn makes time move far more slowly than it does for us outside. We spent months searching for the children, but only two days passed for them."

"Still, eternity . . . !"

"Someone will be foolish enough to let him out eventually," Marudin said evenly. "That is why it would be better if it were Prester John who did so, for he has the magic to control the madman and slay him if he will not repent—which I am sure he will not; he is so mad as to think he is right."

"But until he does . . ."

"Not much time will pass at all—for him," Prince Marudin assured her. "Time within the crystal seems to be keyed to the prisoner's mood in some way. That is why I am still young even though I have been locked in prison for centuries of sleep—time was bottled with me, always just a little more than I could tolerate."

"It's a sort of waking stasis," Matt explained, but that didn't seem to make things any clearer for either of them.

"Think of Prince Kaprin," Marudin explained. "Angel that he was, he took responsibility for the younger ones, trying desperately to keep them amused so that they would not be afraid. Since he had them enjoying themselves by the games he made up, mere days passed for them—they would have been content to stay much longer."

"Kaprin, however, was definitely near the end of his tether," Matt said, smiling. "He was running out of ideas for keeping them happy, so he was more than ready to get out."

"By that token," Balkis said thoughtfully, "Arjasp should be ready to exit only moments after going in, for he will surely be raging at his imprisonment."

"Yes, and it serves him right," Matt said, seething. "Fortunately, it could be a year or more in this outside world before Prester John is ready to deal with him. He very easily may step out to find himself surrounded by Prester John and his priests, about to deliver judgment."

"I hope he fumes and frets every second of that year," Prince Marudin said, "but I fear it will be the reverse—that it will seem only seconds to him."

"I thank you, Prince." Balkis seemed quite relieved. "It is not so harsh a punishment, then."

"Not a scrap of what he deserves," Marudin said grimly.

Maracanda was a free city again, ruled by a monarch, perhaps, but a monarch of its own people. Guests of the Crown, Alisande and Matt walked the terrace of the palace in the dusk, gazing out over the lights of the city and inhaling the fragrance of exotic blooms.

"I rejoice that the three younger children seem to have emerged from the gem unharmed," Alisande said, but sadness tinged her face. "I fear, though, that our boy will be scarred by the experience."

"Doesn't seem all that bad to me." But Matt was concerned because she was.

"Have you not noticed how much more solemn he has become?" Alisande protested. "He is far too responsible for his age!"

"Oh, I think he'll recover, given his normal ration of playtime," Matt said with what he hoped was a reassuring smile. "Besides, an overdeveloped sense of responsibility might not be a bad thing, for a boy who's going to grow up to become a king."

"Well, that is so," Alisande admitted. "But that is all the more reason to ensure that he has much time to play while he may!"

"We'll get a tutor who knows how to ration the lessons," Matt agreed. "One good result you can't deny, though—he's made a real hit with the djinn twins. Our children and Lakshmi's will be fast friends all their lives."

"That is surely so." Alisande smiled, gazing into his eyes. "Trust you to find the bright side of the coin, my love."

Later that night Prester John took Matt aside and asked, "The young one, the maiden who is a wizard—has she emerged from these trials unscathed? For surely I know that the hearts of the young are most vulnerable when they must witness human cruelty."

"She seems to be coping pretty well," Matt said. "In fact, she was a little worried that Arjasp's fate might be too harsh."

"She is sound, then, and has a good heart indeed." John's

smile became brittle. "Even so, I do not think she would have
been so merciful if she had witnessed the barbarians' taking
of the city sixteen years ago."

"Sixteen years," Matt said slowly. "Balkis is sixteen."

"Then you have noticed?"

"Noticed what?" Matt asked.

"She is of our breed."

Matt stared at Prester John a moment while he sorted it out
and made sense of it. Then he said softly, "Of course. That's
why your people seemed to have a familiar look. That's why
you thought she was our local guide."

Prester John nodded.

"And that," said Matt, "is why she kept having the feeling
that she'd been here before."

"Because she has," John affirmed. "Let us bring her to my
gardens."

The moonlight made Prester John's garden a place of
magic, tranquil and mystical, the only sounds the susurrus of
leaves and the tinkling of the brook that ran through it,
turning model mill wheels and tugging at miniature boats
moored for the night at fanciful tiny boathouses. The breeze
that stirred the leaves wafted the perfume of exotic blossoms
to the three wizards. Around them, flowering trees took fanciful shapes, the product of dozens of years of patience. Wind
chimes filled the night with music. The turquoise lawn
seemed deep green in the moonlight, bejeweled with dew. Topiary shrubs in sculpted forms framed an ivory gazebo of ornate screens.

"This . . . this all seems . . ." Balkis pressed a hand to her
forehead. "Lord Wizard, is this another of those déjàs you
mentioned?"

"I think it's a bit more than that." Matt watched her closely,
concerned.

"There is a way to be sure," Prester John said softly. "Call
upon the spirits who surround you."

Balkis began to tremble. "They will be angry if I trouble
them to no purpose!"

Matt noticed that it never occurred to her that she couldn't
do it.

"It will be to a purpose, and a good one," John assured her. "If they bear you goodwill, they will be pleased. Maiden, call."

Balkis cast a look of desperation at him, then stepped out into the garden and called out, "O Spirits of Water and Tree! Phantoms of Earth and Wind! If any of you know me, come forth now, I beg of you, and tell me who I am!"

There was only silence, the wind whispering condolences.

Balkis bowed her head, her shoulders sagging. "There is nothing. It is to no purpose."

"Give them time," John said, reassuring her.

There was a splash in the river, too large for a trout or even a sturgeon. There was another splash.

Balkis looked up, hope lighting her eyes. Then she ran.

Matt and Prester John had trouble keeping up with her.

Balkis dropped to her knees on a little pier, looking down into the water. "Whoever you are who has come in answer to my call, show yourself, I beg you!"

Matt braced himself in case the answer was unpleasant.

But it was very pleasant indeed. Seaweed seemed to rise from the water, but it framed a greenish face, and Matt saw that it was hair. The spirit rose farther, and he saw a gentle roundness that he thought was a bust but saw an instant later was a cluster of lotus. Lily pads formed the flatness of a belly, and below it glistened the scales that might have covered a tail, but might just as easily have covered legs.

Another rose behind the first, and gasped. "See, Sister Shannai! Her aura!"

"I see indeed, Arlassair!"

John and Matt both turned to Balkis, inspecting, seeing nothing. She herself turned, looking first over one shoulder than over the other. "Aura? What . . . what is that?"

"The color of light that glows about you, silly mortal!" Shannai laughed. "No two are the same! Each soul makes a different pattern! You cannot see it with your poor weak eyes, but we can! Can we not, Arlassair?"

"Of course we can—and we know it, too, do we not?"

"Certainly, sister! However could we forget the baby set adrift in the trunk?"

"Trunk?" Balkis stared. Then her words tumbled over one

another. "A little chest crafted of ivory? Bound with straps of gold?"

"Like that? Do you think it was like that, sister?" Shannai asked.

Arlassair screwed up her face, considering—and dragging the moment out until Balkis looked as tense as a cat sensing a storm. At last the sprite relented. "Yes. The trunk was exactly like that. And there can be no doubt—you are the very babe who was in it."

Balkis cried out and held out her arms. "Bless you, good spirits!"

Arlassair laughed. "We are not so good as all that, but we remember you, yes. Your poor mother! Those horrible horsemen who chased her down and carried her off to sacrifice! But she called on us to protect you, oh yes, and we did, didn't we, Shannai?"

"We did indeed, sister." Then to Balkis, "We nudged your trunk down the stream as far as we could, then called upon the dryads to care for you. Since you are alive and well, it would seem that they did."

"Well, then! We have finished the task we never promised to complete!" Arlassair flirted her flukes above the water. "And since we have, there is an end to it! Feed the fish if you would show thanks, mortal, for they feed us!"

"Farewell, and be good to the river!" Shannai called. Then both nixies turned, splashed in dives, and were gone.

Balkis knelt on the pier, face in her hands, sobbing.

"Come, be comforted." John came up and gently took her by the shoulders. "You have come home now, maiden, to the place where you were born, and where you belong."

"But . . . but who am I?" Balkis raised tearful eyes to him.

"You are the daughter of the Princess Kanachai, my own niece," John said. "We thought she had died in the invasion, and now we know it."

"What . . . what was my name?"

"Balkis, even as the Franks call you," John told her, "and her title now is yours: the Princess of the Dawn Gate."

"So Balkis was indeed my name!" the girl cried. "I did not know why, only knew that it was!" She turned to Matt accusingly. "It was you who named me Balkis."

"Then it's no accident that she came home, is it?" Matt asked quietly. To Balkis, he said, "Remember why you came with me when I started east?"

"Yes—because something pushed me, something within me insisted I come."

"Tearing yourself away from a really cushy place you had just made for yourself in a royal palace." Matt turned to Prester John. "The flip side of the spells the nixies and dryads wove to protect her?"

"I would so conjecture," John agreed. "Mind you, there is always a link between a mortal soul and its native soil, but when magic has been woven there, the link would be forged into a geas."

"A magical compulsion." Matt turned back to Balkis. "You may not have sent me east, but something within you knew you had to come."

"I can only thank you so very, very deeply for bringing me home," the princess whispered.

"And I can only thank you for getting me here alive," Matt returned. He looked up at Prester John. "Just don't let her claw the furniture, okay?"

Finally Matt and Alisande were able to close the door and be alone in the guest room John had assigned them. Matt took his wife in his arms. "It's nice having the kids back, but it's nicer having a babysitter for them."

"It is good of Balkis to still serve them so." Alisande sighed, resting her head on his chest.

"She's just forging future diplomatic relations," Matt said. "After all, she might need Kaprin's help someday, when you've retired and he's become king."

"Retired . . . an interesting thought . . ." Alisande looked up at him as the other shoe dropped. "But why might Balkis need his help?"

"Well, the horde is still out there," Matt said, "several of them, in fact—and now they know what they can do if they all band together."

Alisande smiled and rested her head on his chest again. "We need not worry. They have been beaten; they will be too wise to attempt it again."

But Matt wasn't so sure. The khans knew now that they needed to attack the Western nations one at a time—and that they needed to find a source of magic that would be stronger than that of Islam and Christendom put together. Not very likely, of course, but they were no doubt burning for revenge. All they lacked was a leader.

"Retired . . ." Alisande returned to the new idea he had given her. "A novel notion." She looked up at him again. "But if I were to retire, what should I do with all my time?"

Matt grinned down at her, knowing a cue when he heard one. "Oh, I think we could find something."